Blackwater

Also by Thomas H. Williams

Fiction
Greenbrier! Valley of Hope
Into the Mountains
Backbone Mountain

Nonfiction
A History of Bonafield School

Blackwater

A Novel

Thomas H. Williams

To order additional copies of this book, contact:
Xlibris
1-888-795-4274
www.Xlibris.com
Orders@Xlibris.com
775895

Acknowledgements

I wish to acknowledge those who provided assistance and encouragement in the completion of this book. Over the years, I worked with many professionals who have devoted their lives to teaching, research, and writing. I thank them all for the work they do. I especially thank those researchers who, on occasion, allowed me to tag along, sometimes dragging measuring tapes, making tedious stem counts and DBH measurements. Since I am not a research scientist, their instruction was invaluable.

Thanks goes to those who volunteered to read early drafts of the manuscript. Janet Myers provided help with continuity and the story line. Thanks for your help, Sis. T.M. Bautista made recommendations to improve the story, suggested the title for the book, and took the cover photograph of the author. Thank you, my friend. Anita Craig provided expertise in editing. Thank you for taking time from your busy life to complete this tedious task, Anita. Danny Miller suffered through my constant obsession with the writing process during our early morning walks. Thank you for listening. Thanks to Jim Yost for a quote used in this novel. A special thank you goes to Erin Greb for her work on the map of North Central West Virginia. Any errors that have found their way into this book are the author's responsibility.

The places, highways, rivers, mountains, and streams in this novel are real and are described as faithfully as possible. In all other respects this is a work of fiction. Adams County, where much of the story takes place, is entirely fictional as are the county sheriff and his deputies. The names of incidents, characters, and places, are either used fictitiously or are the result of the author's imagination. Any resemblance to any actual persons, living or dead, is entirely coincidental.

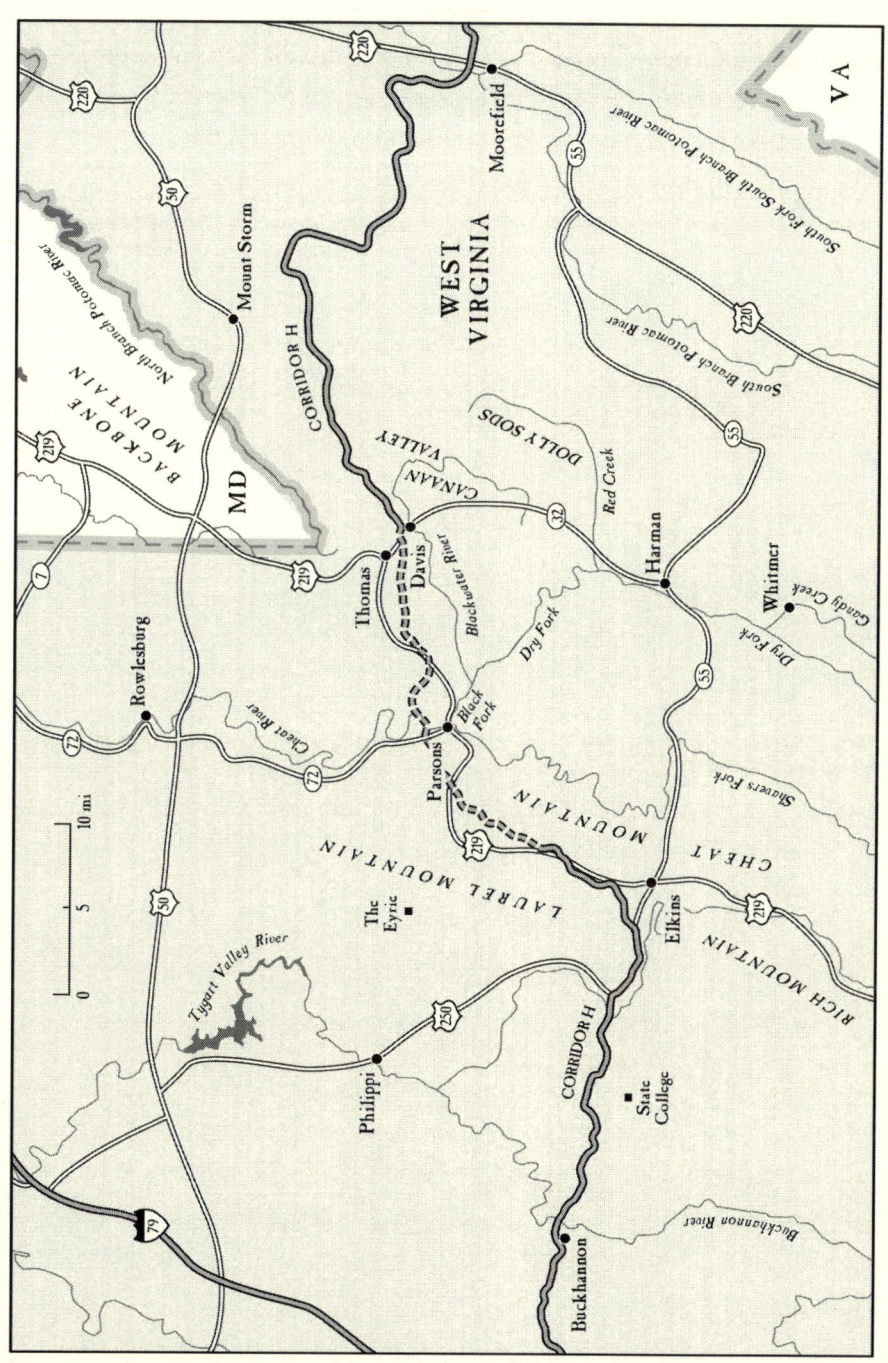

Map Design by Erin Greb Cartography

Prologue

The sheriff and his deputy stood in the darkening forest, looking upward into the limbs of a large maple tree. Fine snow sifted down through the bare branches adding to the thin layer already coating the forest floor. The snow-covered boughs of red spruce trees drooped forlornly with their burdens. Partially melted drifts spotted the stark landscape of Dolly Sods. It was early March and Father Winter was reluctant to release his grip on this high Appalachian ridge.

"How do you suppose he got up there?" the deputy asked, referring to the human body lying atop a large, horizontal tree limb. Chris Franklin was twenty-eight years old and a newcomer to the force. He had completed his basic training the preceding fall. "He looks peaceful except for what the birds did to him." The man in the tree lay on his back with his hands clasped over his stomach. Tattered strips of cloth hung from the corpse, undulating in the frigid breeze that filtered through the forest. Rotting flesh showed through openings in its shroud made by ravens and turkey vultures.

"I've been with the sheriff's office for over twenty years, and this is the damnedest thing I've ever seen," the sheriff said, shuffling his feet in the damp leaves. "I've found bodies just about every crazy place you can think of, but this is a first. A dead man in a tree."

"What do we do now, Sheriff?" the deputy asked, wrinkling his nose at the fetid smell that drifted down from the body. "He smells pretty ripe, but I guess it would be a whole lot worse if it wasn't so darned cold." He pushed his hands deeper into the pockets of his uniform jacket, hunching his shoulders against the stinging wind.

"We wait for the tech van to get here and let Vicky do her thing." Dr. Victoria Whitehead, MD, worked the emergency room at the local hospital and occasionally served as Adam County's medical examiner. "She'll work with the tech guys to get him down, and they'll gather whatever evidence there is to be found. We just have to stay out of the way." A sudden blast of wind rattled the bare tree branches and almost swept off their hats. "Meanwhile, we need to talk to the hikers who found him."

They walked back along the rocky trail, past the entrance to a wooden boardwalk that extended into a large, moss-covered glade and approached the narrow parking area along the forest service road. Two young men waited in the back seat of the sheriff's cruiser which bristled with antennae like a large glossy insect. The sheriff department name and logo were stenciled on its doors. The sheriff opened the back door and leaned in toward the hikers, resting his forearm on the roof of the cruiser.

"Tell me how you came to discover the body," he said.

"We came up here to do some hiking. We're both students at State College, and we just wanted to get outside for a bit of fresh air," the larger of the two men said. Both were dressed in heavy coats and hiking boots. "We left our car at the first overlook and were just hiking along the road when my dog, Duke, started barking over there in the trees along the loop trail."

The second man spoke up, "We could tell from the way he was baying that something was wrong. When we got there, he was looking up into the trees and barking as if he had something treed. When we saw what it was, we called 911 and waited until you got here."

"Did you see anyone else? Anyone drive by while you waited?"

"No," the smaller man said, "this road doesn't have snow removal in the winter. A month ago, no one could have made it up here without a snowmobile. Even now, it's nearly impossible to predict if the roads will be open."

The sheriff questioned the men for a few minutes more but was interrupted when a tech van drove carefully down the rough road, rocking from side to side as the driver maneuvered around large potholes. It pulled into the parking area, and Dr. Whitehead powered down the passenger side window. She was a smallish woman with dark brown hair streaked with silvery strands of gray. She wore a parka with a fur-trimmed hood.

Her face lit up when she saw the sheriff. "Did I hear right, Bill? You've got a body in a tree? Any idea how it got there?"

"Hi, Vickie. Yep, you heard right. There's a man in a tree, dead as a doornail. Looks to me like he's been up there for a while. I have no idea how he got there. I was hoping you'd figure it out for me," Sheriff Bill Donovan said, grinning at her.

As the tech crew began dragging large equipment boxes out of the van, the sheriff asked the deputy to get the hikers' names and tell them to come into the office the next day to give a formal statement. He walked along the trail with Vickie, briefing her on what he knew, which was pitifully little. They stopped near the tree and the sheriff pointed upward. "There he is," he said. "What do you think?"

"Well," the pretty medical examiner said, "unless he fell out of an airplane or something, there's only two ways I can think that he could have gotten there. He climbed up there to commit suicide, or someone killed him and put him there. Either way, I haven't the slightest idea *why*."

The sheriff studied the corpse for a long moment, and then said, "I think it's like the old saying: If you find a turtle on a fencepost, you can bet it had help getting there."

Chapter 1

Professor Houston leaned back in his office chair and frowned slightly at the red-haired coed who sat in his visitor's chair. She was young and pretty, maybe twenty, and was flirting with him. She was enrolled in one of his introductory botany classes and needed help. She was struggling with the course content and had come to his office for a little extra tutoring. He could hear the busy hum of student conversations in the hallway outside his office. Dr. Jimmy Houston, single, in his mid-thirties, tall and attractive with dark hair, often had to deal with students with crushes on him. He reviewed the material he had just covered in his last lecture with her and recommended that she re-read—or more likely, read for the first time—the chapter he had assigned in the text.

They ended the tutoring session and the young lady left. Jimmy walked to the window of his second story office and looked out over the campus. State College, located in the mountains of north-central West Virginia, boasted an enrollment of eight thousand students, many of whom commuted from the surrounding area. Trees and shrubs on the carefully manicured campus were almost in full leaf. The large sweet-gum tree that grew near the parking oval cast a cooling shadow over the lawn. Robins searched for worms, and a cardinal sang from the top of a nearby oak. Final exams were scheduled for the following week.

He returned to his desk and picked up a letter from the dean and read it again. It contained good news. His application for tenure had been approved. He smiled to himself, remembering how difficult it had been to reach this milepost in his career. Among college professors, tenure was a big deal. A *very* big deal. His employment at the college was guaranteed. It was one of the perks of the job—employment security. Unless he really screwed up, his job was assured. He loved his work and had every intention of staying for a long time.

He looked up as a woman rapped her knuckles on the door facing. She was attractive, of medium height with mahogany-colored hair drawn back from her face. She wore jeans and a tight-fitting blouse that accentuated her figure, and Jimmy guessed she was in her mid-forties. "Professor Houston?" she asked. "Your secretary said it was okay to interrupt you."

"Yes, of course. Come in. What can I do for you? Please sit down," he said waving a hand toward the chair the student had recently vacated.

"I'm Frankie Richmond's mom. He's in one of your classes."

"Frank Richmond? Yes, he's in my plant communities class. He goes by Frank here."

"Yes, but he's always been Frankie to me." She had a sad look in her eyes, something deep and lasting.

"Frank's a strong student and is doing fine. I'm afraid I can't go into detail. He's an adult, and his records are confidential."

"Oh, I know. Frankie's a good student. Almost straight A's. It's not about him."

"I don't understand, Mrs. Richmond."

"I don't want to take up a lot of your time, Professor, but let me start from the beginning. I'm a widow. Frankie's dad was killed in a mining accident when he was only three years old. Tiffany, Frankie's sister, was six. They're both grown now and I'm an empty-nester. Tiffany joined the military right out of high school and seems to be satisfied with her career. After the kids left home, I started dating a man who lived in Canaan Valley. They liked him and was happy that I had found someone. We started out just being good friends; he was a widower, but it developed into much more than that. We were thinking about getting married." She looked down at her hands clasped in her lap. "He was killed last fall; more than six months ago."

"I'm sorry to hear that, Mrs. Richmond. You must have cared very much for him."

"Yes, I loved him. I never thought I'd find someone who I could care for after my husband died, but I did." Tears welled up in her eyes, threatening to overflow. "He was murdered."

"I don't understand. What is it you want me to do?"

"I want you to find whoever killed him and put him away."

"Mrs. Richmond, I'm not a detective. I'm a teacher. I know nothing about how to catch a murderer."

"Aren't you the professor who was accused of killing one of your students? Frankie kept me informed as all that was going on—just last year. You caught the killer and proved your innocence. He's in prison right now, isn't he?"

"Well yes, but that hardly qualifies me to be a detective. That was just plain luck. Besides, I had a lot of help from a friend. He's a retired state policeman, a detective."

"Sam Miller. Frankie told me about him, too. The two of you found out who killed your student and brought him to justice. Maybe you could do the same for my fiancé. Find out who killed him and put him away for life." She frowned and balled one hand into a tight fist.

"I have a job, Mrs. Richmond," Jimmy said not unkindly. "I just can't take off and…"

She interrupted, "Please call me Wendy. Aren't you off for the summer? Frankie said he had exams next week, and the semester will be over. He doesn't have classes again until next fall."

Jimmy chuckled. "Mrs. Richmond, Wendy, I have a lot of work to do this summer. I conduct research, attend conferences, and I'm teaching a new course next fall that I have to prepare for. There's a lot most folks don't realize college professors do as part of their work."

Her shoulders slumped as she said, "I don't know what else to do. Sheriff Donovan has worked hard to find the killer, but he's just about stumped. He told me that he had no objection if I wanted to hire someone to do some investigating. I can pay you. I have a little money stashed away, insurance money from my husband's death."

Jimmy leaned back in his swivel chair and looked with sympathy at the woman. He knew from experience the police wouldn't want outsiders nosing into their investigation and said as much.

She said, "The sheriff said he's understaffed and has been spending most of his time dealing with the opiate problem that's causing so much trouble in our state. He said it was all he could do to keep the drug dealers from taking over the county."

Jimmy was doubtful. "What was your fiancé's name?" he asked, trying to remember if he had read about the killing in the papers.

"Mitchell. His name was Scott Mitchell. He was forty-eight years old and lived on an old farm up in Canaan Valley."

"The name rings a bell, but I can't place him."

Wendy took a big breath and said, "He's the one they found in a tree up on Dolly Sods. They said he'd been up there since last fall."

"Oh yes," Jimmy said, "now I remember. I read about it in the papers."

"Scott had been missing since last fall, just after Thanksgiving time. He didn't answer my texts, and I went to his house to check on him, and he was just gone. The search and rescue people looked all over the valley for him, and everywhere else they could think of, but they never found him." She looked out the window and twisted her hair with slim fingers. A large tear slid down her cheek.

"I remember hearing about the search. At first, they thought he'd gone into the nature preserve. They did a grid search for him but didn't find anything," Jimmy said.

"Yes. He liked to hike there looking for birds. His farm borders the preserve. He was a birding enthusiast. The bobolink was his favorite."

"I do a lot of research there. Much of the preserve is marsh; most people call it a swamp, covered with speckled alder. It's difficult to get through. If he'd died in there, they might never have found him."

She squirmed in her chair, grimacing. "The sheriff interviewed me, trying to get an idea of his general routine, trying to figure out where he'd gone. They talked to his niece, Sandy Lynch. She lives in the valley. She's all the family Scott had left. Sandy hadn't seen him since they'd had Thanksgiving dinner together. Sandy's single and doesn't have anyone other than Scott. They were pretty close." Wendy sniffed and searched in her purse for a tissue. Jimmy offered her a box of Kleenex he kept handy on his desk for tearful coeds. She pulled several tissues from the box and loudly blew her nose. She looked around for a waste basket, and Jimmy pointed to one beside his desk.

"Anyway," Wendy continued, "they looked everywhere and didn't find him. I think the sheriff figured that he'd run off somewhere. Maybe with another woman. I knew better. We were happy together and were going to get married," she said, repeating herself.

Jimmy sat upright in his chair and snapped his fingers. "Now I remember. It was on Scott's farm that the U.S. Fish and Wildlife people found an endangered fern."

"Yes. He was so proud. His farm is just about the only place it's been found. He told me all about it."

Jimmy muttered to himself, "*Dryopteris canaanensis.*" To Wendy he said, "Canaan Valley wood fern. It caused quite a stir among the science community several years back. I've been on Scott's property to look at it, but I don't think I'd ever met him. The wildlife people have an easement on his property, and they took me there. I wanted a specimen for our plant collection here at the college, but since it's endangered, I had to settle for photographs."

"Yes, Scott gave them written permission to access his property any time they wanted."

A group of noisy students walked by Jimmy's office door, laughing and talking all at once. "I hesitate to ask, Wendy, but how did Scott's body end up in a tree? I read about it in the paper, but they were short on details."

"Nobody knows. Someone put him there. The killer. But, I don't have any idea why he'd do that." She hesitated and added, "I suppose it could have been a woman, but that's…" Her voice trailed off. Suddenly, her composure seemed to drain away, and she put her hands to her face and sobbed. She snatched more tissues from the box and dabbed at her eyes. "I'm so sorry, Dr. Houston. I don't want to come across as a sniveling sissy, but I did love him so."

"There's nothing to be sorry for, Wendy. I understand completely."

"I'd hoped that you'd be able to help me find out what happened to Scott. Who killed him and why." She stood abruptly and started toward the door. "I have to go to work. The boss doesn't like for us to be late."

Jimmy stood behind his desk. "What kind of work do you do?" he asked.

"I tend bar at the Red Creek Saloon, near Harmon. I have a small place on Dry Fork." She sniffed and dabbed again at the corners of her eyes with the tissue.

"I'm sorry, Wendy, but I don't think there's anything I can do to help you. I'm not a detective, as I said before, and you'd be better off finding a licensed private detective or something."

"I've tried that, Professor. Do you have any idea how many of them there are in this area? None. That's how many," she said with a small resigned voice. "I found one in Morgantown, but he wanted too much money. Mileage back and forth each day, and all kinds of expenses. I just couldn't afford to hire him."

"I understand. I'll tell you what," he said reluctantly, "I'll talk to Sam Miller. Maybe he'll know someone who can help you. He retired last summer and since then, he's been traveling and having a big time. Last I heard he was in Key West doing who knows what."

She brightened and said, "Oh, thank you. I just knew that you'd help me. Frankie thinks the world of you, and he said that if anyone could help, it'd be you."

Jimmy listened as Wendy's footsteps receded down the hallway, wondering what he had gotten himself into. He returned to the window in time to see her get into her car and drive away. There was a knock at his door and he turned to see one of his students clutching an oversized cell phone. He had a worried look on his face.

* * *

Later that evening Jimmy sat on the deck of his cabin on Laurel Mountain, or as his friend Sam called it, his "nest." His father had called it the Eyrie—his refuge. Jimmy liked it because it was high on the mountain, relatively inaccessible, and he could see for miles. The small cabin was perched on the rocky side of the mountain and resembled a fire tower—one side rested on the ground and the other was held up with posts set into the rocks on the steep mountainside. It had a steeply pitched roof, many large windows, and a deck that wrapped around three sides. The view was breathtaking.

He thumbed through his bird book and found the description of a bobolink. Its scientific name is *Dolichonyx oryzivorus*, he read, and the birds are about seven inches in length. The female is sparrow-like, but the male is mostly black with a white rump and straw-colored nape. Now, his curiosity was sated. He wasn't much of a bird watcher. Botanists tend to look toward the ground where the plants grow, not high in the air. One of his colleagues jokingly said that as far as he was concerned there were two kinds of birds—crows and non-crows.

His large yellow dog trotted across the walkway that led from the parking lot to the deck setting up a tremor that rattled the wooden shutters on the windows. He flopped on his belly near Jimmy's feet and looked up at him. Jimmy rubbed his ears. Yellow Dog had been a gift from a former lady friend and had quickly become an important part of his life. Unfortunately, the lady friend hadn't. Jimmy was trying to train him but wasn't sure who was training whom. Jimmy picked up a sock stuffed with rags and tossed it across the deck. Yellow Dog promptly retrieved it but wouldn't give it to Jimmy. He sighed and watched the dog chew on the sock.

Jimmy leaned contentedly back in his chair and put his feet up on the deck railing. The sun was falling through a scattering of clouds, and he looked forward to another spectacular sunset. It was a perfect May evening. A slight breeze ruffled his hair, and he could hear birds twittering in the surrounding forest.

He thought about his meeting with Wendy Richmond. He admired her greatly for her spunk. He had no idea what it would be like to lose a spouse or someone you had grown to love. It had to be almost unbearable for her. If he were in her place, he'd want to find the killer and put him away, too. To make matters worse, Scott had been missing for six months before they'd found his body. How had she held up? Just thinking about him up in a tree, high on the mountain, with the birds working on him made Jimmy shudder. He had no idea how he could help Wendy, but maybe Sam would know what to do. Maybe he'd know someone who could ask some questions and help the sheriff solve this mystery. Jimmy frowned and scratched the back of his head. How the hell did the body end up in a tree on the top of a remote mountain?

As the sun settled behind the ancient mountains, the sky was streaked with vermillion light. Cumulus clouds, backlit by the setting sun, glowed red, lighting up the darkening sky. Jimmy watched raptly, enjoying every second of the spectacle. Yellow Dog, less impressed, paced back and forth on the wooden deck.

Jimmy had spent the winter in a small apartment in town because the cabin wasn't winterized. Now that the weather had improved, he'd given up the apartment and moved back to the Eyrie. He was happy to be back. The home he'd inherited from his parents had been burned to the ground, leaving him homeless except for the cabin. He'd put off having the house rebuilt. He wasn't sure why, but he just couldn't get motivated enough to start the arduous process of housebuilding. He'd received a settlement from the insurance company that would provide enough money to rebuild, but he'd think about that some other time. Maybe tomorrow or the day after.

The sun set behind the mountains and darkness quickly crept in around him. Night creatures began to creak and moan in the surrounding forest. He heard the descending whinny-call of an eastern screech owl far below in the trees. House lights flicked on, scattered here and there across the mountains. Far away, along one high ridge, he could see a smattering of car lights as they sped at seventy miles per hour along the Corridor H highway. A faint glow, low on the horizon, marked the location of Clarksburg, a small city along I-79.

The dog went to the cabin door and looked expectantly at Jimmy. Yes, he thought, the dog has me well trained. He got up from his chair and opened the door. The dog trotted into the cabin to his food bowl and finding it empty, curled up in his bed. He worked industriously on his front paws, gnawing at the pads and webbing between his toes, clicking his teeth. He carefully licked his paws clean.

Jimmy sat at his desk and pulled his phone from his pocket. He wanted to talk to Sam, but who knew where he was. He wasn't very good at answering his cell. He punched in the number and waited patiently as he heard the phone ring. He could hear Sam fumbling with the phone. Music blared in the background. Someone was laughing uproariously, and a jumble of voices almost drowned out Sam's tinny voice.

"Hullo?" Sam said.

"Sam? Is that you? I can barely hear you."

"Yeah, it's me. I haven't heard from you for a long time, Jimmy. Where are you? Are you still living in your nest up on the mountain?"

"Well, yeah. I spent the winter in town, but I'm back up here, at least for the summer."

"You're an old hermit. You know that, don't you? You should get out more." Sam had become a good friend to Jimmy, helping him clear his name and catch a killer.

"Yeah, thanks for the advice. Speaking of getting out, where are you?"

If anything, the music had gotten louder—a Jimmy Buffet tune. "I'm still in Key West. I've been here for several weeks. Right now, I'm at Margaritaville. You know, the real one on Duval Street."

Sam told Jimmy to hold on a second and stepped out of the restaurant to the relative quiet of the street. They talked for a few minutes, catching up with what each had been doing for the last several months.

Jimmy explained why he was calling, briefly describing Wendy's request. "When are you coming home, Sam? Will you be back in town any time soon?"

He laughed. "Yeah, I'm flying back early next week. I'm about out of money. Do you have any idea how much it costs to stay here? The cheapest hotel room I could find was over two hundred dollars a day. But, I'm having a great time."

An image of Sam came to mind as Jimmy listened to him describe in some detail the good time he was having—something about a woman he'd met. Sam was retired from the West Virginia State Police. It had been mutually agreed between Sam and the captain that he should retire. They hadn't parted friends. In his late fifties, Sam was big and broad-shouldered with a slight paunch. He was a former football player with thick arms and strong hands. He had been an excellent detective with an impressive case clearance rate. His wife, Ruth, had died a few years back.

Jimmy could hear music coming from the street. People laughed and talked as they passed Sam on the sidewalk. Faintly, from well down the street, a throbbing rhythm could be heard as a street musician drummed on upturned plastic buckets. "Well, Sam, when you get back in town let's get together. I'll buy your lunch. In the meanwhile, let's try to figure out how to help Wendy."

"Yeah, okay, but I'm not too anxious to get tied down. I had enough detective work to last a lifetime. Besides, I'm thinking about going on a cruise."

Jimmy laughed and said, "Looks like you've found a new lease on life, Sam. You've turned over a new leaf."

"When you get to be my age, you begin to think about having a good time while you can. As a friend of mine used to say; 'If you don't spend your retirement money, your kids will.' Well, I don't have any kids, but *someone* would step up to the plate to spend it."

Jimmy laughed again, pleased his friend was enjoying himself. He could hear a woman's voice calling to Sam, asking him to come back in the restaurant and listen to the music. Jimmy was almost sure she'd called him "Sammy."

Chapter 2

Jimmy sat on a stool behind the long slate-covered lab table at the front of the classroom, looking intently at his laptop screen. It was nine o'clock in the morning. Students, at desks scattered around the room, labored on their laptops, taking their final exams. When they were finished, they'd send their answers to the grade-maker software in his computer. It would crunch the numbers with other course grades and spit out a final letter grade for each of them. All he had to do was review the results, make any adjustments or corrections necessary, and then send the grades on to the registrar's office. He'd also send final grades for his courses to his students—they'd have them on their cell phones before they ate supper this evening. The registrar would send official records to all students within a few days.

He scrolled through the Google searches he'd made, reviewing newspaper articles about the body in the tree. There wasn't much about Scott's disappearance last fall, only a couple of short blurbs buried deep in the paper. It wasn't that unusual for a person to go missing.

A student raised her hand, and Jimmy went to her table to explain a question on her exam. He carefully re-stated the question, avoiding giving the answer away. He made a quick survey of the room, and then returned to his desk.

A reporter at the local newspaper had written a long article about the discovery of Scott's body. It was long on conjecture and short on facts. Another article from a paper in Charleston was more detailed. Ray Lambert, the reporter, had written a thorough article that contained information from police press releases and interviews with a variety of people who were near the case. He found a few other news items that had bits of information he thought might be of use. Jimmy flagged the articles and moved them to a folder on his computer. He closed the lid of his laptop and gave his attention to his test-takers.

One by one, the students completed their exams and stopped by his desk to say good-by. He would see many of the biology majors again in his advanced classes or in and around the department offices. Others, he would never see again. Most told him they had enjoyed his class—others just smiled and headed for the door, happy to be done with the semester and on their way. Summer vacation was something to anticipate. Some would graduate and enter the real world after spending four years in the cloistered environment of the college. Commencement was scheduled for the weekend and marked the end of the semester and the academic year.

Jimmy returned to his office and sat at his desk. He was thinking about Wendy Richmond and all she had gone through, when he heard a knock at his door. It was Frank Richmond.

"Come in, Frank," Jimmy said. "Or should I call you Frankie?"

"You've been talking to my mother," he said, grinning. "She has called me that ever since I was a baby." He was a good-looking kid of medium height with an unruly mop of dark hair. He wore the uniform all students wore; jeans, a dark t-shirt and tennis shoes. "She said she had come to see you."

"Yes. She told me what happened to her friend, Scott." Jimmy invited him to sit down.

Frank sat with his arms folded across his chest. "She said you were going to find out who killed him."

Jimmy hesitated. "That's not exactly what I said. I told her that I'd talk to Sam Miller, the retired police detective. He might be able to recommend a person who could do some investigating. Since he left the state police, he's been traveling and living the high life. I doubt that he'd be willing to take it on himself."

"Oh. She had the impression the two of you were going to start investigating right away."

"No, I don't know anything about detective work, and Sam seems to be happy being retired. He didn't exactly leave his position with the state police voluntarily. At best, it was a mutual agreement that he should leave. I don't think he wants anything to do with police work."

Frank leaned back in his chair. "I'm sorry to hear that. Mom will be disappointed."

"Maybe Sam can find someone to help her. She said she'd tried to find a private detective in the local area, but without luck."

"Yeah. She called everyone she could think of. You're about her last hope."

"Tell you what," Jimmy said reluctantly. "Let me talk to Sam, and we'll see what we can do. I'm not making any promises, but between the two of us, we should be able to come up with a way of helping out."

"Thank you, Dr. Houston. I would appreciate any help you can give her—my sister, too."

"Frank, do you have any idea how Scott's body ended up in a tree on the top of a mountain?" Jimmy's curiosity was getting the better of him.

"No. That has us all stumped. When he went missing, Mom just about worried herself to death. She called the sheriff's office just about every day, pushing them to find him. She knew that he hadn't just left without telling her where he was going. I think she knew deep down that he was dead. I thought the same thing. Scott was a private person, living up in the valley on that farm of his, but he and Mom were close. She knew him better than anyone."

"I have to ask the obvious question. Did Frank have any enemies? Anyone who'd want to do him harm?"

"That's the curious thing. Everyone who knew him, liked him. The sheriff couldn't find anyone who might have wanted him dead."

"Where does the sheriff's investigation stand now?"

"I think he's stumped. He's followed up all the leads they had, and it seems the investigation is at a dead end. As you know, there's a drug epidemic going on here, and the sheriff's focusing on that. People are dying from overdoses, so I can understand that he has to make some hard choices."

Frank was one of Jimmy's advisees, so they spent some time reviewing his program of studies. Jimmy brought Frank's records up on his computer and they discussed the classes he'd enrolled in for the fall semester. Together they reviewed his checklist for the completion of his degree and decided that with the advanced placement credits he'd brought with him from high school, he might be able to graduate a semester early. Frank smiled at that, saying, "That's great. That'll save me the cost of a full semester. Mom will be thrilled."

Frank told Jimmy about his summer job as an intern with the forest service. He'd be assisting with research on the effects of increased coyote populations on the state's white-tail deer herd. "Thanks again, Dr. Houston, for helping me get this internship. It'll be a great addition to my resume."

"That's what an advisor is for, *Frankie*," Jimmy said, laughing.

After Frank had left his office, Jimmy swiveled his office chair sideways to his desk, tapping a pen on its edge. He looked out the window, deep in thought. Frank was a good kid. He was polite, always had a quick smile, and was an excellent student. He seemed to be genuinely interested in his major field of study. But, what did a professor ever know about his students? He wasn't naïve enough to think that students *ever* told their parents or teachers everything they did. He hadn't when he was in college, and he knew students had lives of their own, sometimes secret lives.

He shook his head and smiled grimly. He turned back to his desk and looked at the stack of work he had yet to do before the semester was over. He picked up his to-do list and studied it carefully.

*   *   *

When Jimmy arrived back at the cabin, there was an hour of light left before dusk fell. Yellow Dog greeted him enthusiastically when he opened the door, then made a beeline for the grassy spot beside the tiny parking area to take care of business. Jimmy tossed his briefcase on the sofa and changed into faded blue jeans and a tee-shirt. He set up his father's old, brass telescope on the deck and focused on the farmhouse on a far mountain slope. The old house had recently been renovated. New paint and windows had made a vast improvement in its appearance. The old, leaky shingles had been replaced with shiny new metal. The garage doors, newly installed on the shed beside the house, were closed. He couldn't tell if the owner's truck was parked inside, or not.

Moving the telescope carefully with his fingertips, he followed the long, two-track driveway from the house to the gate at the entry to the property. The gate was always open—the owner didn't have livestock that might escape—but Jimmy was looking at the top of the gate-post. The house wasn't visible from the state road, and to save any potential visitor the trip over the rough driveway to the house, an old plastic bucket was placed upside-down over the top of the post if the owner was home and receiving guests. There was no bucket on the post. Laughing Woman wasn't home.

He stepped away from the telescope and leaned against the deck railing. He smiled to himself when he thought about her. She was slim and beautiful with wild hair and a quick smile. She came and went, living alone part-time in that old house with a large black dog. She had a telescope of her own, and they'd caught each other looking. She called him "Watcher." They'd laughed when they'd realized each was watching the other across the miles that separated them.

She'd invited him for dinner one night, and they'd enjoyed a pleasant evening in her house, but when he'd left, he realized he didn't know any more about her than before they'd met. Her first name was Dana, but she hadn't given a last name. She'd disappeared soon after, leaving the farm for who knows where, and he'd moved back into town for the winter. Now, he was hoping to catch her at home again.

Yellow Dog sat beside him, leaning against his leg, nosing Jimmy's hand, encouraging him to scratch his ears. Jimmy obliged as he always did. The dog thumped his tail against the rough planks in the deck floor. He returned to the telescope, scanning—as Louis L'Amore wrote—"the far blue mountains." Spring was almost done, and the acid-green leaves of the trees had given way to the green-black color of summer foliage. At the horizon, the mountains faded into every imaginable shade of blue. A Cooper's hawk screeched from a nearby tree. As the day ended, the temperature dropped quickly. Jimmy went inside, followed closely by the dog, to make his supper.

As a young man, Jimmy had learned that it was better to learn to cook for himself than to go hungry. He wasn't especially good at it, but he had quickly figured out how to read a cookbook. Cooking was a lot like performing a chemistry experiment. You measure out some of this and a little of that, heat it to the proper temperature, add some herbs and spices, stir it once in a while, and when it's done, serve it up on a plate.

He heated his old iron skillet on the gas hotplate and added a dash of olive oil and a dollop of butter, finely chopped onions, carrots, celery and garlic. A roughly chopped tomato, some chopped parsley, a splash of white wine and some of his special blend of Cajun spices were added next. He turned down the heat and let it reduce for a few minutes, then tossed in a handful of raw shrimp. While it all cooked, blending together, he put a pot of water on the stove and added a pinch of salt. When it came to a boil, he added some linguine pasta and set the timer for nine minutes.

The dog watched with great interest as Jimmy plated the food, covering the pasta with a generous spoonful of steaming Cajun shrimp. He broke off a chunk of bread from the loaf he'd bought at the deli in the grocery. Jimmy put some linguine in the dog's bowl and sat at the table by the window to eat his supper. He watched the last remnant of light fall beyond the mountains and listened to his old CD player as Alison Krauss and James Taylor sang *How's the World Treating You?*

Chapter 3

Jimmy and John Compton drove through Elkins and then took U.S. 219 south from Huttonsville. Many mountainous miles later, they drove past the turnoff to Snowshoe ski area. At the top of Elk Mountain, they turned west onto scenic Route 150 and soon arrived at Williams River. At that altitude, the mountains were just coming to life, showing a touch of green leaves on the trees. Splotches of crimson color marked red maples in full bloom. Mountain magnolia trees sported pale yellow-green blossoms as large as a man's cupped hands. Spring wildflowers were approaching their peak, and it was all Jimmy could do to keep from stopping along the way to do some botanizing. Williams River flowed to the west surrounded with mountain peaks soaring to heights well over four thousand feet. The boundary for Cranberry Wilderness lay nearby. It was a beautiful and wild mountainous terrain.

The two men got stiffly out of Jimmy's old Cherokee, stretched and pulled their fly fishing gear out of the cargo space. They assembled their rods and pulled on their waders, all the while keeping an eye on the tumbling waters of the river. They talked quietly as only close friends do, anticipating the coming of an evening hatch of mayflies.

They had left John's condo that afternoon, making the two-hour drive to fish the river during the prime time just at dusk. It would be a long drive back home in the dark, but they had done it dozens of times in the past.

They had been fishing partners since high school. After graduation, John had joined the Navy, and Jimmy had gone to college. Upon discharge from the military, John had opened a successful automobile repair shop. Jimmy had completed a PhD and was hired by State College to teach botany. They spent a lot of time together, mostly fly fishing.

Jimmy fished the deep pocket in the river just above the bridge, and John walked down the road to the confluence of the river and Tea Creek. They each caught several nice brown trout, releasing them back into the cold, rushing water. When it became too dark to see well, they met back at the Cherokee, talking excitedly about the fish they had caught. They packed their gear and climbed reluctantly into the vehicle. As Jimmy drove toward home, he told John about the body in the tree.

"Let me get this straight," John said. "The sheriff found a dead man in a tree up on Dolly Sods. Do they know who it is?"

"Yeah, his name is Scott Mitchell, or maybe I should say 'was.' He'd been there for months, and the birds had worked on him."

John grimaced and said, "That's not a pleasant thought. How did they identify him?"

"I don't know. Maybe he had identification on him, or they could have used DNA, I suppose. All I know about the case is what Wendy and Frank Richmond told me." He explained who they were and what they'd asked him to do.

John laughed, "So you say you're not going to get involved, huh? You don't think Sam will be interested? Who are you kidding? How can he resist a case like this? A dead man in a tree! Nobody knows how he got there or why. I'll bet you ten dollars it won't be a week before both of you will be neck deep in the case. Why, I'm curious myself, not that I'm going to get involved, but you must admit it is fascinating. What else do you have to do for the summer? I wish I had a job where I didn't have to work for three months of the year."

They had been through this argument before. Jimmy had tried to convince John—and a lot of others—that he worked all year round; teaching, doing research, going to conferences. He had long since given up the argument.

"No, I have too much work to do. I have a research grant, and then there's research in Costa Rica I'd like to do."

John snorted and shook his head. "Sounds like a pretty cushy job to me. You could take the time if you wanted to."

"I suppose, but I have no intention of getting involved. Besides, what do I know about being a detective?"

John wasn't convinced. He knew his friend better than almost anyone, and he'd gotten to know Sam in the last year. He'd bet his best flyrod that neither of them could resist the challenge of finding out who had killed Scott Mitchell and why he'd been stuck up there in that tree.

Jimmy dropped John off at his condo and drove up the winding mountain road toward his cabin. As he neared the narrow parking area, he could see that light streamed from the cabin's windows. Yellow Dog rushed down the road to greet him. Had he forgotten to turn off the lights when he left earlier in the day? And, he thought that he'd left the dog in his kennel. What was he doing running around free? Then, he saw that his parking space was occupied by a large, new SUV he'd never seen before.

He climbed out of the Cherokee and closed the door carefully, making as little noise as possible. As he walked across the catwalk toward the deck, a familiar voice said, "It's about time you got home, Professor. I've been waiting on you for hours."

Jimmy relaxed. "Former detective Sam Miller, what are you doing here? I thought it'd be another week before you showed up."

"I caught an early flight." The two men shook hands and slapped each other on the shoulders.

"How'd you get in, Sam? I'm sure I locked the door before I left this morning."

Sam snorted. "It didn't take me more than thirty seconds to open that rickety old door." He pulled a credit card from his wallet and shook it at Jimmy. I just slid this in the opening by the door lock and turned the handle. A first-grader could do it. You should be more careful. Someone could break in here and rob you blind, or worse yet, be waiting in the dark and brain you with a club."

Jimmy grumbled to himself. He'd heard this lecture before and was happy to change the subject. "I'm glad you're here, Sam. Have you eaten? How about a cup of coffee or something cold to drink?

"I had a hamburger in town before I came, but a cold glass of iced tea would be good."

Jimmy banged around in the small kitchen until he had made drinks for them.

Sam sat slumped in the old overstuffed easy chair by the woodstove while Jimmy sprawled on the couch. The dog lay on his side by Jimmy's feet, snoring softly. The two men drank their cold tea and talked quietly, catching up on each other's lives. A cool breeze had picked up, whistling around the cabin's eves. Finally, the conversation came around to the subject that both knew would come up.

Sam said, "You know as well as I do the sheriff wouldn't like having civilians poking around in his case."

"Wendy Richmond said the sheriff was swamped with the drug epidemic that's sweeping the county and the rest of the country. He's shorthanded as it is. She said he'd welcome the help."

"Well, I guess he might, but only if he was confident that he could trust whoever it was that decided to do it." Sam looked at Jimmy and raised an eyebrow. "You're not thinking about taking this on, are you?"

"No, not really. I have a lot of work to do this summer."

Sam snorted again and shook his head. "Yeah, sure. I know how busy you are. You've finished the spring semester, and you're as free as a bird until the end of August when classes resume."

Jimmy knew better than try to argue with him. "You have to admit, it is an interesting case. Not that I'm going to get involved or anything, but why would someone stash a body in a tree? There's a million places you could dispose of it without going to all that trouble. Whoever did it had to be pretty strong to drag it up there."

Sam frowned and asked, "Have you talked to any of the officers on the case?"

"No, I only know what I read in the papers and what Frank and his mom told me." He told Sam about their visits to his office.

They sat quietly for a few moments, listening to the wind blowing outside. They could hear the clatter of tree branches and the deep gonging of the large wind chime that hung from a beam at the corner of the cabin. The dog raised his head and listened to some faint sound only he could hear and then lay down again and went back to sleep.

Finally, Jimmy asked, "Do you know anyone who you could recommend to Wendy to help her with this? Maybe a former colleague who's retired and would like to make a few extra dollars? Someone she could trust not to rob her blind? She said she'd called all the private investigators in the area, and that they charged too much."

"No, not just off the top of my head. Most of the retired state policemen I knew have moved to Florida or some such place. I can't think of anyone."

Jimmy grinned at him and said, "I can think of one. I'm looking at him."

"No, now wait a minute. I told you that I'm tired of doing police work."

"What I think you're saying is that you're tired of dealing with the captain you worked for and all the bureaucracy that came with the job. Don't you miss the investigations? Just a little bit?"

"Well, maybe just a little," he conceded. "The investigation part was interesting. I have to say that I was never bored."

"I'd think the best part about being a private investigator would be you could do things your way. You'd have to keep some records and write reports for clients, but other than that you'd be your own boss."

"I guess that's right, but I don't ever want to work for the captain again. I got my fill of that."

Jimmy laughed and said, "From what I heard, you don't have to worry about him begging you to come back to your old job."

Sam laughed and grinned at Jimmy. "No, there's no danger in that. We didn't exactly part on good terms."

"So, you're free to do whatever you want. You could take on the job. What else do you have to do? Oh, I forgot. Didn't you say on the phone that you were going on a cruise? When will you be leaving?"

Sam grinned ruefully, "Oh, that fell through. The lady who was going to go with me decided not to go. Not much fun going on a cruise by myself."

"Who was she, if you don't mind me asking?"

"Her name was Lilly and she was a Conch I met in the Keys. A real nice lady, but whatever we had going ran its course and we decided to move on." He quickly changed the subject. "Wait a minute, Professor. I know what you're doing. You want me to take on this investigation, so you can tag along and satisfy your own curiosity."

Jimmy said seriously, "There is that, but more to the point, I'd like to see Wendy have some closure on this grim chapter in her life. She's lost two good men, and she deserves better. I talked to her for quite a while in my office, and I like her. I like her son, Frank, too. They're good people."

"I'm not promising anything, Jimmy. I'll sleep on it. Maybe I could go talk to the sheriff and see if he really wants someone poking around in his case."

"Do you know Sheriff Donovan?"

"I've met him a few times. I was stationed in another county, but the state police cooperate across county lines. I've seen him on various task forces and talked to him a couple of times. It's a small state, Jimmy, and everybody knows everybody in law enforcement."

"When do you think you'll get started?"

"Now, wait a minute. I haven't said I'd do it. You sure are getting pushy, Professor. Are you like this with all your friends?"

Jimmy laughed again. "I suppose it's in my DNA. Maybe you could call Sheriff Donovan and set up a meeting. Maybe tomorrow or the next day."

"Not so fast. I just got home and have a ton of things to do. If I don't get my lawn mowed soon, the neighbors will kick me out of the homeowner's association. Come to think of it, that might not be such a bad thing. I have a bunch of laundry to do, and I need to pick up my mail at the post office, pay some bills, and a dozen other things. Tell you what, I'll think it over and let you know."

Jimmy nodded. "Okay, that'll be fine."

"And if I meet with the sheriff, I suppose you'll want to tag along, that is if you can fit it in your *busy* summer schedule."

"Well, yes, if you don't think I'd be a bother."

As Sam drove his new SUV down the mountain, he wondered what he'd gotten himself into. In the cabin, Jimmy absently scratched Yellow Dog's ear and wondered why a killer would put his victim's body in the top of a tree.

*   *   *

A few days later, Sam and Jimmy met near the entrance to the State College campus. They climbed into Jimmy's Cherokee and drove eastward on the four-lane Corridor H highway, passing the exits to Elkins. They continued to the end of the new highway at Montrose, and onto U.S Route 219, a two-lane, secondary road.

Upon completion, Corridor H highway would extend—west to east—from I-79 in central West Virginia, to I-81 in the Shenandoah Valley near Front Royal. Only the unfinished ten-mile section remained from Montrose to Davis for the completion of the highway. The proposed route, when completed, would span the Cheat River just north of Parsons.

Jimmy and Sam sat in Sheriff Bill Donovan's messy office in the basement of the Adams County Administration Building, perched on a hillside. It had the usual array of framed photographs of policemen and dignitaries on its walls. A photograph of two grinning teen-aged children—a girl and a boy on a ski slope somewhere in the nearby mountains—occupied a prominent place among the stacks of papers on his desk. A middle-aged woman in a police uniform sat at a desk in the outer office and served as guardian to the sheriff's inner sanctum.

A short hallway led to a large, low-ceilinged room that was divided into individual work cubicles by sound-deadening panels. Some were occupied by deputies. The room smelled of burned coffee and sweat. Fluorescent light panels in the ceiling provided a white glare in the windowless room. A low thrum of voices was punctuated by ringing phones and laughter.

The sheriff was a big man, almost as big as Sam, tall with broad shoulders that stretched the fabric of his shirt. Sandy colored hair poked out from under his cap. In his middle forties, he had recently been reelected for another four-year term. Sam and the sheriff exchanged work histories and a couple of old cases they had in common. Sam introduced Jimmy. The sheriff's eyebrows rose when Sam told him Jimmy was a professor. They sipped lukewarm coffee that could easily have been used for paint remover.

The sheriff's swivel chair squeaked as he leaned back and moved it back and forth with his toes. "So, you and your friend are interested in my case, the man in a tree. Is that right?"

Sam said, "Yes, Jimmy told Mrs. Richmond that we'd try to find someone to look into her friend's disappearance and murder. Somehow, he volunteered my help." Sam turned to Jimmy and said, "Tell him what she asked you to do."

Jimmy told the sheriff that Wendy Richmond had asked him to investigate the murder since she couldn't find a private investigator she could afford. The sheriff frowned at him and pursed his lips. He swiveled back and forth. He suddenly sat forward, snapped his fingers and pointed at Jimmy with a sausage-like finger.

"Now I remember. You're the professor who was accused of killing one of your students. You were proved innocent—or at least not guilty. They're not always the same, you know."

"Yeah, sheriff, that was me. Sam, here, did the investigating and was able to find the killer. It was a colleague and friend of mine, or at least someone who I thought was a friend. He almost killed me before we figured everything out."

"You vouch for this man, this professor, Sam? He doesn't look like your usual private investigator."

Sam chuckled and said, "Yeah, he's okay, I guess." Sam looked solemnly at the sheriff. "We don't want to step on your toes. We don't want to interfere with your investigation. We'll drop it right now and go home if that's what you want us to do. But, if we can be of help, we could ask a few questions, see what we can find out. We'd keep you informed, give you updates as we go along." Sam paused, giving the sheriff time to think. "Mrs. Richmond said that you're strapped for manpower and have other irons in the fire. Namely the opioid epidemic that's sweeping the country."

"Yeah, we're stretched pretty thin. We invested a lot of time on the case before it went cold. Sam, I'd be pleased to have you look into it. With your experience in law enforcement, I'd be crazy not to accept your help. I can give you a temporary, special consultant appointment. I'll give you a badge, but I doubt that my higher-ups would allow me to give you a weapon. Too many legal and liability questions. I'll have to jump through some hoops to get the paperwork done but let me worry about that. But, your friend there is a different problem." He nodded toward Jimmy. "I doubt that you had many law enforcement seminars on your way to a PhD. Can't give you a badge, but I won't object if you tag along with Sam now and then. Just let Sam handle any of the technical stuff."

Jimmy said, "You're right, sheriff. I'll do what I can to help, but I don't know the first thing about investigating a crime. I'll be more than happy to let Sam do the heavy lifting."

The sheriff nodded. "It's a smart man who knows what he doesn't know." To Sam, he said, "Once you sign a contract, I'll see that you get copies of the case files. Unfortunately, there's not much in them. We interviewed the people closest to the crime, but mostly drew blanks. I can put you in contact with the medical examiner. She can go over the autopsy report with you. I'll tell the crime scene techs to cooperate with you, too. If you run into any roadblocks, let me know. I'll straighten them out."

"Great. We'll get started right away."

"As far as pay is concerned, well, there's not much leeway in my budget. I'll see what the folks on the county commission say, but I'd not expect anything more than a small honorarium, if that. I'll see what I can do, but don't get your hopes up. Don't go out and buy a new car or anything."

Sam said, "That's what I expected, Bill. A little help with expenses is about all I could hope for."

"Sam, I probably should tell you that when you called for an appointment, I called your old captain at the state police office. I'd heard about your run-in with him that resulted in your retirement—the whole law enforcement community heard about it. You were the talk of the town, for about fifteen minutes. After talking to him, I got a pretty good idea of what happened. Anyway, that's in the past. You had a distinguished career in law enforcement, and I'm pleased that you're on board with us."

As they left the office, the sheriff introduced Jimmy and Sam to the deputies who were at their desks and said that he'd make an announcement to the entire force that they would be working for him.

Chapter 4

The following morning, Jimmy and Sam returned to the sheriff's office to pick up copies of the case files. The sheriff had been right; the files were thin. They sat at a window table in a local restaurant and spread them between them. Diners came and went around them, eating their breakfasts and preparing for their workdays. The restaurant was constructed of hand-hewn poplar logs reclaimed from an old cabin and had a roof of green sheet metal. It sat beside a river under a canopy of large sycamore trees. They could hear the peaceful murmur of the river and see flashes of whitewater as it tumbled over a jumble of rounded boulders.

"Sam, where do we start? As you have rightfully pointed out, I don't know a thing about being a detective," Jimmy said.

"Well, it's pretty simple. We collect as much information as we can, and eventually something will float to the top. Some small clue will prompt something bigger, and that will lead us to something else. Before you know it, we'll have a suspect. Then, the hard work begins. It's one thing knowing 'who done it,' but another proving it in a court of law. That means we'll have to be careful with any evidence we find, following police procedures."

As they read, a waitress came by their table to take their orders. She was young, bright-eyed with a big smile. She wore a colorful apron with the restaurant's name and logo imprinted on the front. Jimmy guessed her to be right out of high school, or maybe, a college student. She served them coffee, took their orders and disappeared into the kitchen in the back.

Sam said, "The sheriff and his deputies did a pretty good job of interviewing people, although you can see that some deputies were better at making notes than others. They used a combination of complete and incomplete sentences and a lot of abbreviations. If we have questions, we'll have to go back to the officer to get a translation." Sam handed Jimmy a stack of files. "How about you make a list of the people interviewed. Include full names, addresses and phone numbers, so we can locate them when we're ready to talk to them."

"Will we re-interview all of them? There's going to be quite a list."

"Probably, unless we can rule some of them out. But, even if we rule them out as suspects, you never know when someone will tell us something important."

Jimmy began his list, recording the names in his cell phone. Sam frowned at him and said, "Can you print out hard copies, using that thing?" He nodded at Jimmy's phone.

Jimmy laughed and said, "Oh, I forgot. You want everything on paper, don't you? You need to join the twenty-first century, Sam. I can keep all our files on here," referring to his new phone. One of the perks of working for a college was that he was periodically given the newest version of phone for his work. He didn't have to pay for one of his own.

"Yeah, but if I wanted to review a file, I'd have to run you down to look at your phone." Sam was kidding. He knew that Jimmy could transfer everything to his phone, but somehow, paper copies were easier to read and handle, and you could put them in proper order, and well, paper copies were just better. Jimmy knew all that but couldn't help himself from giving Sam another jab.

"Are you still using that old flip-phone?"

"No! I bought one of those new smart phones." Then, he grinned at Jimmy and said, "I almost know how to use it."

As Jimmy completed his list, Sam flipped quickly through the autopsy report checking only to see if it was all there. Thankfully, the sheriff hadn't included any of the photographs taken during the procedure. He'd left a note in the folder saying if Sam absolutely needed to see them, he could come in the office and look at them. He didn't want such sensitive photographs getting out to the public, especially the media. The last thing he wanted was for a gruesome photograph of the body to show up on the front page of the local newspaper.

Sam said, "Let's hold off on reading the autopsy report until we interview the medical examiner. Sometimes it's better to hear the short version first. We can always go back and read for details later."

The waitress brought their breakfasts, and they pushed the stacks of files aside long enough to eat. She refilled their coffee cups and retreated behind the front counter, propped her elbows on it, and began flirting with a young man who sat on a stool. They leaned toward each other, laughing occasionally.

Sam and Jimmy read through the police files, exchanging folders occasionally, each with a frown of concentration on his brow. Customers glanced at them as they passed by but paid little attention to them. They were probably mistaken for salesmen, or maybe lawyers preparing for a case.

When they had finished reading, Sam pulled a binder from his weather-beaten briefcase and put it on the table. "This'll be our murder book. We'll keep everything in it; our notes, documents, copies of things we find, and so on." He nodded at the binder and said, "That way we'll have everything we need in one place. You can keep all the stuff you want on your phone, but copies of everything go in here. Okay?"

"Sure, Sam. I was just kidding before. What about the sheriff's files? Do they go in there, too?"

"No, we can put them in a folder and stash them in the safe in my house."

Jimmy laughed. "You're the only person I know who has a safe in his house. You see them in the movies, but you're the first person I've ever met who actually has one. Somehow, I'm not surprised."

"Comes from being a cop, I guess. I had all kinds of stuff that I had to keep secure, and it was often more convenient to keep it at home than having to drive back to the station. Besides, I had a sidearm that had to be secured—I kept it in there, too."

Sam was quiet for a moment, then leaned back and looked sternly at Jimmy. "This is what you professors call a teachable moment. I'll be the professor, and you can be the student. Now that you've read through all the files, what do you think we should do next?"

Jimmy thought for a moment. "I'm tempted to say that we should start re-interviewing people, but that seems kind of random. How do we know who's important and who isn't? Seems to me that we could waste a lot of time without some way of prioritizing them."

"You're right about that. We may have to re-interview them all, but maybe not."

"I think we should start with the body. The medical examiner might be able to help focus our investigation. And then, the crime scene tech people can help translate the evidence they found."

"Bingo! You might make a cop yet. The autopsy is written in technical terms, and I'd like to have Dr. Whitehead translate it. She serves as the medical examiner, doesn't she?"

"Yes, Dr. Victoria Whitehead. According to the file, she's an emergency room doctor at the local hospital."

Sam closed his murder book and crammed it back into his briefcase. He bunched the case files together and pushed them toward Jimmy. "Here, Professor, make yourself useful. You can carry them out to the car." He called the hospital to make an appointment with Dr. Whitehead.

*   *   *

It was late afternoon by the time they arrived at the hospital. It was a large brick structure that sprawled over most of a city block. Over the years, additions had been built in what appeared to be a random pattern. A large air conditioning unit labored on the roof of the main section of the complex. It contained a large, many-bladed fan that vibrated and roared. As they approached the visitor's parking lot an ambulance, it's siren screaming, came to a screeching halt at the emergency entrance. A man, wearing a technician's uniform, jumped from the driver's side and rushed to the back of the van to help unload a hapless victim. They pushed the laden gurney through automatic doors and disappeared inside.

Sam and Jimmy stopped at the information desk in the lobby to ask for directions.

"We're looking for Dr. Whitehead. Can you direct us to her office?" Jimmy asked.

The receptionist, a tall woman with gray hair, wore a name tag that identified her as a hospital volunteer. Judging from her appearance, Jimmy figured she was retired and looking for something to occupy her time. She gave them a complicated set of directions that entailed a lot of twists and turns into the bowels of the building.

They walked along the narrow hallways, listening to the sounds of misfortune and misery that emanated from the numbered rooms along the way. Sam's forehead glistened with sweat as he remembered the endless hours he'd spent in a hospital with his wife as her life slowly drained away. The unmistakable odor of disinfectant and floor cleaner assailed his nostrils. He wiped the moisture from his face with the handkerchief he kept in his back pocket.

The door led directly from the hallway into the doctor's office and stood open a crack. A brass plate announced her name. Jimmy knocked gently.

"Come in," the doctor said.

"Dr. Whitehead?" Jimmy asked.

"Yes. Come in and have a seat." She nodded toward two uncomfortable-looking visitor's chairs. After they were seated, she offered them coffee or water. They both declined. Dr. Victoria Whitehead was an attractive woman, in her late forties with graying hair done up in a no-nonsense arrangement on top of her head. She wore hospital scrubs and was petite with an engaging smile.

Jimmy and Sam introduced themselves, and they exchanged the usual greetings. They explained why they were there.

She sat at a small, metal desk that contained stacks of files and a laptop. Framed medical diplomas were displayed on the wall behind her. "Sheriff Donovan called me and said that you'd be coming by. He explained what you wanted. Frankly, I'm surprised that you showed up so quickly."

Sam said, "We won't take much of your time, Doctor. We know you're busy. We have not yet read the autopsy report. We thought it might be best if you gave us a condensed version first. You know, the *Autopsies for Dummies* version. We'll read the full report later."

She laughed. "Oh Sam—you don't mind if I call you by your first name, do you? —Bill told me about your background. All those years of doing police investigations! I suspect you've read more autopsies than I've written. I doubt you need me to interpret."

Sam chuckled. "Yeah, I've read a few, but it's always important to get the opinion of an expert."

Jimmy spoke up, "Although I'm a scientist, I don't know anything about autopsies. I'm just along for the ride. Your explanations would be a big help to me."

She smiled and said, "Yeah, Bill told me about you, too. He said you're a botanist. I can see how it would be a whole new world to you." She turned back to Sam and said, "Okay, what can I tell you?"

Sam asked, "What was the immediate cause of Scott Mitchell's death?'

She leaned toward them, looking first at Sam and then at Jimmy with a grim smile on her face. "He was killed by a blow to the back of his head with a blunt object. It left a rounded indentation in his skull 7.2 centimeters in diameter. That's almost three inches. I'd say that death was nearly instantaneous. He would have lost consciousness immediately. I won't go into the gruesome details of how I know that— it's all in the report. Suffice it to say, his brain was badly damaged. I couldn't find any evidence of defensive wounds. There weren't any skin scrapings under his fingernails that might help identify the killer."

"So, he was surprised by the attack?" Jimmy said.

She smiled again. "Well, I don't know if he was surprised to be hit on the head or not. Let's just say he was probably struck from behind without warning."

Jimmy nodded, conceding his inexperience in asking technical questions. He tried again. "Was the weapon found?"

"You'll have to talk to the crime scene technicians for an official answer, but from what Bill told me, it hasn't been found."

"Was there any indication of what the weapon was? Was there any residue in the wound that might indicate what kind material it was made of?" Jimmy asked.

She hesitated a moment before answering. "Don't hold me to this, but I think it was a rock. I found a single grain of what appears to be sand in the wound. I noted that in the autopsy report, but I can't officially say that's what it was. If it's important to your investigation, I suppose someone could analyze it, but that'd be expensive, and there wouldn't be anything left of it after the test."

"Well," Sam said ironically, "that narrows the murder weapon down to just about a zillion rocks."

"Actually, it was probably something like a river rock, if that helps. Something rounded and smooth," she said. "But, I can only tell you what the end that struck his head was like. The other part of the weapon could have had any shape. It could have been spherical or long with a rounded end. There's no way of telling."

"Can you give us any idea of when he was killed?" Jimmy asked.

"I can only speak in general terms. He was found in early spring, when it was still cold, but you know how it is here in the mountains. The temperature goes up and down like a yoyo, so it's impossible to tell how fast the body decomposed. The birds had been at him. He'd been up there for a while, probably for months. The body was wrapped in an old blanket, but the birds had opened it in several places. There were a few tooth marks on some of his bones like a rodent had been gnawing on him. He disappeared sometime after Thanksgiving, so you can do the math. Say, three or four months. I can't be more specific than that."

"No help there," Sam said. "No way to check a suspect's alibi."

Jimmy asked, "How sure are you that the body was that of Scott Mitchell?"

"Absolutely sure. First, he had identification on him. He had a wallet in his hip pocket that contained his driver's license, and we did DNA tests on the body to compare with samples taken from his house. You know, from his toothbrush and hair from his bathroom. He was a good housekeeper, but they had lots of choices. The Sheriff took samples right after he disappeared."

Sam asked, "Were you at the scene where the body was found? I mean, before the tech people took him down from the tree?"

"Yes, I always go out to the scene if the cause of death isn't obvious. I don't go out to car accidents and things like that, you know, where the cause isn't a great mystery. I do autopsies in our morgue if I'm asked. But, you must admit this was a special case. Bill called me out right away. As you probably know, Sam, most autopsies are done in Charleston at the state morgue. Bill asked me to do this one so that he'd have the results quickly."

"Do you do a lot of autopsies?" Jimmy asked.

"No, as I said before, only for special cases. I'm an emergency room doctor, not a coroner."

Sam said, "We reviewed copies of the case files from the sheriff's office. Crime scene reports didn't reveal any evidence that the victim was killed at the site. They believe he was killed elsewhere and transported to the scene. Do you agree with that?"

"I don't have any reason to believe otherwise. The corpse was tightly wrapped with a blanket and bound up in a neat bundle with rope. Someone hoisted him up into a large maple tree." She nodded toward Jimmy. "I believe it was a *red* maple and secured him there with more of the same kind of rope, and before you ask me how I know this, I was still at the scene when the technicians took him down. That's part of my duty—to just be there observing as the technicians do their work. If there were questions in court, I can testify that they collected evidence in a reasonable manner."

"Tell us what you saw when you got to the scene," Sam said.

"The body was found on national forest land. There's a long gravel road that leads along the mountain crest at Dolly Sods. Someone had put him on a tree limb about three quarters of the way around Northland Loop Nature Trail. Since you're a botanist, Dr. Houston, you've probably been there."

"Oh yes, many times. There's an interesting glade there, and I visit it often with students. The entire area is a botanist's dream."

Dr. Whitehead paused, shifting around in her chair. Hospital sounds, and odors drifted in through the door. "Anyway, there's a large maple tree with a limb that extends over the trail. The body was tied to the limb about thirty feet above the ground. The technicians had a heck of a time getting it down. They used an extension ladder, and one of the techies climbed up there and cut him down."

"Did they lower the body with ropes?" Jimmy asked.

"No, the technician just put it over his shoulder and climbed back down the ladder. It wasn't very heavy, having lost a lot of fluids. A body desiccates, dries out, as it decomposes. The body weighed about a hundred pounds. We sent our biggest techie up the ladder to get him."

The doctor's phone buzzed, and she looked at it. "Sorry, gentlemen, I've got to go. They're bringing in a car accident victim, and I'm needed. If you have more questions, maybe you could call me, or send a text. I'll help any way I can."

Jimmy and Sam walked back down the hallway. Dr. Whitehead hurried through a side door that displayed a sign that warned only authorized personnel were permitted to enter. As they walked back to the parking lot, a gust of wind swirled dust and grass clippings around them and sent a Styrofoam cup skittering into the street. A dark cloud hung over the horizon to the west—they heard a rumble of thunder. A spring storm was approaching. They trotted across the lot and climbed into the Cherokee.

Chapter 5

Gusts of wind battered the Cherokee as decorative shrubs and trees bordering the parking lot whipped back and forth. Rain strummed on the roof, and the windows quickly fogged. Jimmy and Sam waited out the storm before heading home.

"So, what's next, Sam? Do you think we need to interview the crime scene technicians, or can we depend on their report?"

"Let's depend on their report for now. It was comprehensive, and we can always interview them if we need clarification or more detail."

"Did anything catch your eye? Anything we need to follow up?"

Sam scratched the back of his head and thought for a moment. "I'm wondering how the killer got the body up in that tree. Whoever it was had to be one strong dude."

"Do you suppose he had a ladder like the technicians used? Even at that, I'd hate to try to tote a grown man up a thirty-foot ladder. I wonder how much he weighed before he was killed."

"That's a good question. It would have been on his driver's license. I wonder if the sheriff got copies of his medical records. I didn't see them in the files. If he's ever had an office visit to a doctor, they'd have weighed him. My doctor always has a nurse do it and then complains that I should lose weight." Sam unconsciously rubbed his stomach. "That's something we need to know." He opened the murder book and made a note.

"Do you suppose there was more than one killer? Two men, or women for that matter, could have found a way to hoist him up there.

Maybe with ropes. I didn't see anything in the tech report that supports that, did you?"

Sam said, "No. So far, there's no evidence there was more than one killer, but that doesn't mean there wasn't. We don't know if ropes were used."

"If they used ropes, there should be fibers on the blanket."

Sam chuckled. "You've been watching too many crime stories on TV. I doubt they tested for them. This isn't a big-city police department, you know."

Jimmy ignored the comment. "Is it common for more than one person to be involved in a murder?"

"It's not unheard of. In a case like this, though, I'd bet it was one person. I suppose someone could have killed him then enlisted another person to help get rid of the body. That person would be guilty of a crime, too. An accessory after the fact, even if he didn't do the actual killing."

"If we can figure out how the killer got the body up in the tree, it might tell us if there was more than one. It might tell us something about the killer's size, too. However it was done, it took a lot of physical strength. I think we need to make a trip to Dolly Sods to look at the crime scene."

"That's not a bad idea. We'll take a ladder."

The rain finally stopped, and streams of sunshine broke through the clouds. A robin began singing in a nearby tree. They rolled down their windows and let the fresh smell of mountain air wash over them. Jimmy put the Cherokee in gear.

*   *   *

Jimmy awoke to a serenade of bird songs outside his cabin window. Sometime during the night, he'd pulled his blanket over his head. He pushed it aside and sat up. Sunshine streamed through the window beside his bed, making the small room dazzlingly bright. He squinted his eyes, allowing them to adjust to the glare. The clock on the nightstand informed him it was seven-thirty. Yellow Dog sat in the doorway looking at him hopefully. When he saw Jimmy look his way, he pounded his tail on the floor and tossed his head.

Jimmy got out of bed and pulled on a pair of jeans and a t-shirt. He spent a few minutes in the tiny bathroom and then walked in his bare feet to the kitchen. The dog followed him, his nails clicking on the wooden floor. When he trotted to the cabin door, Jimmy let him out to do his morning routine. Jimmy turned on the radio to catch the morning news and filled his old coffee pot with cold water and ground coffee. He smiled as he remembered his father making coffee in this same "percolator." He wondered how many of his students had ever seen one. They probably drank chocolate-flavored stuff—with a shot of whipped cream on top—from Starbuck's if they drank coffee at all. The pot was the 8-cup model, made of blue-speckled, porcelain-covered metal. The glass bubble in the lid was stained with years of use.

He cooked bacon and scrambled eggs in a cast-iron skillet as the coffee brewed. The cabin filled with its pleasing aroma. When all was ready, he ate his simple breakfast on the deck, savoring the sharp morning air that ruffled the tree leaves nearby. The valleys below were filled with fog, giving the appearance of a large lake, sharp and bright in the morning sun. The dog sat at attention, hoping for any morsel that Jimmy might give him. "No begging," Jimmy said to the dog. "It's not dignified. You have your own kibble." The dog lowered his head and licked his lips. Jimmy tossed him a piece of bacon.

After he washed the dishes and put them away, he loaded the dog into the Cherokee and headed down the mountain to town. When he arrived at the college campus, he parked in his usual spot behind the science building. He sneaked the dog into the building through a side entrance, telling him to be quiet. Once in his office, he pointed toward a rug conveniently located in a corner. The dog lay down on it and began licking his paws.

Jimmy sat at his desk, sorting through a stack of phone messages. Even though he had the latest technology at his fingertips, the department still fielded most of his calls. Otherwise, he'd never get anything done. He spent a half hour responding to e-mails. He walked down the hall to the department chair's outer office and greeted Sylvia, the department's administrative assistant, who typed furiously on her computer.

She looked up and smiled. "Why, Dr. Houston, I didn't expect you today. Did you have an appointment or something?" She was a middle-aged woman, pretty with dark, graying hair. She and Sam had gone out a few times, but Jimmy didn't know any of the details. He didn't think they were seeing each other now. Sam hadn't told him much and he hadn't asked.

"No, I just came in to catch up on a few things," he said. He sat down in one of the visitor's chairs beside her desk, extending his legs, crossing his ankles. During the summer, faculty members came and went as needed. Most worked away from their offices, traveled to meetings, did research, and went on vacations. They chatted about her children and grand-children, and she asked about his sister who lived in Wyoming with her family.

"Is Dr. Tapper in? I need to talk to her about the research I hope to do in Costa Rica." Belinda Tapper was the newly hired chair of the department.

"Yes, you can go right in. She just got off the phone." She leaned toward him and said confidentially, "Your trip has been approved. You've been there before, haven't you?"

"Yes, a couple of times. I'm doing research on tropical ecology."

"What's it like there?" she asked.

Jimmy laughed and said, "Mostly rain and howler monkeys. They wake us up every morning at daylight. It rains almost every afternoon, and the monkeys raise a ruckus. I guess they don't like getting wet." They laughed together as he told her about the research station and the work he was doing.

Jimmy rapped on the office door. A pleasant voice from within told him to enter. She was a stout woman, in her mid-forties, with piercing blue eyes. She wore jeans with a plain cotton top. She smiled and shook hands firmly with him and led him to two armchairs near a window.

They talked briefly about the goings-on at the college, and then she said, "I'm glad you came in, Dr. Houston. I've been wanting to talk to you privately. I don't know just how to say this, but I'd like to clear the air. I hear by the grapevine you were interested in the chair's position before I was hired. This is kind of awkward. I've heard the dean's version of why you withdrew your application, and now, I'd like to hear yours."

Jimmy chuckled. "Dr. Tapper, you don't have anything to worry about. I'm not interested in the chairmanship. Oh, at one time I was, and maybe sometime in the future I'll be again, but for now, I'm very happy with my status as a faculty member. I was just granted tenure this spring, and I like teaching. I have a lot of research I'd like to do." He told her about being charged with murder, losing his job, and being cleared when the murderer confessed. "I was just happy to be cleared and reinstated to my old job. While all that was going on, I bumped noses with the president and dean, but we've worked out our differences. We're all professionals. We can work together even if we disagreed in the past."

"It's a relief to hear that. I was nervous taking the job, thinking maybe others in the department might not want me here."

"No, it's nothing like that. I'm sure you know how a college faculty works. One minute we're squabbling like a bunch of kindergarten kids, the next we're getting along. You'll be just fine. I haven't heard any rumblings among the faculty you should be concerned about."

They discussed the details of his trip to Costa Rica and his fall schedule. She signed his travel request with a flourish and handed it to him. "Sylvia will make your travel arrangements, and I assume you will take care of accommodations at La Selva. I've never been there. What kind of a research station is it?"

Jimmy told her about the *Organization for Tropical Studies* and its mission. He suggested that they explore avenues of funding for undergraduate research for some of their students. She said that since she was a cellular biologist, she'd have to depend on him to take the lead on that. Ecology wasn't her specialty. They talked about college politics and exchanged personal information, getting to know each other.

Sylvia was on the phone when he dropped the travel request form on her desk as he left, mouthing a thank you. When he entered his office, Yellow Dog stood and stretched. Jimmy took time to complete his monthly travel voucher—Sylvia had reminded him that it was overdue—and was startled when his cell phone vibrated. It was Sam.

"Where are you?" he asked.

"I'm in my office. At work. Why?"

"When are we going to the murder scene? Are you free this afternoon?" Sam asked.

"I only have a few more things to do, and then I can meet you. It's not noon yet, so we should have enough time. It doesn't get dark until almost nine. It'll only take us an hour or so to get there."

Jimmy left his Cherokee in a Hardee's parking lot and got into Sam's SUV. A long aluminum extension ladder was lashed to the luggage rack on top. The dog climbed into the back seat and tried to lick the back of Sam's neck. He pushed him away.

"I like your dog, Jimmy, but I don't think I need my ears washed."

"He's just trying to be friendly. He likes you. You're lucky he doesn't decide to chew them off," Jimmy said, laughing.

They took the onramp to Corridor H highway and sped by the exits to Elkins, continuing until it ended abruptly. They drove through Parsons, Thomas and Davis where they followed Route 32 through Canaan Valley. A sharp turnoff led them on a narrow, winding road along the side of the mountain to the bridge over Red Creek. The SUV bucked and groaned over the rough, unpaved road as they climbed the mountain to Dolly Sods on Forest Service Road 75. They soon reached the parking area for the loop trail where the body was found. The dog jumped from the vehicle and began searching the shrubs and trees along the road, his nose to the ground.

They took the aluminum stepladder off the top of the SUV, and Jimmy pulled on a backpack filled with equipment Sam had brought along. Sam removed the murder book from his briefcase, and they each grabbed an end of the ladder. They walked down the rough, rock-strewn trail, past the boardwalk that extended into the glade, and soon arrived at a large maple tree that stood along the trail. Yellow police crime scene tape was tied around its base. Ravens called to one another from the forest.

"Well," Sam said, "we could have walked along the back part of the loop and saved some time. The tree's only a few hundred feet from the forest service road. That's probably the way the killer brought in the body."

"Yeah, next time we'll come in the back way and save a few minutes."

They stood on the trail looking up at the large branch that extended from the tree, about thirty feet up. It was shady on the trail, and red spruce trees crowded in around them. Jimmy also recognized mountain-laurel, service berry, a few yellow birch saplings, and closer to the bog, alder. The trail was edged with diminutive trailing arbutus vines and teaberry. Reindeer lichen and ground pine spotted the ground here and there. Sam pulled a crime scene photograph from his murder book and held it up, looking from it to the tree branch, and back.

They stacked their gear in a pile on a large flat rock and began an examination of the ground. The crime scene people had done a meticulous search, but Sam insisted that they do it again. They searched in ever-enlarging circles around the trunk of the tree, soon becoming entangled in the heavy brush and down-falls that littered the ground. They didn't find anything of significance. They examined the ground directly under the tree searching for any indentation a ladder might have left in the soil. It had been almost nine months since the murder took place, so it was unlikely any sign of a ladder would still be there. Not to mention the result of the tromping back and forth of policemen, hikers, crime scene technicians, emergency medical technicians, and so on. But, they looked anyway.

"Dr. Whitehead said the technicians used a ladder to get the body down. We didn't even find evidence of that," Sam said.

They extended their ladder and set it against the tree limb. It barely reached.

"How about climbing up there and taking a look? You're a lot younger than I am. Besides, I'm not fond of heights," Sam said.

Jimmy climbed the shaky ladder while Sam held it. When he reached the limb, he called back down to Sam, "Just what am I looking for? You're the expert."

"Evidence. Remember that we're trying to figure out how the killer got the body up there. Look for skinned bark or anything else that might indicate that ropes were used."

Jimmy stood on the ladder and looked carefully at the bark on the limb. He could see places where it was roughed up, probably where the body was lashed to the limb. He'd want to look at the crime scene photos again to be sure. He snapped a few pictures with his phone. He bucked the ladder along the limb, making it clatter and shake, trying to move closer to the trunk.

"Jeeze, Jimmy, don't do that. I thought for sure you were coming down outta there. You scared the crap out of me."

Jimmy laughed. "I need to get closer to the main trunk." He climbed down to the ground, and they moved the ladder. He climbed back up and examined the limb where it joined the trunk. He found an arc of rope burns over the top of the limb. "I found something. Whoever did this, used a rope. It wore off some of the bark." He described the rope burn to Sam and took more pictures.

Back on the ground, Jimmy and Sam sat on a pile of rocks, looked at the pictures in Jimmy's phone and talked. Even if the killer used a rope to get the body up in the tree, how did he move it out the limb and tie it there? Crime scene photos showed the body at least five feet from the main trunk of the tree.

Jimmy said, "Let's say he threw a rope across the limb and tied the end around the body. If he pulled it up, it would end up just under the limb. How did he get it out on the limb?"

Sam thought for a few minutes. "Maybe he used the rope to climb up in the tree himself. Then he pulled up the body. If that was the case, it would take almost inhuman strength. We still need to know how much Scott weighed."

Jimmy pulled out his phone and called Wendy Richmond. Within minutes they had an answer. Scott Mitchell weighed almost two hundred pounds. Jimmy looked at Sam and said, "Women always know these things."

Sam nodded solemnly in agreement. "Ruthie knew how much I weighed—to the ounce. If I put on a pound or two, she'd know it, and tell the doctor on me." He smiled, thinking about his late wife. "She knew all my clothing sizes, too. Shoes, included."

"Can you imagine someone sitting thirty feet off the ground, hauling two hundred pounds of dead weight, hand over hand, up onto that limb? I don't think so."

"No, he must have used a block-and-tackle or something. That means he had to have a point of attachment even higher in the tree." Sam looked up at the branches, shielding his eyes from the sunlight that filtered down through the forest canopy. "I don't think you can get up there. The ladder's not long enough."

"No, and I don't climb trees. Maybe when I was a kid I'd have tried it, but not now."

Sam searched through the backpack and pulled out a compact pair of binoculars. He moved back from the tree and scanned the upper branches. "There's a branch up there that he might have used, but I don't see any damage to the bark. I can't tell." He checked from several angles, but with no luck. "Here, you try it. Your eyes are younger than mine."

Jimmy looked, repeating Sam's movements from one area to another, but he couldn't tell if a rope had been attached. "It's possible, but I can't tell for sure. But, using a block-and-tackle is the only way I can figure one man could have done this. It brings up the possibility that there were two of them."

"Yeah, maybe he, or they, used a combination of a rope *and* a ladder. One man could have climbed up a ladder to the limb, and the other man pulled the body up on a rope he'd tossed over the limb. Then, the first man wrestled the body onto the limb. It would still take a lot of strength to do that. Have you ever had to move a dead body?"

"No, Sam, I can't say that I have. I don't see too many of them in my line of work."

"Well, I have, and I can tell you from experience, a dead body is just about the most awkward thing you can try to carry. Once you get it over your shoulder it isn't so bad but picking it up is a real job. I don't know if I could carry a two-hundred-pound dead body more than for a few minutes."

Jimmy didn't like thinking about carrying dead bodies around. "A few years back, I had an arborist trim some of the trees around my house. The man who did the limb-trimming hung from ropes. He moved around the top of the trees like a monkey on a vine. He was good at it. Maybe our killer is a tree-trimmer. He'd know how to rig ropes and climbing a tree like that would be a snap for him."

"Let's not get ahead of ourselves. We need to stick to the evidence and let it lead us wherever it will." While Sam made notes in the murder book, Jimmy searched the area for interesting plants.

The dog came trotting up the trail. He'd been in the bog and was covered with black, smelly mud. He shook himself, slinging gobs of muck in a wide arc. Sam took one look at him, shook his finger at Jimmy and said, "He's not riding in my new SUV."

Chapter 6

Sam met the sheriff for an early breakfast. They sat in a booth along the back wall of the restaurant. The sheriff had taken a seat that allowed him to scan the entrance and room's interior. A waitress came by and set scarred mugs on the table before them. Each contained steaming, black coffee. A metal spoon stood in each mug like a buoy in a hot tub. The sheriff emptied a yellow packet of sweetener in his cup and added cream. He stirred lazily.

"Thanks for taking time to see me, Sheriff. I know you're busy," Sam said.

"Where's your buddy, the professor. He hasn't bailed out on you, has he?"

Sam laughed. "No, nothing like that. He's as curious about this killing as I am. He's out somewhere doing field work on a big project he's working on. I don't have the faintest idea what it's about. He keeps talking about doing quadrant counts or something. Whatever that is." Sam motioned toward the murder book he'd placed on the table. "We're going to start interviewing people and thought you might have some thoughts about who to talk to first."

"Well, I'm at something of a loss, too. None of the people we interviewed seemed to have a motive to kill Scott. At least, not a serious one."

"What do you mean?"

"Back about a year ago, Scott had a run-in with Kelly Rice. You probably remember her from the files. She's originally from New Jersey.

She's what would have been called a hippie, back in the seventies. From what we've been able to piece together, she started a war with her neighbors up there over her chickens. It was in all the city papers, and on TV—what reporters called 'the chicken wars.' She had a whole flock of them right in the middle of an upscale housing development and was eventually forced to get rid of them. She went to town hall, and then to court. Seems she threatened everyone in sight. Then, after she sold her chickens, just to spite her neighbors, she planted her yard in corn. She said the neighborhood association could go to hell. That didn't go over so well, either. She eventually sold her house and moved down here. Bought a little bit of land, went off the grid and began farming. Lucky us. She's a real piece of work."

"What was her argument with Scott about?"

"Oh, more of the same. She has a flock of goats and some of them got through her fence and onto Scott's property. Her land adjoins his. They ate everything they could find, including some of Scott's rare ferns. Seems they're protected by that federal endangered species act. Scott complained to us, and she threatened to make him into a gelding, and it just went from there."

"Do you think she's a real possibility as a suspect? You think she's capable of murder?"

The sheriff hesitated for a moment. "You know, I could see her working herself up into a rage and whacking him on the head with a rock or something. But, she's probably a long shot." He stirred his coffee again and placed the spoon along his knife and fork, aligning them carefully. "Her property isn't worth a lot. She only has a few acres, but the land developers are chomping at the bit to get their hands on it. Most of the available land up there near the ski resort is already developed into vacation cottages. They're boxed in by national forest land and the nature preserve. From what I hear, they've made her a few offers, but she told them to take a hike, or something more colorful. It's my guess that having been run out of New Jersey, she's dug in her heels. She's not about to budge. Where would she go this time?"

"What about Scott's land? Isn't it worth a lot, too?"

"Yes and no. Remember, there's the endangered ferns. By federal law, that land can't be developed. As sheriff, I'm also the county treasurer. The sheriff's department collects property taxes. The assessor and I went through all this when she placed a value on his property. For tax purposes, it's almost worthless. We can only collect taxes on it as undeveloped property. He pays almost nothing. If it wasn't for those ferns, it'd be worth millions."

"Can't they just dig up the ferns and move them?"

"No way. If someone digs them up, the feds will slap him with a fine, and I mean a huge fine. There's also a prison term involved. No, they're untouchable."

"That brings up my next question. If his land isn't worth anything, who profits from Scott's death?"

"No one that we could see. He has a few thousand dollars in the bank. We found a couple of hundred dollars in a desk drawer in his house. He was living on a small military pension and odd jobs. The pension ended with his death, and he wasn't old enough to collect social security. He seems to be one of those rare souls who wasn't interested in accumulating wealth. He didn't have life insurance.

"His only relative, Sandy Lynch, will inherit whatever his estate is worth once probate is completed. She's his only sister's daughter. There was another child, a son, but he was killed some years ago in Iraq. There was a rumor going around that he had a child with a woman near his base in Texas, but we could never substantiate that. Sandy said she didn't know anything about it."

Sam played with his napkin, tying it into a knot. The waitress came by again to take their orders. They said they only wanted coffee. She frowned and walked away.

"So, the adage, follow the money, doesn't seem to apply here."

"Not unless Scott had a bundle squirreled away somewhere. Believe me, we looked, but came up dry. He had some personal possessions in that old farmhouse, but nothing worth much. There's an inventory in the case file. Oh, and he had an old beat-up pickup truck. Worth maybe a few hundred dollars."

"Anyone else we should be looking at, Sheriff?" Sam asked.

"Stephen O'Neil owns some property that also adjoins Scott's. He's a retiree from Delaware who worked in technology. Local gossip says he made a bundle when he sold his business. He wanted to buy Scott's property. He sold off most of his own property bit-by-bit to developers. I think he only has a couple of lots left. You could check that out at the assessor's office, or on the land maps in the courthouse."

The sheriff continued, naming others who had come to his attention during his investigation. Buddy Smith, a construction worker, wanted to lease Scott's land for his hunting club. Scott had turned him down. He'd only offered a few hundred dollars a year. Jonathan Wright, thirty years old with no visible means of support, drove an expensive Lexus automobile and dressed like a fashion model. He lived in a large cottage near Scott's farm, traveled around the world extensively, and spent money like it was going out of style. The sheriff had investigated Jonathan only because rumor abounded in the valley that he was into something illegal. Drugs, maybe. The sheriff said he was unable to get a search warrant to look at his finances. The judge had said that rumor alone wasn't probable cause to issue a warrant. The sheriff mentioned a few others who were in the files but offered no real help.

"Did you find out where Scott was killed? It's unlikely that he was killed up on the mountain."

"No, I don't have any idea where he was killed. If we knew that, we'd be able to collect evidence from the scene. We didn't find any indication he was killed in his house. Victoria and the tech crew would have found blood splatter, so he wasn't killed there. It's unlikely the killer drove him up on the Sods and killed him there, but I suppose it's possible."

Sam paid the check at the cash register at the front of the restaurant. They walked out to the parking lot and stood beside the sheriff's cruiser. The morning sun had finally cleared the surrounding mountains, casting bright sunlight onto the parking lot.

"I'm sorry I wasn't more help, Sam. If anything comes to mind, I'll give you a call."

"Thanks, Sheriff. We'll re-interview these people and add any others that we run across. You never know what'll turn up once we begin stirring the pot."

"I don't have to tell you to be careful. If the killer feels you're getting too close, he'll be capable of anything. And, tell your buddy, the professor, to be careful, too."

*   *   *

Sam sat in his SUV, making notes on his meeting with the sheriff. He opened a new page and compiled a list of the people the sheriff had named. He compared his list to the one Jimmy had made of the interviews the sheriff and his deputies had done to be sure no one had been left out. Then, he compiled a short biography for each person from the information the sheriff had given him and what he could glean from the files.

He drummed his fingers on the steering wheel while he thought. Who were they leaving out? He grunted to himself, then added three more people to the list whom the sheriff hadn't interviewed; Wendy Richmond and her two children, Frank and Tiffany. He knew Jimmy liked Wendy and Frank and would object to adding them to the list, but he'd deal with him when the time came. It was important to have them on the list if for no other reason than to cross them off as suspects.

Wendy was an unlikely candidate as the killer since she had asked them to investigate the crime. If she was the killer, the last thing she'd want was someone poking into the case. But, children sometimes reacted in unpredictable ways when their parents began dating again. Especially, after the untimely death of the spouse. Tiffany was in the military and was also an unlikely candidate. They should be able to eliminate her if they could get a copy of her military schedule. Frank was a different matter.

Sam put his vehicle in gear and drove to Canaan Valley. From the highway, he could see ski slopes along the side of the mountain. Cabin roofs peeked through the heavy foliage of the forested mountainside. Access roads led from the valley floor to the lodges and shops strategically located at the bases of the slopes. To Sam, it all seemed to be packed together to the bursting point. A sharp demarcation line marked the boundary of the housing developments and forest service and private lands. If more development were to happen near the ski slopes, it would have to be in the private holdings.

The highway was straight as an arrow through the heart of the valley. An unimpressive concrete bridge marked the passage of the slow-moving Blackwater River. Much of the land on both sides of the highway was incorporated into the nature preserve. The valley floor was flat, crowded with alder and shrubs, interspersed here and there with red spruce and quaking aspen.

He turned off the main highway and followed a narrow road through the open valley floor, skirting the base of the mountain. Fields bordered the road along one side, and the nature preserve, with low shrubs and scattered red spruce, lay on the other. A few houses and small farms were scattered along the road. After he passed the entrances to the ski areas and cabins, the road became narrower. Soon, the blacktop ended, and the gravel forest service road began. He parked the SUV along a pull-off and got out. There was no traffic on the road.

It was a beautiful, early-summer day. The sun had climbed into a cloudless, azure sky, and its warmth felt good on his arms and back. Somewhere along the river a mallard duck quacked loudly. A pair of ravens gamboled in the sky, lazily swirling around each other, their loud *quark* calls echoing off the mountains. A myriad of bird calls arose from the low shrubs along the road, none of which he could identify.

He leaned against the SUV and surveyed the terrain around him. A narrow driveway, not much more than a weed-filled track, ambled toward the mountainside. Posts on each side of the driveway supported a metal gate held closed by a length of chain and a padlock. A large no-trespassing sign was stapled to each post. At the road's end, a ramshackle house sat on a low rise, its sides cobbled together from rough-sawed lumber. It was protected from the elements by a roof constructed of sheets of metal of varying colors. Goats, chickens and ducks wandered around a makeshift barn whose roof was covered with a bright blue tarp. One corner flapped in the light breeze. A tall hoop greenhouse, covered with ragged sheets of plastic, stood forlornly behind the barn. There was no one in sight. This must be Kelly Rice's homestead, he thought.

He walked along the road until he came to a second driveway. Its leaning mailbox was stenciled with the name *Mitchell* and a street number. Every third post of the woven-wire fence that extended parallel to the road held a sign proclaiming the property to be a private nature preserve. Access was allowed only by written permission.

Sam stepped to the middle of the road and looked at the overgrown farmland. The driveway disappeared into the trees—the farmhouse wasn't visible. Clumps of saplings and shrubs had become established in parts of the pastureland. The section closest to the river was sparsely covered with ten-year-old trees. Judging by the boundaries laid out by the fencing, Sam guessed the property sloped from the mountainside, down to the river. Almost one hundred and fifty acres. The Rice property bordered one section of the farm. Higher up on the mountain, behind the Rice property, he could see a cluster of cabins crowding against the farm's property line.

Sam climbed over the fence, ignoring the signs, and walked toward the river. The ground soon became wet and spongy interspersed with humps of vegetation consisting of moss and a low-growing vine with green berries. Plants of all kinds crept over the ground. Ferns abounded, but he was at a loss to tell which the endangered species were. He was tempted to snip off a sample but knew that Jimmy would pitch a fit if he did, so he settled for a few photographs taken with his cell phone.

He waded through the weeds back to the fence and clambered back over. He walked along the road, snapping pictures, then climbed into his SUV. He took a few minutes to write notes in the murder book before starting the vehicle and making a three-point turn. As he neared the entrance to the Rice property, a banged-up old pickup truck turned into the driveway. A large, stout woman dressed in an old shirt and coveralls climbed out and began unlocking the gate. Her short, straw-like hair poked from under a ballcap. She gave Sam a hard look as he drove by.

He stopped at each mailbox along the road and noted the name and street number. It could be that he and Jimmy would need to talk to Scott's neighbors.

His stomach began to growl, and he decided that he'd find something to eat before making the hour's drive home. He parked near the Cooper Knob Ski Lodge and walked inside. It was a beautiful log structure with soaring timber-frame beams supporting the roof. The slate floor was appointed with thick scatter rugs, and rustic wood furniture beckoned to the casual visitor. He waited at the entrance to the dining room and was seated by the hostess beside a window that overlooked the grass-covered ski slope. Towering snow-makers stood silent, awaiting cold temperatures and the ski season, still months away. The table was covered with a fancy tablecloth and set with crystal glasses and heavy silverware wrapped in cloth napkins. The chairs were plush and soft.

The waitress came by his table and expertly filled his glass with ice water. She was middle-aged, slim and attractive, wearing black slacks and a white blouse. Her feet were clad in sensible crepe-soled shoes. She'd wore her blond hair up on her head—a few stray tendrils swirled around her neck.

"You want anything else to drink? A coke or something?" She asked. She stood with her pencil poised over her order pad.

"How about some ice tea?" Sam asked.

She swept away, returning quickly with his drink. "What can I get for you?"

"If you were going to eat your lunch here, what would *you* order?"

"That depends on who's paying. If you're paying, I'd have the lobster dinner. You can't go wrong there. But, if I'm paying, I'd have the cheeseburger and fries. The hamburger is black angus, grass-fed, and the fries are hand cut. Never been frozen."

Sam chortled and said, "Ok, I'll have the cheeseburger."

The waitress took his order and swept away again, disappearing into the kitchen. Sam leaned back in his chair and looked over the restaurant. Only a few tables were occupied. He was a little late for lunch and too early for dinner. An older couple sat at another table near the windows, the woman looking wistfully outside while the man flipped through a pile of brochures. They whispered occasionally, pointing to the pictures in the glossy publications.

Another table was occupied by a young family. The woman was young and pretty with fashionably long, blond hair. The man was tall and handsome with an expensive haircut. Two children, a boy and girl ten to twelve years old, sat hunched over cell phones. They all wore designer clothing—the man and boy long shorts and sandals, the woman and girl white shorts, expensive blouses and shoes. The all-American family. Sam figured after their meal, the woman and children would hit the pool and the man the golf course.

When it arrived, Sam ate his cheeseburger and fries while leafing through the murder book. He made notes occasionally, pausing to think about what he was reading. The waitress refreshed his drink and asked how he liked his food. He said everything was very good and thanked her for her recommendation.

Sam asked, "Do you live here in the valley?"

She faked being shocked, "My momma told me to never let a strange man know where I lived. You might be some kind of pervert, or something." She smiled at him.

"No, no. I'm not asking for your home address or anything. I'm a police officer." He showed her his new badge. "I'm looking for someone who has lived in the valley for a while, you know, someone who knows everyone."

"Well, that wouldn't be me. I'm just staying here for the summer. I live in Florida. I come up here to work and get away from the heat. Besides, there's not much work down there in the summer. I'll go back in the fall."

"So, you don't know many people here?"

"No, just the people who work at the lodge here, and a few of the ones who own cabins. They come and go. But Wally said he's lived here all his life. He seems to know everyone." She pointed through the window toward the ski lift. "He runs the lift. Tourists ride it up on the mountain for the view. Maybe you could ask him."

Sam thanked her, paid his check and walked out to the lift. Wally sat on a bench beside the huge wheels that powered the lift up and down the mountain. A row of lift chairs was interspaced up the slope, dangling from the massive cables like empty seats on a carnival ride. No one was waiting for a ride up the hill. Sam showed him his badge and told him he was working with the sheriff's office.

Wally said, "I thought I knew all of the deputies. You must be new."

Sam explained that he was on temporary assignment. "I'm helping the sheriff with one of his cases. You heard about the body they found in a tree, didn't you?"

"Oh sure, everyone's been talking about it. Scott Mitchell, wasn't it?" Wally was a large man with calloused hands. Sam wasn't sure, but he was probably in his early sixties. He wore heavy trousers and a short-sleeved blue shirt. A worn ballcap with a Steelers logo was pulled firmly on his head.

"That' right, Scott lived on a farm near here. Did you know him?"

"Yeah, I live here, have all my life, except for a few years in the Army, so I know most everybody. He wasn't from here originally. I mean, he bought that farm years ago when he got out of the service. We weren't fast friends, but he's always been around. Kinda quiet, stuck to his own business."

"Do you know anyone who would want to do him harm?" Sam asked.

Wally shook his head solemnly, "No, not that I know of."

"Any rumors going around? You know, people talking about what happened to him."

"Oh, there were plenty of those, but nothing I would put any stock in. Everything from drugs to witches and warlocks. Space invaders, too. No, I've thought a little bit about it, but nothing I've heard makes any sense."

Sam leaned back on the bench and waited while Wally got up to run the lift for a young couple. They held hands and laughed when he folded down the restraining bar that held them in the seat. The machinery groaned and banged when he put it in gear. The lift lurched forward and began its ascent to the top of the mountain. Wally used a hand-held radio to notify the worker at the top that a load of visitors was on the way.

He returned to the bench and sat down. "Johnny will turn it off when they get to the top."

Sam asked him if he remembered Scott's wife. He replied that he'd seen her with Scott years ago and that she'd died. He thought she'd had cancer. When questioned further, he didn't know anything about her family. He thought maybe she'd been from out of state but wasn't sure. He remembered Scott's sister—he'd gone to high school with her. He recalled Sandy, Scott's niece, as a child. "I think she left for a while but came back. She owns a gift shop now."

"What about Kelly Rice? Do you know her?"

Wally laughed, "Oh lord, everyone knows Wild Rice. That's what they call her behind her back. She's a real piece of work. Just about everyone around here has had a run-in with her. She's a Yankee from up north somewhere." He described her farm, laughing again. "Not that I've ever been there. But you can see most of it from the road. She had a real run-in with the assessor. Said they'd tried to gouge her on her property taxes. She had the assessor and sheriff running around in circles." He chuckled, just thinking about the scene. "One of the clerks that works in the assessor's office told everybody about it at her kid's soccer match. The whole town was laughing."

"Do you think she's capable of murdering Scott?"

"Probably." He hesitated, then said, "Well, no. I shouldn't say that. She has a fiery temper, but I don't have any reason to think she might have done it. Sometimes, it's the quiet ones you have to look out for."

"She had an argument with Scott when her goats got out. They ate some of those endangered plants," Sam said.

"Yeah, I heard about that, but that's hardly a reason to kill someone. You ask me, Scott should have been mad at the EPA for making his land worthless, all because of some rare plants. They should keep their noses out of a property owner's business!" Wally's face had started to get red.

Sam ignored his outburst. He asked Wally about Stephen O'Neal and Buddy Smith, but he said he didn't know them.

"Scott was seeing a woman, Wendy Richmond. Do you know her"

"Oh sure, Wendy's a real nice person. She works at that saloon down on Red Creek. Before she started there, she worked at the state park.

Lost her husband a few years back. There seems to be a lot of that going around. Most everyone around was happy to see her and Scott hook up. Two people like that have a right to a little happiness. I heard they were planning to get married. It's a real shame."

"What about her kids? Do you know them?"

"Some. You know how it is. There's always young people around, going to the high school, playing sports, working here and there. I can't say I know anything much about them. I think the girl went into the military, and the boy's going to school somewhere. That's about it."

The lift suddenly came to life, creaking and groaning again. Empty lift chairs came down on the cable, made a sweeping turn under the gear wheel, and began their mindless ascent up the mountain. Soon the young couple got off the lift and walked back toward the lodge, hand in hand. Wally turned the machine off and walked back toward Sam.

"Thanks for talking to me, Wally. If I have any more questions, I'll give you a call, if that's all right."

"Oh sure, deputy. Be happy to help."

Sam wrote Wally's name and phone number in the murder book, thanked him again for his help, and walked to the parking lot. He got in his SUV and began writing notes. He'd meet with Jimmy and tell him what he'd learned, which was practically nothing. At least, nothing he hadn't heard elsewhere, but this was a big part of what an investigator did. Confirm and reconfirm what he already knew. He'd match one person's story against another's, looking for discrepancies, and sometimes, lies. Especially, lies.

Chapter 7

Sweat poured from Jimmy's face as he laid out yet another quadrant. He used a hammer to drive a four-foot section of steel rebar into the forest floor and tied a florescent-orange piece of surveyor's tape to its top. He added three more stakes to form a ten by fifty-meter rectangle. That done, he formed a border by running a piece of heavy twine around the stakes, tying it securely to each one. The result was a 500-square meter plot in which he'd make plant species counts.

He sat against a large tree and opened his backpack. He placed the tools of his trade on a plastic tarp—a DBH tape used to measure the diameter of trees at breast height, hand lenses, sample containers, a laptop computer, a hand-held GPS unit, and a variety of other instruments.

He identified and measured every tree over three centimeters in diameter in the plot, methodically marking each with a piece of chalk to be sure he didn't count them more than once. Then he surveyed woody plants *under* three centimeters in diameter in a ten by ten plot.

The next step was the most tedious. He laid out a one square meter plot randomly inside the larger plot. It contained numerous herbaceous plants, some a few centimeters in height, but most only consisted of a couple of tiny leaves and a thin stem. He identified and counted them all, entering the data into the laptop. By training and experience, he knew all of them by common and scientific names.

Jimmy entered a variety of other data in the laptop including the slope, altitude, and aspect of the quadrant. He drove a two-foot section of rebar in the exact center of the plot and took a GPS reading, carefully recording latitude and longitude. The rebar would be left in place. If another scientist wanted to replicate the count sometime in the future, he or she would be able to find the quadrant. The four corner stakes were no longer needed. He pulled them up, tied them to the outside of his backpack, wound the twine and tape into a ball and stuffed it into the pack.

He policed the area carefully, slung his pack on his back and hiked back to the Cherokee. Jimmy's mind was on his research as he drove back to the Eyrie. He and his colleagues would complete species counts in hundreds of quadrants before the project was complete. They were working along a transect line that began on Blennerhassett Island in the Ohio river and reached across the state to its eastern border with Virginia. The idea was to produce scientific descriptions of the plant communities in a west-to-east profile that included the low hills of the western section, the central mountains, and the Ridge and Valley Province to the east.

The resulting description of these chief phytogeographic regions would be published in a book. It would become a reference for other scientists, students, foresters, farmers, agronomists, geologists, and others, as they conducted their own research projects. The data would also serve as the basis for numerous papers read at conferences and published in juried, scientific journals—the saving grace for those professors who had to publish or perish. Jimmy was one such professor.

Jimmy raced a frontal weather system home. A dark line of clouds marched across the sky from the west. The air was still, but he knew that wouldn't last long. As he drove up the mountain to the Eyrie, the sky darkened as the black clouds covered the sun.

Sam's SUV was in the parking area near the cabin when he arrived. He let the dog out of his kennel and slung the backpack containing his laptop and plant specimens over his shoulder and walked across the deck to the door. When he opened it, the dog entered quickly and made a circle around the room, sniffing at the floor and furniture. He approached the closed door of the spare bedroom slowly and placed his nose to the crack under the door. He sniffed loudly, then trotted to his food bowl and began eating kibble, crunching loudly. He lapped water from his bowl. Jimmy put his ear to the door and listened. He heard the soft snore of a sleeping man. Evidently, Sam had made himself at home.

Jimmy stripped off his sweaty clothes and took a quick shower. He put on a clean pair of jeans and a shirt. He was well into making supper when Sam came out of the bedroom. He had a sheepish grin on his face.

"Hey man, I'm sorry about crashing your pad, but when I got here, I was so sleepy, I could hardly stand up. I've been staying up too late watching TV. I hope you don't mind me taking a nap." He yawned and stretched his hands high over his head.

"Nope. Anytime, but I haven't heard anyone call a house a *pad* since my father died. You're going to have to get up to date, *man*," Jimmy said, laughing.

As he prepared the food, the wind picked up and raindrops splattered against the windows. It was soon pouring. He laid out a couple of steaks and cleaned two potatoes to bake in the microwave. He'd rather cook them in the oven but didn't want to take the time. He found a quart of home canned green beans overlooked in the back of the food shelf and put them on the stove to heat. He'd planned to cook the meat on the grill but would have to keep an eye on the sky. His grill was protected from the weather by a large canvas fly, but the wind would be a problem if it didn't calm. Maybe it would settle down when the front passed through.

They talked about food, as men often do. Sam said he missed Ruthie's cooking, and that he was getting tired of eating frozen dinners. Eating out was getting old, too. "I eat out so often, the waitresses know me by name, and they ask if I want the usual. Guess I'm getting in a rut."

"I know what you mean, Sam. I like to eat at home as much as I can, but my cooking isn't great. I only know how to cook simple recipes."

"Well, you can't go wrong with meat and potatoes," he said philosophically. "I know women like fancy dishes and all that greenery they eat, but men just want basic food, and lots of it."

"If I were you, Sam, I wouldn't let too many people hear you say that. That's a stereotype if ever there was one."

"Yeah, I guess it is." Yellow Dog padded across the room and put his chin on Sam's knee. Sam absently stroked his head. "And, can you imagine one of those fancy French chefs cooking at a professional football training camp? You know, the ones that put a couple of thimbles-full of fish and a green bean or two on a plate, swizzle a little fancy sauce on it, and call it a meal? Put that in front of a three hundred pounder and see what happens. The chef is likely to become the main course."

Jimmy chuckled. "I suppose. But, I doubt there are too many French cooks in football camps."

Sam nodded thoughtfully. "You're a fisherman. Do you eat all those fish you catch?"

"No, not usually, but sometimes I keep a couple and cook them up. When I surf-fish, I like to keep a speckled trout occasionally, and bluefish aren't bad if they aren't too big. They get pretty strong-tasting if they're over twenty or twenty-five inches."

They discussed the pros and cons of seafood versus beef and compared Chinese to Mexican food. They discussed the best restaurants in the area, and Jimmy told Sam a little about the food in Costa Rica. By the time their discussion ended, the storm had passed, and the sun was peeking through the clouds to the west. Water dripped from the eaves of the cabin, and the birds began to twitter.

Jimmy put the steaks on the grill and within minutes, the tantalizing smell of grilled meat reached their nostrils. Jimmy plated the food, and they sat at the table by the window and ate, watching the sun fall in the sky. Golden sunlight back-lit the mountains. Long streamers of steam rose from the mountainsides and valleys.

Sam told Jimmy about his visit with the sheriff. "He gave me some insight into who to interview first, but it's my opinion that we should talk to Scott's niece. She might give us some idea of who to talk to. You remember her name, don't you—Sandy Lynch. She lives in a small community in the valley. I thought maybe we'd drive up there and interview her. Are you available first thing in the morning? I called her and set up an appointment."

"Sure. I have some more field work to do, but I can spare some time tomorrow."

"I also drove up in the valley and looked around a little bit. I think I figured out where Scott's farm is. Oh, and I saw Kelly Rice drive into her farm." He described her farm's layout. "She's a hard-looking character. The sheriff said she's been giving him and the assessor hell about her taxes. She's a real piece of work."

"Are we going to interview her, too?" Jimmy asked.

"Well yeah, I'd like to talk to her, but from what the sheriff tells me, we'd better take a platoon of deputies with us." Sam grimaced and said, "I'm exaggerating, but only barely so. I'd hate to tangle with her. She looks like she could take care of herself."

Sam brought Jimmy up to date on his discussion with Wally, the ski lift operator. "It's all in the murder book. I took some notes. I'll leave it here with you. You can read through it and give me your thoughts."

Jimmy began clearing the table as Sam left for his house. Yellow Dog walked him to his SUV and returned promptly, hoping for table scraps in his food bowl. He wasn't disappointed. He crunched a bone loudly with his strong jaws and licked his lips. He licked the bowl clean with his big red tongue, pushing it around on the floor.

When the dishes were done, Jimmy sat on the deck, listening to the radio in the failing light. The dog stretched out on his side and was soon asleep. Jimmy thought about Dana, aka Laughing Woman, wondering who she was. Where did she go when she left her farm? Sometimes she was gone for weeks at a time. She was a very attractive woman who liked to laugh and had a warm smile. She was interesting, knowledgeable about any topic, and seemed to be interested in him, too. He'd looked at her farm occasionally through his telescope, hoping to see the bucket on the gatepost, indicating she was at home, but had been disappointed. He tilted his chair back on two legs and put his feet on the lower rung of the deck railing. Tree frogs trilled, and little brown bats circled the sky in the last glow of the day's sun. He had decided that he'd try to see her again, maybe take her for a long drive to show her *his* West Virginia. The one that few saw beyond the stereotype pushed by unknowing critics. The one you couldn't see while entombed in the steel of a car.

He'd gotten the impression she was a city girl, someone who had traveled widely. Where was she now? Maybe she'd gone on a trip, a vacation. For all he knew, she could be on the other side of the world, trekking through a steaming jungle, or sitting at a sidewalk café in Paris, watching the people who walked by.

Dew began forming on the deck and railing, His clothing soaked up the moisture in the air, suddenly giving him a chill. The dog walked to the cabin door and looked expectantly at Jimmy. When they entered the cabin, the dog got in his bed, turned around a couple of times and laid down. It was bedtime. Jimmy got undressed and turned out the lights. He climbed into bed and drew the comforter up to his chin. When he drifted off to sleep, he dreamed about buckets on gateposts and a beautiful woman who lived on a lonely mountain.

*   *   *

Sandy Lynch was an attractive young woman, thirtyish, give or take a few years. Her tanned arms and face indicated a life lived outside. There was a light sprinkle of freckles across her nose. She wore tight jeans and a colorful, long-sleeved shirt. Her brown hair was tied up in a ponytail that swung back and forth as she talked. She faced Sam and Jimmy across a picnic table in a small park on the edge of town. The dark water of the Blackwater River flowed by with a quiet whisper. Birds dipped and swirled over its glossy surface. The sun's warmth felt good as it peeped above the nearby mountains. It promised to be a pleasant, summer day.

Sam said, "Thank you for agreeing to see us, Ms. Lynch. We won't take a lot of your time." He introduced himself and Jimmy and told her they were helping Wendy Richmond—trying to find Scott Mitchell's killer. "We'd like to ask some questions, and please don't be offended. We're talking to everyone even remotely involved."

She told them to call her Sandy. She shrugged and said she'd be happy to answer their questions if it would help find the killer.

"Do you have any idea who would want to harm your uncle?"

She shook her head, making her ponytail bounce. "None at all. Uncle Scott was a good man. He lived a quiet life on the farm, and I was shocked to hear that he'd been killed. He was just about the only relative I had left. He and Mom were the only two children in their family, so I don't have any relatives who live in the area. My father died when I was in first grade. Mom died several years ago, and my brother was killed in Iraq."

"What do you think of Wendy? Did you get along with her?"

Sandy brightened, and said, "Oh, Wendy is a wonderful person. She was really good for Uncle Scott. They were going to get married. They spent a lot of time together, and they traveled together some. Not anyplace exotic, mind you, but just nearby, around the state. She would have made him a good wife."

"What did Wendy's children think about her plans to marry Scott?"

Her brows knitted together as she concentrated on the question. "Oh, as far as I know they were fine with it. I don't know her daughter very well, she's in the military, but Frankie's a nice person. He's going to school at State College." She looked at Jimmy and asked, "Do you know him?" Jimmy explained that Frank was one of his students.

"Did Scott have a will?" Sam asked.

"Yes. Since I'm his closest living relative, I'll inherit whatever he had. It's still in probate, but there's not much to inherit. He was planning to give the farm to the nature preserve. He wanted the land looked after. He was really interested in that kind of thing, preserving the land. As far as I can tell there will only be a few thousand dollars' worth of personal property and a little money in the bank. His old truck isn't worth much, but I think I'll keep it. Maybe have it fixed up a little."

"What about other valuables in the house?" Jimmy asked. "Something of value that someone might want to steal?"

She smiled at him again. "Like what?"

Jimmy thought for a moment, "Did he have a stamp or coin collection? Maybe an old motorcycle that would be worth a lot of money to a collector. Something like that."

She shook her head. "No, nothing that I've ever seen. Of course, I wasn't in his house every day, so I suppose anything is possible."

Sam knew the answer to the next question before he asked. "I'd imagine that the farm is worth a lot of money. There were, what, a hundred and fifty acres?"

"One-forty-eight," Sandy said.

"Aren't developers interested in buying it? Wouldn't they be eager to develop it?"

Sandy chuckled ruefully, "Yes, it would be worth millions, if it wasn't for the endangered plants there. It's practically worthless for anything other than a preserve. It was all he talked about. He was so proud of those ferns. Whenever anyone came to visit him, he'd take them around the farm, pointing them out." A tear escaped from her eye and slid down her cheek. "I'm going to see that the farm goes to the nature preserve. It's what Uncle Scott wanted, and I'm going to see that it happens. I've talked to a lawyer, and as soon as the estate's settled, I'm going to deed it over to them."

Jimmy said, "That's very generous of you, Sandy. I know a little about the ferns, and it's important that they be preserved."

Sandy nodded sadly, "Thank you. Uncle Scott was adamant that they be saved."

Sam asked, "What kind of work do you do, Sandy?"

She smiled and sat up straighter, "I was a business major in college. I've opened a variety shop. I sell local art and hand-made items, all West Virginia made. I really enjoy being self-employed. I've worked for others, but there's nothing like being your own boss."

"Congratulations," Sam said. "I'm sure you'll do well with all the tourist traffic the area gets."

She beamed and said, "Thanks. You'll have to stop by my shop. Maybe buy something for a special friend." She looked pointedly at Jimmy, who smiled at her.

"Do you live here in town?" Sam asked.

"Yes. I bought an old house here, and I'm planning to remodel it. It's going to be expensive, but I love this area and think it'll be a good investment."

Sam flipped a page in the murder book and wrote a few notes. He asked her where she'd gone to school.

"I attended the local high school. That was before Mom died. Then, I went to the university. I wasn't a strong student, but I got by. I liked living in a large town, but when I graduated I wanted to come back home. Isn't it often that way? People leave, go somewhere to work for a while, but many want to return home. It's too bad there's not a lot of work here. I think more people would return if they could."

"Sandy, I'm about out of questions. Jimmy, how about you, any questions?" Jimmy shook his head.

Sam asked, "Would it be all right if we called you if anything more comes to mind?"

"Sure. I'll do whatever I can to help. Stop by the shop if you need anything else." She smiled at Jimmy again.

They said their good-byes and watched as she walked back toward town. Sam asked, "Well, what do you think?"

Jimmy grinned and said, "I think she's very attractive. She has a nice smile."

Sam sighed, "No, that's not what I meant. What do you think about her answers? Any warning bells go off?"

"Warning bells? No, she seems like a nice person," he said with a big smile.

Sam sat quietly for a few moments, picking at his lower lip. "Yeah, I suppose you're right."

Chapter 8

The sun had just topped the mountains behind the Eyrie when Jimmy drove down the long driveway to the secondary road below. Yellow Dog pressed his nose against the passenger's window of the Cherokee, making a long, wet smear on the otherwise clean glass. Jimmy turned on the car's radio, listening to the local station, tapping the steering wheel to the beat of the music with his fingers. A half hour later, he arrived at his property near the Cheat River. He parked in the driveway to the house site, listening to the murmur of Canada Geese on the pond. He looked forlornly at the burned-out building site where his house once stood. He'd hired a man with a bulldozer to clear away the rubble. The two-story house had been built by his great-great-grandfather more than a century ago and had held many pleasant memories. Except for the time he'd spent at university, he'd lived here all his life. The man who had framed him for killing one of his students had burned it to the ground and killed his dog.

He stepped out of the jeep and walked around the property noting the partially burned trees and shrubs. Several had valiantly attempted to produce new leaves, but he knew that they would not survive. Grass struggled to reclaim the circle burned by the intense heat of the fire. It was a prime building site, and he planned to rebuild one day. The dog explored the trees along the driveway.

He walked down the lane and crossed the narrow road that ran parallel to the river, approaching the riverbank. The river stone he'd placed at Max's grave had tilted over the winter, and he pushed it back into an upright position. He tamped the sandy soil around the base of the stone with his boots. Max had been a good companion and hadn't deserved to die. He stood for a few moments, remembering the dog and his antics. He touched the headstone with his fingertips and nodded, acknowledging the close relationship he'd had with the animal. After a few minutes, he rapped the stone with his knuckles and walked to the river.

It was a glorious, early summer day. A warm breeze rippled the calm waters near the shore. Sunlight streaked the water's surface, highlighting the swift current toward the middle of the river.

Cheat River is unique. It is one of the few rivers that flows northward. Formed from the Black Fork River and Shavers Fork near the town of Parsons, it flows northward for many miles until it empties into the Cheat Lake impoundment and then the Monongahela River near Morgantown. The Monongahela River continues northward to Pittsburgh. Historians were undecided how the river got its name. One theory is that the river had cheated many people out of their lives from drownings and other mishaps. Another is that it was named for a family that had once lived on its shores.

However it had gotten its name, it is a beautiful, wild river, flowing through some of the most spectacular scenery in the country. Steep mountains, cloaked with a dense hardwood forest, border the river. At times, the river is calm and smooth, and at other times, it could become a raging torrent sweeping away everything in its path. Jimmy loved the river—it represented everything good about his native state.

He stooped to pick up a flat rock, skipping it across the water as he had done hundreds of times as a child. The rock skipped along the river's surface until it lost momentum and sank from sight. For ten minutes he skipped rocks and thought about his family who had lived here, on this spot, for generations. Undoubtedly his father had skipped rocks here, and his father before him. He would rebuild the house. Suddenly, he couldn't wait to get started.

He returned to his jeep and took out the blueprints for the new house he'd had an architect from Charleston draw up. He unrolled them on the hood of his vehicle and used a couple of books to keep the paper from curling. He tried to visualize the new house that would arise from the ashes of the old. He'd argued with the architect, who had wanted him to build a modern home, on the style of Frank Lloyd Wright, with massive stone edifices and acres of glass. He wanted something more fitting to the setting—stone, wood and glass, yes—but smaller than she had proposed. What did he need with a three thousand square foot house? The result was a single-story dwelling of modest proportions with hints of the federal style, hewn beams, stone accents and strategically placed windows. The geese raised a chorus of protest as the dog ran along the edge of the pond, and Jimmy called him back to the house site.

Cut stone blocks from the foundation of the old house would be used to build a large fireplace and chimney. He'd instructed her to design small, glassed portals high on the great room walls that would allow sunlight to stream onto the fireplace on the winter and summer solstices. She had spent hours calculating where the portals should be placed.

The architect had incorporated his ideas into the plan and she'd smiled when they'd reviewed the final product. Jimmy thought that his great-great-grandfather would have approved of the new house. The next step was to find a dependable contractor to do the work.

Upon return to the cabin, Jimmy dragged an old duffle bag out of the back of the closet and opened it on the bed. He began filling it with the equipment he'd need for the trip to Costa Rica. He had everything he needed at the cabin, having stopped at his office the day before to pick up a boxful of supplies. He packed the delicate instruments carefully, filling voids with crumpled newspapers. He pulled a smaller bag from under the bed and packed it quickly with clothes. He included rain gear, knowing he'd need it; after all, the biological station was in a rain forest. The dog watched him carefully. His head drooped, knowing that Jimmy was going on a trip, and he would likely not be included.

Jimmy sat on the edge of the bed and called Sam. He answered immediately.

"Did you remember that I'm leaving in the morning for Costa Rica?" Jimmy asked.

"Oh, I forgot. I thought you were leaving next week."

"No, tomorrow. I'll be gone for almost two weeks."

"Gee, it must be nice going on vacation and getting paid for it," Sam said. Jimmy didn't bother trying to convince Sam that he'd be working every day, and that field work in a rain forest could be dangerous, dirty work. The last time he'd been there he'd almost stepped on a fer-de-lance, a highly venomous pit viper. Jimmy knew Sam was just jerking his chain.

"What will you be working on while I'm gone? Are you going to do some more interviews?" Jimmy asked.

"Yeah, I want to interview Stephen O'Neil. He owns property adjoining Scott's farm. I may as well talk to Buddy Smith, too, while I'm at it. He's the hunting enthusiast who wanted to lease the hunting rights for Scott's property. I also want to look at Scott's house and farm."

"Are you thinking that Scott may have been killed there?"

"The sheriff and his deputies searched the house and out-buildings. There's a report in the files. They don't think it's the murder scene, but I just want to get a feel for who Scott was and how he lived. It always helps to get to know the victim. Going through his house is one way to do that," Sam said. "I'll decide what to do next after I get all that done."

"Okay, Sam, but remember what the sheriff told us. There's a killer out there, and the closer we get, the more desperate he'll become. Be careful."

Sam chuckled mirthlessly, "You don't have to tell me that, Jimmy. I've done a few of these investigations before. I know what I'm up against."

Jimmy grimaced. "I didn't mean to tell you what to do, Sam. I know you know what you're doing. I just don't want to see anyone get hurt on my account. I'm the one who got you involved."

"I know, Jimmy. I'll be careful. You're probably in more danger tromping around in a jungle than I am. So, we'll both be careful."

Sam agreed to take care of Yellow Dog while Jimmy was gone. He wasn't sure how that would work out, but the dog would be company and would have the run of his house. Sam just hoped he wouldn't eat his furniture while he was out. They talked for a few minutes more, then Jimmy put his phone back in his pocket and resumed packing. The dog watched with great interest.

Early the following morning, Jimmy put Yellow Dog in his kennel where Sam would pick him up and drove to the airport in Bridgeport. He boarded a small commercial jet that would take him on the first leg of his journey.

Chapter 9

It was a bright, sunny morning when Sam called Stephen O'Neal and asked if he could come by his house to talk to him. O'Neal agreed, saying he was planning to leave town by noon, but would talk to Sam if he could come immediately. Sam said he could be there within an hour.

Sam looked at the dog who sat on the floor thumping his tail. As Sam moved toward the front door, the dog went with him. Sam stopped, looking at him. "Oh, come on. You might as well go, too." The dog jumped around in circles and yipped. "Don't get so excited. You'll have to wait in the car while I talk to the man." Yellow Dog didn't seem to care and clambered into the back seat of Sam's SUV. He sat proudly on the blanket Sam had used to cover the clean upholstery.

Within forty-five minutes, Sam pulled into O'Neal's driveway in Canaan Valley. The large cabin was constructed of massive logs, stacked with their ends showing at the corners. A massive stone chimney dominated one end of the structure. A porch spanned the length of the front of the cabin with outdoor furniture arranged in a pleasing pattern. The lawn was landscaped with native plants and flowers. An expensive car was parked in the gravel driveway. Sam could see the metal roof of the ski lodge through the trees. The dog hung his head out a back window of the SUV and watched Sam ring the doorbell.

Sam could hear footsteps approaching, and the door was opened by a man immaculately dressed in chinos and a light-colored button-down shirt. He appeared to be about sixty years old and had close-cropped dark hair speckled with gray. He extended a hand and shook with a firm grip.

"I'm Stephen O'Neal, officer. Won't you come in?"

He led Sam to a couch and chair that faced a massive river-stone fireplace. They sat at a ninety-degree angle to each other, and Sam turned so that he could see his face. Stephen offered water or coffee, but Sam declined. Sam explained that he was working with the sheriff's office as a special investigator.

"What can I do for you? You didn't say why you wanted to talk to me."

"I'm investigating Scott Mitchell's death. Did you know him?"

"Yes, but I don't see what I can do to help you. I don't know anything about his death."

"I understand," Sam said patiently. "I'm just trying to get a feel for Scott and how he lived. I'm talking to all his neighbors. Let's start from the beginning. Tell me a little bit about yourself. What do you do for a living, where are you originally from, are you married?"

He reluctantly replied, "No, I'm not currently married. I guess you could say that I'm between wives. I've been married a couple of times, but it didn't work out. I'm originally from Delaware and I worked in technology. I developed some software that made it easier for businesses to track their customers' buying habits, sold it for a bundle, and essentially retired. I still dabble in real estate, buying and selling property, and so on."

"Did you know Scott well?"

"No, not well. I tried to buy his property. That was before I found out about the endangered plants that grow there. As far as I can tell, they essentially make his property useless. It can't be developed."

"That's what I've heard," Sam said. "Have you run into a problem like this before when you've bought property for development"

"No, but I've heard war stories from other developers. I'm just glad I wasn't successful in buying the land. It could have ruined me. You buy a piece of property for big dollars, then find out that you can't develop it. You could be out millions of dollars."

"How did you find out about the ferns"

"The what?"

"The ferns. They're the endangered plants you were talking about."

"Oh, yeah. I don't know one plant from another. Scott told me about them when I approached him about buying his farm. He just laughed and said I wasn't the first person who had tried to buy it. He said he was going to give it to some environmental group. Can you imagine that?"

"Did you and Scott part on good terms? Were you angry that you couldn't buy the land?"

"Oh, I wasn't angry. Why should I be? You'll probably find out anyway, so I'll just tell you now. I sold my last lot a couple of weeks ago, so I'm out of the development business until I can buy another section of land. I'd have liked to have his land, but that's the way it goes. I'll just have to find some other property to subdivide. It won't be too hard. It won't be prime land like Scott's, but I'll still make money. Mountain land and vacation cabins are in high demand right now. When the state finished the Corridor H highway to Davis, it opened this whole valley to development. It'll be even better when they finish that last section through Parsons."

"So, you were okay with Scott not selling to you?"

"Sure. No problem."

"What do you know about Scott? Did you see him socially?"

"No, I really didn't know him. From what I heard, he kept to himself. Didn't do much socializing. It's kind of sad, but I don't think I'd ever seen him around anywhere. At least, not in the social group I hang with."

"Do you know Wendy Richmond?"

"No, who is she?"

"She was Scott's girlfriend," Sam said.

"Oh yes, I know who you're talking about. I'd heard that she was dating Scott. She works at the Red Creek Saloon, but I don't know anything else about her."

"What about Kelly Rice? Do you know her?"

"Oh Jeeze, everyone knows Wild Rice. I've had the pleasure of meeting her a couple of times—the whole area talks about her. She's a hippie from up north somewhere. New Jersey, I think."

"How did you meet her?"

"She attends some of the county's chamber of commerce meetings. Everyone hates to see her coming. I've talked to her a time or two in passing. Not a pleasant experience," he said frowning.

"What have you heard about her?"

"Oh, just that she's about as nasty as they come. She'd just as soon spit in your eye as look at you. Lives on a farm over there," he said, waving an arm vaguely, "with a bunch of goats and chickens." He continued, telling about her run-in with a hunter who had lost his dog and wandered onto her property looking for it. She'd accused him of trespass, took his name and filed charges against him with the police. The hunter had to pay a fine. "All he was doing was trying to get his dog back. What kind of person would do that?"

"Do you think she'd be capable of killing someone?"

"Oh Lord yes. Of all the people I know, she's the one who's most likely to fly into a rage and knock someone on the head."

"Do you live here year 'round?" Sam asked.

"Yeah, I do now. When I bought this place, I was still living in Delaware. I like to ski, so I bought this cabin and several extra lots. I don't ski much anymore. When you get to be my age—I just turned sixty—you begin to re-think some of the things you used to do. I like the area, and plan to stay. I sold everything I owned in Delaware and moved here. One of the best things about living here is that I'm a long way from my ex-wives," he said with a chuckle.

"How did you hear about the Canaan Valley ski resort? I mean, when you first bought the cabin? Did you see some of the state's advertising in a magazine or something?"

"No, I met a man at the gym back home where I used to work out. He was from West Virginia and kept telling me how great it was. Said he wanted to go back home when he retired. Over the years I met several people from the state, and every one of them sang the state's praises.

Given half a chance they'd sing a few bars of that song about country roads," he said, laughing.

"Mr. O'Neal, do you have any idea who might have wanted to kill Scott? Other than Ms. Rice. Maybe you've heard something in the community?"

"Call me Steve. No, as I said before, I don't have the faintest clue as to who might have killed him. All I really know about it is what I read in the papers. Sorry I can't be more help."

Sam thanked Steve and left him standing on the cabin's porch. He drove away from the cabin and stopped at the first pullover. He pulled a pad and pen from his briefcase and made notes on the meeting. He had a very good memory for details and soon had filled several pages. When he got home, he'd scan them into his computer and e-mail them to Jimmy's phone. If Jimmy was willing to reduce his notes to paper for the murder book, he should be willing to do the reverse and at least send him a photo copy of his scratching.

He gazed out the windshield while he thought about Steve O'Neal. The nature preserve stretched before him, alder-covered and daunting. A pair of ravens perched in the top of a spruce tree, occasionally sounding a mournful *quark*. He tended to believe Steve. Yes, he'd wanted to buy Scott's farm, but didn't seem to be disappointed when his offer had been turned down. He seemed to be just what he claimed to be—one of a thousand divorcees trying to get on with his life. At a time like this, it would have been good if Jimmy were here. They could talk about the interview—two points of view were always better than one. He sighed and put his pad back in his briefcase and put the SUV in gear. It was still early, not yet noon, and he had time to make another stop. But, first he'd find somewhere to eat lunch.

*   *   *

Sam sat at a picnic table behind a restaurant along the highway. He'd ordered a pizza and the waitress had agreed to bring it outside to the table for him. He'd known about the restaurant for years and when he was a state policeman, tried to arrange his schedule occasionally so he could eat there. As he waited for his food, he called the sheriff and asked if it was possible for him to look at Scott's house.

"Sure, Sam. I can get you in the farmhouse. Where are you?"

"I'm in the valley eating lunch." He gave him the name of the restaurant.

"I'll send a deputy with the keys. He should be there in about thirty minutes. Sandy let us keep them in case we needed to get in."

"Thanks, Sheriff. Has she removed any of his belongings?"

"No, not to my knowledge. I think she's waiting until the will is probated."

"That's good. I'd like to see the house just as Scott left it."

"Sam, it's about time you called me Bill. All the deputies call me Sheriff or Chief, but since you're a special employee and probably have more experience than I have, call me by my first name."

"Okay, Bill. Tell the deputy I'm at the picnic table behind the restaurant."

"All right. He'll leave here in a few minutes."

"I talked to Steve O'Neil this morning." He gave the sheriff a brief description of the interview. "I tend to believe him. I don't see him as a suspect unless something new turns up."

"I agree, Sam. He seems like a straight shooter. What do you hope to achieve in looking at Scott's house? We're confident it wasn't the murder scene."

"Yeah, you're probably right. I read all the reports. I just want to get a feel for who Scott was. You know, walk through his house, look at his things, get a feel for the man."

"Well okay, Sam. It's your call."

The waitress brought Sam his pizza; He ate slowly, savoring the mingled flavors of tomato sauce, cheese and pepperoni, washing it down with a tall glass of unsweetened tea. He leafed through the murder book, reviewing what he had recorded there. It was always good to review the book occasionally, looking for details he'd overlooked. Sometimes something he read sparked a new line of thinking, taking him to something he'd not thought of before.

The deputy arriving with the keys to Scott's farmhouse found Sam at the picnic table. He looked enviously at Sam's pizza as he handed them over. Sam asked if he'd like a slice of pizza and the deputy quickly said he hadn't had lunch yet. He deftly picked up a piece, folded it in half longways, and crammed half of it in his mouth. Through a mouthful, he said, "This is really good."

Sam paid the check, leaving the waitress a generous tip. She hadn't frowned at the cash Sam had used to pay the bill. He'd heard, and he believed it to be true, that some restaurants no longer accepted cash. They wanted credit cards, or preferably payment from a cell phone. Tough, Sam thought. They'd just have to deal with it. He liked to pay with old fashioned cash, and that was that—end of story.

Sam returned to his SUV and gave the dog the remaining slice of pizza. "You're lucky to get that," he told the dog. "That deputy would have swallowed the whole thing if I'd let him." The dog licked his lips and tossed his head.

Sam drove back through the valley, the way he'd just traveled, to Scott's farm. He used a key to unlock the padlock on the chain that secured the gate and drove up the long driveway to the house. It was an old-fashioned, two story farmhouse of white-painted wood siding. A narrow brick chimney stood at one end, and a long porch spanned the front of the house. The house was surrounded by a white picket fence, badly in need of paint. Several lilac bushes stood in the yard, encircled by grass in need of mowing. Dandelions dotted the lawn. A small shed stood forlornly behind the house. Farther on, a small barn with sagging double doors leaned precariously on its foundation. It was obvious that this had not been a working farm for years.

Sam mounted the creaking steps to the porch and opened the door with the key the deputy had given him. A stale odor, that of a house closed for months, assailed his nostrils. It was not unpleasant, just the stuffy aroma of a once lived-in home, closed away from fresh air. He found a switch on the wall and flipped on the lights. He stood in the living room—just inside the front door—and scanned the interior. The room was neat and tidy with matching sofa and chair, an armchair, a coffee table, a large flat-screen TV, and various stands and lamps. The floor was covered with a large Indian rug. It was a cozy and inviting room, very masculine, with attractive, framed pictures on the walls.

Pictures of family members, some new and others older, were arranged on tables and book cases.

He looked at each picture carefully. In one, a man and woman in their Sunday best stared back at him solemnly. They were likely Scott's parents, or perhaps grandparents. Another, a framed black and white photograph, was of an Indian pueblo taken somewhere in the southwest. Other black and white photographs and watercolors of mountains and tumbling streams, tastefully done, were hung prominently. A light coating of dust covered everything.

A short hallway led toward the back of the house and a recently remodeled kitchen. A kitchen table was cluttered with junk mail and magazines. A smaller stack of bills was held down by a large, irregular rock pocked with fossils. Sam sorted through the bills, noting that the latest date was for late November of the previous year. They were of the expected variety; electricity, phone, satellite TV, and so on. Nothing unusual. The kitchen was neatly kept. One bowl of the double sink held a drying rack with a few plates, cups and silverware. Otherwise the counter top was bare.

A mudroom off the kitchen held the usual coats, boots, and outdoor gear. Two metal pet food bowls were pushed into one corner, and a well-worn pet bed indicated that Scott had owned a large dog at one time. An open bag of dog food sat on a shelf attached to the wall. A peg held a long leash. Other pegs held coats and sweaters.

Sam climbed the narrow stairway to the second floor. A quick look around revealed two bedrooms and a bath. He took a quick look at the smaller bedroom, undoubtedly a guest room, and found only some old clothes and a winter coat in the closet. The bed was neatly made and covered with a patchwork quilt. Sam looked carefully at the stitching on the quilt and determined—to his untrained eye—that it was hand made.

The master bedroom was sparsely furnished. He saw a double bed, a night stand with a lamp, more pictures on the walls, and a large rug covering the hardwood floor. The night stand drawer held a few personal items that a woman would use. A small, plain, clay pot on the night stand held an assortment of loose items; old keys, Chapstick, loose coins, a couple of rubber bands, a tie clip of silver and turquoise, and a small travel clock. The closet held an assortment of men's clothing neatly arranged on hangers. Shoes and boots sat in a neat row on the floor. He looked more closely and found a woman's house coat on a hanger and a small pair of house slippers among Scott's shoes. Probably left there by Wendy Richmond. Sam pushed aside the clothing and found a .22 caliber rifle standing in a corner. The top shelf held neatly folded sweaters and a variety of other clothing. A partially empty box of cartridges for the rifle was shoved to one side.

There was nothing unusual in the bathroom. He found stacks of towels on wall shelves, shaving equipment on the sink, prescribed drugs for blood pressure in the medicine cabinet, a modest collection of shampoo and sanitary aids, hair brush, tooth brush and toothpaste, etc.

Sam went back downstairs and found a door that led to the basement steps. He made a quick tour of the basement, finding a laundry area and a lifetime collection of junk covered with a thick layer of dust. Nothing of interest there.

He returned to the living room, sat on the couch and studied the room again. If there was a clue as to who killed Scott here, he just didn't see it. What he did see was the home of a man who had few possessions, was neat and tidy, and lived a simple life.

He locked the house and climbed into his SUV. The dog stretched and sat looking at him. Sam searched through his briefcase until he found the sheriff's report on their search of the house and outbuildings. He read through it carefully noting the description of the contents of the shed and barn. There was nothing unexpected there, so he didn't bother doing a search of his own.

He sat back in his seat and stared out the window, thinking. He suddenly left the vehicle and re-entered the house. He looked again at the Indian rug on the living room floor. It looked genuine to him, but then, he wasn't an expert on textiles. He lifted a corner of the rug and felt its texture, noting it was thick and heavy. It looked to him like it was made of tightly woven wool. The rug was woven into a zigzag pattern of bright colors; reds and blacks, and yellows. To his untrained eye, it was pleasing. Beautiful. He estimated its size to be at least six by ten feet. He moved a coffee table to one side to get a better look, then fumbled his phone from his pocket and took several pictures, each from a slightly different angle.

He sat back on his heels looking at the rug. Where did Scott get it? What was it worth? A rug that size and quality must be worth thousands. But, if someone killed Scott for the rug, why was it still here? He stood, hearing his bones crack and pop, still looking at the rug. It probably wasn't important, but he'd follow up. Where *had* he gotten it? It was the only thing of any value in the house. Buying such an expensive item was out of character for Scott, and therefore, something Sam needed to figure out.

Sam drove back to his house in town, stopping at the local grocery for food and more dogfood. On impulse, he bought a small bag of doggy treats. When he entered his kitchen loaded down with grocery bags, he noticed that the light on his old-fashioned, land-line answering machine was blinking.

Chapter 10

Sam stacked his grocery dry goods in the kitchen cabinets and put the perishables in the refrigerator. Yellow Dog stood by impatiently while Sam filled his food bowl and refreshed the water in the cooking pot he'd found in a drawer under the stove. The dog alternated between crunching his food and noisily lapping up water. He made a mess on the linoleum floor, but Sam would mop it up later.

As he worked, the light on the phone's answering machine blinked monotonously. Each blink was followed by an annoying beep. He didn't recognize the number on the handset's small screen. He debated just deleting the message unheard, but curiosity got the better of him. It would probably be a telemarketer telling him that he could get a reduced rate on his student loans, but he listened to the recorded message anyway.

"Hello? Anybody there?" a gruff, male voice asked. "I'm trying to contact Sam Miller. If that's you, I need to talk to you. It's important. Call me as soon as you can." He recited the same number that had appeared on the phone's screen and hung up.

Sam stood in the kitchen with the phone in his hand, wondering who the caller could be and what he wanted. What was so important? He placed the phone in its cradle and searched among the detritus on the counter for paper and pen. He wrote down the number before he forgot it. It was still in the phone, but he didn't want to have to figure out how to retrieve it if he needed it. Paper and pen worked just fine.

Sam took the handset with him to the living room and collapsed into his favorite armchair. He used the remote control to flip on the

TV, found a sports channel that was broadcasting a Pirates game, and settled in. The dog curled upon the rug in front of the fireplace. He hadn't built a fire in the fireplace since his wife had died. She used to like to watch the flames and read on cold winter nights. He'd sat in his chair, she at the end of the couch within arm's reach. He still missed her desperately. He looked around the room, thinking he needed to do some cleaning. She wouldn't have approved of his lifestyle. Maybe he'd find a cleaning lady to come in every week or so to keep the place in order. He wondered if the dog thought the fireplace was giving off heat. Probably not. It was almost the middle of the summer, and the room was warm and stuffy.

He punched the number into the phone and listened to it ring— three, then four times. The same gruff voice answered.

"Yeah?"

"This is Sam Miller. I'm returning your call."

"Thanks for calling back, detective. I have a couple of questions for you."

"Questions? Who is this? What do you want?"

"I'm Ray Lambert. Does that name mean anything to you?"

"No, I can't say that it does. I repeat. What do you want?"

"I'm a reporter. I write for the *Kanawha Daily Bugle*. That's why I thought maybe you'd know who I am."

"Oh yes, I remember now," Sam said. "I've read a few of your articles."

"Good. I heard by the grapevine that you and a college professor are trying to find the killer of the man found in a tree up on Dolly Sods. Is that right?"

"Who told you that?"

He chuckled, "Reporters never give up their sources. You should know that, Detective. I've written several articles about the murder. I probably know just about as much as you do about it. From what I've heard, you just started working on it a couple of weeks ago."

"Yeah, you probably do," Sam said grudgingly.

"So, is it true? Are you and the professor working on this case?"

"I don't think I want to answer any of your questions."

"Oh, come on, Detective, you can answer a couple of questions, can't you? You can help me get the facts straight."

"It's your job to get the facts straight, Ray. Not mine. But, I will tell you that I'm helping the sheriff's department on a part-time basis. I'm retired, so I have some extra time on my hands."

"What about the professor? Who is he, and what's his part in this?"

"I didn't say anything about a professor. Let me ask *you* a question. What do you know about the murder?"

"I'll be honest with you, Sam. I only know what I've written in the paper, and that's pitifully little. The sheriff gave me a few details, but as you can imagine, he's pretty closed lipped. If you've read my articles, you know everything I know. The editor asked me to do a follow-up article, and I'm just trying to come up with a new angle."

"Sorry. I can't be of much help, but I'll give you this much, off the record. Yes, I'm working the case as a special deputy. The professor you mentioned has little to do with the investigation. As a matter of fact, he's out of the country right now. I've just begun the investigation and don't have any new leads. Right now, I'm going over the work the sheriff and his deputies did. Otherwise, I'll just keep plugging away at it until something significant happens. That's about all I can tell you. Don't use my name. I don't want every Tom, Dick and Harry in the county calling me. Maybe I'll have more to tell you later. Oh, and you might say that if anyone has any information about the murder to call the sheriff's office. They have an anonymous phone number you could list. Call the sheriff's office for it."

"Okay, Sam. That will give me enough to write the story. I'll rehash what we all already know and keep you as an anonymous source."

"Oh lord, don't call me an anonymous source. When I was a cop, we hated that. Just keep me out of it."

Ray laughed and said, "You got it. But, I'll be calling again. This is quite a story. I hope you crack it. I'd hate to see the murderer get off Scott free. No pun intended."

"You and me, both," Sam said as he hung up the phone.

Sam sat back in his armchair and stared at the television screen. He wondered if he had made a mistake talking to the press at all. Even the best of them got the facts wrong more often than not. He'd have to call Jimmy and warn him that his name would probably be in the paper. He'd also call the sheriff in the morning and tell him about his conservation with Ray Lambert. One thing he knew for sure about law enforcement officers; they didn't like surprises. Neither did he.

The next morning, Sam called the sheriff to let him know a reporter had been nosing around, and that there would likely be a new article about the murder in the Charleston paper.

"I just wanted to keep you informed. I don't think Lambert knows much, but that won't stop him from writing a story. He'll probably emphasize that I'm working for you and that Jimmy is involved in the investigation. I didn't give him Jimmy's name, but it won't be too hard for him to find out who he is."

"Don't worry about it. It was a gruesome murder, and his readers will be interested. I just hope he doesn't make up too much of the story."

Sam took the opportunity to update the sheriff on what he had been doing. He told him about the Indian rug in Scott's house. They talked about its significance and wondered if Scott had bought it for himself or if someone had given it to him.

"So, what do you plan to do next?" the sheriff asked.

"I have a few more interviews to do." He shuffled through his notes until he found Jimmy's list of people to interview. "I want to talk to Jonathan Wright. As you probably remember, he's the man who has no visible means of support and lives near Scott's farm."

"Yeah, I remember. We couldn't get a warrant to search his financial records. The judge said there wasn't enough probable cause. One of my deputies interviewed him. Did you find his report in the stuff I gave you?"

"Yes, but there wasn't much in it. As far as I can tell, the deputy didn't *ask* him how he made his living. Maybe he'll just tell us if we ask him. I didn't see that in the report. Did he refuse to tell the deputy?"

"I don't know. Maybe the deputy didn't ask. I'll talk to him and let you know."

"It doesn't really matter. I'll ask him myself. Maybe he'll explain everything." Sam looked through the list again. "I also want to talk to

Buddy Smith and Frank Richmond. Maybe Wendy Richmond, too. I'm guessing Frank or Wendy can tell me where Scott got the rug."

"Do you really think the rug's important?"

"Probably not, but it's inconsistent with the way Scott lived. It'll bug me until I get an answer."

"Why do you want to talk to Frank? Do you really believe he's involved in the killing?"

"No, probably not, but you never know. But, Wendy might know something important and just not realize it. As you know, Sheriff, sometimes it's the little things that lead to a break in the case."

"Yeah, I suppose so. Just go easy on Wendy. I don't want her complaining to the papers or something. After all, she's the one that hired you to begin with."

"I'll be careful with her, Bill. But, so far, I haven't found a single clue as to who might have killed Scott Mitchell."

"Aren't you going to interview Kelly Price? You didn't say anything about her."

"Oh, I haven't forgotten. I'm going to wait until Jimmy returns before I go talk to her."

The sheriff guffawed loudly into the phone. "You'd better take more backup than the professor, Sam. She'll eat him alive."

After he'd hung up with the sheriff, he called Jimmy. It never ceased to amaze him that he could call someone in another country as if he were just across town. He could still remember having to use a phone booth to make calls, and you had to pay extra for long distance. It made him feel old. If he remembered correctly, Costa Rica was an hour or two behind his time, but Jimmy answered immediately.

"Hey, Sam. What's up?" Jimmy asked. There was a low roar in the background somewhat like a waterfall, frogs peeped loudly, and he could hear someone yelling close by.

"Where are you, Jimmy? I can hardly hear you for the racket there."

Jimmy laughed. "I'm in Costa Rica, Sam. It's raining—hard. That's what it does in the rain forest."

"You mean that roaring noise is rain?"

"Yeah, it's really pouring. I'm along a trail in the preserve collecting data. My hands are wrinkled like prunes, and even with rain gear, I'm soaked to the bone. Luckily, it's really warm."

"What's all that yelling about that I can hear?"

Jimmy laughed again, "Howler monkeys. They make a racket when it rains. There's some parrots screaming, too. Whenever it rains, the natives get restless."

"Well, I'm glad you're there and not me."

"How's the investigation going? Have you found any important clues yet?"

"No. I've done a couple more interviews, but nothing important has come up. I sent you my notes and some photos. Did you get them?"

"Yeah, but I haven't had time to read them. I'm really busy. I only have a limited amount of time here, and I want to make the most of it. I won't even begin to analyze my data until I get home. I'm just dumping it all in my computer and will wait until later to do anything with it."

"Well, if you get a chance, look them over. But, the reason I called, a reporter by the name of Ray Lambert called me last night. He said he's going to do a follow-up article on the murder and was trying to pump me for information. I have a feeling you and I are going to become famous. Don't be surprised if both our names are featured prominently in the piece. He didn't have much new information, so I think he'll focus on a retired policeman and a college professor who are acting like detectives."

"Oh. That's not good, but I'm not worried about what the college will think about my involvement. After all, I have tenure. Do you think it will hinder our investigation?" Jimmy asked.

"No, not really. The news of our involvement is probably out anyway. I asked Ray to include the sheriff's anonymous phone number in case someone knows something. We'll get a prank call or two, but you never know when someone will give us something that will be helpful. Anyway, I just wanted you to know that your name will probably be in the paper. When do you plan to come home?"

"I have about a week left. The days tend to run together when you're doing this kind of work. The rest of the research team will be going home then, too."

"Ok. Have a good time. I'll keep you posted on my progress. Or, more likely, on my lack of progress."

They talked for a few minutes more, then Sam hung up and began putting the murder book back in order. He closed the file and stuck it in his briefcase. He picked up the phone again and called Jonathan Wright. He had a young-sounding voice and seemed friendly enough. He agreed to talk to Sam and suggested that he come by right away. Sam told him he lived in town near the State College campus, and it would take forty-five minutes to get there. Wright said that he was going to be home all day and would see him then.

It was a pleasant drive up on the mountain and into Canaan Valley. It was late morning, and the traffic was light. The day was crisp and clear, and the air temperature was pleasant. Sam pulled into the paved driveway to Jonathan's house. The ski resort was nearby, and the house sat on several acres of wooded property. It was an expensive-looking log cabin with stone and shingle trim. He guessed the house had four or five bedrooms. A current model Lexus SUV was parked in front of the detached two-car garage. Sam guessed the landscaping surrounding the cabin cost more than his house. Judging from the home and SUV, Jonathan was worth some serious money. The deputy's report indicated that Jonathan didn't work. Family money? Not everyone had to work for a living. That didn't include anyone Sam knew, but he'd heard there were such people. Maybe he was into illegal drug sales.

Sam told the dog to stay in the car and rolled down all the windows to provide ventilation. He mounted the expansive porch and pushed the button for the doorbell. He heard a gong sound deep in the house's interior. The door was opened by a tall, handsome young man of about thirty dressed in expensive, casual clothing.

"I assume you're Sam Miller," he said. "Come in." He stepped back to allow Sam to enter. "Come on in to the family room. We can talk there."

The room was attractively decorated with a leather couch and matching arm chairs, drapes on the windows, and expensive-looking rugs on the hardwood floors. A massive stone fireplace arose along one wall.

Jonathan offered coffee, and Sam accepted. While Jonathan went to get the drinks, Sam observed the room carefully. Expensive paintings of bucolic scenes from the valley decorated the walls, and shelves and bookcases were loaded with souvenirs from his travels. A coffee table contained maps and travel manuals.

"Here you go," Jonathan said, handing Sam a large porcelain mug of steaming coffee. "I get the coffee beans from a free trade consortium in Central America. I grind them myself. I hope you like it."

Sam sipped the coffee. "It's very good. Thank you." It *was* good. Easily the best coffee he'd tasted for a long time. Much better than the stuff Jimmy brewed in his antique coffee pot.

"So, Detective, what brings you to my home asking questions?"

"I'm investigating the death of Scott Mitchell. You remember the case, don't you?"

"Oh yes, I can see the roof of his house from my front porch. It was unnerving, to say the least. But, I'm afraid I don't know anything that would help you. I've already told the deputy everything I know."

Sam asked a series of probing questions establishing Jonathan's background. He was a university graduate with a major in journalism, had a large family who lived in another state, and was dating a young woman who taught English at the local high school.

"I only have a few more questions for you, then I'll be out of your hair. Did you know Scott personally?"

"I didn't know him well, but I've talked to him a couple of times."

"Where did you come in contact with him?"

"I go to the Red Creek Saloon sometimes. I saw him there once or twice. He and Wendy, she's the bartender, had a thing going. We talked a couple of times. He was my neighbor, so I was just trying to be friendly. And then, there was a meeting we both attended. It was a conference about the nature preserve. You know, how it should be managed, setting policies, making decisions about its future."

"At this meeting, did he say anything about the endangered species on his property?"

Jonathan thought for a moment, picking at his lower lip. "No, not that I remember. I don't know anything about that. What is it, some kind of rare plant or something?"

Sam explained that it was a rare fern. "Do you have any idea who might have wanted to do Scott harm?"

"Oh, heavens no. Scott was a good guy. He stayed to himself, minded his own business as far as I know. I was shocked when I heard he'd been murdered." He hesitated a moment, then frowned at Sam. "May I ask you a question, officer?"

"Sure. Go ahead."

"What was it that prompted you to come to interview me? There are lots of others who knew Scott. Why did you single me out?"

Sam paused before answering. "You're probably aware that your neighbors and others who live nearby sometimes gossip and spread rumors, aren't you?"

"Oh, now I understand. It's that old rumor that I'm into drugs, or that I'm from a wealthy family, or that I'm a genius who plays the market."

"Yes, that's the one. You came to the sheriff's attention because you live near Scott, seem to be very wealthy, but don't have to work. It's just a loose end that needs to be tied up. We're talking to all his neighbors. Did the deputy ask you about how you make a living?"

"No. He didn't actually ask many questions."

"Well, are you going to answer the question?"

Jonathan threw his head back and laughed. "Sure, Detective, I'll be happy to explain. Come with me." They walked into another room that was originally a den. It had been converted into a work space with a large computer screen and a variety of tablets, keyboards, and other electronics. A large television screen was attached to a wall. Post-it notes were stuck on the sides of the screens and on other surfaces. An empty coffee mug sat precariously on a stack of books.

"I'm a writer. It's what I do for a living, and I've been very successful at it. As you can see, this is where I work."

"So, you're not independently wealthy? No family fortunes?"

He laughed again, "Oh, heavens no. I come from a long line of teachers, fire-fighters, policemen, and military men and women. We've never been accused of being wealthy."

"What kind of stuff do you write? Are you a novelist?"

"No, sadly, nothing like that. I could only wish. I'd like to claim to be another John Grisham, but I can't. I write news items. Not quite the stuff of legends."

"No offense, but I can't see how you could make a lot of money writing news stories."

"Do you remember the news item back during the presidential campaigns that one of the candidates was involved in the human trafficking trade? It made quite a splash on the cable news networks. I didn't write the story, but that's the *kind* of story I write."

"You mean fake news?" Sam asked incredulously.

"Yep. I guess that's what it's called." He looked at Sam with a sly grin on his face. "And, I make a lot of money at it."

Sam shook his head. "Where do you get the information for your stories? Do you do research?"

"I don't do much research. Only enough to make my stories believable. I just make them up. People tend to believe just about anything that conforms to their preconceived ideas."

"Can you really make money doing this?"

"Yes. The stories are posted on the Internet; blogs, Facebook, anywhere there's a large readership. I write both conservative and liberal political stories. It doesn't matter to me. The more outrageous the better. The more hits the story gets, the more I get paid. It's all about the advertising on the webpages. The more people who read the pages, the more the advertisers pay, and the more I make."

"Isn't this unethical or something?"

"Not in my way of thinking. It's entertainment. It's fiction. The stories Mr. Grisham writes are fiction. They're not real. Well, my stories aren't real either, and people *must* get some enjoyment out of them or they wouldn't read them. Besides, if you're naïve enough to believe anything you read on the Internet, you get what you deserve."

"How much do you get paid for a story?"

"It depends on how many people read it, but I can get eight or ten thousand dollars for a good story. That's for thirty or forty minutes of work. Not bad, huh?"

Sam shook his head. The Internet represented a new world where reality was whatever the webmasters wanted it to be. Facts were no longer important. It made him feel older than dirt.

Chapter 11

The following day dawned bright and sunny. Sam arose early and made coffee in his untidy kitchen. He'd promised himself that he'd call today to find a housekeeper—someone to come in once a week or so to do the cleaning that he'd neglected, wash the laundry, and clean up the kitchen. The more he thought about it, the better he liked the idea. It couldn't be too expensive.

He fried bacon in an old skillet while the dog milled around his feet. He knew Ruthie would have pitched a fit if she knew what he was eating for breakfast. He put the bacon to drain on some paper towels and cracked three eggs into the grease. They crackled and sputtered pleasantly. When they were cooked, he plated the food, adding a couple of slices of buttered toast. He poured a mug of coffee, not nearly as good as Jonathan's had been, and ate at the kitchen table. He gave the dog a slice of bacon. It disappeared in one gulp.

He washed the skillet, put it in the rack to dry and loaded the dishes into the dishwasher. He'd have to clean the kitchen a little before the cleaning lady came—the living room and bedroom, too. And then there was the upstairs bathroom. He couldn't have her thinking he was a slob.

He walked down his short driveway to get the newspaper while the dog saluted the shrubs and bushes and did his business on his neighbor's lawn. Sam looked around to see if anyone was watching. He returned to the front porch and sat in the swing. He opened the paper to see photographs of him and Jimmy staring at him from the front page. The headline proclaimed in bold letters:

Local Sleuths Promise to Find Scott Mitchell's Killer.

He read the story quickly, muttering under his breath. His face got redder with each paragraph. Lambert had written background information about him, emphasizing his career as a police detective and highlighting his run-in with the captain. The story didn't claim he'd been fired but made it clear that he had left under a cloud. Jimmy's career as a professor was described, and the story stated that he'd been arrested for murder but had successfully cleared his name. It went on to say Sam and Jimmy had worked together to find the murderer. The part that most irritated Sam was Lambert's claim that he and Jimmy had bragged they'd find Scott's killer and bring him to justice. The known facts of Scott's murder were stated, with the sheriff's office being blamed for not solving the crime.

Sam tossed the paper aside and rubbed his face with his hands. This was what he was afraid of when he talked to Lambert. Everything Ray had written was accurate, more or less, except for the claim they'd find the killer. It hadn't been written as a direct quote and only implied that they'd made the claim. He shook his head, wondering what the sheriff would think when he saw the paper. Thank goodness, he'd given him a heads-up that the article was coming. Sam pulled his phone from his pocket and called the sheriff.

"Yeah, I read this morning's paper. It's about what I expected. Ray's a good reporter, but he doesn't pull any punches. Don't worry about it. I have thick skin." The sheriff paused, then said with a chuckle, "Where did they get your picture? I didn't realize you were that handsome."

Sam snorted, "Probably from the state police files, or the Internet. You can find anything you want on there." He told the sheriff about his interview with Jonathan Wright.

"He's a writer? Well, I guess that puts it to rest. You say he makes money writing false stories for the Internet? I didn't know you could do such a thing."

"I guess it's protected under the First Amendment, but I'm not a lawyer. What do I know?"

"Sam, you understand what all this means, don't you?"

"Yes. If the killer gets nervous about us working on the case, he might try to stop us. We'll have to watch our backs."

"You got that right. It's been my experience that the second killing is easier than the first. The penalty for two killings is about the same as for one—life in prison. What does he have to lose?"

Sam ended the call and walked back inside the house. He booted up his laptop and searched through the newspaper's website until he found the article and sent it to Jimmy's phone. Oh, the wonders of modern technology. Misery could be sent around the world in a flash.

Sam poured a fresh cup of coffee and returned to the swing on the front porch. So far, his investigation hadn't turned up anything of use. Nothing he'd read or learned from his interviews had gotten him any closer to solving the crime. He had more interviews to do, but he was dubious that they'd reveal anything helpful. But, as he'd told Jimmy on several occasions, you never knew when you'd stumble onto a clue that would crack the case. He swung back and forth slowly, mulling over the facts. Scott's body had been left to rot in a tree. What was that about? Why would the killer go to the trouble of putting it in a tree? Was it part of a sick ritual of some kind? Was the killer taunting the police? No, that didn't make sense. If he wanted to tease the cops, why drive all the way to Dolly Sods to do it? Was it something a bunch of kids would do? He made a mental note to follow up on that but doubted it would lead to much. It didn't feel right. It didn't sound like something kids would dream up, like a weird science project. The body was much too neat, bundled in a blanket, tied up like a leg-of-lamb and stashed on a tree limb. Kids were more impulsive. More likely to do the killing and leave the body where it fell. He'd ask the sheriff if he knew of any gangs or groups of crazy kids living in the area that might be involved, but he was doubtful of anything coming of it. He mulled through several other theories, but in the end, he was no closer to a solution than when he began.

His coffee had grown cold. He took the cup back in the kitchen, rinsed it under the faucet, and put it in the dishwasher.

He climbed into his SUV with the dog clambering in beside him on the front seat. Sam looked at him and shook his head. "Who said you could sit up front?" he asked. The dog looked back at him with serious eyes, then sat down. "Oh, I guess you can ride up front. Why not?"

They drove to Canaan Valley, then continued on Route 32 toward Harmon and down the mountain to the bridge over Red Creek. Sam pulled into the expansive gravel parking lot of the Red Creek Saloon, just off the two-lane highway. A dozen cars, SUVs and pick-up trucks in about equal numbers, were parked in the spaces delineated by lines sprayed in white paint onto the gravel. It was newly built; a large wooden structure, stained a pleasant cedar color with a green metal roof. Small, dark windows broke up its lines, and a narrow porch spanned a good portion of the front of the building. Tiny white lights were strung on the porch posts and exposed rafters. Several large wooden tubs were planted with brightly blooming plants that cascaded pleasantly onto the porch floor. Wooden benches and rocking chairs were arranged along the wall. Dense smoke rose from behind the saloon, emanating a smoky, brown sugar odor. Yellow Dog tested the air with his wet nose.

A narrow, gravel road lead toward the back of the property and a large metal building. A long box truck was backed up to its loading dock. Two men worked at unloading its cargo.

The interior was a large room with a bar along one wall. A line of stools stood along the bar. A long mirror behind the bar was flanked with shelves containing an impressive array of bottles and glasses. Above the mirror was a large painting of a nude woman reposed on a bed of moss and flowers. A dreamy smile graced her comely face. Wendy Richmond, her head down, worked behind the bar, taking beer cans from cartons and plunging them into waiting ice chests. Like all the other workers, she wore a dark green polo shirt with the name of the bar stenciled on the breast pocket and tan dockers.

A small stage illuminated by an array of lights hanging from the ceiling dominated the opposite wall. The members of a four-piece band were setting up for the evening gig. Sam recognized Chris Franklin, the lead guitarist. Chris was one of the sheriff's deputies who, evidently, also moonlighted as a musician. Sam remembered from a report that he was on the scene when Scott's body was recovered. A cramped dance floor of parquet flooring lay immediately in front of the stage. The remainder of the room was crowded with tables and chairs. The wait staff was industriously preparing the room for a busy night.

Several large stuffed animal heads looked down mournfully from the walls—moose, elk, deer, and a large black bear. A full sized, stuffed grizzly bear stood in a corner, its face frozen into a snarling grimace. Large, paddle fans rotated in lazy monotony in the high ceiling of the room.

Toward the back, double, swinging doors led to the kitchen. Sam peeped through one of the windows on the doors. The kitchen was clean and bright. Stainless steel stoves, preparation tables, and refrigerators filled the room. Three young men clad in clean, white aprons and baseball caps worked frantically chopping, cutting, and dicing. Preparation for a big night was well underway.

"Something I can do for you? We're not open yet."

Sam turned to see a large man, in his mid-forties, standing with his hands on his hips. One arm was covered with a full sleeve of tattoos. He had attractive, chiseled features, a strong jaw and piercing brown eyes. He wore faded jeans and a tight t-shirt that showed off his well-muscled arms and shoulders.

"I'm Sam Miller. I need to talk to Wendy. It will only take a few minutes," Sam said.

The man frowned at him and asked, "What do you want with her? She's busy. We're getting ready to open, and we have a lot of work to do."

Sam fished his badge out of his pocked and showed it to the man. "It won't take long. Who are you?"

The man looked at the badge and shook his head. "You people are always trying to give me a hard time. All I'm trying to do is make a living here. I employ fifteen people, and in this area, good jobs are hard to come by."

"I'm not going to give you a hard time. I'm investigating Scott Mitchell's murder. As far as I know that doesn't have anything to do with you, or your business. What's your name?"

The man sighed and said, "Seth Buckman. I own this place."

"Ok, that wasn't so hard, was it? Wendy asked me to try to find Scott's killer. I need to ask her a few questions, then I'll be out of your hair."

Seth frowned down on Sam. "I just don't want anyone pushing her around. She's had a hard time dealing with Scott's death. It was terrible for her. First, he was missing, and then they found him up there on the mountain."

"Did you know him?"

"Oh, sure. He came in here occasionally. He wasn't much at socializing. Drank a few beers. Sometimes he'd pick Wendy up after closing. Take her home. Make sure she was okay."

"Do you have any idea why someone would want to kill him?" Sam asked.

"No. I can't imagine why anyone would want to do him harm. The cops found his body up in a tree. What was that all about?" Seth looked toward Wendy as she worked behind the bar.

"That's what we're trying to find out." Sam looked around and said, "Tell me about your business here. You've only been open a short while, haven't you?"

"What does my business have to do with Scott's death? Why are you questioning me?" he asked with a hard look in his eye.

"Just curiosity. It looks like you're very successful."

"Yes," he said proudly, "It's working out well. I'm beginning to make a profit. I opened a couple of years ago, but it takes time to get things going. We brew most of the beer we sell here in the bar. You probably saw the large building out back. When the state changed the laws to allow micro-breweries, it opened a huge market. Besides selling our beer here, I distribute it all over the east coast, but mostly West Virginia and Northern Virginia. When Corridor H was completed from Davis to the Virginia border, it made distribution easier."

"What's your brand name?"

"Well, we have several brands, but the most popular is Red Creek Ale." Seth had warmed to Sam as he talked about his business. "We also have a dark ale and a blond pilsner. We stock the other brands— Budweiser, Miller, you know, the usual. But, the locals are slowly learning to like ours. I just signed contracts with some of the large resorts in the area to stock their bars and most of the groceries carry it."

"I'm glad to hear you're doing well, Seth," Sam said not unkindly. "We need all the businesses we can get in the area. Fifteen jobs aren't anything to sneeze at. I hope you continue to be successful."

"Thanks. If you need a private place to talk to Wendy, you can use my office. She knows where it is."

Wendy smiled at Sam as he approached the bar. "Hi, Sam. I wondered when you'd get around to talking to me." She extended her hand and shook his firmly.

"Yeah, when Jimmy and I met with you earlier, I didn't get to ask a lot of questions, and I'd like to get you up to date on our progress. Or, I should say, lack of progress."

"I know you and Dr. Houston are working hard on the case."

"You know that I'm working for the sheriff's office, don't you? Officially, I'm working for them, but since you hired me first, I thought I'd keep you posted on what we're doing."

"Is Dr. Houston working for the sheriff, too?"

"No, not officially. He's still involved in the case, but only as a volunteer. He's still employed by the college, so his time is limited."

"I thought he was off for the summer," she said.

Sam laughed. "No, he has work that he does while he's off from teaching, so he's still working. As a matter of fact, he's in Central America somewhere right now."

"Central America?" she said incredulously.

"Yeah, doing some kind of research. But, while he's gone, I'm continuing the investigation."

"I read the article in the paper. Did you really say you'd solve the crime?"

"No, but I'm confident we'll get to the bottom of this. It may take some time, but sooner or later, we'll figure out who killed Scott."

"Okay. Fire away. Ask your questions."

"It might be best if we talked in private. Seth said it was okay to use his office."

Wendy led the way across the dining area, weaving around tables, to a side door. The office was small and cramped with video monitors, a lap top, stacks of papers and invoices, and a small safe sitting in one corner. A large, wooden desk dominated the room with an office chair and two folding chairs for visitors. They sat in the visitors' chairs.

When they were comfortably seated, Sam said, "First, Wendy, let me warn you. I may ask some questions that could be uncomfortable for you. Don't take offense. I just want to be thorough. If you don't want to answer, just tell me, but I hope you can see your way to be as forthcoming as you can."

"Okay," she said nervously. "I've never been interrogated by the police before."

Sam chuckled, "I promise to go easy on you."

Wendy settled into her chair with her hands clasped in her lap, a determined look on her face.

"Did you and Scott ever argue?" Sam asked.

"No! Never. Scott was such a kind soul. He wouldn't have argued with me if I'd tried."

Watching her closely, Sam asked, "Did you kill Scott?"

It was as if he'd slapped her. She sucked a huge breath into her lungs. Her eyes grew large and her face turned crimson. "No! Of course not. I loved him." Her hands shook in her lap. "Why would I hire you to find the killer if I'd killed him myself?"

Sam was confident she was telling the truth, but then, he'd been fooled before. "I'm sorry, Wendy. I needed to know. Do you have any idea who would have a reason to kill him?"

"No. As I told the sheriff, everybody loved and respected him."

"When I searched his house, I noticed an Indian rug on the floor in the living room. Do you have any idea where it came from? It didn't seem like something he'd buy, an expensive item like that."

"No. It's been there for as long as I've known him. I always thought it was a reproduction. Did you check the label? Maybe it was made in China or something."

Sam grimaced. No, he hadn't checked for a label. He'd just assumed it was expensive. Maybe it wasn't. He made a note in his notebook. Another loose end.

He asked, "You have two children, right?"

"Yes. Frankie and Tiffany. You know Frankie. He's a student at State College—one of Dr. Houston's advisees. Tiffany's in the military," she said proudly. "She's a supply sergeant."

"Where is she stationed?"

"Iraq. She's been there for almost a year. Her tour will be over soon, and she'll return stateside."

"In the year she's been in Iraq, has she been home on furlough?"

"No. They usually stay there for the full year, unless there's an emergency at home or something. You know, a death in the family or something." She glowered at Sam. "Why are you asking about her?"

"Just being thorough," Sam said. "What about Frank? How did he and Scott get along?"

"Just wait a minute. Why are you asking about Frankie? You're not thinking he killed Scott, are you? You can't be serious." She started to stand, then slumped again onto the chair.

"Did Frank and Scott get along?" Sam asked, repeating the question.

"Yes, of course. Frankie liked Scott. They got along fine."

"No arguments, disagreements, anything like that?"

Wendy hesitated and looked down at her hands clutched in her lap. She raised her face, looking over Sam's shoulder, avoiding his eyes. "Oh, there was one time when they got in an argument. It wasn't anything. Just a misunderstanding."

Sam said, kindly, "Tell me about it."

"It was last fall, a week or two before Thanksgiving." She stopped speaking. A tear ran down one cheek. After a moment, she said in a tiny voice, "Frankie had gone with me to Scott's house. Frankie wanted to talk to Scott. It was something about the rare ferns that grew on the farm. Frankie's a biology major, so he's interested in such things."

Sam interrupted, "They argued about the ferns?"

"Oh no, not about the ferns." She sighed and looked Sam in the eye. "Scott caught Frankie smoking a joint out in that old barn. Scott had a thing about drugs, and he said something to Frankie about it. They argued, but not violently or anything. Just raised voices. I was surprised that Scott would even say anything to him about it. Anyway, Frankie stomped off and went and sat in the car. That was the last time Frankie saw Scott."

"Did they have any other confrontations, that you know of?"

"No. I'm sure they didn't. As I said before, Frankie liked Scott, and he was pleased that I'd found someone and that we were talking about getting married. I think it was a relief to him that Scott would be around to look out for me."

"Your husband was killed in a mining accident, wasn't he?"

"Yes. It was a freak accident. He was crushed by a large coal loading machine. It was awful."

"How did Frank take his father's death.?"

"Frankie took his father's death hard, but he seemed to have adjusted. At least, as well as any of us did."

Sam abruptly changed the subject, "When was the last time you saw Scott?"

She thought for a moment. "It was Thanksgiving week. We had dinner at my house. It was the day before Thanksgiving, a Wednesday. I had to work Thanksgiving Day. Seth puts on a big Thanksgiving dinner, with turkey and all the trimmings. He closes the bar because he wants it to be a family thing. Lots of locals eat here instead of at home. And, it's in the middle of deer season, so there's lots of hungry hunters, too. Anyway, I made dinner for him at my house." She pulled a handkerchief from a pocket and dabbed at the corners of her eyes. She sniffed loudly and said, "There. See what you've done? I've ruined my makeup."

Sam could hear the band members tuning their instruments through the closed door. They played a few bars of a familiar country-western tune, stopped abruptly, and began laughing.

"How long have you worked here?" Sam asked.

"I've worked for Seth since he opened the place. I'd been a bartender before, long ago, before I was married. So, I had the experience, and really needed the job."

"Do you like working here?"

"Yes, I do. It's not like working in a regular bar with drunks and everything. It's more like a restaurant. The evening crowds get a little loud sometimes, but Seth doesn't stand for any foolishment. Anyone who gets out of hand is kicked out on his ear. The pay's good with tips and all. We all get health insurance and can set up a retirement plan if we want. Seth has been very kind to me, kind of like a big brother."

"It's unusual for a business like this to provide such a generous benefits package, isn't it?"

"Yes, but Seth said that if you want to keep good workers, you have to pay them well."

"Does everyone get the same benefits?"

"I assume they do, but I've never asked."

Sam said he'd like to talk to Frank and asked if he was at her home today, and she said he was. She gave him directions how to get there. He asked a few more questions, carefully taking notes as he went. "I'm sure you need to get back to work, Wendy. I'll let you go. Can I call you if I have any more questions?"

"Sure. Do you have a card in case I need to call *you*?"

Sam didn't have a card. He made a mental note to have some printed. He gave her his home number and encouraged her to call if she thought of anything that might be helpful. They left the office, and Wendy took up her station behind the bar. Sam waved toward Seth as he left and got a nod and a frown in return.

Chapter 12

Sam left the bar and drove less than a mile toward Harmon, turned off Route 32 and crossed a rickety metal bridge over Dry Fork. The narrow road turned downstream, closely paralleling the swiftly flowing creek. Birds trilled in the trees and brush along the road, and a half-grown groundhog scurried into the tall grass along the lane as he approached. A half-mile along, he turned into the short driveway of an attractive cottage. It sat on a well-tended lot with attractive shrubs and trees and a freshly mown lawn. Pots of ferns dangled from the porch beams, and potted flowers were attractively arranged near the front door. A small garden plot was close by, bordered by a ten-foot high, woven wire fence. Sam guessed deer were a problem for any gardener in the area. An older pickup truck was parked beside the house.

As Sam got out of his SUV, he could hear the mutter of conversation behind the house and the clank of metal on metal. He walked along the house, stepping carefully on the flat river rocks that lined the walkway. As he turned the corner, a large English setter spotted him and ran to sniff his shoes and trousers. Frank Richmond looked up at Sam's approach and stood wiping oil from his hands with an old, greasy rag. A large riding lawnmower sat with its hood up, and its battery on the ground beside it.

"Hey, Frank," Sam said. Your mother said you'd be here. Looks like you're having a problem with your mower."

"Hello, Sam. Yeah, I just got the lawn mowed and it quit before I could get it in the shed. I think it's the battery. The posts are all corroded."

"Yeah, mine does that, too. All you have to do is scrape the crud off the terminals and it should take right off."

"Yes, I've had to do that before." He pointed to the dog and said, "Don't mind him. He won't bite, but he'll want to sniff you."

"He probably smells my dog's odor on me. He's out in the car. What's his name?"

Frank looked sheepishly at Sam and said, "His name's Sam. Some coincidence, isn't it?"

Sam laughed and leaned down to scratch the dog's ears. "It's a fine name, Frank. I like it." Sam looked around. "I thought I heard you talking to someone back here."

Frank looked embarrassed. "I guess I was talking to the dog. I do that sometimes when I'm here alone."

Sam laughed. "No need to be embarrassed. I'm keeping Jimmy's dog for a while, and I talk to him all the time."

Frank led Sam in the back door of the cottage, through a mud-room hung with the usual coats, hats and boots and into a tidy kitchen. A faint odor of bacon lingered in the air. Plates, silverware and a small skillet were stacked on the counter. Sam sat at the small table covered with books and scientific journals. Frank dumped out the cold coffee in the coffee maker and refilled it. He pushed the books aside and sat opposite Sam. The coffee pot gurgled and groaned.

"Mom called and said you were coming by to talk to me. She sounded concerned. Any reason I should be?"

Sam wasn't surprised that Wendy had called her son to let him know Sam was coming to talk to him. He'd have done the same thing in her place. "No, not at all. I'm talking to everyone even remotely tied to Scott. It's how detectives do their detecting. I'm trying to eliminate as many people as I can. That way, I can focus on the ones left. I'm not having a lot of success."

"Where's Dr. Houston? I thought he was working with you."

"Oh, he is." Sam chuckled, "Right now, he's in Costa Rica doing research. That's all he thinks about. That, and fly fishing."

"I remember now. He has a big grant. I'm not sure what he's researching, but it'll probably go on for months."

"I only have a few questions for you, Frank. Were you and Scott close?"

Frank squinted his eyes and said, "No, not really. I mean, he was a lot older than I am. I liked him a lot, and he was good for Mom. They got along well and had a lot of interests in common. But, we weren't best buddies, if that's what you're asking."

"Did you and he ever argue.?

"Yeah. Mom said she'd told you about us butting heads. There wasn't much to it. It was sometime last fall. I was at his house with him and Mom. I wanted to ask him some questions about the rare plants on his property, but he really didn't know much about them other than they were endangered. Although he wasn't a botanist, he fully understood their significance. He was going to give the property to the nature preserve."

"How did you feel about that? Did you think that was a good idea?"

Frank's eyes brightened. "Oh yes, they have to be preserved. I'm glad he was going to donate the property. I hope whoever inherits the land will do the same."

"You were telling me about your argument," Sam said, prompting him.

"Right. After we talked about the ferns, I got bored. He and Mom were talking in the kitchen, and there wasn't much to do, so I snuck out to the barn and lit a joint. I don't smoke the stuff very often. Scott came looking for me because Mom was ready to leave. He caught me red-handed. I was embarrassed, and he was mad. We got into a bit of an argument. I stomped off and sat in the car until Mom came out, and then we left. That was all there was to it."

"Did the two of you ever work out your differences?" Sam knew the answer to the question, but he wanted to see if Frank would tell the truth.

"No. He disappeared shortly after that. They didn't find his body until the spring. I wish I'd been able to talk to him, you know, to make things better. If not for our sake, for Mom's. But, I didn't get the chance."

The coffee maker had stopped its racket and Frank poured them each a mug of coffee. He sat down again, facing Sam across the table.

"There's an Indian rug in Scott's living room. Do you know where Scott got it?"

Frank looked blankly at Sam. "To tell you the truth, I've never noticed. I guess there's a rug there, but I never paid any attention to it. I wasn't in his house very often. Not like Mom. Why, is it important?"

Sam ignored his question. "Did you ever hear Scott, or anyone else talk about it?"

"No. As I said, I didn't even notice it was there."

"Okay, another question. What do you know about Seth Buckman, the owner of the Red Creek Saloon?"

"Well, I go there sometimes. Mom works there. Tonight will be a big night—it's Saturday and the place is always busy then. As far as I know, he's a good person to work for. Mom makes good money, has insurance and a retirement plan. People seem to like him. It's one of the reasons the bar is successful." Frank looked toward his feet and frowned.

"Something bothering you, Frank? You look disturbed," Sam said.

"No, not really. It's just that..." His voice trailed off.

"Just what? Something on your mind?"

"I don't want to start any rumors, Sam. Seth has a thing for my mom. She hasn't said anything about it to me, but I can tell when I see them together. He's pretty possessive of her. Doesn't like the patrons talking to her, especially men her age. Even some of the younger ones. It isn't anything he said, but you can tell he's fixated with her. I guess it's none of my business, but she's my mom and I don't want to see her get hurt. You know what I mean?"

"Of course. I'm sure your mother knows how to handle men. What do you know about Seth? Is he from around here?

"No. I grew up in this house. I've lived in this community all my life and know just about everyone. He just showed up two, three years ago, and built that big bar and set up a microbrewery. He said he was originally from Beckley, but nobody knows for sure. As you can imagine, there are rumors galore about him. Some say he's laundering drug money through his business, but that's pretty far-fetched."

"Did he know Scott?"

Frank sucked in a breath, "You don't think he had anything to do with his death, do you?"

Sam answered quickly, "Let's not jump to conclusions. I ask a lot of questions that end up not meaning a thing."

"Yeah, he knew Scott. Once in a blue moon, Scott would come to the bar, mostly to see Mom. I've seen Scott and Seth talking, but I didn't notice anything going on between them. As I said, Scott rarely came to the bar, but then, I don't go there very often myself. It's about the only place to go to meet people nearby, but I only go when they have a band playing that I like. And, of course, it's a good place to meet chicks," he said grinning.

"Are you into music, Frank. Do you play or anything?"

He laughed and said, "No, I can't play a lick, or sing. I just like good music."

"What do you know about the band that's playing tonight?"

"That's the *Ramp Supper Band*. They're a bunch of locals. Not too bad. I've heard them several times."

"Chris Franklin plays lead guitar, doesn't he? What kind of music do they play? Bluegrass?"

"Yeah, Chris is pretty good. He can sing, too. They play some bluegrass stuff but lean more toward new-grass. Why are you asking about the band?"

"Chris's a county deputy. He was on site when they found Scott's body." Sam paused, then said, "I'm a curious man, Frank. What in the world is new-grass music?"

Frank laughed again, "It's like bluegrass, but with a more contemporary sound. I like it. Why don't you stick around and listen to them since you're already in the area?"

"Maybe I will," Sam said. He looked seriously at Frank and asked, "What did you and your sister think about your mother starting to date again? Did the two of you ever talk about it?"

"I know you have to ask these questions, Sam, but Tiffany and I were okay with it. Yes, we talked about Mom dating Scott, but we both thought it was good for her to get out and date again."

"Did Tiffany meet Scott?"

"Yes, she was home on furlough last summer and Mom made dinner for us. We all had a chance to get to know him a little. She liked him just fine and thought he'd be a good match for Mom."

"Did she know that your mother and Scott were talking about getting married?"

Frank glowered at Sam. "I don't know where you're going with this, but, yes, she knew and thought it was okay." He leaned back in his chair and looked away from Sam. "You're on the wrong track here, Sam. I didn't kill Scott, and I know that Tiffany didn't either. You're wasting your time if you think anything different."

Sam stood and walked toward the door. He said, "Thanks for your time, Frank. Tell your mom that I'll keep her informed of my progress on the case."

Sam the dog followed him out to his SUV. Yellow Dog looked out the window at the strange dog and whined. Sam got in the vehicle, started the engine and sat for a few minutes thinking about what he should do next.

He drove back to Route 32 and found a convenient pull-off. He spent fifteen minutes updating his murder book. He snapped a few photos of his notes and sent them to Jimmy's phone. They'd be hard to read, but he could figure them out. He put his SUV in gear and continued to the town of Harmon where he turned west onto Route 55 toward Elkins. There, he intersected Corridor H and continued home.

When he opened the door of the SUV, Yellow Dog shot by him, making a bee-line to his neighbor's lawn. Sam went inside, not wanting to know what the dog was doing. Ignorance is bliss. A few minutes later, Sam went out on his front porch to check on the dog. Sam called him inside and went to his office where he booted up his computer. The sheriff had given him pass codes that would allow him to access police data-bases. As a state policeman, he had routinely tapped into police records.

He typed in Seth Buckman's name and sat back as the computer did its magic. The search didn't take long. Seth Buckman was a forty-five-year-old Army veteran. His only police record was for speeding. He'd been given five tickets over the years. Not so good for his automobile insurance. He owned three personal vehicles; a new SUV, a two-year old sedan, and a late model pick-up truck. He had owned a bar in Beckley until a couple of years ago, and a couple of large trucks were titled to the business. Sam assumed they were being used at the new bar. Other than the speeding tickets, there had been no arrests or warrants. His background was clean—at least as far as Sam could determine. Perhaps a more thorough search would turn up more, but Sam didn't think it would be worth the effort, at least not for now.

Chapter 13

Early the next morning, Sam sat at his desk in his house and opened the murder book. Over the last couple of weeks, it had grown in volume. He'd jammed notes and other papers in it at random, and it was disorganized. His morning task was two-fold; re-organize the book, and review everything from start to finish. He placed the interview notes and reports made by the Sheriff and his deputies in individual stacks. He placed the lab reports in separate stacks. He added his and Jimmy's notes of their interviews to the appropriate stacks. The result was an individual file for each person interviewed. He used tabs to identify each file. The sheriff hadn't interviewed Seth Buckman, so that file only contained his notes.

He spent the next two hours reviewing the murder book. The reorganization had helped tremendously, and he was able to quickly review each file. He had hoped that something important would come to his attention, but he had no such luck.

He leaned back in his chair and perched his reading glasses on top of his head. He still had to interview Kelly Rice and Buddy Smith. He thought about Rice. The sheriff had interviewed her, but he hadn't turned up anything conclusive—except for the fact that she had a violent streak, had argued with Scott, and her property bordered Scott's. The sheriff's hand-written notes left little doubt that he didn't like the woman. Sam decided he'd wait until Jimmy got back before re-interviewing her. He wasn't looking forward to it.

He picked up his house phone and dialed the number the sheriff had listed for Buddy Smith. A young woman answered by reciting the name of an excavating company and saying, "This is Joanie. How can I help you?"

"I'm Sam Miller, a deputy policeman with Adams County. I need to talk to Buddy. Is he in?"

"Who may I say is calling?"

Sam hesitated, "Umm, Sam Miller?"

"One moment, please." The phone went dead as she put him on hold, then the silence was replaced with canned music.

After a few minutes, a gruff voice answered, "This is Buddy. Who did you say you are?"

Sam explained. "I need to talk to you about a case I'm working on. Is there a time when we could meet?"

"I'm really busy. I have several contracts going at the same time, and one of my end loaders broke down. Even worse, one of my best men is out sick. I don't have time to talk to you. What's the case you're working on?"

When Sam told him he said, "I've already talked to a deputy about that. I don't have time for this."

"How about this? Give me five minutes, and we can do this over the phone." Sam didn't like phone interviews, but he'd do a face-to-face interview later if he thought he needed to.

"Oh, all right. You've got five minutes. My phone's ringing off the hook."

"The deputy's notes say you tried to lease the hunting rights on Scott's farm. What was that all about?"

"As I told the deputy, I'm a member of a hunting club. We lease land to hunt on. Scott's land borders the national forest. We thought it would give us a place to camp because the national forest people wouldn't allow camping. It would have been a good deal. It would have given us easy access to thousands of acres of prime hunting."

"What kind of hunting do you do?"

"Mostly for deer and turkeys. A couple of the guys hunt bears, but I've never been into that. Grouse sometimes."

Sam asked, "What did Scott say when you asked to lease his property?"

Buddy sighed, signaling to Sam that he was not happy to be wasting his time answering questions. "He said he didn't want a bunch of guys tromping around on his land. Something about some plants he wanted to protect. Just between you and me, I think he was a little off in the head. We made a good offer, and all he had to do was sit back and cash our checks. We said we'd pay for any damage we might do."

"Were you disappointed that you didn't get the lease?"

"Well of course. We were upset that we couldn't work out a deal. But, if you're thinking I killed him or something, you're out of your head."

"I'm not accusing you of anything, Buddy. I'm just trying to get a feel for what happened. What about the other men in your club?"

"No, as a matter of fact, they weren't upset. We're still trying to work out a deal with the forest service to camp there. Their main hang-up is sanitation. They say we got to have port-a-pottys or something. Can't just go in the woods. I think we'll be able to work out something."

"Did you approach anyone else about leasing property"

Buddy laughed grimly, "Oh yes. We talked to that Rice woman. Her property would have worked for a hunting camp, too, but no way. She's a real piece of work. She told us to get off her property and never come back. We were happy to leave in one piece. You ask me, she's the one you should be looking at. She'd as soon knock you in the head as look at you."

They talked for a few minutes more, then Buddy said he had to go. He said his secretary was standing in his office door with her hands on her hips, glowering at him.

After he'd hung up the phone, Sam walked to the window in his office and looked out at his back yard. The grass was badly in need of mowing, and his neighbor had been on his case to get rid of the dandelions. He said their seeds were blowing over on his lawn. His neighbor was a neat freak. His lawn and hedges were trimmed just so. Sam was sure he'd soon find out that Yellow Dog was using his lawn for a bathroom and all hell would break loose. For some strange reason, he really didn't care. Let him rant and rave. Since Ruthie died, he just didn't have an interest in mowing and trimming and weeding—keeping up with the neighbors. Before her death, his yard had been the envy of the neighborhood.

He sat behind his desk again and flipped through the murder book until he came to his notes on his visit to Scott's house. The Indian rug was still bothering him. Was it authentic, or was it a reproduction? Wendy had suggested that it might have been made in China. Did it really matter? If it was a clue, it was a thin one. He scrolled through his camera until he found the pictures he'd taken of the rug. He was amazed how sharp they were, but still couldn't tell if it was the real thing. He sent the picture files to his printer and soon had paper copies for the murder book. He took a magnifying glass from a desk drawer and used it to study the photographs. If there was a tag, it was underneath the rug.

There was only one way to know for sure. He called Yellow Dog and filled his bowl with water. He gave him a small scoop of kibble and waited impatiently at the front door until he'd eaten. It didn't take long. Sam stuck the murder book under his arm and checked his pants pocket to make sure he had his phone. He told the dog to get in the SUV but had to wait as the dog did his business in the bushes along the property line.

Forty-five minutes later, Sam pulled in Scott's driveway where he used the keys the sheriff had given him to unlock the gate. He left it open, knowing he'd only be there for a few minutes. Besides, there wasn't any livestock that might get out. He drove on to the house where he let the dog out of the vehicle. He watched as he ran excitedly around the house, sniffing every bush and clump of grass. He ran onto the porch and raced back and forth smelling the floor and the front of the door, snuffling loudly.

Alerted by the dog, Sam drew his gun from the holster in the small of his back and walked carefully around the house, looking in the windows. The interior of the house was too dark for him to see what was inside. He stepped cautiously to the back door and tried the knob. It was locked. He worked his way back around the house to the front door. When he tried the doorknob, he found it was locked, too. What had the dog smelled? Was it a person, or was it an animal of some kind? Was he making too much of the dog's behavior?

He relaxed and put the gun back in its holster. He was getting jumpy. He unlocked the door and stepped inside. He stopped, listening carefully. He heard nothing. He flipped on the lights and walked straight to the rug. As he bent over to check it for a tag, the front window exploded, throwing glass over him. It had been broken by a rifle shot. He dived to the floor, rolling in the glass and crawling for cover. There wasn't much available. Shots were coming rapid-fire now, blasting through the thin walls of the old house. A wooden wall was little protection from a high-powered rifle. His experience as a policeman told him that the shots were coming from a semi-automatic. Something like an AR-15. By reflex, Sam covered his head with his arms and rolled into a corner.

There was a slight lull in the shooting, but it soon began again in earnest. The shooter had taken time to change clips, Sam thought. How was he going to get out of this alive? He rolled quickly across the room as pictures on the walls danced and jittered in the onslaught of bullets. Knickknacks rained onto the floor, and a bullet struck the back of the couch just above his head. A small vase exploded nearby as he crawled down the short hallway into the kitchen.

The shooting stopped. Sam sat in a corner in the kitchen, his back against the cabinets, trying to make himself as small as possible. He pulled a sliver of glass from his hand and wiped the blood from the wound on his pants. Somewhere along the crawl down the hallway and into the kitchen, he'd drawn his gun, but he had no memory of it. It was a small, seven-shot semi-automatic. Against a rifle, it wasn't much but better than nothing. His hands shook as he checked the weapon to make sure there was a cartridge in the chamber. He pulled his phone from his pocket, but he didn't have service. He stuck it back in his pocket.

Everything was quiet. Somewhere, off in the distance, he could hear crows calling. He sat hunched in his corner. He shifted around, the glass in his clothing gritting and grinding as he moved. A trickle of blood ran down his forehead and onto his nose. He wiped it away with the back of his hand. He waited.

Five minutes passed. Then ten. Had the shooter left? Or, was he waiting for Sam to come out? Maybe he thought Sam was dead and had gone away. Sam shifted again, his muscles protesting. He pushed himself up with his back to the wall. He hurt in a hundred places. He had just decided to chance a look out the window when he heard footsteps on the front porch. Someone walked cautiously toward the front door. Sam looked quickly down the hallway toward the front of the house but saw nothing. The door stood open, but no one was there.

A shadow passed over the kitchen window just as the shooter used the stock of his gun to smash out the glass. Sam squatted in his corner again. The shooter opened fire through the window, spraying bullets randomly around the room, emptying a full clip. Sam could hear the bullet casings bounce off the exterior wall. Sam fired two of his precious rounds through the wall at the point where he thought the shooter might be. He was rewarded with a startled yelp.

Gripping his gun tightly in his hand, he ran across the kitchen and hit the back door with his shoulder. It buckled but didn't open. He suddenly realized that house doors opened *inward*. He turned the knob and yanked it open, stumbling in a panic into the yard. He knew he had only seconds before the shooter would come around the corner and fire on him. He ran around the opposite corner of the house and plunged into the shrubs and bushes that crowded in on the house. He could hear footsteps and heavy breathing as the shooter pursued him. He ran blindly, the brush and briers ripping at his skin and clothing. Shots rang out behind him. Twigs and leaves rained down.

As he ran, the forest became denser, the trees larger. He found a windfall, a large tree that had been blown down, its exposed roots providing a bit of shelter. He slid behind it, breathing heavily. His heart thundered in his chest. He felt as if he were going to have a heart attack. He could hear his pursuer running toward him. He fired three quick shots toward the sound. The running stopped. Sam hunkered down behind the root mass and used his phone to dial 911. To his relief, he was answered. He quickly told the operator what was happening to him and where he was. He was told to stay on the line.

He yelled at the shooter. "I called the cops. They're on the way. You better run."

He was answered by a fresh volley of bullets. He sprawled on his belly behind the tree, clutching the phone in his hand. The operator told him to stay calm. How could he stay calm when the shooter was probably flanking him at this moment? He looked frantically from side to side and behind him. The hair on the back of his neck stood on end as he anticipated a bullet striking him at any time.

Although adrenaline surged through his veins, his limbs felt heavy—a terrible weariness settled in on him. His reaction time was slowing down, and he couldn't seem to get enough oxygen into his lungs. He heard a rustling in the brush behind him and turned in time to see a hint of movement and the flash of gunfire. Bark flew from the tree near his head, and he scrambled around to the other side of the root mass. He held his gun unsteadily in his hand, trying to remember how many rounds he had remaining. Should he stay behind the root mass, hoping the police would get there in time, or should he run?

The shooter fired another volley, and Sam was struck in the side. A gout of blood splattered the leaves and debris that covered the forest floor. The pain was excruciating. He gritted his teeth and fired two more shots toward the shooter. The shooter returned fire with a short volley. Sam was struck again in his upper left arm. It quickly became numb and flopped uselessly at his side. Blood ran down his fingertips and dropped onto the ground. He fumbled with his belt, thinking he'd make a tourniquet, but he couldn't get it in place. Blood flowed.

The forest became quiet again and Sam slumped onto the leaves that had piled up around the tree trunk. More time passed. Surely the shooter was flanking his position again, circling around, trying to get a clear shot at him. His wounds were bleeding profusely, and he was becoming lightheaded. He thought briefly again about running but knew he didn't have the strength. He rolled over onto his stomach and rose slowly onto his hands and knees, his head hanging down. He was horrified at the volume of blood that pooled on the ground beneath him. Little wonder he was so weak.

He heard cautious footsteps approaching. He was so tired. All he wanted to do was lay down and sleep. The shooter came closer. He tried to raise his head but couldn't. The shooter came closer still. He fell awkwardly onto his side and pointed his gun at the dark figure that loomed over him. It took all his remaining strength to raise his arm and pull the trigger. Nothing happened. The gun was empty.

The dark figure approached confidently and fired at him pointblank. An unimaginable pain hammered his chest like the fist of an angry god. The forest became quiet again as a profound darkness closed around him.

Chapter 14

Jimmy sat in the crowded airport terminal in San Jose waiting for his flight to Houston where he'd catch connecting flights to Bridgeport. Other travelers milled around, talking and texting on their phones. A young couple sat huddled together with two small children playing on the floor at their feet. A young man slumped in a corner chair, his arms crossed over his chest, snoring lightly. There was a pleasant mix of Spanish and English spoken, with a smattering of Portuguese. It had been a successful trip. He'd collected the data he needed for the project and would have a winter's worth of reports and papers to write. He was pleased. He stretched his legs in front of him, noticing that his boots still had mud stains from his work in the rainforest. They'd need a good cleaning and oiling when he got home.

He'd worked hard doing research and collecting data in two short weeks, sometimes in pouring rain that came down so hard that he could hardly see his hand before his face. White-faced monkeys had watched him from their lofty perches in huge fig trees that dominated the forest, and parrots of many kinds shrieked from daybreak to dark. Brightly colored poison dart frogs, no larger than his thumbnail, crept over the moss-covered forest floor. He'd had fleeting glimpses of Coatimundi and Capybara as they shambled through the undergrowth and had hoped to see a jaguar. He hadn't been that fortunate. Plants of every kind with brilliantly colored flowers crowded every nook and cranny, and vines dangled from limbs hundreds of feet above. It was a botanist's dream.

He recalled steamy nights visiting a small cottage near the research station owned by a renowned scientist who specialized in tropical ecology. They talked plants and research and Pre-Colombian culture and drank a strong local brew from tin cups. His Costa Rican wife prepared the most wonderful traditional dishes served on banana leaves held together with wooden skewers. Bats flew in and out of the cottage's open windows while graduate students sat on the floor along the walls soaking up the great man's knowledge. They learned from each other, better than in any classroom, describing their day's work with the delightful odor of black beans and rice and tortillas in their nostrils. Jimmy smiled to himself as he recalled the experience. Yet, he was anxious to get back home to *his* mountains.

He was startled from his musings when his phone vibrated in his pocket. It was John Compton, his long-time fishing buddy. Jimmy could tell from the seriousness of his voice that something was very wrong.

Jimmy asked, "What is it, John? What's wrong?"

"It's Sam. He's been seriously injured. The doctors don't know if he'll make it or not. It's bad. The sheriff knows we're friends and asked me to let you know."

"Injured? How? What happened?" Jimmy's voice shook as he spoke.

"Someone shot him. He was at Scott Mitchell's house, up in the valley, when someone ambushed him."

"He was shot?" Jimmy's voice had risen, and a woman sitting beside him turned to look at him. "Where was he hit?"

"That's the thing, Jimmy. He was hit three times. Whoever did this was serious about killing him."

"Where?" Jimmy asked, lowering his voice to avoid attracting any more attention.

"As I said, up at Scott's place." A little exasperation crept into John's voice.

"No, where did he get hit. What part of his body?"

"Oh. I don't have all the details. The sheriff didn't tell me a lot, other than he wanted you to know. Where are you? How soon can you get back here?"

"I'll be back tonight. I'm sitting in the airport, waiting for my flight home right now. I'm due to land in Bridgeport at about six this evening. Where is Sam? Did they take him to the Elkins hospital? That's probably the closest."

"No, they life-flighted him to Morgantown. They're better equipped to handle a case like this."

Jimmy's flight was called over the intercom, and travelers began lining up to board the plane.

"Look, John, they've called my flight. I won't be able to talk while I'm on the plane, but I'll call you when I land in Houston. I have about an hour's layover there. See what you can find out about his condition. Damn, this is awful. I feel guilty because I talked him into getting in this mess. If I'd kept my nose out of this case, he wouldn't have gotten shot." Jimmy shuffled along in line as it inched toward the boarding gate.

"Come on, Jimmy. You know better than to blame yourself. There's only one person to blame for this, and that's the shooter."

"Yeah, well, maybe. Look, I have to hang up. My boarding pass is on my phone. I'll call you when I can."

He broke the connection and searched his phone apps for the pass. The gate attendant smiled at him as he checked in, and then he walked down the narrow boarding ramp, a heavy burden weighing him down.

*   *   *

Jimmy's flight into Bridgeport was delayed because of thunderstorms, and it was well after seven when he arrived. He'd talked again with John during his layover in Houston, but he had little new information, only that Sam was in intensive care and that his condition was grave. Jimmy had quickly deplaned, left the terminal, and trotted out to the parking lot. He threw his luggage into the cargo space of his Cherokee and pushed the old vehicle to its limit northward on I-79 to Morgantown. It was almost nine o'clock when he pulled into the hospital's parking lot.

He climbed wearily out of the Jeep and stretched his back. It had been a long day. He looked up at the towering structure that sprawled over many acres. Even at this late hour, visitors and doctors dressed in scrubs poured into and out of its entrance. It was a massive hospital and seemed to grow larger each time he visited it. A large crane, idle at this hour, stood ready to lift building materials to yet another wing.

He stopped at the visitor's desk in the lobby long enough to receive directions to the intensive care unit. He rode the elevator to the fifth floor, and the doors opened onto a narrow hallway. A hospital worker at a desk asked him for the patient's name, then led him through a maze of narrow hallways to a waiting room. The worker left him abruptly before he could ask about Sam's condition. He wasn't a family member, so she was unlikely to tell him anything, anyway. He looked around the room for a familiar face.

Small groups of people huddled together, talking in subdued voices. Others watched the television screens suspended from the ceiling with blank looks on their faces. A young mother with red-rimmed eyes cared for an infant of about six months. She sat holding the child, rocking and humming. Nearby seats were loaded with baby bags, toys, and a large box of animal crackers. Hospital workers hurriedly came and went. Jimmy didn't see anyone he recognized.

A tall, thin man, in his middle sixties, approached Jimmy. He was wearing chinos and a button-down shirt. His cleanshaven face was weathered and wrinkled, and he wore wire-rim glasses. A woman, dressed in jeans and a long-sleeved shirt rolled to her elbows, stood by his side. She was almost as tall as the man beside her. Her long, gray hair was rolled into a bun on the back of her head.

The man asked, "Are you Dr. Houston?"

"Yes, I am," Jimmy said.

"I'm Sam's brother, Donald. The sheriff said you'd be coming by, but he thought it might be several days since you were out of the country. He gave us your description."

Jimmy shook their hands and said he was pleased to meet them.

"This is my wife, Joan," he said, nodding toward her. "Sam spoke highly of you. I'm glad you're here."

"How is Sam? All I know about his condition is that he was shot several times and that he's here in the intensive care unit. I'm really worried about him," Jimmy said.

Donald shook his head and said, "Not good. He was shot three times and left for dead. He was way up there in Canaan Valley, and it took the police a while to find him and get him on a life-flight. He lost a lot of blood. When the paramedics got there, he had almost no blood pressure. It was really touch and go."

"Is he conscious? Has he said who did this to him?"

"No. He hasn't regained consciousness. He was hit once in the upper arm and once in the side. The sheriff said the third shot was fired from close range into his chest. Whoever did this, intended to kill him. I don't know how he survived."

"I feel responsible for this. If I hadn't talked him into taking this case, he wouldn't have been shot."

"No, you mustn't think that. Sam was a policeman. He knew the risks, and we all knew that someday, something like this could happen. It's a hazardous occupation." His wife nodded her head in agreement.

Joan said, "My father was a city cop in Baltimore. My mother and I always worried about him. He retired after twenty-five years of service without firing his weapon. But, you never know..."

They sat in a corner of the waiting room, talking quietly. Jimmy told them a little about his work and outlined the case he and Sam had been trying to solve. Donald said he and Sam had a sister who lived out of state. She'd arrive later tomorrow. After a several minutes of silence, Donald asked Jimmy if he wanted to go in and see Sam.

"Yes. Will they let me in, since I'm not a relative?"

"Sure. I'll tell them to put you on the approved visitor's list. That way, you can go in and see him anytime you want to. They'll only let two people in there at a time." He turned toward Joan and asked, "Do you want to take him in, or do you want to wait out here?"

She said that he should do it. She'd wait. Donald led Jimmy through a door and into a long corridor with a nurses' station toward the middle. He asked the nurse on duty if it was all right to visit Sam, and he said it was okay, but only for five minutes.

They stood awkwardly by Sam's bed, neither man knowing what to do or say. Jimmy looked at his friend who, somehow, seemed to be much smaller than he remembered. His left arm was bound by a heavy dressing, and numerous tubes pierced his body, carrying away fluids he'd rather not think about. His otherwise bare chest was heavily wrapped with bandages. A yellowish stain marked his skin where antiseptic had been generously applied. IV packs drained life-giving blood and other fluids into him through a series of tubes. A monitor panel, held in place on a portable stand, beeped monotonously and displayed a cluttered array of numbers and graphs. Sam's eyes were closed and sunken into his pale face.

"They had him on a breathing tube for a while when he first got here, but they took it out when he started breathing on his own," Donald said. "He has a living will that stipulates he didn't want to be put on a ventilator, but the doctors didn't know that. They said it saved his life."

A dozen questions went through Jimmy's head. Would Sam survive? Would he be able to walk and lead a normal life? How long would it take for him to recover? Did he have enough insurance to cover all the care he'd need? Who would care for him until he could take care of himself? Who had done this to him? And, on and on.

They stood there, beside Sam's bed, listening to his labored breathing and the beep and gurgle of the life support equipment. The room smelled of antiseptic and cleaning fluids. With nothing more to see or do, they walked silently back to the waiting room.

It was after midnight when Jimmy curled up in a corner with a blanket and pillow a worker had given him. He was exhausted. Donald and Joan had gone to a local motel to try to get some sleep. Jimmy twisted and turned through the night with his sleep interrupted occasionally with the continuous activities of the busy hospital. He awoke just after daylight, tossed the blanket aside and rubbed his back. He was told at the nurses' station there was no change in Sam's condition. He went looking for coffee. A short ride on the elevator took him to the floor that housed the cafeteria, and he found what he was looking for; coffee and a bagel.

When he returned to the waiting room, Sheriff Donovan and Deputy Chris Franklin were waiting for him.

"There you are, Professor. The nurse said you were around here somewhere. How's Sam doing? They won't tell us much. Privacy rules, I guess."

Jimmy shook hands with both men and told them there was no change in Sam's condition.

The sheriff looked around for a private place to talk. A nurse led them to a small conference room just off the waiting room, and they sat around a small table. Jimmy wondered how many people had learned of the fate of their loved ones in this room.

The sheriff told Jimmy what had happened to Sam. "He was lucky to get out of the attack alive. The house was all shot to hell, and we found some blood. We think it was Sam's, there in the house. It'll all be tested. There were shell casings all over the place—over a hundred rounds. Probably from an AR-15 or something similar. The shooter just stood back and let fly at the house. The best we can tell, Sam was inside but bolted out the back door. He ran through the woods with the shooter after him. There was a trail of shell casings along the way. We found him down there in the woods, behind a clump of roots from a tree that had been blown over. The shooter kept circling Sam until he hit him. The spent shell casings told the story."

"Was there only one shooter? Could there have been more than one?"

"No, we think there was only one, but I guess it could have been possible for another person to have been involved. One thing for sure. Whoever it was, wasn't much of a shot."

"How did you find out Sam had been shot?"

"He called 911 on his phone. He told the dispatcher where he was and that someone was shooting at him."

"Did the shooter take his phone?" Jimmy asked.

"Yeah, he did. We tried to track its location, but he must have taken the battery out of it. We couldn't trace it."

"I don't understand. Sam told you he was at Scott's farm, right? Did he say exactly where he was in the woods?"

"Yeah, he gave the dispatcher a pretty good description of his location. Said he was about a quarter of a mile from the farmhouse, toward the nature preserve. We didn't have much of a problem finding him. Once the paramedics got there, we carried him out to a field on a stretcher, and the 'copter set down beside us. He was on his way to the hospital in minutes."

"Didn't Sam have a gun? I think he carried one while he was out questioning people."

The sheriff scowled, "All he had was a little ole pea-shooter of a gun. Seven rounds. We found all his casings. We used a sniffer dog to locate them. Not much of a weapon to go up against a military style rifle."

"Did you find anything that would help to identify the shooter? Blood, or maybe fingerprints on the shell casings?"

"No, nothing like that. We'll check all the casings for prints, but it'll take a while. There were so many of them. More than likely, they'll be clean."

Chris Franklin, the deputy, spoke up, "We found a big yellow dog at the farm. Do you know if it belongs to Sam?"

"Oh crap. I assumed he'd left the dog at home. He's probably mine. Sam was keeping him for me while I was out of town."

"Is this him?" the deputy asked. He showed Jimmy a picture of the dog on his phone. "When we got there, he came crawling out from under the old shed behind the house. He was shaking all over. It looks like he found a hole when the shooting started. It's a wonder he wasn't killed."

Jimmy sighed with relief, "Yeah, that's him. His name's Yellow Dog. Where is he now?

The deputy laughed. "That's some name. Very original. He's at the station in our pound. He's not too happy. He's keeping the neighbors entertained with his barking."

"One more thing, Sheriff. Was Sam's murder book in the SUV?" Jimmy asked. "He kept all of his notes in it."

"No, there wasn't anything in the vehicle except for an old blanket with dog hair all over it. Are you sure Sam had it with him?"

"No, but he usually carried it with him while he worked. Maybe it's at his house."

"I'll send someone over there to check, but I wouldn't bet it'll be there." The sheriff hitched up his gun belt and looked seriously at Jimmy, "I want you to listen carefully, Professor. As of now, you're off the case. If you think you're going to go nosing around to find the shooter, forget it." The sheriff paused to let his words sink in. "From now on, this case is ours. We don't take kindly to someone shooting one of our own, and that's what Sam is—*one of our own*. Even though he was hired temporarily, he was a sworn police officer. We'll find the shooter. You can bet on it."

"You don't have to try to convince me, Sheriff. I'm just a professor. I don't know a thing about police work. Besides, I have a lot of my own work to do before the fall semester begins."

The deputy looked at him seriously and said, "I thought you professors were off all summer."

Chapter 15

Sam's sister, Susan, arrived in the waiting room in a swirl of motion, hugging Donald and Joan tightly. She was of medium height with dark brown hair cut in the fashion of the day. She wore expensive, designer jeans and an expensive silk blouse. Jimmy guessed her age at fifty—the baby of the family. She cried when Donald told her how serious Sam's wounds were. She shook Jimmy's hand, and then hugged him tightly. She, too, told him how often Sam had spoken of him.

Donald took her hand and led her to Sam's room. They were gone only minutes before they returned. Susan cried again, and Donald told Jimmy that the nurses were changing his bandages and they'd been asked to leave. They all sat down and talked quietly. Sometime later, a nurse came by to tell Donald and Susan they could go see Sam. When they returned, Donald gave them an update on Sam's condition. There had been some improvement overnight. Sam had shown signs of regaining consciousness. When he was fully conscious, he'd be moved to a private room. His vital signs were improving, and the doctors seemed to be pleased with his progress, little as it was. They were now thinking that he'd recover, but it would be a long convalescence.

Jimmy was relieved. With Sam's family in place, he felt comfortable leaving his friend for a while and going home. Donald promised to keep him informed of Sam's progress and to call him if his condition worsened. He assured him they would watch over Sam and could spell each other as needed.

Jimmy called John Compton before he left the hospital parking lot, and he volunteered to go to the sheriff's pound and get Yellow Dog. He'd meet Jimmy back at the Eyrie. Jimmy's eyes felt gritty, and he was sure he was in bad need of a shower. He drove south on I-79 until he reached the Corridor H highway and turned east. Within thirty minutes he'd passed the State College campus and turned onto the narrow road that led to his cabin. It was good to be home. The sun was setting when he pulled in his small parking spot and climbed out of the Cherokee. The cabin was dark and uninviting, but he soon had the lights on and a pot of coffee on the stove.

He carried his luggage and several duffle bags filled with his research instruments into the cabin and stacked them on the floor by the woodstove. He'd unpack his bags tonight and take the other gear to his office at the college tomorrow. He had just gotten out of the shower when he heard a car door slam and the clatter of nails on the wooden floor of the deck. When he opened the door, he was almost bowled over by the dog. He jumped and yipped, running circles around Jimmy. John stood in the doorway with a large pizza box in his hand, laughing at the dog's antics.

John said, "I don't know what you need a girlfriend for with a friend like that."

Jimmy grinned and said, "Who says I have to choose?"

They sat on the deck and ate pizza while the last of the sunlight faded along the ridges in the distance. Jimmy turned on the deck lights and leaned back in his chair with his feet on the deck railing.

He told John that Sam was showing some signs of recovery and gave him a quick summary of the sheriff's description of the attack.

John said, "I'm really happy that Sam's going to be okay, even though he's not out of the woods yet. He's a good guy." He pulled another slice of pizza from the greasy box and bit off a mouthful. When he had chewed and swallowed, he asked, "Do you have any idea who the shooter is?"

"No, none. I've been gone for over two weeks, and I don't know what Sam was doing while I was gone. He sent me some notes and a couple of pictures, but I really didn't spend much time looking at them.

I was busy with my research. I'll look more carefully at them tomorrow, and if there's anything important in them, I'll send it to the sheriff. But, here's the problem; Ray Lambert wrote that piece in the paper, so it could be anyone. Even someone we haven't interviewed. Everyone in the country knows we're working the case."

"You're thinking Scott's killer and the shooter are one and the same person?"

"Yes. Someone wants us, or at least Sam, off the case."

"You said the sheriff warned *you* off the case. What are you going to do about that? Can you just walk away, not knowing who the shooter is?"

"Well, he made it pretty clear—he wants me to stay away from the case." He drank slowly from the coffee mug he held in his hand. "Yeah, I'm not a detective. I'll do what he says. Mostly."

"Mostly," John repeated. "That's what I thought. You won't be able to let it alone. First thing you know, you'll be right back in the thick of it."

"No, the only thing I'm going to do is try to reconstruct Sam's murder book. The sheriff called me on my way home from the hospital. He sent a deputy to Sam's house looking for it. He said it wasn't there. That means the shooter took it. I have copies of the sheriff's reports, including Scott's autopsy. The originals are in Sam's safe at his house. He sent copies of most of his notes to my phone, so I can print them. I think I can reproduce most of it. Then, I'll give it to the sheriff."

John tossed the dog a piece of pizza crust. He grunted and said, "Yeah, I'll bet. If you do send it to the sheriff, I'll wager you keep a copy for yourself."

Jimmy rocked in his chair as moths and other flying creatures of many sizes and colors circled the deck lights. He scratched the dog's ears and said, "We'll see."

*   *   *

The following day, Jimmy drove to the college and lugged the duffle bags full of equipment into his office. He returned to the Cherokee and retrieved a folder containing copies of the reports the sheriff had given him and Sam. He sat behind his desk and tried to put them in some semblance of order. There was a lot missing. He searched through his phone files and sent the notes and pictures Sam had sent him to the printer. He soon had an impressive stack of Sam's records. He then put the files in order and carried them down the hall to the department chairperson's outer office.

Sylvia, the departmental executive assistant, greeted him warmly when he entered.

"You're back from Costa Rica. How was your trip?" she asked.

"It was great, but did you hear what happened to Sam?" Sylvia and Sam had dated occasionally some time back.

"Yes. It was in all the papers. I've been worried about him, but not being a member of the family, the doctors wouldn't tell me much about his condition."

"I just returned from the hospital yesterday. He's gravely ill. He was shot three times and barely survived." Jimmy told her what he knew of Sam's state.

"Well, next time you visit, tell him I'm thinking about him. Maybe I'll send him some flowers."

"He'd like that. If I know Sam, he'll be rearing to go home before we know it. He's a tough old bird."

Jimmy asked to use the department's copier. The college allowed faculty and staff to make copies for personal use but charged them a fee. By the time he'd copied everything in the murder book, he'd run up a substantial bill. Sylvia wrote out an invoice and handed it to him as he left the office. He'd pay it in the bursar's office the first chance he got. The office was all the way across campus.

Back in his office, he put the sheriff's copy in a small box. He'd hand deliver it to him. Jimmy put his copy of the murder book in a binder and looked at it with satisfaction. Sam would be proud, he thought.

He flipped through the binder until he came to the photos of Scott's Indian rug. He studied them carefully. He read through the notes Sam had made the day he searched Scott's house. Why was Sam so fascinated with the rug? He'd written the rug was expensive and it was out of character for Scott to buy such a luxurious item. He read the notes Sam had written when he interviewed Wendy. She's suggested the rug might have been made in China and wasn't expensive after all. She'd said that Sam should check the tag on the rug.

Jimmy stared out his office window as he rocked in his swivel chair. Somewhere, on a far corner of the campus, a lawnmower chugged, intruding on the otherwise quiet day. Was that why Sam had returned to Scott's farm? To check the tag on the rug? Had the shooter waited there for him? If so, how had he known Sam was going to be there? Or, had he followed Sam to the farm? Either way, it hadn't been a random shooting. It was premeditated, attempted murder. The shooter hadn't shot at him as a warning—he had a cold-blooded killing in mind. He wanted to stop Sam's investigation.

That brought the next problem to mind. Would the shooter come for him? Or, would he think of Jimmy as a blundering professor who didn't know what he was doing? Maybe he would be satisfied with taking Sam out of the equation and stealing the murder book. Maybe the sheriff would find the shooter quickly, and all this would become a moot point.

There was a bright side to all this. The medical examiner hadn't been able to determine a precise time that Scott had been killed. It had been months before his body had been discovered up on Dolly Sods. Therefore, the sheriff hadn't been able to check the suspects' alibis. But now, the sheriff knew precisely when Sam had been ambushed. Sam had called in the attack, so the time of his call was easily determined. The 911 dispatcher had recorded his call, and it had a time-stamp. With the time of the attack in mind, checking suspects' alibis would likely be the sheriff's next step.

Jimmy hoped and prayed that the sheriff would catch the shooter quickly, and it would all be over. Catch the shooter, and he'd caught Scott's killer. But, what if he didn't? Jimmy didn't want to think about that.

He put the murder book aside and began unpacking his gear. Equipment had to be cleaned and oiled, chemical supplies replenished, and specimens categorized. He had a lot to do. Data waited to be crunched. Papers and reports had to be written. He was anxious to get started. He worked unhurriedly, methodically putting things in order.

He stopped suddenly and sat on the edge of his desk. The killer was out there somewhere, and Jimmy knew he'd be coming for him. He could feel the hair on the back of his neck standing on end.

*   *   *

The next day, Jimmy sat in the sheriff's office with the extra copy of the murder book on his knees like a misbehaving child sent to the principal's office.

"Didn't I tell you to stay out of this case, professor? What are you trying to do, get yourself shot, too?"

"Don't worry, sheriff. All I want to do is give you a copy of Sam's murder book. I've pieced it together as best I could. I think most of it's there. Sam was pretty good about sending me copies of his notes and stuff. He sent it to my phone. All I had to do was run copies." He placed the box on the sheriff's desk and pushed it toward him with a finger.

The sheriff took the murder book from the box and flipped through it carefully. It was organized, tabbed, and easy to read. He looked at Jimmy and said, "Well okay. Just as long as you keep a low profile. I don't want you getting shot." He riffled through the book again and said, "Why don't you give me the short version. What's in here?"

"As you can see, it includes copies of the notes your men made when they did the initial interviews, autopsy and tech reports, Sam's and my notes, and some photographs."

The sheriff ran his thumb down the tabs reading off the names of those who had been interviewed. "I see that Sam interviewed Seth Buckman. He's the owner of the Red Creek Saloon. We didn't interview him. Why do you suppose Sam talked to him"?

"I think he went to the Saloon to talk to Wendy Richmond and just ran into him. It didn't seem to be a detailed interview. Sam noted that he seemed to be protective of Wendy. He wondered if Seth might be a love interest or something."

"Okay, I could see that. I've run into him a time or two when we had to go to the Saloon to break up fights. It didn't happen very often, but Seth seemed to consider himself the cock-of-the-walk. Let's just say he didn't seem to lack self-confidence. We'll go talk to him." He shuffled through the tabs again. "There seems to be one interview missing. Did he talk to Kelly Rice?"

"No, not as far as I could tell. I think he was waiting for me to go with him."

"We interviewed her, but nothing much came of it. You have a copy of our notes in there. Maybe we should go back and talk to her. We need to find out where she was when Sam was shot."

Jimmy looked carefully at the sheriff and said, "I could go with you. You know, just to get another person's assessment of her truthfulness."

"Nice try, Professor, but we'll handle it. And, believe me, I'll take all the back-up with me I can get." He looked seriously at Jimmy and said, "What I want you to do now is go back to your day job and leave all of this to me and my men. Believe me, we'll leave no stone unturned."

"Okay, okay, Sheriff. I've got a lot of work to do, so I'll leave the detective work to you. I would ask just one thing, though. Keep me posted on your progress. Sam is a good friend and I want to see his shooter get what's coming to him. He's a danger to society and needs to be put in jail. I hope you don't mind if I check in with you occasionally."

The sheriff grudgingly said, "Okay. I suppose you deserve at least an occasional up-date."

As Jimmy drove back to the Eyrie, his mind kept turning over the central questions of the case. Why had Scott Mitchell been killed? Why had his body been placed in a tree? Who had tried to kill Sam? Would the killer come for him next?

When he arrived at the cabin, he let the dog out of his kennel and followed him down the catwalk and onto the deck. He let them in through the front door and Yellow Dog made a beeline for his food and water bowls. Jimmy prepared a quick lunch of leftovers and sat on the deck in the hot midday sun. The sun's heat was pleasant on the back of his neck and shoulders, and he could hear seventeen-year cicadas grinding in the oak trees nearby. He washed the last of his lunch down with ice water and returned to the cool interior of the cabin.

On a whim, he set up his old brass telescope and focused on the farmhouse on the mountainside far away. There was a truck parked near the house and a white plastic bucket hung upside down on the gate post. Laughing Woman was home.

Chapter 16

Jimmy looked at the farmhouse though his telescope and wondered what to do next. Dana was an attractive woman, and he'd like to see her again. For the millionth time, he wondered who she was and where she was from. When he'd had dinner with her, most of their conversation had been directed away from her. He'd asked for her phone number, but somehow, although she hadn't refused to give it to him, he'd come away without it. How could he get in contact with her? He'd thought about using a mirror to signal her but dismissed the thought as juvenile and impractical. What would he do, send a message in Morris Code? He didn't know code, and neither would she. He settled on the simplest solution. He'd drive to her house.

He took a quick shower, the second of the day, and pulled on his best pair of jeans and a t-shirt with a local bluegrass band's logo on its front. He put Yellow Dog in his kennel, much to his displeasure, and drove down the hill to the main road. He missed a turnoff and had to double back to the road that led to her farm, having only been there once before. He soon arrived at her gate and drove up the narrow lane to the house. A large black dog bounded out to meet his Jeep. Jimmy got out nervously and let the dog smell his pantleg. The dog bristled and produced a deep rumbling growl.

A sharp whistle from the woman on the porch brought the dog up short. It trotted nonchalantly back to her side.

"I wondered when you'd come to see me, Jimmy. The bucket has been on the gatepost for a couple of days now. I was beginning to think you'd forgotten me."

Jimmy laughed and said, "No, I didn't forget you, but I'd begun to think you'd not be coming back." She was an attractive woman, thirtyish, with shoulder-length auburn hair, just as he remembered her. She wore a faded pair of jeans and a long-sleeved cotton shirt. Her feet were clad in sturdy work shoes. Her most striking feature was a pair of startlingly blue eyes set in a face with flawless, porcelain skin. She was tall, almost as tall as Jimmy, and she shook his hand firmly as he approached and looked him in the eye.

She invited him to come sit on the porch. She led him to a pair of wicker chairs arranged around a small table. The black dog stood by her side and stared at Jimmy. "This is Brutus," she said, nodding toward the dog. "I got him from the local dog pound—they were just about ready to euthanize him. They'd already given him a name, and when I tried to give him a new one, he ignored it. So, I guess we'll stick with Brutus." The dog looked up at her at the mention of his name. "I'd tell you that he won't bite, but that's probably not true. He's very protective of me. I guess under the right circumstances, all dogs will bite."

She offered iced tea and Jimmy accepted. While she went to get it, Jimmy sat with the dog who stared unflinchingly at him. Jimmy decided it wouldn't be a good idea to try to pet him. A deep rumbling came from the dog's chest and Jimmy realized his decision was a good one. Dana returned with a tray and two glasses of iced tea and a bowl of sugar cubes.

Once they were settled and had sipped their drinks, Dana said, "I see through my telescope that you're still living in your cabin on the mountain. I check on you occasionally. I hope you don't mind. I don't mean to intrude. When you came for dinner last fall, I thought you said you were going to rebuild your house, the one that was burned."

"I plan to. As a matter of fact, I've been working with an architect, trying to finalize the plans. It will be built in the same location as the old house, but I've been busy, and just can't seem to find the time to get on with it."

"Maybe you could show me the plans sometime. I'm interested in home construction and design in general."

"Sure, anytime." The conversation lagged as they sipped their iced tea. The dog grew tired of staring at Jimmy and sprawled on the floor near his master's feet. "Let me change the subject for a minute," Jimmy said. "When I was here for dinner before, I really didn't get to know much about you. Somehow, the conversation always seemed to be about me. I don't even know your last name."

She threw her head back and laughed, making her silky hair dance around her face. "I guess I just wanted to know all about you. After all, how many attractive bachelors live on the top of a mountain in a glass house?" She looked frankly at him over the top of her glass of tea. "I didn't want to dominate the conversation. My name is Dana McGregor. What do you want to know?"

"Where are you from, and what do you do for a living?"

"Actually, I'm a native of this area. I grew up in the country near Kingwood, attended the public schools there, and graduated from WVU. My major was business and I did a graduate degree in finance. Sounds exciting, doesn't it?"

"Yes, it does, but I'm afraid I don't know much about business. I had to take a class in economics as a part of my undergraduate program, and it wasn't one of my best courses. I took a gentleman's B and let it go at that." He chuckled as he thought about it.

Dana said, "After graduation, I went to work for a company that specialized in mortgages and other bank loans. I was doing well until the recession hit. I lost my job, then was employed by an investment firm in New York City. I've spent the last several years working in Manhattan. I make a decent salary, but it's extraordinarily expensive to live there. I wasn't really happy living in a large city like that. I'm basically a country girl. I've resigned, but the company asked me to stay on for a while until they can train a new person to do my job. Right now, I'm working for them part-time. That's why I'm in and out of the farm. I'll soon be here full time."

"Ok, mystery solved. Do you plan to live here at the farm permanently? It's pretty remote."

"Oh, I don't know. I inherited the place from my grandfather, so I'll always keep it, but I may decide later to move on, to live somewhere else. I'm unattached, so I can do whatever I want to do. Go anywhere I want. But, for now, I'm going to settle in and see what happens."

"May I ask another personal question? You don't have to answer if you don't want to. I won't get mad."

"Sure, go ahead."

"You said you're unattached. Does that mean that you've never been married?"

She paused and touched the top of the dog's head with her fingertips. "No, I was married once. I was very young, in my early twenties, and it didn't last long." She paused again and looked away in the distance, trying to decide how much to tell this man.

Jimmy said quickly, "I'm sorry. I shouldn't intrude in your past. Forget I asked."

"No, it's not that you're intruding. My past isn't a big secret. David and I had a good marriage, but it didn't work out." She looked frankly at Jimmy. "Here's the thing. I could tell you that I was sorry that we divorced and that I was pining away for him, hoping that one day he'd return to me, but that wouldn't be true. The fact is, I just didn't like being married. It was a huge relief when I signed the final papers. Isn't that awful? I enjoy my freedom." She leaned toward Jimmy, warming to the subject. "I like making my own decisions and not having to answer to anyone. I come and go as I wish. I have a lot of friends, and I am very close to some of them. I still have family who live in the area, and I enjoy being with them. But, I don't miss having a husband." She looked at Jimmy again, a challenge in her eyes.

"Does that mean that you'll never marry again?"

"No, not necessarily, but let's just say it's highly unlikely. My parents are constantly after me to get married again and settle down, especially my mother. She wants a bunch of grandkids. I'll leave that to my sister. She's married and has two kids already." She smiled at Jimmy and asked, "What about you? It's your turn to tell all."

Jimmy told her that he'd never married although he'd come close a time or two. He gave her a quick description of his past, leaving out most of the details.

He quickly changed the subject, telling her about the murder he and Sam had been trying to solve. He described the interviews they'd done, the progress they'd made and told her of Sam's injuries.

"I read the article in the paper about you and Sam. So, what are you going to do, Jimmy? Are you going to take the sheriff's advice and stay out of the investigation? Aren't you afraid the killer will try to shoot you, too?"

"I'd be lying if I said I wasn't concerned, but I promised Wendy I'd try to find out who killed Scott. Besides, I'm basically a curious person. I hope the sheriff finds the killer, but if he doesn't soon, I'll keep trying. The killer should have to pay for his actions."

They sat on the porch in the late afternoon sun, talking and getting to know each other. Dana pointed out the location of Jimmy's cabin, far away on a distant mountainside. He could see the faint glint of sunlight on its windows. She told him of her plans to clear away more of the brush and brambles that had reclaimed parts of the farmland over the years. He could see scorched spots on the ground here and there where she'd burned brush. She proudly showed him the palms of her hands and the callouses and blisters she'd earned from the work.

As the sunlight began to fade, they exchanged phone numbers and made vague plans for a dinner date in the next few days. She gave him a lingering embrace and a quick kiss on the cheek. Jimmy liked the feel of her against him and the faint smell of her shampoo. She watched him with her hands in the pockets of her jeans as he climbed into his Cherokee. He drove slowly down her lane, toward the main road, mindful of her image in his rearview mirror.

*   *   *

He'd no sooner gotten home and fed and watered Yellow Dog when his cell phone rang. It was Donald, Sam's brother. Sam's condition had worsened.

"He was doing well, his vital signs were good, and he was showing some indication of regaining consciousness when he had a relapse. The doctors don't know what happened for sure, but they suspect that he has some internal bleeding. There was a lot of damage, especially in his chest, and they think some of the repairs they made have come undone. I thought you'd want to know," Donald said.

"Oh no," Jimmy said. "Just how serious is his condition? What are his chances for survival?"

"It's pretty serious. He's back in the ICU. They'd moved him to a regular room, but that didn't last long. The doctors are prepping him for surgery now. They need to find where the blood is coming from. They won't even guess what his chances are."

"I'll be right there, Donald. It shouldn't take me much more than an hour."

"Jimmy?"

"Yes."

"You'd better hurry. The doctors told us we should call in his family," he said, his voice cracking.

Jimmy threw a change of clothing into a bag—he didn't know how long he'd be there—and put the dog back in his kennel. He filled the automatic food hopper and made sure the water dispenser was full. Yellow Dog would be good for several days if necessary. He'd call John to come walk him and give him some attention.

The drive to the hospital seemed to take forever. There'd been an accident on I-79 and traffic slowed to a crawl. He finally reached the accident site and was waved into the left lane by emergency responders. A small car lay on its side in the ditch with its front end badly crushed. Police cars sat at various angles, their emergency lights flashing. As he drove by, an injured man was being loaded onto a gurney by EMT responders. Once past, he pushed the Cherokee beyond the speed limit and finally pulled into the hospital parking lot.

When he entered the ICU waiting room, Donald's face told him everything he needed to know. Things were not going well for Sam. Joan and Susan huddled together on a couch in the corner of the room, their faces pale and drawn. Donald sat dejectedly beside them. He stood when Jimmy approached.

"He's still in there," he said, nodding vaguely toward the door that led to the operating suite. "It's been almost two hours. I'm really worried."

"Have the doctors told you anything?"

"No, they said they'd come out here and talk to us as soon as they could. The wait is killing us."

"Okay. I guess we'll just have to wait it out. Let's just try to relax. Can I get you something to drink?" Jimmy asked, looking from one worried face to the next. They all declined his offer.

They sat together on the couch, talking quietly as friends and relatives do while waiting for word of their loved ones' fate. People came and went, and hospital personnel entered occasionally looking for family members of other patients. Each time the door near the operating room opened, they all looked up hopefully. Thirty minutes passed, then another thirty. Finally, the door opened and a tired-looking doctor—a young woman in scrubs—beckoned to Sam's family. She led them to a consultation room, and Donald asked Jimmy to join them.

The doctor said with a kind voice, "Mr. Miller's still in very serious condition. We think we found the bleeder. Several of the major vessels in his chest were damaged by the bullet. We had stitched them back together, but one of them came undone. Because of the damage, we didn't have a lot to work with. It was bleeding badly, and we had to give him several pints of blood to replace what was lost. Frankly, it was touch and go for a while there, but we think it should be okay now. The problem is, we don't know if more of the repairs will break loose. Only time will tell. He's a very sick man."

She asked if they had questions. Donald and the two women looked numb, not knowing enough to ask a sensible question. Finally, Donald asked, "What are his chances for survival, Doctor?"

She replied guardedly, "If he can get through the next few days without another bleeder, his chances are fair to good. The longer he goes without springing another leak, the better the chance the repairs we made will heal. He's stable for now."

Jimmy spoke up, "Assuming he survives okay, what kind of life will he have? Will he be able to live a normal life?"

The doctor turned toward him and said, "Good question. Assuming no more emergencies, he should make a good recovery physically. But, his body has experienced a severe trauma. Including his brain. We don't know how long it might have gone without oxygen. Remember, his blood pressure was almost zero when they brought him in, and he's been unconscious for several days now. That's not a good sign. So, the short answer is that we don't know."

The doctor answered several more questions, then left in a rush. They returned to the waiting room and sat again on the couch. They rehashed what the doctor had told them, trying to make sense of it all. They waited until Sam was taken back to the ICU, and Joan and Susan went in to see him. Jimmy and Donald talked while they were gone. Donald told Jimmy they'd called in the rest of Sam's family, but he decided to call them back and let them know that Sam had successfully made it out of surgery and was stable again. They'd have to decide if they wanted to come in to see him or not. He walked out into the hallway to make the calls.

Jimmy moved to a chair in the corner and listened to the rush and clamor of the hospital. Announcements were made frequently over the public announcement system, and patrons came and went. Visitors talked quietly while others watched the muted televisions located around the room. It was as if he was caught in a rerun of an old movie.

He leaned back and closed his eyes. Whoever had done this to Sam deserved to be caught and put in prison for the rest of his life. He hoped the sheriff would find him quickly, but what if he didn't? Would this become just another unsolved crime? Jimmy had no doubt the sheriff would search doggedly for the shooter, but would he find him? Was there something he could do to help—to speed things along? The sheriff had told him in no uncertain terms to stay away from the investigation, and for the most part he would, but what harm could there be in asking a few simple questions? What the sheriff didn't know wouldn't hurt him.

Jimmy shifted into a more comfortable position in his chair and frowned as he thought about it. What was it that police detectives always said? If you don't catch the killer in the first few days, you weren't likely to? Well, it had been more than *a few days*. Sam was a good friend, and he wasn't about to let this crime go unpunished. If the sheriff didn't find the shooter, he would.

Chapter 17

It was late the following afternoon when Jimmy arrived back at the cabin. The evening before, Sam's condition had stabilized somewhat, and the doctors had moved him from ICU back to a regular room. A nurse carefully monitored his condition. Jimmy had wanted to stay by his side, but Donald, Joan and Susan had insisted that he should go home. They'd be able to watch over Sam as they had before. He had reluctantly agreed.

He puttered around in his tiny kitchen, sipped a can of beer and thawed a steak in the microwave oven. He fired up the gas grill on the deck and allowed it to heat while he prepared the rest of his meal. He put a potato in the microwave to cook and tossed a small salad. He drizzled the meat with olive oil and dusted it lightly with Cajun seasoning. It sizzled pleasantly when he put it on the grill, its aroma pleasant and sharp. When his meal was ready he ate it at the table on the deck while he thumbed through the murder book.

He read Sam's notes on his interviews with Wendy and Frank. He was surprised that Sam had decided to interview them. Jimmy thought it a waste of time but didn't question Sam's decision to talk to them. He read about Frank and Scott's disagreement when Frank had been caught smoking pot in Scott's barn. That was interesting, but hardly a reason to kill someone. Besides, he knew Frank and didn't believe he was capable of killing Scott.

Sam had written a few notes about Seth Buckman and his ownership of the Red Creek Saloon. In the margin of the page, he'd written "*jealous boyfriend?*" He'd drawn a circle around the words. Jimmy went back and reread what Frank had said about Seth being possessive of Wendy. Interesting.

He washed the dishes and used a brush to scrub the grill and wiped the grate clean with a folded paper towel. He paused long enough to scan the evening sky. A dark bank of clouds approached over the western horizon, and he thought he saw a flicker of lightning. It was going to rain. He pulled the vinyl cover over the grill and put a flat rock on top to keep it from blowing away in the coming storm.

He went inside and sat at the table by the windows. Opening the murder book again, he reread Sam's notes about Seth Buckman. Was Sam thinking that Seth could have killed Scott in a jealous rage? Was there something Sam had heard or seen but hadn't written down? Jimmy knew that Sam was a very perceptive investigator. Little got by him when he did interviews.

Jimmy checked the dates and found Sam had talked to Seth the day before he was shot. Was that a coincidence? Had Seth become nervous because Sam was asking questions about Scott's death and decided to take him out? Jimmy knew Sam didn't believe in coincidences, but Jimmy had done enough research to know that correlation did not *imply* causation. It was a basic research principle that because one event followed another did not mean the first event *caused* the other. It follows that just because Sam talked to Seth one day, it didn't mean that Seth shot him the next. There *was* such a thing as coincidence, but the same research principle also postulated that Seth *could* have shot Sam. Sometimes correlation *resulted* in causation. He shook his head. He was beginning to get a headache just thinking about it.

He closed the murder book and returned to the deck. He watched as the storm approached. Lightning flickered, outlining the towering clouds briefly with silvery light. The molecules of air were charged and expectant. A light breeze preceding the storm rattled the leaves in the trees nearby. A distant rumble of thunder rolled through the mountains, resounding again and again. It would be an exciting night—high on a mountain in a cabin made mostly of glass. He looked forward to it.

Jimmy went inside and got ready for bed. Tomorrow, he'd go see what he could learn at the Red Creek Saloon. He'd have lunch there; how could the sheriff object to that? He'd update Wendy on Sam's condition and let her know that he wasn't giving up on the investigation. As he drifted off to sleep, he could hear the thump of Yellow Dog's tail—he was under Jimmy's bed. A great storm was coming.

*　　*　　*

The following morning, Jimmy swept leaves and twigs off the deck in a light drizzle of rain. The storm had been a powerful one, crashing and banging through much of the night. Rain had poured in torrents from the eaves of the cabin, and he found a leak in the ceiling of the kitchen. He put a cooking pot on the floor to catch the rainwater. He'd have to get up on the roof and make repairs when it dried out. It had taken a lot of coaxing to get the dog to come out from under the bed. He'd rolled his eyes and stayed close to Jimmy as he worked.

The rain picked up as Jimmy drove up on the mountain to the Red Creek Saloon. Creeks and rivers roiled with muddy water, nearing the tops of their banks. Gravel and debris had washed onto the mountain roads, and Jimmy drove slowly as he swerved to avoid the worse of it. On one section of the highway near the top of the mountain, a large tree had been blown down by the storm. It had partially blocked the road, but someone had used a chainsaw to cut out a section large enough for cars to pass. It took almost an hour for him to reach the saloon.

As he pulled into the parking lot, he was impressed with the new building. It was quite large with cedar siding and a green metal roof. A large building stood out back. He was equally impressed with the saloon's interior. A young woman wearing a uniform of khaki pants and a dark shirt led him to a table. She said that the waitress would be by soon to take his order. As he waited, he noted the stuffed animal heads on the walls, the small stage, and the long bar along one wall. He saw Wendy working behind the bar—she hadn't seen him enter. Several other diners sat at tables nearby.

The waitress brought water, gave him a large menu, and said she'd be back for his order. She left in a whirl. The menu contained the standard lunch fare; hamburgers, sandwiches, salads, soup. When the waitress returned, he ordered the soup-of-the-day and a large salad.

"Have you worked here long?" he asked. "This is my first time here."

The young woman stuffed her pad in a back pocket and cracked her gum. She was attractive in a tom-boyish way with short, dark hair. A fashionable pair of glasses were perched on her nose. "Yeah, I work here every summer. I live just down the way," she nodded vaguely in the direction of the bar. "I'm in college," she said.

"Do you like working here?" Jimmy looked around the room. "It seems pretty quiet."

"Oh sure. We don't get a lot of lunch traffic, but things pick up in the evenings and weekends are really busy."

"Mr. Buckman's the owner, isn't he? How do you like working for him?"

"Oh, he's okay. He's always busy, running around like a chicken with his head cut off. He treats us okay. I don't have any complaints."

Jimmy couldn't think of other questions to ask her, at least questions that she would be likely to answer for a stranger. His questioning skills were not up to Sam's standards. She hurried to the kitchen door with Jimmy's food order clutched in her hand.

Jimmy enjoyed his meal. The soup turned out to be a crab bisque served with a bread roll the waitress said had been cooked on the premises. The house salad was crisp with just the right combination of ingredients. The food was excellent. Jimmy asked to see a dinner menu and browsed through it as he ate. He decided that he'd come back sometime and try some of their dinner entrees. Just as he was finishing his meal, Wendy stopped by his table.

"Dr. Houston, I thought that was you. I didn't see you come in." She was dressed in the restaurant's standard uniform with her long hair pulled back in a loose arrangement. She was an attractive woman.

"Oh hello, Wendy," he said. "I thought I should come and fill you in about Sam. I'm sure you've read about the shooting in the social media." He asked if she'd like to sit down, and she slid gracefully into a chair opposite him.

"Seth doesn't like for us to sit with the customers, but it won't hurt for a few minutes." She drew her eyebrows together into a frown. "How is Sam doing? I feel responsible for getting him involved in all this. Will he be okay?"

"His condition is very serious, Wendy. He was shot three times, once through the chest. Right now, he has two major problems; he hasn't regained consciousness, and some of the vessels the doctors repaired have started bleeding again. For now, he's stable and his chances for recovery are fair. Wendy, it's not your fault that he was shot. The shooter is completely responsible for that."

"That's kind of you to say, Dr. Houston. I hope he'll be okay. I pray for him every night. He's a good man."

The waitress came by with the check. Jimmy asked, "Is there somewhere we could talk for a few minutes? I'll bring you up to date on the investigation."

"Oh sure. There's a break room in the back for employees. We can use that. I'm not busy right now, and won't be until later, about dinnertime. Then, it gets pretty hectic."

Jimmy paid the check and Wendy led him through a back door to a small room with a long table surrounded with brightly colored chairs. Schedules, notes, and scraps of paper with items for sale were pinned to a cork bulletin board attached to the wall. A soft drink machine hummed in a corner, and a microwave oven sat on a long counter. Various personal items were scattered about. One lone sweater, forgotten by its owner for the summer, dangled from a hanger on a long, metal coatrack.

Jimmy told her about the interviews he and Sam had done, and she said that Sam had told her much of the same. He brought her up to date as best he could. Jimmy told her that the sheriff wanted him to stay out of the investigation.

"What are you going to do, Dr. Houston? Do you think the sheriff will find the killer?

"Yes, I think it's likely he'll eventually find who shot Sam, and I believe that the same person killed Scott. That doesn't mean that I can't ask a few questions myself. I'll just have to be careful not to step on the sheriff's toes. I'm going to go talk to him again to see if I can weasel my way back in the investigation. He might let me sit in on some of their interviews. I'm going to let him cool off a little first," Jimmy said with a grin.

"I'm glad you're not giving up. I think the sheriff's a good policeman, but he's so busy. I'm afraid he'll get distracted again if he doesn't find the killer right away."

"I know you have to get back to work, so is it okay if I ask you a few quick questions?"

"Yes of course. Sam asked a lot of questions, too."

"I have his notes, so I won't have to repeat them." Jimmy took a deep breath. "Sam was especially interested in Seth."

Wendy interrupted him, "Seth? What does he have to do with this?"

Jimmy didn't want to rat out Frank to his mother, so he carefully said, "Sam had reason to believe that Seth might be interested in you romantically. Have you noticed him being especially possessive of you?"

Wendy's face got red. She shook her head, "No." She hesitated. "No more than with some of the other girls. He's...friendly. You know what I mean?"

"No, not really. You'll have to spell it out for me." Jimmy didn't want to put words in her mouth. She'd have to just come out with it.

She sighed, and her shoulders slumped. "This is embarrassing." Her face had gotten even redder. "He asked me out a couple of times. I said no. He's my boss. Even if I wanted to go out with him, and I don't, that wouldn't work. I'm an employee, and the other workers wouldn't like it. They'd say he was playing favorites. Anyway, I said no, and he seemed okay with that for a while. But, he kept pressing me. Nothing terrible, but it was really uncomfortable for me."

"When did this happen? Was it before or after Scott's death?"

"Oh god, you don't think he killed Scott, do you?"

"Wendy, you can't think that way. As Sam liked to say, we ask a lot of questions that don't go anywhere."

"Let me think. Seth didn't seem to be interested in me until after Scott died. I remember because the first time Seth asked me out was on Valentine's day. So, that was several months after Scott went missing." Wendy seemed to relax. "No, Scott was already gone when he asked me out, so he couldn't have done it, killed Scott." She almost whispered the last words—killed Scott. "I don't remember him paying much attention to me before that."

"Sam seemed to think that Seth was possessive of you. Didn't want men showing you attention. He thought Seth was even jealous of you when male customers talked to you. Did you see any signs of that?"

"Oh, this is a bar. Men drink and do stupid things. I know how to put them off. I just shoo them away. I never thought much about it. It's an occupational hazard. Besides, a lot of the people who come here are locals. I've known them forever. Many of them are my friends." She slumped in her chair, "But, now that you mention it, Seth is always rushing people away from the bar. He told me to get them their drinks and move them away. I never thought much about it, but yeah, he's a little possessive."

Jimmy thought about asking about Frank's and Scott's argument about the pot but decided that Wendy was unlikely to add anything new on the subject. He asked if she knew where the Indian rug in Scott's house came from, but she gave him the same answer she'd given Sam. She didn't know.

"Did Scott have a special attachment to the rug? Was it a special souvenir, maybe from a trip he'd taken?"

"No. He didn't pay any attention to it. It was just there, like a part of the furniture."

"So, he never talked about it, told you a story about where he'd gotten it?"

"No. Why are you so interested in it? It's like asking someone where they got their refrigerator. After a few years, you don't remember because it isn't important. You know?"

They sat quietly for a few moments, each lost in his own thoughts. The soft drink machine suddenly shut off, and the silence crept in around them.

Jimmy cleared his throat and asked, "Did Scott date anyone before you started seeing each other?"

She laughed ironically and said, "No, I don't think so. He'd been widowed for a long time, and I think he'd just about given up meeting someone. I'm not sure he was even interested. To tell you the truth, I was the bold one. I liked what I saw in him, and I finally got him to ask me out. It took some doing."

"What about others in his family? Anyone who would object to him getting married again?

"No, nothing like that. He didn't have many close relatives. They were all gone."

"Wendy, I'm grasping at straws, so bear with me. How well do you know Sandy Lynch, Scott's niece?"

"Not well. She was around while Scott and I were dating. She went out to dinner with us a couple of times, and we all did some hiking together. Nothing real strenuous. Scott liked to fish, and she went with us a couple of times. You know, like that."

"Did she and Scott get along well?"

"Oh yes. They weren't real close, you know, about like normal uncles and nieces. There was quite an age difference. She'd help him around the farm sometimes, and I think she cleaned his house a little from time to time. All that stopped when I came on the scene."

"How did she feel about that? Do you feel she thought you were taking her place?"

Wendy made a face and said, "She didn't care. She still saw him, and they seemed to have a good relationship. It wasn't like she was there all the time, but she still made dinner for him sometimes after Scott and I started dating. If I remember correctly, she made Thanksgiving dinner for him because I had to work that day. I think I told Sam that."

The door to the workroom suddenly opened, startling them both. A large man with a muscular build stood in the doorway, almost filling it. They looked up from the table at him.

"There you are," he said to Wendy. "I wondered what happened to you."

"Seth, this is Dr. Houston. He's Frank's advisor at State College," Wendy said.

Jimmy stood and extended his hand, "Pleased to meet you, Mr. Buckman. I just enjoyed a nice lunch here. It was very good."

Seth shook his hand firmly and said, "I'm sorry to interrupt Wendy, but we need to get ready for tonight's rush."

Wendy looked at her watch and blushed. "I'm sorry, Seth. The time got away from me. Dr. Houston's working with the police to find Scott's killer, and we were talking about that, too."

"Yeah, I read about that in the paper. Sounds like you're a regular Sherlock Holmes, Doc." He grinned at Jimmy.

They passed a few pleasant moments, and then Wendy rushed back to work. Seth walked with Jimmy to the front door. He invited Jimmy to come back for dinner sometime, and Jimmy said he certainly would. The food was very good. They shook hands again and Jimmy climbed into his Cherokee. He saw Seth watching him as he left the parking lot.

Jimmy crossed Red Creek and drove up the mountain to the entrance to the state park in Canaan Valley. He pulled off the road at a wide spot and began writing notes in the murder book. Sam had taught him that note taking was an important investigative technique that must be done as soon as possible after the interview—while his memory was fresh. He wrote everything he could remember about his conversation with Wendy. He paused to look out the Jeep's window at a doe and fawn that grazed on the lush grass that grew along the entrance road. The fawn was half-grown, and its spots had almost faded away. They switched their tails rapidly as they ate, swishing away the deer flies that pestered them. They ignored the cars that sped by no more than ten feet from them. Occasionally, tourists slowed long enough to snaps pictures with their cell phones.

He hesitated with his pen poised over the note pad. He didn't know what to write about Seth Buckman. He seemed likeable enough. He'd talked pleasantly with Jimmy and shook his hand firmly, but not aggressively. He'd suggested nicely that Wendy needed to get back to work and had accepted her excuse of losing track of time. He'd invited Jimmy to come back for dinner sometime. Maybe Jimmy was reading too much into it, but Seth just didn't seem sincere. It was like he was gritting his teeth behind his pleasant smile. Jimmy jotted down a few notes and let it go at that.

The dog began to whine and dance around. Jimmy had almost forgotten about him. He drove down the road a way and led him into a clump of quaking aspens. The dog did his business quickly and Jimmy looked around expecting to see a ranger writing him a ticket. He wondered what law he and the dog had broken. Surely there was one. Jimmy chuckled, thinking if a wild bear could go in the woods, so could Yellow Dog.

Chapter 18

Jimmy drove through the valley and into the community where Sandy lived. There was a smattering of businesses along the main street; a couple of good restaurants, art galleries, and a grocery. Side streets spread away from the main drag and were lined with Victorian houses and small bungalows.

He parked along the street and entered a restaurant to ask directions to Sandy Lynch's shop. He was directed to a broad side street. The shop was small and tidy with a display window facing the street. A variety of hand-made collectables were arranged in a nice display enticing the casual window shopper to come in and buy something.

A bell tinkled as he entered, and Sandy looked up from her station behind a counter. The shop was crammed with stock—jewelry, carvings, weavings, candles, paintings, wooden spoons, and every imaginable craft item. The pleasant odor of potpourri lingered in the air. Two elderly women browsed through the store.

"Why hello, Dr. Houston," Sandy said pleasantly. "I was hoping you'd stop by one day." She wore tight jeans with an expensive looking blouse that fell to her narrow hips. Her hair was down on her shoulders and he could see silver earrings peeking through it. Her eyes were bright and sparkled with mischief. "Are you here to buy a gift for that special person?"

Jimmy jokingly said, "I'm looking for a new pair of fishing waders. Do you have anything in my size?"

"Let me think for a minute." She stood with one arm across her chest and the other with a carefully manicured finger tapping her lips. After a moment of thinking, she said, "No, I don't think I have anything that will fit you. How about a nice candle or maybe a bag of potpourri?"

The two ladies looked first at Sandy, then at Jimmy and grinned, enjoying the banter. They placed their purchases on the counter and Sandy rang up their bill. They paid and left the shop tittering, looking over their shoulders at them.

"Are you a fisherman, Dr. Houston? I hear the Blackwater River is prime trout fishing."

"Yes, I am. I've fished the Blackwater many times. But, I'm not here to buy waders. I'd like to ask you a few questions."

"I read about Deputy Miller being shot. Is he going to be okay?"

Jimmy updated her on Sam's condition. "He'll be in the hospital for a long time, and then he'll have to do a lot of physical rehab."

"I'm sorry to hear that. He seemed like a very nice man. What kind of questions do you have for me? I'll be happy to help you any way I can."

Jimmy asked if there was somewhere they could sit and talk. She said she couldn't leave the shop. She was working alone today but had hired a salesperson who came in on weekends to help out. They stepped outside and sat on wooden benches that flanked the shop's entrance. Jimmy dragged his bench around, so he could see her better. The afternoon was pleasantly warm and the clouds that had produced rain earlier had broken up. Patches of blue sky peeked through the clouds.

Jimmy said, "You have a very nice shop here, Sandy."

"It's difficult running a business by myself. It's nothing like I imagined when I was in business school," she said. "It's so restrictive. I'm here six days a week, and it's hard to find time to go to the bathroom. But, I like being my own boss."

"I can understand that. I'm sure it's very fulfilling."

"In the retail business, it's all about buying stock that will turn over quickly. I buy wholesale and sell retail, and if I buy an item that won't sell, I have to eat the loss. It's hard."

"How's it going?" Jimmy asked. "Are you making a go of it?"

"Well, I'm not getting rich, but I'm getting by. Thank goodness I have a little nest egg to see me through the hard times."

"Well, Sandy, I wish you the best of luck. Now, if you don't mind, I have a couple of questions for you."

"Sure. Fire away." She smiled warmly at him. She was a nice-looking woman.

He cleared his throat and asked, "When was the last time you saw your uncle alive?"

"Thanksgiving last year," she said without hesitation. "He came to my house for dinner. Wendy had to work at the saloon, so I invited him to come eat with me. We're about the only family we have left." Her eyes welled with tears. "I guess I should speak in past tense. He's gone, and I have little family left."

"What was his mood? Did he seem worried? Distracted?"

She shook her head. "No, not that I remember. He seemed to be his old self. He was always friendly and pleasant."

"Are you aware of any financial dealings he might have had at the time of his death?"

"Nooo," she said, dragging out the word. "Not that I know of. As I told you and Sam before, he was going to give his property to the nature preserve, but I don't think he ever finalized that. At least, I haven't found anything to that effect. I'm the executor of his will."

"In going through his finances, did you find any indication that he'd traveled recently?"

"Do you mean like airline tickets, or something?"

"Yes."

"He only had one credit card, and I've looked at his past records. I didn't find anything like that."

"Did Scott ever say anything about having an argument with Frank Richmond?"

She laughed, her eyes sparkling, "Oh, heavens yes. Uncle Scott caught Frank smoking a doobie in his barn. He had a fit. They argued about it." She laughed again, "I thought it was funny. He was old-fashioned that way and he'd go on and on about the states out west that are legalizing pot. He wasn't terribly angry with Frank, but he didn't like it."

Jimmy pulled his phone from his pocket and swiped through it until he found the picture he wanted. He showed it to her. She took the phone from his hand and looked closely at the photo.

She said, "This is the rug that's in Uncle Scott's house. It's in the living room." She handed the phone back to him. "How did you get the picture? As far as I know, it's still a crime scene."

"Sam took it. He's a deputy, so the sheriff let him look through the house."

"Oh. What about it?"

"I was wondering where Scott got it. It looks expensive, and it would have been out of character for him to buy an item like that."

"I'll have to add it to his estate for probate. I haven't gone through all his stuff yet. Do you think the rug has anything to do with his killer?" she asked, her eyes getting big.

"No, probably not," Jimmy said. "Sam seemed to think it was a loose end. He's a great one for tying up loose ends."

"Do you think the rug's valuable? I know some Indian rugs can bring in big money."

"I really don't know. Have you ever stocked them in your shop?"

"No, I don't think they'd sell here. Besides, I can't afford to put a lot of money in a single item like that and have it sit on the shelf a long time before it sells. I'm more comfortable stocking smaller items and trying for rapid turnover."

A young boy peddled by on a bicycle followed by a large, awkward puppy. The bicycle wobbled badly as the boy freed a hand to wave at them. Sandy smiled and waved back, calling him by name, "Hey, Bobby. Stop by on your way back for a lollipop." He said he would and continued down the street.

Jimmy watched the boy pass by. "Sandy, have you thought of anything that might be helpful to us since we were here before?"

"No, and I've thought about it. I don't have any idea why someone would want to kill Uncle Scott. He was a kind soul, and everybody liked him."

"What about Kelly Rice. Did she like him?"

Sandy's face clouded. "Oh, that woman! I didn't think about her. I guess she could have done it. She's mean. She and Uncle Scott argued, but it wasn't enough to kill someone over."

"What was the argument about?"

"Her goats got out and ate some of the endangered ferns. Uncle Scott wasn't really mad. He just wanted her to keep her goats off his property. She called him some pretty nasty names, but she took her goats home and fixed the fence. That was about it. As far as I know, they didn't have another run-in. She stayed on her side of the fence, and he stayed on his."

Jimmy asked, "In your opinion, was Ms. Rice mad enough to kill your uncle?"

"Oh, I don't think so. She's all bluster."

Jimmy thought about her answer for a moment. "One last question. Do you have any idea where Scott was killed? The sheriff said there's no evidence he was killed at his house, and he doesn't believe he was killed on Dolly Sods where his body was found. They just don't know where it happened."

Sandy's eyes welled up again. She pulled a tissue from a pocket and dabbed at the corners of her eyes, then blotted them carefully. "Sorry. I don't have any idea. Why is that important?"

"If the police can find where he was killed, they might be able to collect evidence that would be helpful in solving the crime."

She dabbed at her eyes and said, "Oh, I see. Sure, that makes sense. No, I don't know where he was killed. As far as I know, it could have been anywhere."

Jimmy leaned toward her, touched her arm with his fingertips and said, "I'm sorry to have to ask these questions, Sandy. I know it's hard for you. But, be assured we're doing everything we can to find whoever did this."

"Thank you, Dr. Houston, I..."

He interrupted her saying, "You can call me Jimmy. Everyone else does."

She smiled at him. "Thank you, Jimmy. From all your and Sam's investigations, do you have any suspicion who killed Uncle Scott?"

"No. It's very frustrating. We've looked at a lot of evidence, talked to a lot of people, but so far, nothing. But, we won't give up. We'll keep at it until we find him."

With the questioning over, they talked, getting to know each other. She was an outdoors person. She had been a mountain biker in her younger years but had gotten away from it lately. She liked to kayak and canoe and did a lot of hiking.

"I don't have a lot of time for recreation since I opened the shop, but I get out when I can. What about you? I know you're a fly fisherman. Do you get to fish often?"

"Not as often as I would like." He told her about some of his fishing trips, fearing his enthusiasm for the sport would bore her. He needn't have worried.

"I've always wanted to learn how to fly fish," she said, almost batting her eyes at him.

"Well, when this is all over, I'd be happy to teach you. One of the best fly fishing streams in the county is just a stone's throw away from your shop."

She asked if he liked bluegrass music, and he said he did. She said there was a place in a nearby town that had live music almost every night, and she went there, mostly on Saturday nights. "Maybe I'll see you there sometime."

"Maybe," he said.

They moved the benches back to their original positions and Sandy extended her hand. Jimmy grinned at her as he shook it, noting her strong grip. There was nothing like a woman with a strong handshake. They said goodbye and Sandy returned to her work in her shop. Jimmy climbed into his Jeep and rubbed the dog's ears. He'd find a place along the road to write some notes, and then he'd go home. He needed to think about what he'd learned today, but it all boiled down to two words—not much.

*   *   *

When he got home, Jimmy called the sheriff. "I was wondering if you'd made any progress on Sam's shooting." He'd been surprised when the sheriff answered his cell phone.

"Before I answer any of your questions, how's Sam doing? Is he going to make it?"

Jimmy gave him an update on his condition. Jimmy had talked to Donald and found that Sam was beginning to show signs of waking up. He'd opened his eyes a couple times, and his vital signs had stabilized. He told the sheriff what he knew.

"I told you to stay out of this, Professor, but to answer your question, we haven't found diddley-squat. None of the cartridges had fingerprints, but we weren't surprised. Only a fool wouldn't wipe them clean. We didn't find any footprints, tire prints, or anything else that might give us a clue who did it. My deputies have put the word out on the street hoping someone would come forward. The hotline number Ray Lambert put in his newspaper article didn't produce anything useful. Just a bunch of kooks and weirdos looking for attention."

"I assume you canvassed the neighborhood around Scott's house. Did that turn up anything suspicious?"

"Professor, I told you to butt out of this investigation, but here you are sticking your nose in it."

Before the sheriff could get off on a rant, Jimmy interrupted and asked, "I'm just curious what you've found out about Sam's assailant. What harm could there be in that? Did anyone in Scott's neighborhood hear or see anything. After all, it happened in broad daylight."

Grudgingly, the sheriff answered. "One of the neighbors thought she heard gunfire, but at the time assumed it was firecrackers. No one saw anything unusual. They probably wouldn't have noticed since there are people coming and going to the nature preserve all the time, and some of the guests from the ski area get lost and drive out to the end of the road. The workers at the lodge weren't of much help." He gave Jimmy a detailed description of his investigation of the shooting.

"Did you talk to all the neighbors? What about Kelly Rice?"

"Oh God, don't remind me of her. Yeah, we talked to her. We went to her house, but she wouldn't let us in. She asked if we had a warrant.

Of course, we didn't—no probable cause. So, we said she could talk to us there or at the station. She chose the station."

"What did she say?"

Jimmy could hear the sheriff drumming on his desktop with his fingers. Several seconds passed before he answered. "We filmed the interview. She gave us permission, so we recorded it. Nothing much came of it. She wasn't cooperative, to say the least." The sheriff drummed some more on his desktop. "I shouldn't do this, but do you want to see the interview? I can send it to your phone. Maybe you'll see something in it we didn't."

"Yeah sure, Sheriff. I'd like to see it. Sam and I didn't have a chance to interview her, so maybe this will do instead."

"Look, Jimmy, sticking your nose in this is really dangerous. One person has been killed, and another was badly wounded. I don't have any doubt the shooter intended to kill Sam. He won't hesitate to try to kill you, too, if he thinks you're a threat. I have my deputies on high alert, especially the ones who are out questioning people. They travel in pairs. We aren't taking any chances. You shouldn't either."

"I'll be careful, Sheriff. I don't think I'm doing anything to attract his attention."

"Do you have a gun? If so, I advise you to start carrying it. You don't need a permit in this state to carry a concealed weapon."

"Yeah, I have a gun."

"What kind is it?"

"Well, it's a .22 rifle."

Jimmy could hear the sheriff sigh with exasperation. "I guess that's better than nothing. You'd better keep it handy."

Chapter 19

Jimmy downloaded the file the sheriff had sent him to his laptop. He wanted to view it on a screen larger than the one on his cell phone. He sat at the small table near the window and clicked the play icon.

The video was surprisingly bright and clear with good sound. It showed the sheriff, a female deputy and Kelly Rice sitting at one end of a long wooden table. The sheriff told Ms. Rice that she wasn't under arrest but had been asked to come in to answer a few questions. She could leave anytime she wanted to. She mumbled that she would answer their questions, but for them to be quick about it. She had things to do.

She was a stout woman with strong-looking arms and hands. Her short sandy hair looked like it had been done in a blender. She wore heavy, canvas pants and a man's shirt. She glared across the table at the two officers.

"Would you like something to drink?" the deputy asked.

"No. This isn't a social gathering. Let's get this over."

"Ms. Rice, we only have a few questions," the sheriff said. "As you're probably aware, someone tried to kill a police officer who was investigating Scott Mitchell's death. He was alone at Scott's farm when someone shot and wounded him. We were wondering if you heard or saw anything that might help us find the shooter. Scott's house is only a few hundred yards from yours." The sheriff gave her the time and date of the attack.

"Yeah, I heard some shooting over there. At first, I thought it was firecrackers. You know, kids setting off fireworks."

"Have kids done that before?"

"No, but they could have. There's a lot of snot-nosed kids running around here. They try to sneak onto my land sometimes."

"Did you hear anything besides the shooting?"

"Like what?" She glared at the sheriff.

"I don't know. You tell us. Any other sounds? Anything?"

She leaned back and folded her arms over her chest. "No, I didn't hear anything else. There might have been some shouting, but I'm not sure. Sometimes I hear people talking all the way up at the lodge and ski slope. Depends on what direction the wind's blowing. I guess it could have come from Scott's place, but I'm not sure."

"Anything else? Did you see anything that might help us?"

"I saw a car. After all the racket stopped, I walked down by the gate. I was thinking the kids would try to cut across my land on the way back home. I don't allow anybody on my land."

"Do you mean the kids who you thought might have set off the firecrackers?"

"Yeah. You're real smart, Sheriff. Who do you think I was talking about?" she said, her voice dripping with sarcasm.

The sheriff ignored the remark. "Tell us about the car."

"I didn't get a good look at it. By the time I got there, it had already passed my gate. I just saw the ass-end of it going around the bend down the road."

"Could you tell what make or model it was?"

"No. As I told you, I didn't get a good look at it. Besides, I didn't know it would be important, so I wasn't paying a lot of attention to it."

"You probably didn't get a license number, did you?"

Kelly Price rolled her eyes. "What part of 'didn't get a good look at it' don't you understand?" She made quotation marks in the air with her fingers.

"Was it an in-state or out-of-state license plate?"

"Don't know."

"What color was the car?" the sheriff asked.

Ms. Rice thought for a moment. "There was some dust, but I think the car was white."

"Do you *think* it was white? Or, are you *sure* it was white? Which is it?"

"I'm sure it was white. It was a small car, a sedan. It wasn't a big SUV like you see everyone driving, polluting the air, and using up our natural resources."

"Did you see the car during the shooting, or after?"

"Why, after, of course. The shooting had stopped."

"How long after?"

Jimmy could see her concentrating, trying to remember. "Ten minutes, maybe. I don't know. When the shooting stopped, I walked down my driveway to the gate. That only takes a few minutes. But, after the shooting stopped, I waited at my house a few minutes to be sure it wasn't going to start again. So, probably ten minutes total."

The sheriff asked, "Did you see any other cars on the road after you saw the white car go by?"

"No," she said, "not until all the emergency vehicles arrived."

"How much time elapsed between when you saw the white car and the emergency vehicles got there?"

"It wasn't very long. Another ten minutes? Maybe a little less. They got there pretty quick."

The sheriff clasped his hands on the table before him. Laughter erupted in the hallway outside the room. "Had you ever seen anyone on Scott's property before the shooting? After Scott's death, I mean."

"Yeah, once in a while someone would go tromping around over there. Scott didn't seem to care. He'd talk to them and ask them to leave, but he didn't seem to think it was a big deal. I'm busy, so a whole army could have set up camp over there, and I'd not have noticed. There are a lot of trees between my house and his property."

"Ms. Rice," the sheriff said, "where were you when Sam Miller was attacked?"

An incredulous look passed over her face, and then it flushed red. "What do you mean, you stupid..." She sputtered and grasped for words. "I just told you where I was. I was at home, working. Like I am almost every day."

"Can you prove you were there? You could have made all this up. Was there anyone there with you?"

"No, there wasn't anyone there with me," she shouted. "I answered all your stupid questions. Now, we're done." She jumped up from her chair and marched out the door.

The deputy looked at the sheriff and shrugged. She laughed and said, "I thought that went well." The sheriff leaned forward and pushed a button on the table and the screen went blank.

Jimmy watched the interview again, looking for any sign of deception in Ms. Rice, but couldn't detect anything. She seemed to be telling the truth. If that were so, it meant that she hadn't killed Scott, unless the killer and the shooter were two different people. That didn't seem likely to Jimmy.

He called the sheriff. When he answered, Jimmy could tell that he wasn't thrilled to be talking to him again so soon.

Jimmy said, "I watched the interview."

"Okay, Professor. What do you think? Was she telling the truth?"

"I tend to think she was. If that's true, she didn't kill Scott."

"I'm not sure I agree with you. She's a real nut case. She'd as soon lie to you as spit in your eye. She could have made up everything."

"True, but I've worked with people all my professional career. I can usually tell when my students are lying to me. She came across to me as telling the truth."

"I guess I've grown cynical in my old age, but here's something to think about. She doesn't have an alibi. She admitted she was at home when Sam was attacked, and no one was there with her. She was alone. What better way to throw us off her trail than to come up with the story about the car?"

"Oh, I hadn't thought about that. I suppose that would have been a neat way to create an alibi."

"And, Professor, here's something else you should consider. You work with students, and I'm sure you're very good at reading them. But, they're not criminals. Criminals are very good at deception. They're expert liars. It's their stock and trade. I'm not saying Ms. Rice is lying, but it's a distinct possibility. She could have killed Scott. She lives next door to him, she'd argued with him, and she certainly has the temperament to whack him with a rock. I'd love to search her property looking for trace evidence. There will be blood evidence wherever Scott was killed, even after all this time. Right now, though, that's out. No judge will give us a search warrant with what we have so far."

"I understand, Sheriff. So, you're not going to cross her off your suspect list just yet?"

"No, I'm not. I'm not saying she's the shooter or the killer, but she's not off my list yet."

"Have you begun checking alibis for the other suspects?"

"As we speak. I have my deputies out right now asking them to tell us where they were when Sam was attacked. I should have some answers soon."

"I'll be interested in the results, Sheriff."

"Huh! What makes you think I'll share the results with you? You're off the case, remember? And, don't forget to get that rifle out and carry it with you. I don't want to get another 'expert' detective shot."

When Jimmy broke the phone connection with the sheriff, he leaned back in his chair and stared at the ceiling. A round, yellow stain showed where rainwater had soaked through the paneling over the kitchen. Drops of water fell occasionally and splashed into the pot on the floor.

He knew he was out of his element. He'd jumped to a conclusion about Kelly Rice, thinking she was telling the truth. But the sheriff was right. She had reason to be deceptive. He needed to realize that some people were very good at lying, especially when their freedom was at stake. It made him wonder who else had lied to him.

He walked into his bedroom and opened the closet door. He swept the clothing aside on their hangers and opened the hidden panel toward the back. He retrieved his old .22 semi-automatic rifle and a box of cartridges. He'd take the sheriff's advice. He worked the gun's action to make sure it was empty, and the dog, sitting in the doorway, cocked his head at the sound.

*　　*　　*

John Compton called Jimmy early the next morning, just at dawn. Jimmy threw his blanket off and fumbled for his phone. Pale light showed through the windows of the Eyrie as the sky outside brightened. John asked him if he wanted to go fishing.

"What time is it? Jimmy asked grumpily.

"It's time to go fishing, Bro."

"What are you doing up this time of day? The sun's not up yet."

"Time's a wasting. A man brought his car to my shop yesterday. It needed a new muffler. Anyway, he told me that he and a buddy caught their limits of smallmouth bass up at Seven Islands a couple days ago. I figured we'd go up there and catch a few."

"Was there any size to them? Most of the fish in the Cheat tend toward smaller ones," Jimmy said.

"That's the good part. They caught several sixteen-inchers. One was over eighteen. That's a decent smallmouth. What do you say? You going to get your sorry butt out of bed and go with me?"

"Yeah, I suppose. I'm already awake. I might as well go. What time will you be here to pick me up?"

"Now!"

"What do you mean, now?"

"I'm in your parking lot, so get a move on."

"Can I at least have time to go to the bathroom?"

"Yeah, but hurry. I can feel those smallies hitting my fly already."

They loaded Jimmy's gear in the back of John's SUV. The dog watched nervously, and Jimmy didn't have the heart to put him in his kennel.

John said, 'Oh, what the hell. Let him come, too." When invited, the dog bounded into the back seat and thumped his tail against the expensive leather upholstery.

John drove eastward on the Corridor H highway to its end near Elkins where they took US 219 to Parsons. There, they turned north on Route 72. They stopped at a tackle shop near St. George to load up on snack food and soft drinks. Soon, they turned off on the narrow Seven Islands road that wound along the river. John pulled off the road and killed the engine. When released from the confines of the vehicle,

Yellow Dog bounded around exploring the area. The two men sat on the back bumper of the SUV with the hatch door up while they pulled on their waders and assembled their rods.

Jimmy had received an update on Sam's condition the evening before, and he relayed what he knew to John. Sam was still in critical condition and had not awakened. John asked, "How long do you think he'll be in the hospital?"

"There's no way of telling. When he wakes up, the doctors will be able to better assess his condition. Sam can tell them where it hurts, but until then, they'd only be guessing if they made a prediction."

"Yeah, I guess so. I hope he recovers."

They spent a few minutes more talking about Sam, but the conversation soon turned to fishing. They opened their fly boxes and spent a few moments debating with which carefully tied fly to begin. They tied their selections onto the lightweight leaders on their fly lines and walked to the edge of the river. The river bed was made up entirely of a jumble of flat rocks with rounded edges. Most ranged from the size of a man's fist to that of a desktop. The rocks were a deep shade of brown, almost black, and made excellent habitat for the bronze-backed smallmouth bass. The river's water was crystal clear. Jimmy waded into the swiftly flowing stream until it reached his knees, positioning himself so he could cast to just the right spot.

He had chosen a grey ghost streamer fly and cast it across the deeper, main current, allowing it to float downstream. He twitched it occasionally, mimicking a minnow in distress. On the second cast, he felt a solid strike and set the hook expertly. The rod bent in response to the drag produced by the fish as it turned its body against the current. Keeping his rod tip up and a constant tension on the line, Jimmy soon had the struggling fish in his landing net. He gripped its lower jaw and held it against the handle of his rod, measuring its length. It was fifteen inches long. Not quite what John had promised but good enough. He carefully released it into the water and watched it shoot back into the main stream.

They fished away the morning, catching and releasing fish. Most were in the ten to twelve-inch range, and none were over fifteen. Jimmy suspected John had exaggerated the fishing report given to him by his customer, just to get him to go fishing with him. As the sun rose over Limestone Mountain, the day became hot. The direct sunshine on the water put the fish down, and they trudged back to the SUV. The dog was laying in the shade of the vehicle, his tongue lolling from his mouth. He was mud-splattered. His yellow coat was matted with burrs and stickers. John took one look at him and said he'd have to walk home. The dog dropped his head and looked up at him with soulful eyes. Jimmy withdrew an old towel from his gear bag and cleaned the squirming dog. He'd come prepared.

They loaded their fishing gear into the back of the SUV and retraced their route back to Parsons where they stopped at a sandwich shop for a late lunch. They were soon on the road again and arrived back at the Eyrie by mid-afternoon. John said he'd clean all the fish this time—a joke because they always released the fish they caught. As John drove away, Jimmy stowed his fishing gear in the back of the Cherokee and stepped into the cabin. The light on his land-line phone's answering machine was blinking.

"Hey, Dr. Houston. This is Donald. Sam just woke up. He's groggy and can barely speak, but he's been talking a little bit. The nurses won't let us talk to him more than a few minutes at a time, and he sleeps a lot. A lot of what he says doesn't make much sense, but the doctor said that was to be expected. His body has been through a terrible shock. I thought you'd want to know. I tried to call your cell phone, but you must have been out of range of a tower or something. Anyway, we're all excited about his recovery. The doctor said he should be okay. She did a lot of tests on his brain and couldn't find any damage, so it looks like he'll be alright mentally. I guess I'm rambling, but anyway, I thought you'd want to know he's awake. Oh, yes. He's asking for you. Wanted to know where you were." Donald went on excitedly, repeating most of what he'd already said until the answering machine finally cut him off.

Jimmy slumped onto the chair at the table by the window. He put his head down on his folded arms for a few moments and mumbled a few words of thanks. He sighed a big sigh of relief, but he still felt responsible for getting Sam involved in this mess. If he hadn't talked him into trying to find Scott's killer, he wouldn't have been shot. He remembered Sam had been enjoying himself in Key West when he'd called and enticed him to come home and take on the case. Jimmy knew that once he told Sam about Scott's murder and especially where the body had been found, his curiosity would get the better of him. No, Jimmy felt he should have left Sam in Margaritaville where he'd been having fun, minding his own business. He was relieved that Sam would survive but wondered what kinds of lasting injuries he might have. Would he be able to walk? And, if so, how long would his recovery take, and at what cost? Would he have permanent disabilities? He was lucky to be alive but unlucky because he was shot. The analytical part of Jimmy knew the only person who was responsible was the shooter. The emotional part of him knew he was responsible for putting Sam in the killer's sights.

He walked out on the deck and stood at the railing. The sun was making its final arc toward the horizon and beat down on the wooden flooring with a pleasant mid-summer fierceness. Insects, normally vocal and persistent, were silent in the heat of the day, and birds perched quietly in the shadowy forest that surrounded the cabin. It would be dark in a few hours.

Chapter 20

Jimmy called Sheriff Donovan to let him know Sam had regained consciousness. The sheriff said he'd already been notified by the hospital, and that Sam was able to talk and had scheduled a time to interview him. Then, Jimmy sent a text to John updating him on Sam's improvement. On a whim, he texted Sylvia at the college, telling her that Sam had awakened. Once that was done, he threw some clothes in his overnight bag, put the dog in his kennel and drove to the hospital.

He met Donald in the waiting room. They talked quietly as they walked down the long hallway to Sam's room. He'd been moved to a standard room but was still attached to an incredible array of monitors and other equipment. Bags of mysterious solutions dripped into tubes that ran into needles in his arms. His torso was still heavily bandaged, and the bandage remained on his arm as before. Susan sat quietly on a chair in a corner and smiled warmly at Jimmy when he entered.

She said, "He's sleeping now. He goes in and out, sleeping most of the time. He'll want to talk to you when he wakes up. He's been asking for you. Don't expect too much. He can't talk long before he goes back to sleep, but he's making progress. He's way better than he was just yesterday. Why don't you sit there?" She nodded toward the chair. "We'll be out in the waiting room." She left with Donald.

Jimmy stood at the foot of the bed with his hand resting on the metal footboard. Sam breathed in and out rhythmically. He'd lost weight, and his face was narrow and haggard-looking. The skin beneath his eyes sagged, and he had a stubble of gray beard. The skin on his neck sagged as if the air had been let out of him. He stirred in his sleep. He shifted around in the hospital bed, and his right hand twitched much like Yellow Dog did when he was dreaming. Jimmy wondered if Sam was dreaming, too, about the shooter coming for him. Jimmy sat in the chair in the corner and tried to imagine what it must have been like to be hunted like an animal. Had Sam been afraid? Had he tried to run away? What was he thinking while the bullets whizzed and snapped through the air near his head?

Jimmy suddenly remembered what it was like to be shot at. A colleague who'd killed one of Jimmy's students had tried to frame him for the murder and later had taken shots at him. He'd been in his cabin when the assailant had fired at him. Luckily, he hadn't been hit, but not for a lack of the killer trying. He'd narrowly escaped. He'd been afraid and would have run if he'd had the opportunity.

Sam groaned in his sleep and stirred again. A few minutes passed. He opened his eyes and blinked rapidly, trying to focus. He cleared his throat and said in a hoarse voice, "Raise this thing up, so I can see you better," referring to the bed. Jimmy found the remote and raised the head of the bed. Sam nodded when it was where he wanted it. Jimmy held a glass of water with a straw, so Sam could drink, wetting his lips.

"You better watch yourself, Jimmy. Whoever did this to me will come for you, too."

"I know, Sam. Sooner or later he'll try to stop me. Maybe even the sheriff."

Sam nodded. He tried to raise himself in the bed, but fell back, exhausted.

"Did you see who shot you?" Jimmy asked.

Sam shook his head slowly from side to side. "No, just glimpses through the trees. He wore dark clothes. He may have had his face covered because I don't remember seeing any bare skin." Sam stopped talking and closed his eyes.

Jimmy thought he'd gone back to sleep, but he opened his eyes again and said in a weak voice, "I went there looking for that Indian rug."

"Do you think that's why he shot at you? To stop you from looking at the rug?"

"No, probably not. He'd have no way of knowing why I was there. I didn't tell anybody I was going to go look at it." He caught his breath and then said, "Probably followed me there."

"Wendy told me you were asking about it and that she'd suggested you look for a tag. Did you find one on it?"

Sam shook his head weakly again. "No, I didn't have time. He started shooting right away."

A nurse stepped into the room and told Jimmy that he'd have to leave. Sam needed his rest, and she had some bandages to change. Jimmy squeezed Sam's toe and told him he'd be back later. He paused in the doorway to look back at his friend. He'd fallen asleep.

Jimmy returned to the waiting room and sat with Sam's family. Later, Donald and Joan decided to go to the cafeteria for dinner, and Jimmy stayed with Susan. They talked quietly. Susan looked exhausted. She told Jimmy about Sam's slow return to consciousness and asked Jimmy what he'd said. He told her about the rug and said Sam couldn't identify the shooter.

Sheriff Donovan strode into the waiting room and Jimmy introduced him to Susan.

"Have you been in to see Sam, Professor?" the sheriff asked.

"Yes. And before you ask, he can't identify who shot him. He said he saw only glimpses of movement through the trees."

"The shooter stood over Sam while he shot him in the chest. Didn't he see him then?"

"I didn't ask that specific question, but he can't identify the shooter. I guess you'll have to ask him yourself."

"I plan to do that." Turning toward Susan, he asked, "Is it okay if I go in and see him now?"

"Yes, whenever the nurses say it's okay. We've left instructions that it's okay for you to talk to him when he's strong enough."

The sheriff left to talk to the nurses. Jimmy and Susan sat quietly, staring at the silenced television sets suspended from the ceiling until he returned. "He's sleeping now. They gave him a sedative, so he'll be out for a while." He frowned at Jimmy, then asked, "What else did he tell you?"

Jimmy said, "I asked him about the Indian rug. He said he didn't get a chance to look for a tag. The shooting started as soon as he walked in the house. He wanted to see where the rug came from. You know, who bought it?"

"Does he think someone shot him to keep him from looking at the rug?"

"No. He thinks the shooter followed him there. The house is remote. What better place to ambush someone? He said he didn't tell anyone he was going to the farm."

"Frankly, Professor, I don't think the rug has anything to do with this."

"Why do you think that, Sheriff? It was out of character for Scott to buy such an expensive item."

"Maybe so, but if the shooter thought it was important, why did he leave it in the farmhouse after he shot Sam? It' still there."

"That's a good point. Maybe you're right. Do you have a problem with me going there to look at it?"

The sheriff stared at Jimmy for a moment, and then said, "I thought I told you—you're off the case."

"Oh, I know. I'm off the case, but what harm would it do if I just took a look. If it has a tag, it might lead us to whoever bought it. Then, we'd have an answer. We..." Jimmy changed direction, "*You* could move on to something more important."

"I'll say one thing for you, Professor, you don't give up easily. Tell you what. I'll send a deputy up to Scott's farmhouse with you, and you can look for a tag on the darned rug. Then, maybe you'll let the matter rest."

"It's a deal, Sheriff. How soon can we go?"

The sheriff laughed, "Well, not tonight. It's dark and I haven't had my supper. I'll call the office and set up a time. You can meet the deputy first thing tomorrow."

"That'll be great but make it later in the afternoon. I want to stay overnight and see Sam in the morning before I go home."

"That'll work. I'm going to have to come back tomorrow. Sam's going to be out for several hours, and I can't hang around here until he wakes up. Call me if he says anything else important." He said to Susan, "I'll be back tomorrow afternoon to take a formal statement. I hope he's up to it. If not, we'll get it later." He expressed his sympathy to Susan and left.

Jimmy checked into a motel and slept better than he had since Sam's shooting. The next morning, he spent some time with Sam. Sam had asked about the murder book. Jimmy told him it had been taken by the shooter, but he'd been able to recreate most of it. Sam said that pretty well cinched it. If the shooter took the murder book, he must have also killed Scott. He undoubtedly shot Sam and took the murder book to stop the investigation. Jimmy said that was what he thought, too. Sam tired quickly and Jimmy told him he'd be back in a few days to check on his progress.

Late that afternoon, Jimmy met Chris Franklin, one of the sheriff's deputies, at the entrance to Scott's farm. They unlocked the gate and drove their vehicles to the house. When they approached the front door, Chris whistled and said, "Would you look at that. The front of the house looks like a sieve."

Inside, they gawked at the damage that had been done by the barrage of bullets. The front room was shot to pieces. Glass crunched under their feet as they walked. Framed pictures hung at crazy angles on the walls, riddled with bullet holes. Others lay on the floor where they'd fallen. The television set had a bullet hole in its screen, and lamps were shattered and lay on the floor.

Chris said, "I can't imagine how Sam survived this. According to the tech reports, he wasn't hit in the front room. He must have crawled into the kitchen. They found some of his blood there."

Jimmy squatted beside the Indian rug and turned its edge back on itself, exposing its underside. There was no tag. He walked to its other end and did the same. Attached to the edge of the rug, in its exact center, was a small tag. It was made of stiff cloth with a tight weave. It contained a signature written with a fine-pointed Sharpie pen and a city name and state. It read: *Rosa Yazzie, Chinle, AZ.*

Jimmy sat back on his heels and wondered what it meant. He had little doubt the rug was authentic, and probably worth many thousands of dollars. Had Scott bought the rug directly from Rosa Yazzie, or had he bought it secondhand from someone else? Had someone given it to him? If so, who? He used his phone to snap several photos of the tag.

When he stood, he saw Chris looking nervously out the front window. "I hope that dude didn't decide to come back and start shooting at *us*. It makes my skin crawl just thinking about it. You don't suppose he's out there, do you?" He rested his hand on the grip of his Glock.

Jimmy stepped to the window and looked out, too. He shook his head and returned to the rug. He found a broom in the kitchen and swept the glass and debris off it and then turned it completely over. The underside was meticulously done with a tight weave and attractive border. It was as beautiful as the topside. Without a doubt, the weaver was a highly skilled artist. Jimmy turned it back over and returned it to its original position. He stepped back and admired its brilliant colors.

Chris left the window long enough to write some notes about what Jimmy had done to the rug—sweeping it off and turning it over. The sheriff had trained him well. He had Jimmy sign a form stating he had examined the rug and moved it from its original position. Jimmy took a photo of the form with his phone for the murder book. When they'd left Scott's property, Jimmy dutifully stopped along the road and made his own notes. When he'd finished, he sat for a few minutes wondering what to do next. He'd need to find Rosa Yazzie and ask her who had bought the rug. But, Arizona was a big state. How could he find her? Maybe she had a Facebook account. He decided to wait until he got home to start his search.

It was almost dark when he pulled into his parking area. The dog was happy to see him after his absence of more than a day. Jimmy released him from his kennel and laughed at his antics as he ran in circles and tried to get Jimmy to play with him. He found a large stick and carried it to Jimmy, imploring him to throw it for him to retrieve. Jimmy tired of the game of fetch before the dog and took his overnight bag into the cabin. He dumped his dirty clothes in the clothing basket and tossed the empty bag on his bed.

He was hungry but decided to wait until later to eat. He sat at his laptop and began a search for Rosa Yazzie. A Google search of her name revealed a long string of people with the name Yazzie. Evidently, it was a common name, but he didn't find anyone with the name Rosa. A search including her name and the words "Indian rug," brought a bewildering list of companies selling rugs. Computer searches were becoming less and less useful because of companies advertising their products. They pushed out the search results you wanted and replaced them with useless advertising.

He took out his old, battered road atlas and quickly located Chinle. It was in the north-eastern corner of Arizona, at the entrance to Canyon De Chelly National Monument. Another search on his laptop led him to the website for a Navajo trading post in Chinle that posted a long list of rugs for sale. As he scrolled down through the listing, he whistled at the asking prices. Each listing provided a photograph of the rug, the name and photograph of the weaver and a short biography. Rosa Yazzie wasn't listed.

He wondered if it was too late in the day to call the trading post. He did a quick calculation for the time in north-central Arizona, remembering it was one of the few states that didn't observe daylight savings time. He recalled traveling through Arizona some years back with friends on one of his plant-finding excursions. It had been the joke of the day when they stopped for food or gasoline to ask each other, "What time is it *here*?" There was a time zone change out there somewhere—he couldn't remember exactly where—and if he remembered correctly, the Navajo Nation observed daylight savings time although the rest of the state didn't. While he traveled the state, his GPS and phone couldn't figure out what time it was in any given location.

He decided to call the trading post and see if they were open. A pleasant voice answered on the second ring. She stated the name of the trading post and said her name was Betty. She asked him how she could help him.

He told her he was looking for the weaver who had made a rug he'd seen. He didn't tell her the owner had been murdered.

"Yes, I know Rosa Yazzie."

"I looked through your website listing and didn't see her name. Does she sell rugs through your trading post?"

The young woman said, "No. She doesn't."

"Is there some reason she doesn't?"

"Yes. She doesn't need us. She's one of the best weavers in the area. Her rugs sell as fast as she can make them. She has a waiting list. We'd love to have some of her work, but she doesn't sell wholesale."

"Oh, I see. Do you know how I can get in touch with her?"

"Well, that'll be a problem. She lives way out there on the canyon rim. She's traditional. That means that she doesn't have a phone. If you want to talk to her, your best bet is to go talk to her in person."

"I live in West Virginia."

"That's a beautiful state. I drove through there one time on my way to D.C., but it's a long way from Chinle."

"Yes, it is." Jimmy thought for a moment. "Is there someone I could hire to go talk to her?"

"I suppose, but I don't know if she would talk to him. I still think your best bet is to come here and talk to her in person. Look, mister, my boss's looking at me. I have to hang up. He doesn't like for us to tie up the phone."

"Just one last question. Does she come in to town?"

"Yes, of course, but I don't have any way to know when. She doesn't come very often."

"Could I leave a message for her?"

"I thought you said that was your last question," she said, exasperation in her voice. "I suppose you could, but she doesn't come in here. She doesn't have a reason to."

Jimmy thanked her for her help, said goodbye and hung up the phone. He was discouraged. He seemed to be stymied at every turn. How was he going to find out who had bought the rug?

Chapter 21

Jimmy spent two days in his office catching up with correspondence and organizing the research he'd done in Costa Rica. He wanted to get everything organized before he began to forget details. He cleaned up data files on his laptop, wrote two outlines for papers he planned to submit to scientific journals, and put plant specimens in presses to be dried for eventual mounting and identification. The results would be a nice addition to the college's herbarium.

The next day, he drove to the hospital to visit Sam. He perched on the foot of his hospital bed and talked to his good friend. He was pleased to see that Sam had improved significantly in the last few days. His face had filled out, and the IV bags were gone, but the boxlike monitor was still there, beeping and making endless graphs of his vitals. Sam had bragged that he now could go to the bathroom by himself, but it was an arduous journey involving a walker and the watchful eye of a nurse.

"The doctors told me I could go home in another week or two. I'm ready to get out of this place. The nurses wake me up all hours of the night. A man can't get a good night's sleep." As if on cue, a nurse entered the room and studied the vitals monitor. She made notes on a small laptop computer she carried and then rushed out of the room.

Jimmy told him the results of his trip to Scott's farm to look at the rug. "The weaver's name is Rosa Yazzie. She lives out in the desert near Chinle, Arizona."

"Chinle. I was there once. That's near Canyon De Chelly. Ruthie and I went there one time. We toured that whole area. It's a very interesting place. It has lots of history, and it's beautiful, too."

"What do you remember about it? Was there a trading post there?"

Sam pulled on his earlobe. "No, I don't remember a trading post. But then, that was thirty years ago or more. There could have been. I remember we did a tour of the canyon led by a Navajo elder. He told us the history of the place. Tragic." Sam leaned back on his pillow and caught his breath. It would still be some time before he regained his full strength.

Jimmy said, "I'm thinking about flying out there to talk to Rosa Yazzie. As I said, she lives out in the desert and doesn't have a phone."

"It's just a suggestion, but why don't you have the sheriff call the local cops out there and have one of them do the interview? It would save you a lot of time and money."

"I suppose, but I'm getting to be a lot like you. I'd rather talk to her myself. Besides, the sheriff told me to butt out of his investigation."

Sam chuckled and said, "I figured he'd do that. Don't blame him. He's just trying to protect you."

"Yeah, I know, but..."

"He came in and interviewed me. I gave him a full statement, but I don't think it'll help him much. I never saw the shooter's face. Maybe I've blocked it out of my memory or something. All I remember was a dark form standing over me, and then the lights went out. Could have had a mask over his face, I guess."

"Is the sheriff making any progress in finding the shooter?" Jimmy asked.

"No, not much. They have a lot of crime scene evidence, spent shells and such, but none of it has provided a lead on who did it."

"What about you? Do you have any idea who did it?"

The question brought a frown to Sam's face. "I've wracked my brain trying to figure that out. The result is I don't have any idea."

"According to your notes, you interviewed Seth Buckman just before you were shot. Could he have done it?"

"I've thought about him. When I interviewed him, I got the impression he was interested in Wendy, almost obsessive. Frank Richmond said the same thing, that Seth was jealous of her. I suppose he could have looked at Scott as a rival and knocked him in the head with a rock in a fit of jealousy. He wasn't any too friendly when I talked to him."

"Yeah, when I was at the saloon talking to Wendy, he seemed friendly enough, but somehow, I got the impression he wasn't sincere. Like he was trying too hard to be friendly. He's a big guy. He would have had the muscle to get Scott's body up in that tree."

"Maybe you should try to get the sheriff to interview him. He might get something out of him."

"Okay. I'll do that." Jimmy slid off the edge of the bed and walked to the window. He could see a constant stream of people coming and going from the parking lot far below. "So, you're thinking that maybe Seth got worried that you were looking into Scott's murder and shot you to stop the investigation. Is that right?" Jimmy turned to look at him.

"I don't know. He could have done it, but there's not one scintilla of evidence that he did. Maybe if the sheriff could search his home and business and find the weapon it could be proven, but no decent judge would give him a search warrant."

"So, where does that leave us? Where do we go next?" Jimmy asked.

Sam shook his head. "I'm about at a dead end. I guess I'm not thinking too good. The doctor said my brain had been deprived of oxygen for a while. Maybe I'm not thinking as fast as I used to." He leaned his head back on the pillow and stared up at the flyspecked ceiling tiles. "Always before, if I got stuck on a case, I'd go back over the murder book. I'd read every page and look at every report. I'd look at the crime scene photos. Sometimes, it worked. I'd get a new clue. Other times, nothing. Did you bring it with you?"

"Yes. It's out in my Jeep."

"Why don't you give it to me? I've got nothing better to do. I'll go through it again. Maybe something will jump out at me."

"Are you sure you're up to it? I don't want you to have a relapse or something."

"I'm okay. I'll just have to take my time. I'll rest when I need to."

There was a timid knock on the door, and Jimmy turned to see Sylvia standing there holding a large bouquet of flowers and a box of chocolates.

*   *   *

The next day, Jimmy caught a flight from Pittsburgh to Albuquerque. He'd shelled out almost five hundred dollars for the ticket but felt it would be worth it. He landed in Albuquerque early in the afternoon and rented a car. He drove west on I-40 to Gallup, then on Rt. 264 through Window Rock to Ganado. From there, it was a short, scenic hop to Chinle. He hadn't been in the southwest for several years and was enthralled with the hard-rock scenery through which he drove. The trip from Albuquerque to Chinle had taken almost four hours, and he was tired when he checked into a motel on the outskirts of town.

The following morning, Jimmy entered a nearby restaurant and was seated in a booth with worn leather seat covers. A young Navajo woman filled his water glass and gave him a menu. She was pretty and wore a mix of traditional and modern clothing. Her wrists were decorated with silver bracelets that jingled as she worked. Her long black hair was pulled back in a single, loose plait. He ordered a full breakfast of bacon, eggs and coffee.

While his food was being prepared, he looked around the room. There was a mix of booths and tables, and a few early diners sat on stools at the bar. The place was clean and orderly, but all the fixtures were well worn. The diners spoke quietly in a pleasant mix of English, Navajo, and Spanish. He could hear the cooks and other employees in the kitchen talking and laughing as they worked. Waitresses came and went hurriedly.

He enjoyed his breakfast served with hot-sauce and tortillas. It was good. When finished eating, he lingered over his coffee and planned his day. He'd come a long way and hoped he'd be able to find out who bought the rug. If Rosa Yazzie gave him a name, that would make his travels worthwhile. If, on the other hand, she didn't keep records of who bought her rugs, he'd try to get a description of the buyer. Either way, he was determined to get an answer.

He paid his bill and asked the waitress for directions to the trading post. It was just down the road, she said. He couldn't miss it. Her directions had been accurate, and he found it along the main drag through town. It was a smallish, wooden building with a false front. A narrow porch spanning the front of the structure held rocking chairs and a variety of novelty items for sale. A bell tinkled as he entered. Glass-topped display cases dominated the room and were crammed with silver jewelry of every description. Many of the items were set with turquoise and other valuable stones. The walls were hung with a wide selection of paintings of the local area. Many featured stone formations in Canyon De Chelly. Toward the back, wooden racks attached to the walls were hung with brightly colored Indian rugs. Other items, obviously made by native artists, filled every nook and cranny of the store.

Jimmy approached the clerk at the sales counter at the front of the room and smiled. "I'm Jimmy Houston from West Virginia. Are you Betty?"

A look of surprise crossed her face. "Yes, I am." She was a middle-aged woman with piercing brown eyes and long black hair. She wore traditional clothing; long white skirt, long-sleeved velvet blouse encircled with a belt of silver medallions, moccasins, and silver jewelry. "I see you found your way here without a problem, Dr. Houston."

It was Jimmy's turn to be surprised. "I don't recall telling you I hold a doctorate."

Her laughter was musical as she said, "We have computers here. I did a Google search on you. I hope you don't mind. You're quite famous in your state. You're the professor who was framed for murder."

Jimmy laughed and said, "Yeah, I guess I've had my fifteen minutes of fame. I'm glad it's over."

"If you came all this way to find the identity of the person who bought a rug from Rosa, you must be involved in another murder. Is that right?"

"Yeah, I guess I am. Along with a former state policeman, we're trying to find out who killed a man in our community. The rug might provide a much-needed clue."

Betty smiled again and said, "Well, I hope I can help you find the killer. Maybe I'll have fifteen minutes of fame, too. I thought you might show up here looking for Rosa, so I talked to a friend. He's willing to drive you to her house. I'll call him now, if you want me to."

Jimmy said he was pleased that she'd made arrangements for him. Within a half hour, a young man entered the trading post. He was tall and thin and wore jeans and a long-sleeved shirt with pearl buttons. He wore a well-used, wide brimmed hat and strode toward Jimmy confidently. He said his name was Johnny and for a small fee, he'd take Jimmy where he wanted to go. They quickly struck a bargain, and Jimmy led him outside to his rental car. As they drove out of town, Jimmy asked, "How do you know Rosa? Is she a relative."

Johnny chuckled and said, "Yeah, she's my great-aunt, but in our culture, she's more like a second mother." He recited a long litany of relationships that identified his clan.

They fell silent as Jimmy drove as directed along the rim of Canyon De Chelly. The canyon was impressive with vertical walls of yellow sandstone streaked with dark streamers of desert varnish. Stacked rock monuments arose from the canyon's floor, and Jimmy caught a glimpse of ancient cliff dwellings tucked into alcoves in the canyon wall. The rim of the canyon was dotted with juniper trees, pinyon pines and a wide variety of desert plants. Jimmy saw sagebrush, cliffrose, mesquite, and several varieties of yuccas and agaves. Ravens, perched in trees, watched with wary eyes as they drove by. Jimmy longed to stop the car and explore the local flora, filling the car's trunk with a treasure of specimens, but he knew he didn't have time. His return flight was booked for the next day.

Johnny told Jimmy to turn off on a narrow rut of a road toward a small house set against a towering butte. A long spiral of red dust rose behind the car as they approached. The white-painted, wooden house was small and tidy with a large 4x4 pickup truck parked in front. Sheep grazed in the mesquite nearby. A four-posted trellis with a brush roof stood beside the house and cast a dark square of shade on the hard-packed earth beneath it. A large wooden weaving loom stood under the trellis along with baskets of yarn and dyes. Racks of other weaving supplies, whose use was a mystery to Jimmy, stood within arm's reach.

When they stopped in front of the house, Johnny suggested that they wait. "In our culture, it is polite to wait until the occupant of the house is ready to receive guests. When she's ready, she'll let you know it's all right to approach the house. She'll turn on the porch light or step out, so you can see her."

They waited. The temperature in the car began to rise as the late morning sun beat down on them. They rolled down the windows, catching a cooling breeze. After fifteen minutes, Jimmy had begun to think Rosa wasn't home. Johnny grinned at him. "She's getting ready to receive you. She knew you're coming."

"How could she? She doesn't have a phone."

Johnny laughed loudly. "It's called the moccasin telegraph. Believe me, within a few hours of your call to Betty, she knew all about it. She knows why you're here, and she's been waiting for you to arrive."

Jimmy smiled and said, "Back where I come from, we learn things by the grapevine. I guess it's the same thing, but ours isn't quite as efficient."

"I'd guess every culture has something similar," Johnny said.

"I hesitate to ask this, not knowing the proper etiquette, but does she speak English?"

"A little, but she'll probably only use Navajo. I can translate. It's not uncommon for our elders to speak only their native language. Some understand English, but don't speak it well."

A small woman, dressed in her best finery stepped out onto the porch. Johnny opened his door and walked toward the house. Jimmy followed along behind him. She was a beautiful, elderly woman who wore clothing like that Betty had worn. With a sweep of her hand, she invited them to sit on the porch.

Johnny introduced Jimmy, telling her where he was from. Jimmy spoke one of the two words of Navajo he knew. "*Ya at eeh,*" he said, sure that he was badly mispronouncing the greeting.

The woman smiled at him and spoke at some length in return. Johnny said she had given the traditional greeting by listing her ancestors in her Dine. He told Jimmy she wanted to know about his ancestors. "Give her the names of your parents and grandparents," Johnny suggested. Jimmy told her the names of his mother's parents first, then his father's. The woman listened carefully. When he was done, she nodded.

They spent the next hour talking about the weather, his long trip, what he did for a living, and everything except who had purchased the rug. Jimmy told her he thought she had a beautiful place in which to live. She asked about his home, and he described his cabin on the mountain. She grinned when he told her his friend, Sam, called it a bird's nest.

She got up abruptly and went in the house. A few minutes later she returned with coffee served in beautifully painted earthen pots. They sipped and talked. Jimmy enjoyed their conversation immensely. He was disappointed when she abruptly stopped, and he was afraid he'd said something wrong.

Johnny said, "She's ready for you to ask about the rug now." The old woman looked at him expectantly.

Jimmy cleared his throat and said, "A man who lived in our community had one of your rugs in his home. I need to know who bought it from you. I would be grateful if you would tell me."

Through Johnny as interpreter, the old woman asked, "I have made many rugs in my long life. How am I to know which one he had?"

Jimmy showed her a photo of the rug on his phone. She took one brief look at it and nodded. She spoke at length to Johnny.

"She wants to know why the owner of the rug can't tell you who bought it himself," Johnny said.

"The owner is dead. He was killed last fall."

Johnny said, "She wants to know where he was killed. Was it in a house with the rug?"

"No, he died somewhere else. The police don't know where, but they're sure he wasn't killed in the house."

Johnny said, "That's good, because in our culture, when a person dies in a house, we believe his spirit lingers there. It can't get out. Spirits can be bad, even those of good people, causing all kinds of trouble. No one should ever live in a house where someone has died. And, if the rug was in the house, well you can see the problem. She wouldn't even want to talk about it."

The old woman looked seriously at Jimmy and nodded.

Jimmy reassured them that Scott had not been killed in his house. Johnny looked at Rosa and she spoke a few words to him.

Johnny said, "She will tell you who bought the rug now." Rosa spoke again to Johnny, who said, "The person who bought the rug was a *bilagaana*, a white woman. Her name was Sandy Lynch. She bought it three or four years ago. Rosa doesn't keep records of who buys her rugs, but her daughter does, so I'm pretty sure that's accurate. Does this help you?"

"Yes. It doesn't tell me who the murderer is, but it's helpful. I now know that I should talk to Sandy again. She's the deceased man's niece. She must have given it to him. I asked her earlier if she knew where he had gotten it, but she didn't answer the question. I wonder why?"

They talked for a few minutes more, and then Jimmy used the other Navajo word he'd memorized to say goodbye. "*Hagoone*," he said, okay/all right then.

Rosa smiled at him and said, "*Hagoone*."

On the way back to town, Johnny said, "Rosa liked you. That's the only reason she agreed to tell you who bought the rug. You took time to talk to her. In our culture, that's important."

"Well, I liked her, too. She's a very special person, and her talent as a weaver is extraordinary."

Johnny began laughing. "I didn't tell you everything she said to me. She told me she'd like for you to meet my cousin Rosalina. She's named for Rosa, and she's not married. She's thirty years old, and Rosa is worried she'll never find a man. Rosa thought the two of you would be a good match."

Jimmy laughed uncomfortably, "I'm honored, but I think I'm a confirmed bachelor."

"That's not all she said. She gave you a name. From now on, you'll always be known as Bird Man." He couldn't stop laughing, "When you told her your friend said your house looked like a bird's nest, well, that was all it took. So, Bird Man you are."

When he dropped Johnny at the trading post, he went into the store to thank Betty for her help. When he stepped up to the counter, Betty said *"ya at eeh"* and some words in Navajo he didn't understand. When she saw the puzzled look on his face, she burst out laughing. "It means, 'greetings, Bird Man.'"

"How did you know about my new name," Jimmy demanded. "You haven't even talked to Johnny yet."

She was still laughing. "Oh, all you *bilagaana* think we're still back in the nineteenth century. Johnny has a cell phone. He sneaked a text message to me while you were driving back."

"Johnny told me about the moccasin telegraph. He didn't say you used cell phones to get the word out," Jimmy said, laughing.

Betty asked, "Did you find out who bought the rug from Rosa?"

"Yes, I did. It was a woman I know from back home. Her name is Sandy Lynch."

"Sandy? I know her. She was in here all the time a few years back. I haven't seen her for a while, but she hung around a lot, talking to us, asking all kinds of questions about our culture, especially about our religion. She showed up at a lot of the ceremonial dances and at our meeting houses."

"Are you sure it was Sandy?"

Betty described her. "Is that the same person you know?"

"Sure sounds like her."

"I don't want to talk out of place, but she became something of a bother. Some of our ceremonials are strictly religious. We don't allow outsiders, but she showed up anyway."

"Yeah, I can imagine what would happen if outsiders came to *our* religious services to gawk at us. I'm sorry she did that."

"Oh, no problem. We're used to it."

Jimmy said, "So, she was kind of a hanger-on?" He prompted her, trying to get her to tell him more.

"Yes. She even started dressing like we do. You know, moccasins, lots of silver jewelry, velvet blouse. The whole thing. That's okay, but she kind of overdid it."

"Do you know why she stopped coming here?"

"Well," she hesitated. "The telegraph said that she went somewhere else. Someone said she asked a lot of questions about Plains Indians. What would we know about them? Maybe she went up to Montana or somewhere."

He thanked Betty and got in his rental car. He had a four-hour drive back to Albuquerque ahead of him and a plane to catch first thing tomorrow. He looked at the time on his cell phone and decided there might be time for a few stops along the way to do some botanizing. Maybe he could smuggle a few plant specimens on the plane for the herbarium at the college. And, the drive would give him time to think through what he'd learned. Why hadn't Sandy been more forthcoming with him? He was sure he'd asked her if she knew where Scott got the rug but couldn't remember what her exact answer had been.

As he drove, he wondered what Sam would make of his discovery. Maybe nothing. It could be that they were making more of this rug thing than it merited. Just because it was out of character for Scott to have such an expensive item didn't mean it had significance, especially if Sandy had given it to him. He was anxious to get back and talk it all through with Sam. Sam was going back over the murder book. Maybe he'd find something of importance.

He was suddenly stuck with a disturbing thought. Surely the moccasin telegraph wouldn't work all the way back to West Virginia. It would be a disaster if Sam and John found out he had a new name. They'd never let him live it down. He could hear them now, calling him Dr. Bird Man.

Chapter 22

Jimmy stopped at the hospital on his way back from the airport in Pittsburgh. He was pleased to see Sam sitting in a chair by the window when he entered the room. He had improved considerably in the last several days since Jimmy had seen him. A large bouquet of wilting flowers and a half-eaten box of chocolates sat on the stand beside the bed. Sam was dozing with the murder book open on his lap. His reading glasses were perched on the end of his nose. He opened his eyes when Jimmy approached.

"Hey, Professor," he said with a strong voice. "It's good to see you back home. What did you find out?"

"It's good to see you up and about, Sam. You're looking a lot better. When do you get out of here?"

"I'm feeling pretty good. I might even get to go home early. The doctors are still worried about infection, but so far, so good. Enough about me. Did you find out who bought the rug?"

Jimmy sat down in a chair facing him. "Yes. I did, but you're the detective. Who do you think it was?"

"Come on Jimmy, I don't feel like playing games. Just tell me."

"Give it your best guess, Detective. Who do you think it was?"

Sam thought for a moment and then said, "Sandy Lynch."

Jimmy's eyebrows rose. "You're right. How did you figure that out?"

"Simple logic. I was pretty sure Scott didn't buy it. Wendy and Frank said they didn't know where it came from. That leaves Sandy. She's his closest relative. I could see her giving it to him as a Christmas gift or something. Maybe for his birthday."

"If you already knew who bought it, why'd you let me go all the way out there to talk to Rosa?"

"Well, I didn't know for sure. I was guessing. Besides, it's always important to confirm what you already have guessed."

"I suppose so," Jimmy said. He told Sam about Sandy hanging around the Navajo ceremonials, making a nuisance of herself.

"Sounds like she was an Indian wannabe. It happens sometimes. Someone admires another culture so much, they try to become a member themselves."

Jimmy asked, "What does all this mean to our investigation?"

"Beats me. Maybe nothing. Sometimes these things are dead ends. I knew Scott didn't go out and buy that rug. Now we know who did. End of story."

"Not entirely," Jimmy said.

"What do you mean?"

"I asked Sandy if she knew where Scott got the rug, and she evaded answering my question. I wonder why she did that?"

"Hmmm. That's an interesting question. Are you sure she was evasive, or did the conversation just drift away in another direction? That happens sometimes. You ask a direct question, and the person you're questioning has something else pop in his head, and he begins talking about that. Even in normal conversation, not all direct questions are answered directly. Ruthie used to do that to me. We'd be talking about one thing, and the next thing I'd know, she'd be talking about something entirely different."

Jimmy thought back to his conversation with Sandy. He couldn't remember exactly how the conversation had gone. Maybe he was making more of this than he should.

"There's one way to clear this up. I'll talk to her again."

Jimmy told Sam about his trip to Chinle and how much he enjoyed seeing Canyon De Chelly. He said he'd like to make another trip out there. He described his conversation with Rosa, conveniently leaving out any discussion of his new name. He related his conversation with Betty, giving Sam more details of Sandy's intrusion into their culture.

Sam asked questions and told Jimmy of the events of his earlier visit there with his wife.

Jimmy said, "I see you're still reviewing the murder book." He nodded toward the book in Sam's lap. "Any new insights?"

Sam shook his head. "No, not really. Seth Buckman's a person of interest, but there's no law against being jealous of a pretty woman. We could talk to him again, but I doubt anything would come of it."

"I think the sheriff was going to interview him. Maybe I can talk him into telling me how that turned out," Jimmy said.

"There is one thing. Whoever killed Scott had a motive. You don't just brain someone with a rock without a pretty good reason. We just need to figure out what it was. Once we know that, we'll have the killer. Jealousy is one possibility. Money is another."

"But, Scott didn't have anything of value. How could money be a motive for his murder?"

"How sure are we that his property can't be developed? If Sandy figured out a way to develop it, that would be quite a motive. It's worth millions if it can be sold for housing lots or any other kind of project. He was going to give it away."

"It's pretty straightforward. The Endangered Species Act of 1973 was passed by the federal government to protect those species threatened with extinction. I've done a ton of environmental impact statements and have run up against the Act a time or two. The EPA's a terror to work with. They'll protect that fern species with all the might of the federal government. There's no way around that piece of legislation."

"I suppose so. If I remember correctly, Sandy said she was going to donate the property to the nature preserve as Scott wanted. We didn't follow up on that. She said she'd talked to a lawyer about it. I wonder if she actually did."

"I don't know how we could find out. A lawyer wouldn't tell you a thing about her business because of lawyer-client confidentiality."

Sam said, "Maybe you could just ask Sandy. You're going to ask her about the rug anyway. You could ask her then."

"Okay, I will." Jimmy waited until a nurse took Sam's blood pressure and heart rate before he continued. "As far as motive goes, maybe Scott saw something he wasn't supposed to see. Like a drug deal or something. He could have learned something that someone didn't want exposed. A simple, onetime thing."

"Yeah, who's that philosopher you're quoting all the time? The one who believed that the best answer to a question is the simplest one?"

"William of Occam. His philosophy is called *Occam's Razor*. He believed the simplest solution to a problem is almost always the best. He argued that simplicity is better than complexity."

"Yeah, that's the one. Maybe we're over-analyzing this. You might be right. It could be something simple." Sam looked at Jimmy over the top of his reading glasses. "Like money."

A nurse entered Sam's room and told him it was time to get back in bed. He needed his rest. While they were tucking him in, Jimmy stepped into the hallway and called the sheriff. It took a bit of finagling, but he finally told Jimmy what he wanted to know. He ended the call and walked back in Sam's room.

"The sheriff interviewed Seth Buckman again. It seems he objected to being questioned about Scott's murder. One thing led to another, and he took a swing at one of the deputies. He was charged with assault and taken to jail. He's out on bail now. Looks like he has a short fuse and tends to violence."

*   *   *

As he drove back to the Eyrie, Jimmy thought about Sandy Lynch. She seemed like a perfectly normal young woman. She was bright and articulate. She had worked hard to establish a business and seemed to be well liked in the community. Was she capable of murder? Could she hit someone with a rock in a fit of rage. Probably. But then, a lot of people could. People murdered other people in fits of rage every day. Hunting Sam down and shooting him in cold blood was another thing altogether. Could Sandy do that? Had she shot Sam? He hoped she hadn't. He liked her. She was bright, attractive and pleasant. But, he'd been fooled by women before.

When he arrived home, he let Yellow Dog out of his kennel and endured his enthusiastic welcome. He played toss with the dog's sock dummy until they both tired of it. He tossed his travel bag on his bed and collapsed into the easy chair by the woodstove. He was anxious to get back in his usual routine. He'd been away from home more than was usual for him. John had accused him of being stuck in a rut. Maybe he was right, but sometimes being in a rut was good. It gave his life structure.

He put a pot of coffee on the stove to percolate and set up his brass telescope on the deck. The day was pleasantly warm, and the sky was filled with fluffy white clouds, like cotton balls. He focused on Dana's farm and saw a column of white smoke rising from a newly cleared field. She was burning brush again. He panned the telescope to her gate post and saw a white plastic bucket hanging there. He took his phone from his pocket and dialed her number.

She answered immediately. "Hi, Jimmy. You've been gone. I've been checking up on you with my telescope."

"Yeah, it's been a busy couple of weeks for me. I noticed you've been gone, too. When did you get back?"

"A few days ago. I had to make a quick trip back to Manhattan. I finished up my job, and I'm as free as a bird. It's a good feeling."

"Congratulations. Do you feel like celebrating tonight? How about dinner?"

"Sure. What time and where?"

Jimmy gave her the name of a restaurant near the college and suggested they have dinner at seven. They talked for a few minutes, and when he broke the connection, he felt a tingle of anticipation. He'd enjoyed talking to her before and looked forward to getting to know her better.

Later that evening, he went to the closet and looked at his meager collection of clothing. He'd lost all his clothes when his house burned almost a year before, and he'd been negligent in replacing them. He'd bought just enough for work and let it go at that. Jeans and dress shirts were the order of the day in the biology department. He'd purchased one good suit and a sport coat for the rare occasion when a coat and tie was required. Even chinos and a sport coat were a little dressy for the restaurant he'd selected, so he decided on jeans, a well-worn dress shirt and his sport coat. He took a quick shower and shaved. The dog watched with amusement, Jimmy suspected, as he dressed.

Jimmy picked her up at the farm and drove her to what he considered the best restaurant in town. It was upscale with an excellent menu. The food was exceptional. The fact the food was reasonably priced was a bonus. A hostess escorted them to a table and said a waitress would be by to take their orders. They were quiet for a few minutes as they studied their menus.

"Jimmy, I have to admit I was a bit nervous until I saw how you were dressed. I forgot to ask about the proper attire. I was worried I'd be underdressed." She'd worn tight jeans sprinkled with rhinestones, low heels, and a sensible blouse. He couldn't decide what was different about her hair, but he liked it. She said, teasing, "I thought maybe you'd wear a tweed coat with elbow patches. Maybe you'd smoke a pipe. Isn't that what professors wear?"

"Oh, my tweed coat's at the cleaners, so I had to wear this old thing." He gestured toward his coat, grinning. He reminded her he'd lost all his clothing in a house fire, and he hated shopping.

"Yes, I remember you said your house had burned. I have the opposite problem. I have too many clothes. I had to dress the part for my job. Business power suits, high heels, the works. I don't think I'll need them on the farm."

The waitress came by and took their orders. Nearby tables began filling with an eclectic mix of town's people and college personnel. A few students were sprinkled in for good measure. A quiet hum of voices competed with recorded music that issued from speakers arranged around the room. A low stage in a corner was set up for live music.

"Dana, have you thought about what kind of job you'd like to have?"

"Yes, I have. I'm going to take some time off before I go back to work, maybe travel a little, but I'll need to get back in harness soon. I could probably work from home, but I'm not thrilled about that. I'm something of a people person. I'd like to do something where I deal with the public. Do you have any suggestions?"

"Jobs are in short supply here, unless you'd like to teach at the college. We have a strong business program, and you'd fit right in."

"I hadn't thought about that. It would be interesting, so maybe I'll give it a try. I wonder if they have any openings."

"I can put you in contact with the dean. Give him a call. Even if there isn't a tenure track opening, you might want to consider adjunct work at first. That would get your foot in the door."

"Thanks, I'll do that. I'd thought about hanging out my shingle as a financial advisor but teaching sounds much more interesting."

The waitress brought their food, and they talked quietly as they ate. Dana asked him how Sam was doing.

He said, "He's doing much better. He thinks he'll be able to go home soon, but I don't know about that. He'll need help for a few weeks, or maybe several months. He'll have to take physical therapy for quite a while. He's regaining his strength quickly but getting up to speed will take time."

"Is he still working with you on the investigation?"

"Yes. You can't keep him down for long. When I left him this afternoon, he was pouring over the murder book and arguing with the nurses." Jimmy told her about his trip to Chinle. "I just got back this afternoon. It was an interesting trip." He told her Sandy Lynch had bought the rug. "We're not sure what that means. It may be a dead end, but we'll keep looking."

"You live an interesting life, jetting around all over the place, doing research in jungles and chasing killers. I thought professors stayed in their ivory towers, wrote boring papers, and taught an occasional class or two." She wasn't being serious, and he liked that.

"Oh, we do a lot of that, too. Chasing killers is just a hobby," he said, laughing. "You have an interesting career, too. What's it like living in Manhattan?"

"At first, it was very exciting. Everything moves so fast. There's lots to do, and I met many interesting people. I liked my job and the people at work. I made several good friends and we'll try to keep in contact.

Most of the people I worked with have lived all their lives in the city. I'm thinking of inviting some of them to come to the farm to visit. It'll be a real shock to them. Just as much a shock as I had moving to the city."

"Do you think you'll be satisfied here after living such an exciting life in the big city? Life moves slowly here, and this isn't exactly a thriving metropolis."

"Oh sure. I grew up near here, remember? I'm ready to slow down. Life in the city is such a rat race."

"When we talked earlier, you said you didn't like being married. I thought it was every young girl's dream to get married, settle down and raise a family. You seem to be anything but conventional." After saying that, he was immediately worried he'd become too forward.

"Not all relationships have to end in marriage, but when they do, the marriage certificate should read like a legal contract. Think about it. If a man or woman was aware of all the legal ramifications before they signed on the dotted line, they'd probably never do it. If there's a divorce, there will be financial consequences, alimony, child custody and support, disputes over who gets the house, maybe even education expenses if one or the other needs job training. That doesn't even consider the emotional trauma. Half the marriages in this country end in divorce. That's not a very good track record. I know a couple who split up. They fought for years over who got custody of their dog. Their divorce wasn't final until the old pooch finally died. Imagine the legal fees they racked up." She caught her breath. "And if a man or woman is killed, who is the first person the police suspects? The spouse. What does that say about the state of matrimony?"

Jimmy held his hands up in surrender. "Okay, okay. I understand. You have a point. We don't have to get married," he said jokingly. He smiled at her, liking what he saw. She had grit.

"Oh, I'm sorry. I got up on my soap box, didn't I? I didn't mean to. I hope I didn't put you off. It's just that…" She worried her napkin, twisting it into a knot. "I guess I *am* unconventional. I don't make excuses. It's who I am."

"Does this mean you'll pay for dinner tonight?" He grinned at her.

"Heck no. You're on the hook, Buster. You asked *me* out, remember?"

They ended up splitting the check. He drove her back to the farm in his old Cherokee. Its engine was making a strange sound and was smoking a little. He'd have to remember to have John look at it. They sat in her driveway with the windows rolled down. Night sounds flowed through the open windows, and the damp summer air held a slight chill. Far away, they heard a coyote yip and Brutus answered from the darkness with his deep booming voice. Fireflies dotted her fields in a low-lying layer.

"Do you ever get lonely living here, Jimmy? It's so quiet compared to the city."

"No. Being alone is different from being lonely. My friend, Sam, calls me a hermit. Maybe I am. But, to me, this is the best of all lives. I have solitude when I want it, and I can go out and socialize when I want to. I'm in control. Solitude is good, but in small doses, I suppose. I guess that's selfish—seeing friends only when I want to see them."

"As I said before, you're the only person I know who lives on top of a mountain in a glass house, but I've never thought of you as a hermit," she said.

He couldn't see Dana's face to read her expression. Speaking words from darkness was far different from speaking them in broad daylight. He knew what Rosa Yazzie would call him, living alone in his nest. Perhaps one day, he'd tell Dana.

He walked her to her door. The mountain air was clear, and they could see a dazzling array of stars in the night sky. Dana pointed out the milky way, the big dipper and several other constellations. She'd earned a badge for star-gazing as a girl scout when she was a kid, she said. It was one of many things she missed while living in the city. You could never see the stars.

"You're old-fashioned, Jimmy, walking me to my door. A city man would have dropped me at the curb and sped away into the night."

He replied with an exaggerated accent, "As we mountain folk say, my momma brung me up right."

"And, you're a funny man. I like that. You have a great sense of humor."

He stepped close to her. She caught her breath when he drew her against his chest. Their first kiss—the best of all kisses—was long and lingering. The earth continued spinning in its orbit, but for them, it hesitated for just a second.

Chapter 23

It was early morning, and the dog was loudly crunching his kibble when Jimmy called the sheriff. "You'll probably be interested in some information I have."

The sheriff harrumphed and said, "That'll be the day—you giving me information. You're always trying to weasel it out of *me*."

"Come on, Sheriff. You know I have your best interests at heart. Do you want to hear what I have or not?" Jimmy said it with laughter in his voice.

"Yeah, go ahead. Let's hear it."

"Sandy Lynch bought the rug in Scott's house."

There was silence on the other end of the line, and then the sheriff slowly said, "And so…?"

"That clears up the mystery. She bought it in Chinle, Arizona, from a weaver named Rosa Yazzie."

"And, just how do you know this?"

"I flew out there and talked to Rosa."

Exasperation showed in the sheriff's voice when he said, "First, I thought I told you to stay out of this case. Second, it's obvious Sandy gave it to Scott. What does that have to do with who killed him?"

"We're not sure. But at least we know where it came from."

"Okay, so now we know," the sheriff said. "Now, what is it that you want to know from me? It's obvious you have something else in mind."

"You told me earlier that you'd arrested Seth Buckman for assaulting one of your deputies. Did you ask him if he had an alibi for when Sam was shot?"

"Yeah, I asked him, and we even interviewed some of his employees. He said he was at the saloon, but his employees couldn't swear that he was there all day. Apparently, he's in and out, doing whatever it is that business people do."

"So, he doesn't have an alibi?" Jimmy asked.

"No, he doesn't."

"What about Sandy Lynch. Does she have an alibi?"

"We asked her, too. She said she was working in her store on the day Sam was shot."

"Do you consider that a valid alibi?"

"No, not really. I suppose she could have closed her shop for a couple of hours and no one would have been the wiser unless someone she knew came by looking for her. We can't confirm her alibi, but we can't prove otherwise either."

"One more question. Sandy said she was going to give Scott's property to the nature preserve. Did you ask her if she'd actually talked to a lawyer about it?"

"No. It never entered my mind to ask. Why should I? The property's worthless, so why should I ask about it?"

"Just wondering," Jimmy said vaguely.

"Is there anything else you want to know, Professor?" the sheriff asked sarcastically.

"No, that's about it, for now."

The sheriff reminded him again to stay out of his case. And then he said, "Have you taken my advice about carrying a gun? That shooter's still out there, and if you keep asking questions, he'll come for you sooner rather than later."

"Yeah, I have a rifle. I keep it in my Cherokee."

"Is it where you can reach it quickly?"

"Well, no, not exactly. I keep it in the back of the Jeep, in a case," Jimmy said reluctantly.

"Jeeze, Professor, you might as well leave it at home. If someone takes a shot at you, you'll be dead ten times over before you can get to it."

"Okay, Sheriff. I get the message. I'll be more careful."

*   *   *

A few days later, Jimmy was in his office at the college when his cell phone vibrated. He'd been preparing for the new class he was scheduled to teach in the fall. The beginning of the school year was fast approaching.

It was Sam. "Hey, Jimmy. The doctors just discharged me. They finally said I could go home."

"That's great, Sam. I'll bet you're ready to get out of there."

"Yeah, I'm ready. Look, here's the problem. Donald's back at work, and nobody else can come pick me up until later this afternoon. Could you come and get me? I hate to ask."

"Sure, Sam. I'll be right there. I'm at the college now, so I can be there within an hour."

Jimmy made it to the hospital in forty-five minutes. When he pulled under the canopy at the front entrance, Sam was waiting for him in a wheelchair attended by a grumpy-looking nurse. Jimmy got out of the Jeep and opened the passenger side door.

"How long have you been waiting out here, Sam?" Jimmy asked.

"Oh, we just got here," he said.

The nurse rolled her eyes and shook her head. "We've been waiting for a while. He couldn't wait to get out of here, and frankly, we're ready for him to go home." It was obvious to Jimmy that Sam hadn't been a good patient lately, but the nurse patted him on the shoulder and wished him good luck. Sam hobbled from the wheelchair to the Jeep. Jimmy was pleased to see he needed little help.

On the way home, all Sam wanted to talk about was the murder case. With good reason, he was especially interested in who had shot him. Jimmy told him about his earlier conversation with the sheriff.

"You say he actually answered your questions about his mix-up with Seth? I'm surprised he's still talking to you. He told you to butt out, but there you are, still getting him to give you information," Sam said. "I'm impressed."

"I think the sheriff's more bark than bite. He's really a softie at heart."

"Maybe. So, Seth doesn't have an alibi?"

"No, and neither does Sandy. Either one of them could have shot you. Kelly Rice could have done it, too. If you ask me, we're not making much progress," Jimmy said, complaining.

"Didn't Kelly say she saw a white car leaving Scott's farm the day I was shot? What color is Sandy's car?"

"Oh, I forgot to follow up on that. I'm going to talk to her again, so I'll find out."

They drove along the Interstate for a few minutes, each lost in his own thoughts. Sam broke the silence. "It's none of my business, but are you seeing that woman who lives on the farm near your cabin. The one you watch through a telescope?"

"Now, it's not like that, Sam. It's not like I'm spying on her. Besides, she watches me through her own 'scope," Jimmy said, becoming a little defensive.

"Sounds a little kinky, Professor. That includes her. What was it you used to call her? Laughing Woman?"

"To answer your nosy question, yes, I'm seeing her. As a matter of fact, we went out to dinner a couple of days ago, and she raised an interesting point. She said that when a man or woman is killed, the first person the police look at as a suspect is the spouse."

"Yep, that's true. Are you saying that we should look at Wendy as the killer? She wasn't Scott's spouse, but they were planning to be married."

"I know we talked about her before, but maybe we should look at her again," Jimmy said.

"There's one fly in the ointment that we can't get around. She asked us to try to solve the murder. Why would she do that if she was the murderer?" Sam asked.

"Yeah, I remember, but I've been thinking about that. She called and asked me to do some investigating. She didn't ask you to help. I dragged you into it. What if Frank pressed her to talk to me, and she agreed, maybe reluctantly, thinking that a bumbling college professor wouldn't be a threat. Remember it wasn't me who was shot. Evidently, the shooter thought you were more of a danger than me, or I'd have been the one in the crosshairs."

They rode in silence for a few miles while Sam mulled over this new theory. He finally said, "I suppose it's possible, but my radar isn't zeroing in on her as a killer. She seems like a very sincere lady."

"I guess you're right, Sam, but, I'm getting frustrated. The more I think about this, the more I go around in circles. I'm at a dead end. Except for asking Sandy a couple of questions, I don't know what to do next."

"Okay, lets go back to basics. What are the main questions we need to answer? We've talked about motive, and the sheriff checked on alibis. Neither of these are proving helpful. There's a few other questions I think we need answered."

Jimmy snapped his fingers and said, "Why put the body in the tree?"

Sam nodded. "That's one. Another is; Who is strong enough to do it?"

"But the killer might have had help or used ropes and pullies."

"True. He could have. We also need to know who has access to an AR-15. That's what the sheriff said was used to shoot me."

"Good luck with that. It's not a problem to get a weapon like that. Half the people in the state probably own one" Jimmy said.

"Yes, but they had to have background checks done when they bought it, unless it was from a gun show or an individual. Maybe we'll get lucky. The sheriff has probably checked on that already. Maybe you can ask him."

"Maybe, but I think the well's already dry with him. He probably won't want to answer any more of my questions. Maybe you should try him," Jimmy said.

"Okay, I will. We also need to know where Scott was killed, but if the sheriff hasn't already figured that out, our chances are practically nil."

They were still discussing the case when Jimmy pulled into Sam's driveway. There were balloons attached to his mailbox, and a large poster attached to his front door read *Welcome Home.* Sylvia stood on the porch smiling at them.

Sam looked at Jimmy with a pained expression on his face. "Don't get the wrong idea, Professor. She's just here to help me get settled in."

Jimmy smirked, held up both hands and said, "Hey. It's none of my business."

*　*　*

Jimmy looked up the number for Sandy's shop on his cell phone. When he called, she answered with a cheerful voice.

"Hi, Jimmy. What can I do for you today?"

"I have a couple of questions for you, Sandy. I hope you don't mind."

"Oh, I'm disappointed. I was hoping this was a social call."

Jimmy ignored her disappointment and got to the point. "When we talked the last time, I asked about the Indian rug in Scott's house. Do you remember that?"

"Oh sure. I told you I gave it to Uncle Scott for Christmas a couple of years ago. I told you that, didn't I?" She seemed to be unsure.

"No, I don't think you answered the question."

"Well, maybe I didn't. Why is it important?"

"It's just a loose end we're trying to tie up. We didn't think Scott would buy such an expensive item."

She laughed and said, "No, he wouldn't have. I thought he should have something to dress up that dreary old house of his, so I gave it to him. He seemed to really like it. Why are you asking about it?" Jimmy thought he could hear concern in her voice.

"As I said before, we're just tying up some loose ends. Would you mind telling me what kind of car you drive?"

"Why are you asking these questions? Are you trying to say I had something to do with Uncle Scott's death?" she asked, her voice raising.

Jimmy calmly said, "Sandy, we ask a lot of people questions. It's just about the only way we can eliminate them from our investigation. It would be helpful if you'd answer, so we can move on."

"Oh, all right. I drive an old sedan. I've had it forever." She named the make and model.

"What color is it?"

She laughed uncomfortably. "It's mostly white. It's dirty and there's a rust spot or two on it. I still don't understand why you're asking about my car."

"Just bear with me. I'm almost done." Jimmy hesitated to ask the next question, but plunged in. "You told Sam and me earlier that you planned to give Scott's property to the nature preserve. Have you talked to a lawyer about that yet?"

"Jimmy, I like you, but I don't think I want to answer your questions. You're not a policeman, and I don't have to." Jimmy could imagine her pouting as she held the phone. "I'm disappointed in you."

"Sandy, I promise this is the last question. Have you talked to a lawyer yet?"

She hesitated. Finally, she said, "No, but I plan to. I just haven't had time. It's what Scott wanted, so that's what I plan to do. Satisfied?" Jimmy could hear her sniffling. "I don't think I want to talk to you anymore." The phone went dead.

Jimmy sat for a moment looking at the dead phone in his hand. He chided himself. That went well. She was probably filing a complaint with the sheriff right now. He could imagine the tongue lashing the sheriff would give him for meddling in his case. Oh well, he thought, there wasn't anything he could do about it.

He punched a query into his phone and quickly learned that as of the previous year, thirty-six percent of all cars purchased were white. It was the most common color selected. All other colors combined made up the other sixty-four percent. There was about one chance in three that *anyone* driving by Kelly Rice's farm would be driving a white car. Hardly conclusive. On the other hand, it didn't exclude Sandy as a suspect. So far, nothing they had learned had excluded her.

He'd hardly put the phone back in his pocket when it vibrated. The phone's screen showed that it was Sam calling from his home.

"Hey, Sam. Are you settled in already?" Jimmy asked.

"No, but we're getting there. Sylvia's a big help." Jimmy could hear a vacuum cleaner running in the background.

Jimmy told him about his conversation with Sandy. Sam was interested, but Jimmy could tell he had something on his mind.

"That's good, Jimmy. I doubted she'd talked to a lawyer. All of that's important, but I think I've answered one of the questions we talked about earlier."

"Oh? Which question was that?"

"The one about why Scott's body was put up in a tree."

"Well, what's the answer?" Jimmy asked.

"Back when I was in undergraduate school..." Sam began.

Jimmy interrupted. "You mean back in the dark ages? Back when there were no computers or cell phones?"

"Do you want to hear this, or just mess around?" Sam asked, becoming a little grumpy.

"Okay, okay. Go on."

"I took an anthropology class. I don't remember why. I think it was required or something. Anyway, I remember the professor compared burial practices among various cultures. She said that long ago some Native American tribes placed their dead upon platforms. They buried them in the open air rather than in the ground to keep wolves and bears from digging them up and eating them. I remember seeing old photographs of the platforms with partially decomposed bodies still on them. When the whites invaded, they often robbed the platforms, taking anything of value, and in some cases the bones themselves. I'll bet the museums in D.C. are full of that stuff."

"That's right, Sam," Jimmy said excitedly. "I remember seeing those photographs, too. But Scott's body was in a tree. It wasn't on a platform."

"Yes, but it's the same idea, the same kind of practice. When this popped into my thick head, I went online to see what I could find. I looked up mortuary customs in North America and found an article about tree and scaffold burial. It turns out that if trees were available, they used them for burial. But, if they weren't, for example on the Great Planes, they constructed scaffolds."

"What does this mean, Sam? Are you thinking someone killed Scott, maybe in a fit of passion, and becoming remorseful, buried him in a tree?"

"Yes, and we both know who that person might be," he said.

"Sandy Lynch. She was an 'Indian wannabe,' as you called her. She'd know about Native American burial practices." Jimmy's enthusiasm faltered. "Wait a minute, Sam. Sandy spent time with Navajos. They didn't use platform burials. As a matter of fact, they didn't want anything to do with dead bodies and disposed of them as quickly as possible without ceremony."

"Oh. Well, maybe she read about them or saw old photos online like I did. Or, maybe she traveled around to different tribes after she left the Navajos."

"Yes, that's possible. Betty, the clerk at the trading post in Chinle, said Sandy planned to go visit the Plains Indians. Even if she did, they don't use platforms for burial anymore and haven't for more than a century."

"I still think it's a distinct possibility that Sandy mimicked their burial practices," Sam said, hanging on to his theory. "Sandy or some other person."

After their initial spurt of enthusiasm for Sam's discovery, their fervor began to subside. It was a good explanation for why Scott's body was found in a tree but was hardly conclusive. It still didn't provide a motive for his murder. Sam said in a court of law, it wasn't necessary for the prosecution to prove motive. It was a big help in getting a conviction, but not essential. All the state had to do was prove that one person killed another. Proving motive was a bonus.

Jimmy asked, "Where do we go with this? What's our next move?"

"Let me sleep on it, Jimmy. I think Sandy could have killed Scott in a fit of passion, but I'm not sure she has the nerve or talent to shoot me. Whoever that was had one thing in mind. He or she, wanted me dead. Women don't often shoot their victims. Poison is more likely their choice of weapon."

With a grim look on his face, Jimmy said, "Remind me to never eat the lollipops in Sandy's shop.

Chapter 24

Jimmy was at his desk at the college writing a syllabus for the new class when there was a knock on his door. It was Wendy and Frank Richmond. They apologized for interrupting his work.

"Come in," he said, smiling, and ushered them to chairs in his crowded office. He offered them coffee, but they both declined. "What can I do for you?"

Wendy seemed ill at ease, but she asked, "I'm not trying to rush you or anything, but have you and Sam made any progress on Scott's case? It's been several months now. I was just wondering." She looked hopefully at Jimmy.

"No, I'm sorry, we haven't. We were set back while Sam was in the hospital, of course, and I've been tied up with my work." Jimmy felt bad, but he wasn't comfortable telling Wendy what they knew about Sandy's possible involvement. He didn't want her to jump to conclusions and do something rash. He said, "We have some leads, and we're following up on them, but nothing seems to pan out." He told her about their theory of why the body was placed in a tree. "Remember, it's just a theory. We don't have any evidence that's what happened."

"But, why would someone do that? Aren't most funeral services religious? Scott wasn't very religious. He didn't go to church regularly, and tree burial isn't a Christian practice. Why would the killer think he needed to be buried at all?" Wendy was exasperated.

Jimmy leaned toward her and said, "We don't know that's what happened, Wendy. As you can tell, we're grasping at straws. We're as frustrated as you." He leaned back in his chair. "Let me ask you a question. What do you know about Seth's altercation with a deputy? I heard he was arrested."

"Oh, that was a mess. The sheriff and one of his deputies, Chris Franklin, came to the saloon to talk to Seth. They practically accused him of killing Scott. The argument began out in the restaurant area, then they went back to Seth's office. I could hear them yelling back and forth, and when they came out, Seth was in handcuffs. I couldn't hear what they were arguing about. Seth paid his bail and was back at work the next day. I guess there will be a trial sometime unless Seth pleads to a lesser charge or something."

Frank said, "I feel responsible. I told Sam that Seth was jealous of Mom, and he must have told the sheriff because he knew what I'd said. I guess Seth knows, too. That's what the argument was about. Chris told me about it later. To tell you the truth, Dr. Houston, I'm a little nervous about Seth being mad at me. I don't know what he'll do."

Wendy said, "Now, Frankie, you know Seth wouldn't hurt you. He's not like that. He's a pretty good guy when you get to know him."

"Okay, Mom. But, I don't want him to fire you because of something I said."

"Don't worry. He wouldn't do that."

Jimmy asked Wendy, "Had Seth and Scott ever argued?"

Wendy shook her head. "Sam asked the same thing. No, they hardly knew each other. They only met once or twice." She seemed uncomfortable talking about it. "I'm embarrassed that you'd think that Scott was killed because of me."

Jimmy said quickly, "We don't know that at all. We're just trying to follow up on any lead we have no matter how unlikely it seems. As Sam says, you never know when some little clue could lead to a major break. We have to ask all the questions we can think of."

"I know, Dr. Houston, but I'm getting frustrated. I'm sorry. I just want this to be over. I want Scott to be able to rest in peace. I think finding his killer will help him do that. I know it'll make me feel better," Wendy said.

"It's all right, Wendy. I understand."

They talked a while longer, and then they left Jimmy's office. Jimmy felt bad about suspecting Wendy of Scott's killing earlier. He guessed it had been a result of his frustration. She was a nice person, and he didn't know what had gotten into him. She would never do such a thing, and her shooting Sam was out of the question. He shook his head and returned to his work. He finished writing his syllabus and walked down the hall to the department chair's outer office to talk to Sylvia. He hadn't seen Sam for a couple of days and wanted to know how he was doing.

"Sam's doing great, Dr. Houston, but I'm worried he'll overdo it and find himself back in the hospital. One thing for sure, there's nothing wrong with his appetite. I can't seem to fill him up. He's going to physical therapy every day. It won't be long until he'll be able to drive."

"That's good to hear, Sylvia. I'm happy you're there to help him, but it looks like it won't be long until he can live on his own."

"I'm happy to do it. Sam's a good man, even if he gets a little snappy at times."

"Did he ever hire a housekeeper? I know he talked about it before he was injured."

Sylvia chuckled. "Yes, he did. He went online and found someone at one of those placement agencies. I think she'll work out okay, but the first day she was there, Sam followed her around making sure she did what he wanted done. I think she was thinking twice about working for him until he finally backed off and let her do her work."

Jimmy was laughing when he said, "Why am I not surprised? Has he been reading the murder book?"

"Yes, he carries it around everywhere he goes. He's going to wear it out if you two don't find that killer pretty soon."

Jimmy finished his work and picked up a large pizza on the way to Sam's house. He found him sitting on his front porch. His neighbor was standing in front of him wagging a finger at him, obviously angry. Sam had an annoyed look on his face. The neighbor left as Jimmy approached, and Sam grinned at him.

Jimmy sat down, holding the pizza on his lap, and said, "Looks like you and your neighbor were having a little disagreement, Sam. What's the story?"

"It's all your fault, *Dr. Houston*." Sam was still grinning.

"How could it be my fault, *detective*? He's not *my* neighbor."

"You remember when I kept your big dog while you were galivanting around down there in Central America? Chasing the native girls and who knows what else?"

"Yes, I do, and thank you again for taking care of him. And, by the way, I wasn't chasing native girls, I was working."

"So you say. Anyway, your dog, of his own volition, decided to do his business in my neighbor's yard."

"By any chance, did he do this more than once?"

Sam's grin faded a little, and he said, "Maybe."

"Look, Sam. You've lived in town long enough to know it works like this; you put the dog on a leash, walk him up and down the street, and when he does his business, you pick it up in a little plastic baggy and put it in your pocket."

Sam feigned surprise. "Is that right? People do that? What if they forget it's in their pocket? What happens if, for example, their wife or girlfriend or boyfriend, asks for some change and they reach in their pocket and..." By this time both men were laughing.

They took the pizza inside and ate out of the box in the kitchen. Jimmy found drinks in the refrigerator, and most of the pizza was soon gone. He was amazed how much Sam ate.

"Looks like your appetite has returned, Sam. It's good to see you're feeling better."

"Yeah, I'm doing okay. I'm getting around better every day, and the doctor will clear me to drive in another day or two. Even so, it's taken me longer than I expected. I guess my old body doesn't heal up as fast as it used to."

The doorbell rang, and Sam asked Jimmy to go see who it was. Sam could hear a mummer of voices from the front hallway. Jimmy returned to the kitchen with Sheriff Donovan following behind him.

The sheriff said, "I thought I'd stop by to see how you're doing, Sam. I was in the neighborhood. It's good to see you up and around."

"Thanks, Sheriff. Sit down and have a piece of pizza."

He looked at the almost empty box and said, "Looks like I got here just in time." There was only one piece left. Jimmy handed him a drink, and the pizza was gone almost immediately.

They sat around the kitchen table and talked about the case. Sam told the sheriff his theory about why Scott's body was placed in a tree. The sheriff frowned and pursed his lips as he listened patiently. Jimmy sat quietly, watching the sheriff's reaction. When Sam had finished, the sheriff was silent for a minute, strumming his fingers on the table top. Sam and Jimmy looked at him expectantly.

"That's quite a theory, Sam. I guess it's as good as any. Let me get this straight. You think Sandy was an Indian wannabe. Isn't that what you called her? You believe she killed Scott and then put his body up in a tree as a kind of funeral ritual because she was remorseful? She wanted him to have a decent burial?"

"Yeah, that's what we think. It's the only explanation that makes sense."

"What was her motive for killing him?"

Sam hesitated. "Well, we don't know. Maybe they got in an argument, and it got out of hand. But, you don't need a motive to get a conviction, sheriff."

The sheriff snorted and said, "Thanks, I'll tell the prosecuting attorney that. He'll be pleased to have the advice."

"Look, Bill. Here's what we have." He ticked the items off on his fingers. "She was the last person to see Scott alive. She was evasive when we questioned her about the rug. She doesn't have an alibi. She had to know about Indian tree burials. She inherits his property. Maybe she figured a way to sell the farm for a profit." Sam looked at Jimmy for support.

"Wait a minute," the sheriff said. "About not having an alibi. She doesn't need one for Scott's killing because we don't know exactly when it happened. Are you saying she shot you, Sam, and that's why she needs an alibi?"

"Well, someone sure as hell did. Don't you think the person who killed Scott also shot me?"

"Most likely," the sheriff admitted reluctantly. "But, frankly I just don't see Sandy shooting you, or anyone. That was a vicious attack."

"I have to admit that's a weak point in our theory," Sam said.

"Well, there's more than one."

"What we need is a warrant to search her house and car. There must be trace evidence in one or the other. Probably both. Oh, and I forgot. Remember that Kelly Rice said the car she saw near Scott's farm was white. Sandy's car is white."

"There's a lot of white cars around," the sheriff said.

"Thirty-six percent of them are white," Jimmy said. He got a frown from Sam for his effort.

"This isn't nearly enough to get a judge to give me a warrant."

"Can't you find a friendly judge that'll give you one?" Sam was grasping at straws, and he knew it.

"Huh. Are you kidding? We only have one circuit judge, and she's not very friendly," the sheriff said, grimacing at the thought of taking what he knew before her. "If you could find a motive, we might be in business. But until then, forget it."

*   *   *

Dana was to arrive at the Eyrie at any moment. Jimmy had invited her to come for dinner and observe the sunset with him. He hoped it would be a good one. He looked out a window to check on the sun's progress. It was about a half hour away from reaching the horizon.

Jimmy had dressed casually, donning a new t-shirt with the *Organization for Tropical Studies* logo on the front. He'd bought it at the research station in Costa Rica. He wore jeans and comfortable walking shoes. He looked in the tiny mirror in the bathroom and decided he passed muster. He heard the crunch of gravel as Dana's truck pulled into the parking area.

Jimmy and the dog met her at the door. She was dressed casually, too, in jeans and a short-sleeved blouse with a scooped neckline. Her glossy hair was pulled back from her face and she wore large hoop earrings. With the heels she wore, she was almost as tall as Jimmy. She handed him a bottle of wine enclosed in an elaborately decorated, cloth sleeve, tied with a bow.

"I thought I should contribute something to our dinner." She looked toward the stove and said, "Something smells good in here." She pecked Jimmy on the cheek.

"It's just gumbo. I'll serve it over rice with a chunk of hard bread. It's peasant food. It's simple to make. You just make a roux, throw in 'the trinity,' that's chopped onions, carrots, and green peppers, add some chicken stock and shrimp, some Cajun spices and anything else you have, and cook it up."

"Is that an old family recipe?"

Jimmy laughed. "No, our old family recipes tended toward meat and 'taters. My mother was an excellent cook, but I can't remember her ever making gumbo. Fried chicken with mashed potatoes and gravy, yes—gumbo, no."

"Are you a good cook? A lot of men are, you know. My father does most of the cooking in our family. Mom's a good cook, too, but she's happy to let Dad handle the meals. She's always off doing her painting in her studio."

"Oh? Is she a professional artist?" he asked.

"Oh no, not really. She just enjoys dabbling in paints. It's a hobby. She does mostly landscapes. She and Dad go driving on weekends photographing old barns, mountains and streams. She uses the photos as inspiration for her pictures."

"She must be pretty good to warrant her own studio."

Dana chuckled and said, "I made it sound more glamorous than it is. Her studio is an old shed she converted into a studio. She's handy with a hammer and saw, too."

"You have an interesting family. Has your mother sold any of her pictures?"

"Yes. She sells them locally at bazaars and gift shops. That type of thing."

The weather cooperated, and they ate at the table on the deck. The sun set behind the mountains right on schedule. It was an impressive lightshow featuring brilliant reds, yellows, and later, purple. They finished eating just as it became necessary to turn on the deck lights. Late summer insects began their evening serenade, and Jimmy could distinguish the call of tree frogs in the mix of sounds. The stars were beginning to shine when he cleared the table, taking the dishes into the kitchen. He returned with the wine bottle and topped off their glasses. House lights began to come on across the mountains, sprinkled like glitter from a child's hand.

"I understand why you live here on your mountain. It's beautiful. I can't see the sunset from my house. It's blocked by the mountain behind my property. But, the consolation is that I get to see the sunrise. The only drawback is that I have to get up so early to see it," she said wistfully.

"Yes, I like living here, and the sunsets are bonuses. Sometimes I wish I could live here year 'round."

"Why can't you?"

"This cabin isn't winter proof. It's livable for three seasons at best. Sometimes, it gets chilly here in early spring and late fall. My friend, John Compton, let me rent one of his condos last winter, but I think they're all full now. I don't know what I'll do this winter. I'll find something."

"Could you remodel it? Add some insulation, winterproof your plumbing? I'll bet the mountains are beautiful when they're covered with snow."

"I suppose I could, but I'm planning to rebuild my house near Cheat River. That'll take months, so I'll have to find something soon. How about you? Are you living at the farm full time now?"

"Yes. It's my home now. I'm looking forward to spending my first winter there."

Jimmy laughed. "Remember where you are. The winters can be brutal here. We had almost four feet of snow from one storm in January last year. Sooner or later, you're going to be snowed in. You have a long driveway and will need someone to come plow you out."

"Remember, I grew up in Kingwood. I know all about the long, cold winters and the times we were out of school for days. I remember when the National Guard had to use helicopters to help farmers who live near Terra Alta feed their livestock. I'll be okay, but do you know anyone who I could get to plow my lane?"

"Call John Compton. He owns an auto repair shop. He has a big truck with a plow on the front. His men clear my driveway when it needs it. He's reasonably priced, and they'll do a good job."

"Thanks, I'll do that. Have you known him long?"

Jimmy told her about going to school with John and their tendency to go fishing together at the drop of a hat. He asked, "How do you feel about living on the farm by yourself. It'll get pretty lonely at times."

"Oh, I'm not worried. I lived alone in the city. I was surrounded by people, but I was alone nonetheless."

"Maybe so, but the long winter nights can get pretty depressing. Some people suffer from seasonal affective disorder."

"I've never had that problem. Anyway, if I get really lonely, I'll send my drone over and invite you to dinner." She smiled and watched him carefully, trying to judge how he'd react to her ribbing.

Jimmy remembered their first contact. She'd sent a large, four-bladed drone to his cabin with a camera attached. It had scared him and the dog badly because he'd thought he was under attack by the deranged colleague who'd tried to kill him earlier. He'd been surprised, and the dog had hidden under the bed. It turned out the drone carried an invitation to dinner.

He looked at her and laughed. "That's an idea. This time, I'll know what to expect."

They talked until the air became uncomfortably chilly. Jimmy liked what he saw in her. She was outgoing and friendly, not to mention beautiful. Jimmy liked to make her laugh, enjoying their easy give and take.

They went inside, and Jimmy rolled his house plans out on the table. Jimmy pointed out the features of the house he especially liked, and she made helpful suggestions that he'd consider including in the final draft. He described the house his great-great grandfather had built, and he'd remodeled. He told her how saddened he'd been when it had burned. He still owned the property, and that's where he'd rebuild.

Before they knew it, the hour was late, and the wine bottle was empty. Reluctantly, she left for home. They'd held each other on the deck, under the stars, and shared the special intimacy that only two potential lovers could. He'd liked the way she fit against him and the whisper of her breath against his cheek. Their simple embrace gave them each a deep sense of promise.

Chapter 25

Jimmy was startled awake when his clock radio clicked on. He'd forgotten that it would come on automatically unless he turned it off before he went to sleep. It was six o'clock. It was already daylight. If he got up, he'd see the sunshine that streamed over the mountains behind the cabin light up the mountains at the horizon to the west. About now, they would be losing the last hint of pink color that came with each dawn. He didn't get up. He burrowed into the blankets wanting a few last winks of sleep. He'd enjoyed seeing Dana the evening before, and they'd lingered into the night.

He was sure the dog would hear the public radio announcer droning on and on and would soon want to go outside to do his business. But, until then, he'd enjoy a few last minutes of sleep. He was half conscious when the news announcer's words jarred him awake. He caught the tail-end of the report, and fumbled with the volume control, trying to hear what the woman was saying. He hadn't heard it all, but he'd heard enough to know why Sandy Lynch had murdered her uncle. She had a motive, and now he knew what it was.

He dressed hurriedly, checking his cell phone for the time. It was only six fifteen. He would talk to some of his acquaintances in the science community to confirm what he'd heard, but he'd have to wait until they were awake. In the meantime, he'd go talk to Sam.

By six thirty, he was pounding on Sam's door. The doorbell hadn't produced the results he wanted, so he pounded. The door opened, and Sam looked at him through sleepy eyes. He'd pulled on his pants and wore a rumpled t-shirt that showed signs that he'd slept in it. When he saw it was Jimmy who had pounded on his door, he shook his head and motioned him to come in. He led Jimmy into the kitchen where he began filling the coffee pot.

"Do you know it's only six thirty? With all the pounding on my door, I thought the house was on fire or something. What's going on?"

"Sandy Lynch has a motive for killing Scott. I think I know what it is."

Sam turned toward him, a spoonful of ground coffee suspended over the coffee pot. "You do? What is it? And, this had better be good. I was sound asleep."

"I heard it on the radio this morning. Our new president and the conservative Congress are going to eliminate the Endangered Species Act. They're saying it's a job killer, and they're going to get rid of it. According to this morning's news report, it's a done deal. They'll vote on it within a couple of days, and the president will sign it. He's weakened the EPA, and now this."

"I'll be darned. If that happens, it means Sandy will be able to sell Scott's property after all. But, how did she know they'd do it?"

"I need to talk to some of my friends who teach at other colleges. I know someone who keeps up on politics, especially when it comes to environmental issues. I've been out of the country and involved with this murder investigation, so I haven't been keeping up on this. We knew that as a candidate the president promised to get rid of the Act, but no one dreamed he'd be able to get it done. We all just forgot about it. I guess we were wrong."

Sam said, "Your science buddies won't be able to tell us how Sandy might have known about this last fall."

Jimmy slumped in his chair. "No, I guess that's true, but I just know that somehow she knew and that's why she killed her uncle. She knew she'd inherit everything. How are we going to prove it?"

Sam poured them each a steaming cup of coffee and sat down across the table from Jimmy. His face brightened. "We may not have to prove it. Remember, the sheriff said he'd ask the judge for a search warrant if we'd give him Sandy's motive for killing Scott. Even if we can't prove it absolutely, this might give the judge enough probable cause to issue a search warrant for Sandy's house and car. Probable cause isn't the same as absolute proof. It just means that more than likely you'll find something. A lot of search warrants come up dry."

"Don't forget her store. It should be searched, too." Jimmy chuckled and said, "I didn't know that 'more than likely' was a legal term."

Sam ignored his flippant response. "Let's not get greedy. If the sheriff finds anything at her house or in her car, he can get a warrant for the store later."

"Do you really think the sheriff will ask for the warrant? He's pretty cautious."

"He wants to nail Scott's killer as much as we do. I think he'll go for it."

They turned on Sam's small television that sat on the kitchen counter. All the cable news networks were reporting the breaking news. While Sam hobbled around in the kitchen making breakfast, Jimmy called a friend at a college in Maryland.

"Did you see this coming, Bob? "Jimmy asked. His friend was professor of environmental studies at his college. "I haven't heard a thing about it since the campaign."

"No, we were all blindsided with the news. We'd heard whispers about big changes coming to the EPA, but no one had an inkling that doing away with the Act was what the rumors were about. This is terrible."

"Do you think congressional leaders will be able to get this passed? They don't have a very good track record on getting things done. Especially in the Senate."

"I have a source close to the Secretary of the Interior. She's an intern in that office, a former student of mine. Anyway, I talked to her and she said they're very confident over there that it'll pass both houses. Of course, the president will sign it. She's guessing it'll be law by the end of the week."

Jimmy said, "I'm not so sure of that. Everyone thought Congress would be able to repeal Obamacare, but that didn't happen. The Senate leaders have found that trying to get their members to vote on anything is like trying to herd cats. No matter how popular it seems to be."

"Well, I hope you're right, but it looks like this is going to happen."

Jimmy told him about the case he was working on and why the morning's news was so important. They discussed the ramifications of the elimination of the Act on some of the sensitive botanical areas in which they were doing research. When Jimmy broke the connection, he was surer than ever this was Sandy's motive for murder.

Jimmy and Sam talked about the case as they ate breakfast. Jimmy said, "What happens to our case if Congress doesn't repeal the Act? What if their attempt falls apart at the last minute? I'm not sure it will pass."

Sam mumbled through a mouthful of eggs, "Doesn't matter. If Sandy *thought* it was going to happen, that was a motive. If this case ever goes to trial, the prosecutor will have to sort that out. The thing that's important now is to get a search warrant for Sandy's house and car. If the sheriff finds evidence of a fight in the house, or blood or something in the trunk of her car, that should be enough to convict her. End of case."

They spent the next hour going over the argument for a search warrant. They wanted to be able to convince the sheriff he had enough to ask for one. They made an outline of the evidence. They wanted to make it as easy as possible for the sheriff to write the application. All he had to do was fill in the blanks. They decided Sam was the logical one to call him.

"This better be good, Sam. I haven't had time to get my first cup of coffee." The sheriff was still groggy with sleep. They had awakened him at his home.

"What's happening to you, Bill? Are you on banker's hours now?" Sam asked.

"Huh. Sam, you remember how it was when you were a cop. I was out all hours of the night on a drug bust. We caught a bunch of local boys setting up a meth lab. Caught them red-handed. Seems as fast as we catch one bunch, another takes their place. It's a losing cause."

"I remember, Bill. I'm sorry to wake you so early, but we think we have a motive for Sandy's killing of her uncle. Have you had a chance to catch the morning news?"

"No. I was asleep, remember? You woke me up."

"Turn on your television while you put on your pants. How about meeting Jimmy and me at McDonalds in town? In, say, about thirty minutes? It'll take us that long to get there."

"I'm at your beck and call, Detective," he said sarcastically. "This had better be good. And, Sam...?"

"What?"

"You're buying breakfast."

"Okay, Sheriff. You got it."

*   *   *

The sheriff was eating a breakfast biscuit when Sam and Jimmy arrived. A steaming cup of coffee sat on his tray along with a paper sleeve of hash browns. They slid into the booth across from him. A cluster of retired men sat in a corner of the restaurant, drinking coffee and gossiping. They sneaked looks at them and tried to overhear their conversation.

"Aren't you going to eat?" the sheriff asked with his mouth full.

"No, we've already eaten," Sam said. "We've been up since the crack of dawn." Sam looked pointedly at Jimmy.

"Well, at least have some coffee. I hate to eat alone."

Jimmy bought two cups of coffee, and after they'd settled in, Sam asked Jimmy to explain why they were there. Jimmy told the sheriff about the pending repeal of the Endangered Species Act.

Yeah," the sheriff said, "I heard that on the radio as I drove down here. So, you're saying that's Sandy's motive for clubbing her uncle to death? How do you know she knew about it last fall when Scott was killed?"

"We don't know that for sure. But, as Sam says, it should be enough to get the judge to issue a warrant."

"Maybe, but it would make my life easier if we knew for sure. The judge's gonna ask, and I need to have a reasonable answer."

Sam spoke up. "When the president was a candidate, he promised his supporters that he'd weaken the E.P.A., and if I remember correctly, in one speech he actually said he'd do away with the Act. It was way back at the beginning of the campaign when he was making promises left and right. His opponents were making promises, too. If we could find a transcript of that, you could hand it to the judge as proof."

"Well, we don't have it, and I don't have any idea how we can get it. We'd probably have to get a news network that covered the campaign to look it up for us," the sheriff said. "That would take forever."

While Sam and the sheriff were talking, Jimmy was fiddling with his phone. He tapped a couple of buttons and turned the screen toward the sheriff. "Here it is." The three men hunched over the tiny screen. The presidential candidate, wearing his signature red baseball cap, was speaking before a cheering crowd of supporters. He was promising, if he were president, he'd provide jobs for everyone. He said he'd repeal the Endangered Species Act because it was a job-killer.

Sam leaned back and said, "Bingo. How'd you do that, Jimmy?"

Jimmy rolled his eyes and said, "I Googled it."

The sheriff said, "Okay. Maybe that'll be enough to get the warrant. Jimmy, send that link to my phone. I'll attach it to the application for the judge to view. Warrant applications are done electronically now, so that shouldn't be a problem."

Sam asked, "You mean you don't have to do paper warrant applications now? We used to have to hand-carry them to the judge for signatures."

The sheriff explained the department had received a grant from Homeland Security to update their computer systems. "Everything's going electronic, Sam. It's changing so fast, it's hard to keep up."

The sheriff left for his office to get the warrant application started; Sam and Jimmy followed along uninvited. When they got to the station, Sam's badge got them as far as the sheriff's outer office. There, they were told to take a chair and wait. A duty officer asked if they'd like coffee. They said they'd just had a couple of cups and declined the offer. They waited impatiently while phones rang, officers came and went, and the duty officer defended the sheriff's door.

Two hours later, the sheriff's door banged open and he rushed out holding an official looking document. Surprise registered on his face when he saw Sam and Jimmy. "I thought you'd gone home."

"Come on, Sheriff. We want to be in on this. Did you get it?" Sam asked.

"Yeah," he said proudly. "This is it. Fresh out of my printer." He waved the document at them.

"Does it include both the house and the car?"

"Yep. We're in business."

The sheriff assembled his men in the duty room. Sam and Jimmy sat in a corner and watched. He assigned six officers to help serve the warrant and secure the house and car. They'd keep curious neighbors away and manage traffic. The crime scene tech members were ready and would drive to the scene in the mobile lab unit. The sheriff and a senior deputy would manage the crime scene and serve as principal investigators. Jimmy was impressed with the sheriff's efficiency as he organized the operation.

It was after noon by the time the caravan of police cruisers, lab truck, and the sheriff's unmarked car reached Sandy's house. Sam and Jimmy brought up the rear in Jimmy's Cherokee. The officers quickly blocked off the side street where the house was located. There was little need since there was no traffic, but they did it anyway. Jimmy parked along the street as close to the house as they'd let him. They got out of the Jeep and stood close by as the sheriff knocked politely on the front door.

Sandy opened the door and looked at the assemblage of policemen with huge eyes. She stepped outside and closed the door behind her. The sheriff handed her the warrant, explained what it said and told her she'd have to leave the premises while the search was done.

"No, I'm not leaving. You have no right to do this," she blubbered, tears welling in her eyes.

"Yes, ma'am, the judge signed the warrant. We have every right. Now, please step aside. We'll make this as quick as possible. We'll give you a receipt for any evidence we take."

"Evidence of what? What are you accusing me of?" she wailed. "I haven't done anything wrong."

"Yes ma'am, I understand. The warrant lists the types of evidence we're looking for and tells you your rights."

"No!" she screamed. "You're not going in my house." She was becoming more agitated with each minute. She moved to block the doorway.

"Please step aside, Ms. Lynch. Don't make this harder than it has to be."

"I don't care what this paper says, you don't have the right to come barging in my home and taking my things," she shouted. She threw the warrant to the ground and stomped on it. "I'm going to call my lawyer. You can't go in there until I call him. He'll stop you, you'll see."

"You have every right to call a lawyer. But, in the meanwhile, we have authority to execute the warrant. Please step aside," the sheriff said.

She screamed at him, tears and mascara running down her face. "I'm gonna go get him right now. You'll be sorry." She headed toward her car with a purposeful stride.

The sheriff nodded toward a female officer who moved to block Sandy's access to her vehicle. "Sorry, ma'am. We're going to take the car, too."

Sandy pushed the officer with both hands and shouted, "That's my car. You can't take it. I need it. Now, get away from it." When the officer refused to move, Sandy grappled with her, knocked her hat to the ground, and tried to scratch her face. With a movement born from hours of training, the officer took her to the ground face down, pulled her arms behind her and deftly snapped handcuffs on her wrists. All fight left her, and Sandy began sobbing in earnest. Her shoulders shook, and she wept uncontrollably.

The sheriff instructed the officer to arrest her for assault on an officer and take her to the station. As Sandy was dragged away, she saw Jimmy and Sam watching. She implored Jimmy to help her. "Make them go away," she said. "Stop them from searching my house." As the patrol car pulled away, Jimmy could see her slumped in the back seat. She looked out the window at him, her face red and streaked with tears. Her eyes had a terrified look, and she mouthed the words, "Please help me."

Chapter 26

As the patrol car drove away with Sandy handcuffed in the back, the sheriff and his lead detective prepared to enter the house. They put paper booties on their shoes and snapped rubber gloves on their hands. A technician with an assortment of cameras stood by to photograph the crime scene. Other crime scene specialists unloaded boxes and crates of supplies in preparation to collect evidence. A driver with a flatbed truck loaded Sandy's car and hauled it back to the station to be examined.

Sam and Jimmy mounted the steps to the porch hoping to get a peek at the interior of the house. The sheriff stopped them and told them to wait outside. They loitered on the porch and looked in the front windows. An hour passed, and technicians came and went—strobe lights from cameras flashed inside. Sam tried to ask questions, but he was ignored; they were intent on their work.

The sheriff finally stepped out on the porch. "I think we got her. I think we found the murder weapon. Hang on a minute." He stepped back in the house and returned with a large plastic evidence bag with an Indian war club inside. The club was about eighteen inches long with a round stone the size of a baseball lashed to one end with rawhide. It had decorative paintings on its handle and bundles of feathers attached with lashing. It looked old. "I'm betting this is what she used to kill her uncle." He held it out for them to see. "Don't touch it," he said. An evidence label had been attached to the bag, and Jimmy guessed it was used to establish chain of custody.

"There's some other Indian artifacts in there and a stack of books on a coffee table, mostly about Indians. We'll look through them to see if there's any reference to tree burials. The tech guys are going through everything. It'll take hours for them to finish."

A technician stepped out on the porch and said, "We're ready to do the luminol spray now, Sheriff. You wanna come in and watch?"

"Yeah. Did you have any problem getting the room dark enough?"

"Nah. We pulled the blinds and put up some dark paper to block out the light. No problem."

While the sheriff watched the luminol tests, Sam and Jimmy sat on the porch and talked.

"Jimmy, do you know anything about luminol tests?"

"Sure. It's a chemical that glows when it comes in contact with iron. We use it occasionally in our labs."

"That's right. Blood contains a lot of iron in its hemoglobin. You have to darken the room to see the glow. The reaction only lasts a few seconds, so a technician will photograph the results. Any sign of blood should show up even if Sandy tried to clean it up."

"Will they use luminol on the war club to find any blood left when she hit Scott?" Jimmy asked.

"No, probably not. They'll take samples and test them for DNA. That'll be much more conclusive."

"What if they don't find any of Scott's blood? Owning a war club is hardly conclusive evidence she killed him," Jimmy said, "but if the shape and diameter of the stone is the same as the indentation on Scott's skull, that will help."

"Yeah, it's going to be hard to convict her without blood evidence, but even if she tried to clean it up, there'll still be enough iron residue for the luminol to work."

"Maybe they'll find the AR-15 used to shoot you."

"That would be good, but my guess is the gun is long gone. Probably buried out in the woods somewhere." Sam said. "That's what I'd do. Bury it where no one could ever find it."

The sheriff stepped out of the house with a big grin on his face. "We've got blood splatter. The techies think he was sitting at the dining room table when he was hit. Probably from behind, because there's blood on the table and the wall opposite from where he was sitting. There was a puddle on the hardwood floor near the table, too. They think he fell off the chair after he was hit."

Sam said, "That's consistent with the autopsy report. He was struck from behind."

"Yeah," the sheriff said. "The techies will undoubtedly find a blood sample they can use for DNA tests, and that will nail it down. It looks like Sandy cleaned everywhere except the wall. The splatter there was just a fine mist, but it'll be enough to get a good sample."

Jimmy felt like he should be elated to hear the news about the blood splatter, but he wasn't. He and Sam had worked on this case for months and now that it seemed it was almost over, it was a big letdown.

Sam and Jimmy sat in the Jeep while they waited to see if anything else of importance was discovered. Darkness was approaching, and the deputies set up large floodlights on tripods to light up the front of the house. Moths began circling the bright lights and soon a few opportunistic bats circled, finding easy meals. Jimmy soon realized collecting evidence at a crime scene was a slow, tedious process. It reminded him of doing field research.

The sheriff came out of the house and motioned for them to come sit with him on the porch. His face showed lines of fatigue, and he sat heavily on his chair. "I'm surprised you're still here. You might as well go home. We'll be here for a few hours more."

Sam asked, "Did you find anything else, Sheriff?"

"Yeah, a little. We found more blood splatter on a dish that was stacked in a kitchen cabinet with some others. Looks like Scott was eating when he was clubbed."

Jimmy said, "Sandy said Scott had come to her house for Thanksgiving dinner. Do you suppose that's when it happened?"

"Who knows," the sheriff said. "We'll sort that out later. We found a small stash of marijuana and some other drug stuff. We're still looking."

"What about a rifle?" Did you find the AR-15 she used to shoot me?" Sam asked.

"Nope. No guns of any kind, no ammunition, no clue as to its whereabouts."

"Maybe it'll be in her car, or at her store," Sam said hopefully.

"Don't get your hopes up, Sam," the sheriff said. His shoulders sagged, and he rubbed his face with his hands. "I doubt we'll ever find it."

Sam asked hopefully, "Any chance I could get a look inside, Sheriff? An extra set of eyes might be helpful."

"Not now, Sam. Maybe after all the tech work's done. You know I can't risk having the scene contaminated." He held up his hands toward Sam. "Before you say it, I'm not suggesting you'd do anything wrong. Heavens knows, you're more experienced than I am, but a good lawyer might use it against us. The fewer people in there, the better."

"Okay, Sheriff," Sam said. He looked at Jimmy and said, "We might as well go home.

*   *   *

Jimmy was tired when he arrived back at the Eyrie. He sat wearily at his desk and called Wendy. He wanted her to hear the news of Sandy's arrest from him before she heard about it by the grapevine. The phone rang four times before she answered.

"Hey, Wendy," Jimmy said. "I hope I'm not calling too late. I have some news for you. The sheriff is going to arrest Sandy Lynch for killing Scott."

He heard her gasp. "What? Sandy killed him? He was her uncle."

"Yeah, I know. Sam and I suspected her for a while, but we didn't have any proof." He told her about the search of her house and the blood splatter evidence the technicians had found. He was careful to just state the facts and not speculate on their meaning. He'd written enough scientific reports to know better than to start jumping to conclusions.

"Are they sure it was Scott's blood? Have they tested it yet?"

"No, but it shouldn't take too long to get the results back. The sheriff's confident it'll be Scott's." He told her about finding a war club that could be the murder weapon.

"Were Sandy's fingerprints on it?"

"The technicians were still processing the scene when we left, so I don't know. Even if her prints are on it, that's inconclusive. She owns it, so her prints would be on it."

"Where's Sandy now? Is she in jail?" Wendy asked.

"Yeah, she assaulted one of the deputies, and was arrested for that. I'm pretty sure she'll be arrested for Scott's murder tomorrow." He described the altercation Sandy had with the deputy.

"This is crazy, Dr. Houston. I never guessed Sandy was capable of murder." He heard her gasp again. "She tried to kill Sam. I can't imagine anyone doing that, let alone a woman. I don't mean to be sexist or anything, but women don't usually kill people with assault weapons." Jimmy recalled what Sam had said about women using poison instead, but he didn't say anything.

Wendy was quiet for a while. Jimmy could hear her taking deep, gulping breaths, trying to keep from crying. She finally said, "I don't know how I feel about all this. Since those hikers found Scott's body in that tree, it's all I've been thinking about—finding the killer and getting him off the street." She was quiet again for a few seconds and then said, "I guess I should say get *her* off the street. But, why did she kill him?"

Jimmy told her about the pending repeal of the Endangered Species Act.

"Are you saying she heard it might be repealed, and killed him to inherit his land?"

"That's what we think. We can't prove that she heard about it last fall, but the judge agreed it was a distinct possibility and issued the search warrant."

"Oh, I see. I still can't get over this. Sandy was his niece. She seemed like a nice person."

"Wendy, there's one other thing you should be aware of. The media is going to pick this up quickly. It'll be in the papers and on the local television stations. It might go national if it's a slow news day tomorrow. As soon as Sandy's arraigned for murder, they'll be all over it."

"Oh. I hadn't thought about that. I guess you're right, but I think I can handle it. Thanks for calling, Dr. Houston. I'm going to go now.

I need to call Frankie and let him know. I'll let Tiffany know, too. I'll send her a text."

"Okay, Wendy. I'm sorry you lost Scott. I'll keep you posted on any new developments."

"Thank you, Dr. Houston. Thanks for your hard work. Tell Sam I said thanks, too."

Jimmy put his phone back in his pocket. He rocked back in his chair and crossed his arms. He was tired and hungry. He hadn't eaten since breakfast. He went over the evidence again in his mind, putting each item in its place. Had they overlooked something? Sandy *must* be guilty, he thought. How else could Scott's blood splatter be found in her house? He had little doubt that the DNA results would prove it was Scott's, but he'd just have to wait and see. He got up and rummaged around in his tiny refrigerator, looking for something to eat. He had to settle for two-day-old leftovers.

Two days later, Sam came by and picked him up. They drove to the court house to attend Sandy's arraignment. They sat in the back of the courtroom and waited for the hearing to begin. As they waited for the judge to appear, Sam entertained Jimmy with stories about his many appearances in court when he'd been a state policeman. Jimmy remembered going through an arraignment himself when he'd been falsely accused of murder. It hadn't been fun.

Sam told Jimmy about some of the funnier things that had happened in court. He described the time a defendant stripped off his pants to show the jury his injuries after he'd been shot in the buttocks by his enraged girlfriend. Another time, a judge drifted off to sleep in the middle of testimony, and the lawyers had waited patiently until he woke up. When he finally awakened, he proceeded as if nothing had happened.

The hearing lasted only fifteen minutes. The judge asked how Sandy pleaded, and she replied that she was not guilty. Sandy's lawyer, a young public defender, argued valiantly for Sandy to be released on her own recognizance. The prosecuting attorney protested, saying Sandy was a menace to society and should be retained without bail. They argued back and forth for a few minutes, then the judge ordered Sandy to be remanded without bail. A trial date would be set later.

The sheriff caught them as they trooped out of the courtroom. He pulled them into a vacant room to give them an update on the case.

"We were at Sandy's house until midnight. We searched the whole place but didn't find the AR-15. We even searched the empty doghouse out back. It wasn't there. It wasn't in her car either, or her shop. We found some fibers in her trunk that're consistent with the blanket Scott's body was wrapped in. We need to do some more tests, but I think we're okay there. We found some rope in her basement of the same kind that was used to bind up Scott's body. One of my tech guys was able to retrieve a blood sample from the war club. It wasn't very big, but they think it'll be enough. We won't have DNA results for the blood splatter or warclub for a couple of days. It depends on how bad they're backed up at the lab in Charleston."

Sam said, "So, the judge gave you a search warrant for her shop, too?"

The sheriff said, "Yeah. Once we found the blood splatter, she gave us a warrant without argument. We didn't find anything useful there, except more Indian stuff. Silver jewelry, stuff like that for sale. She sure was an Indian nut. We found a lot of the stuff in her house. We found a peace pipe, at least that's what I think it is, with some pot residue in it. Evidently, she smoked the peace pipe in her house because we could still smell it."

Jimmy asked, "Have you interviewed Sandy yet?"

The sheriff shook his head with disgust. "Hell no. That lawyer she has is a real tiger. She's a new public defender. She won't let Sandy say a word to us."

"With all the evidence you have, you'd think she'd be screaming for a plea bargain."

"It's early in the process. Since she's been arraigned now, maybe we'll get to interview her. The prosecutor isn't too worried. I've kept him informed of the evidence we've collected. If the DNA results are positive for Scott's blood, he feels he can get a conviction."

The sheriff didn't seem to be in a hurry to go back to his office, so they sat in the room and talked while a steady stream of unfortunate souls trundled through the halls of the courthouse. He asked Jimmy where he might catch some trout this late in the season, and Jimmy told him about a couple of his favorite streams. Sam began to squirm, and Jimmy knew it was time for them to leave.

Back at his cabin, Jimmy remembered he needed to patch the roof. Every time it rained, water dripped into his kitchen and he had to put out pots to catch it. He found an old can of roof sealant in the shed behind the cabin and pried the lid open. He stirred the sticky, tar-like material inside with a stick and decided it would do to make the patch. He had just put the ladder against the edge of the roof when Dana pulled into the parking area.

"Hey there, Jimmy," she said, smiling. "Looks like you could use a hand." She grinned at him and thrust a covered dish toward him. "I hope you don't mind me dropping in unannounced."

He was happy to see her. He took the food inside and put it in the refrigerator. Before he closed the door, he peeked inside the container. It was peach cobbler, and it smelled terrific. She held the ladder while he made repairs on the leaky roof, and then they sat on the deck and talked.

The dog laid down at her feet and she bent to scratch his ears. "You say you call him Yellow Dog? That's original. How did you decide on that name?"

Jimmy told her the dog had been a gift from a friend. He couldn't decide what name to give him and had started referring to him as the yellow dog. The name had stuck. She laughed and said it was as good a name as any.

Jimmy chuckled and said, "One thing about him—he doesn't like your drone. The last time you sent it over here, he hid under the bed."

She laughed and scratched the dog's ears again. "Smart dog. Let the master handle the scary stuff."

He told her about Sandy's arrest and the evidence the sheriff and his technicians had found in her house. "So, she's sitting in jail waiting to be tried for murder. The sheriff thinks they'll be able to make the charges stick. They're waiting for the results of the DNA tests, but I think the blood will be Scott's."

"I read about it in the papers. That Lambert fellow, the one who writes for the Charleston paper, made you and Sam sound like heroes. You're a modern-day Sherlock Holmes," she said, teasing. "He gave you all the credit."

"Yeah well, the sheriff wasn't too happy about that. He'll run for reelection one day and will need all the good publicity he can get. But, a trial and conviction should help him out. Sam and I are done with the case, so we're out of it. It's the sheriff's baby now."

Jimmy went into the cabin and dished the peach cobbler into his best china—two earthenware bowls, badly chipped around their rims. He called out to the deck, asking Dana if she wanted milk on the cobbler. When she said yes, he knew she was still a country girl. He couldn't imagine a fancy restaurant in Manhattan serving milk over their deserts. They ate the tasty dessert with mismatched spoons and watched the sun fall in the evening sky. He thought; *peach cobbler shared with a beautiful friend. What could be better?*

Chapter 27

Jimmy was working in his lab at the college when the sheriff called him. He was getting ready to interview Sandy for the first time. Her lawyer had given her consent, saying Sandy was innocent. They wanted to talk.

The sheriff said, "Sandy has agreed to tell us what happened, but she wants you to be there. I don't like it, but if that's the only way she'll talk to us, there's little I can do. So, are you willing to sit in on the interview?"

"Yes, of course. I wonder what she wants with me."

"I don't know. Maybe she thinks you can help her. Or, maybe they just want a sympathetic observer present." The sheriff said, "I think they're going to try for a plea bargain, but we have her dead to rights. The DNA results came in. It was Scott's blood. She can't get around that."

"Did you find Scott's fingerprints in her house?" Jimmy asked.

"Yes. In several places. Of course, Sandy's prints were all over the place. We found others, too, that we can't identify. There's no match for them in the data bases."

"Besides Scott's and Sandy's prints, were there any others in the dining room?"

"Yeah. From a couple of different people. But, that's to be expected," the sheriff said. "Lots of people could have been in and out of the house."

Jimmy thought about that for a moment, and then asked, "When is the interview? When do you want me there?"

"It's scheduled for two o'clock this afternoon. Does that work for you?"

"Sure. Is it okay if I ask Sam if he wants to come?"

The sheriff growled, "Sure. Why not. The more the merrier."

They met in a conference room at the sheriff's office. Jimmy, Sam, the sheriff and the prosecuting attorney were sitting around a long table talking when a deputy brought Sandy into the room. Her hands were cuffed in front of her, and she had to shuffle along because of the chains on her feet. The sheriff instructed the deputy to remove them.

She wore an orange jumpsuit, and her hair was drawn back in a ponytail. Dark circles under her eyes were testament to sleepless nights spent in a small jail cell. She was accompanied by Jane Smith, the public defender. Smith was a small woman with dark hair and snapping brown eyes. She lugged a large briefcase and had to use both hands to heave it onto the table. Introductions were made, and the interview began.

The prosecuting attorney notified all present the interview was being filmed. The sheriff reminded Sandy that she'd already been read her Miranda rights and asked if she understood them. Smith waved her hand, dismissing the sheriff's question. She said for the sheriff to get on with it.

Before the sheriff could begin questioning Sandy, Jane Smith said, "We want a deal. Ms. Lynch did not kill Scott Mitchell. He was her uncle. She loved him."

The sheriff looked at Smith with surprise. "No deal. We have her dead to rights. I can go over all the evidence against her if you want me to."

Smith said, "That's not necessary. I've already heard most of it. Anyway, it doesn't matter. She didn't kill Mr. Mitchell. Someone else did it."

The sheriff and prosecuting attorney laughed, and the sheriff said, "You're using the old SODDI defense, huh? Some other dude did it? That's not going to wash."

"Of course, it will. Someone other than Sandy did it, and she's willing to tell you who it was. But first, we want a deal," Smith said. Sandy sat silently with her head down. She picked at the cuticle of a fingernail. Most of the polish on her nails had been gnawed away leaving only flecks of red paint here and there. She wore no makeup and she seemed to have aged years. She raised her head and looked with imploring eyes at Jimmy.

The prosecuting attorney cleared his throat. He was a tall, thin man with a large Adams apple that bobbed up and down when he spoke. Behind his back, the deputies called him Ichabod. "We'll listen to your offer. If Ms. Lynch is truly innocent, we'll find out. What is it you want?"

"A suspended sentence for Ms. Lynch's part in Scott's death."

The sheriff asked, "Are you admitting she was present when Scott was killed?"

"Yes. But, before you start jumping to conclusions, you should hear what she has to say."

The prosecuting attorney said they'd listen but would reserve judgement on her guilt until they heard her testimony. He reminded Sandy that she had the right to remain silent.

All eyes turned toward Sandy. The public defender nodded and said for her to tell them what happened the day Scott died.

Sandy wrung her hands and began in a small voice. "I invited Uncle Scott to my place for Thanksgiving dinner. Wendy, his girlfriend, had to work and couldn't be there. It was just me, Uncle Scott and my boyfriend. We were having a good time, talking and visiting. It was Thanksgiving, and everyone was in a good mood. I'd baked a turkey with all the trimmings, and we'd put it on the table, Scott and me." She looked around the room, seeking approval and encouragement. "My boyfriend had left the room while we set the table. Scott and I had just sat down at the table when he came back in the room. He'd been smoking pot. You could smell it on him, and his eyes were big. He had a goofy look on his face."

Sam interrupted and asked, "Who is your boyfriend?"

The prosecuting attorney looked sharply at Sam and shook his head. "Let her tell her story in her own words."

Sandy continued. "I could tell by the look on Uncle Scott's face that he'd smelled the pot, too. He hated drugs. He didn't allow anyone to use them while they were on his property. It was the one thing that would get him riled up. Anyway, he said something about it. He said he didn't approve of anyone who did drugs, that they were losers. He started preaching, saying how awful drug users were. My boyfriend just laughed at him. They got in a big argument."

Sandy started crying. She sobbed, and tears ran down her face. She blew her nose loudly on a tissue. Jane Smith patted her on the shoulder and made soothing sounds. Smith glared at the men in the room as if this were all their fault.

When she had regained her composure, Sandy went on. "I told them to calm down. It was Thanksgiving. I just wanted to have a nice dinner and for everyone to enjoy themselves. They didn't listen to me. They got louder and louder." She twisted the tissue into a knot with shaking hands. "That's when it happened. He grabbed the war club I had on display and hit Uncle Scott with it. I was horrified. I couldn't believe he did that."

The sheriff said, "Just to be absolutely clear, who was the person who hit your uncle with the war club?"

Sandy said, "It was my boyfriend, Jonathan Wright."

Sam and Jimmy looked at each other with surprise. Jonathan Wright, the fake news writer. The sheriff told Sandy to continue her story.

Sandy was crying softly, her shoulders shaking. She blew her nose again. "I think Jonathan was almost as horrified as I was. He dropped the club and began saying he was so sorry, that he didn't mean to do it. His hands were shaking, and he had a terrified look on his face. He begged me not to report him. He said he'd help get rid of the body. Nobody would know he'd done it. I wanted to call 911 to get an ambulance, but it was obvious Uncle Scott was dead." Sandy stopped talking and stared out a window. Her face was pale, and Jimmy caught a glimpse of the beauty she'd once had.

Jane Smith said, "Go ahead, Sandy. Tell them what you did next."

"Jonathan just kind of took over. He was really scared. He told me what we had to do. He said I was as guilty as he was, and I had to help. He wanted to take Uncle Scott somewhere and just dump him like he was trash or something. In the river, maybe the Blackwater. Weight him down with rocks. I couldn't let him do that. I told him I'd report him if he didn't help me give Uncle Scott a proper burial."

"Is that when you came up with the idea of doing a tree burial?" the sheriff asked.

"Yeah. I like Indian customs. I'd read about tree and platform burials and saw models of them in a museum once. I decided that's what I'd do. I'd give Uncle Scott a tree burial. He deserved at least that. We wrapped him in an old blanket and bound him up with rope, just like the Indians used to do. We took him up on Dolly Sods and put him in a tree. It was hard getting him up there, but between the two of us, we got it done. I said some words like I think Indians would have said, and we left him there with the spirits." She leaned back in her chair and took a deep breath, relieved it was over. She wiped tears from her eyes with the back of her hand.

"What's going to happen to me now?" she asked, looking from one face to another. She looked searchingly at Jimmy. "I didn't kill Uncle Scott. I didn't have a reason to kill him. I loved him. He was good to me. You believe me, don't you, Dr. Houston?"

Before Jimmy could answer, the prosecuting attorney broke in, saying, "Ms. Lynch, what do you know about the Endangered Species Act?"

"The what? Oh, Uncle Scott used to talk about it. It's something about rare animals isn't it? Why? What does that have to do with this?"

"Are you aware of what's going on in Washington regarding the Act?" he asked.

Jane Smith looked quizzically at him. "I'm going to have to stop this line of questioning until I know where it's leading. I'm advising you, Sandy, to not answer any questions about this for now."

Sandy ignored her advice. "What about it? What are you talking about?"

The sheriff told her about Congress's plans to repeal the Act.

Smith said, "How could she have heard about it? She's been in jail. She hasn't had access to television or any other news outlet."

The sheriff asked Sandy. "Were you aware the new president vowed to eliminate the Act? If he does, you stand to inherit a piece of property that's worth millions."

Smith quickly said, "Don't answer that, Sandy." She placed her hand on Sandy's arm.

"No! I want to answer. I don't know what you're talking about. As far as I know, Uncle Scott's land's not of much value." She shook her head, looking from person to person. "I'm going to give it to the nature preserve. That's what he wanted."

"So, you're saying you didn't know the president planned to repeal the Act? He promised he would while he was campaigning," the sheriff said.

"No. I don't follow politics. I can't stand all the bickering and fighting. I didn't even vote." She looked Jimmy in the eye and said. "I didn't kill my uncle. You have to believe me."

Jane Smith said, "So, mister prosecutor, do we have a deal? A suspended sentence for improperly disposing of a dead body. My client isn't guilty of anything other than making a bad decision. Yes, she should have called the police. No, she shouldn't have let Wright talk her into disposing of Mr. Mitchell's body. But, she *did* try to give him a decent burial. In return, she'll testify against Jonathan Wright."

The prosecuting attorney's Adams apple bobbed up and down. Jimmy couldn't help but look at it. "Even if her story is true, there are more possible charges against her than improper disposal of a body."

"Maybe so, but if you want her testimony, that's what she's willing to plead to. Take it or leave it. Otherwise, we'll go to trial, and we'll win."

The prosecuting attorney frowned at her, and the sheriff drummed his fingers on the tabletop.

The deputy returned, cuffed and chained Sandy, and took her back to her cell. Jane Smith lugged her briefcase out the door and disappeared down the hallway. The four men sat in silence for a few minutes. Finally, the sheriff spoke.

"Well, what do you think. Is she telling the truth?"

The prosecuting attorney said, "Beats me. It's a believable story. I think Smith might be able to sell it to a jury. We'll have to see what

Jonathan Wright has to say. We can put them in adjoining interview rooms and go back and forth to see who rats out who."

Sam said, "The one thing that makes me think she might be telling the truth is Scott had an argument with Frank Richmond because he caught him smoking pot in his barn. If what Sandy says is true, I can see Scott and Jonathan getting in an argument over the same thing. But, the question is; was the argument bad enough for Scott to end up dead?"

The sheriff said, "Well, we can sit here arguing one point or another all day, but I'm going to go pick up Jonathan to see what he has to say for himself. We'll get the story from the horse's mouth."

*　　*　　*

The sheriff and a couple of deputies drove up through the valley to Jonathan's house. The sheriff hadn't said they couldn't come, so Sam and Jimmy tagged along in his Cherokee. The sheriff whistled when he saw the size of the place. Jonathan's car wasn't parked in the driveway and a deputy peeked in the garage window. He shook his head at the sheriff who stepped up on the porch and rang the doorbell. When no one answered, he pounded on the door with his fist. "Open up. Police!" he said. After several attempts, he decided Jonathan wasn't home. He called his office and asked the dispatcher to issue a police lookout notice for Jonathan's car.

The sheriff stood back from the house and looked it over. "From the looks of this place, the fake news business is pretty good. Isn't that what he said he did for a living?" He looked at Sam and said, "It looks like we're in the wrong business."

The sheriff sat in his car with the windows rolled down and called the judge to get a search warrant. Sam and Jimmy stood by the car's fenders listening to the sheriff's conversation. He told the judge about Sandy's interview and that she had implicated Jonathan in Scott's murder. Now they needed to search his house. The judge agreed to issue the warrant. She'd approve it the minute she got the application. He hung up and called his office. He told a deputy what to put in the warrant application and to send it to the judge immediately. He told the deputy to send a copy of the approved warrant to his cell phone as soon as it was signed. That would suffice until a hard copy could be driven to Jonathan's house. With all that done, they sat on the porch and waited. The sheriff told them it'd take less than an hour for the warrant to arrive on his phone. While they sat around waiting, a deputy went for food and returned with a large box of pastries. Sam said it was a good thing the house was on a quiet street. It wouldn't do for the public to see them loafing around eating donuts.

The sheriff's phone rang, and he looked at its screen. "Got it," he said.

They broke a small windowlight in the door and were quickly inside. The sheriff made them all don paper booties over their shoes and gloves on their hands. The deputies quickly cleared the house and they did a quick walkthrough.

Sam looked in the computer room. Everything was gone except an old monitor and a tangle of cables and wires. "In here, sheriff," Sam said. "It looks like he's skipped out. This room was full of electronic equipment when I was here before."

Jimmy stuck his head in the door, and said, "His closets are bare, too. He's gone, sheriff."

"Okay. I'm not surprised. I'd skip out too, if I were him. He's in deep trouble. Everybody out. We can't do anything more here except mess up any evidence he might have left behind. I'll call in the tech guys. If there's anything helpful here, they'll find it. I'll have them dust for prints. Maybe we can match Jonathan's with the unidentified prints in Sandy's dining room. That would pretty well cook his goose."

One of the deputies chimed in, saying, "Or his Thanksgiving turkey."

No one laughed.

They waited outside while the crime scene technicians worked their way through the house. Jimmy used his phone to do searches for Jonathan on social media sites. He didn't find anything. For someone as computer savvy as Jonathan, he wasn't surprised. He wondered if he was using his real name. He went to a website that offered background checks for a fee and did a search. Without a social security number, he wouldn't be able to take the search very far. He found several Jonathan Wrights but none that fit his description.

One of the technicians came out to the porch and got the sheriff. He said he had something he wanted him to see before they took samples. Ten minutes later, the sheriff returned and said they'd found a small smear of blood on the inside of the lid of the washing machine. It was in a place that made them think it might have been left by bloody clothing being stuffed into the machine. If the DNA matched Scott's they'd have Jonathan cold.

The technicians and deputies searched every square inch of the house and garage. They crawled under the house and searched the lot. They looked for places the lawn might have been dug up and a gun buried. They checked federal databases to see if Jonathan had bought an AR-15 or any other kind of weapon. They drew a blank.

Jimmy and Sam became bored sitting around waiting and headed home. The sheriff promised he'd let them know if they found anything of importance. Jimmy decided he wouldn't hold his breath waiting. Jonathan Wright was gone, and he wouldn't be surprised if they never saw him again.

When Jimmy got home, he made a few phone calls. The first was to Wendy. He told her about Sandy's confession and her allegation that her boyfriend, Jonathan, had killed Scott.

"I thought Sandy killed him. What about all that evidence in her house?" Wendy said, her voice shaking.

"Sandy explained all that away by saying Jonathan killed him and that they had 'buried' him in a tree together."

"Do you believe her?" Wendy asked.

"I don't know. Unless we get Jonathan's side of the story, we may never know. It'll be hard for the prosecuting attorney to disprove her story."

He could hear Wendy crying quietly on the other end of the line. "I hope they catch him. I'd just about accepted Sandy as Scott's killer. Now this. I wish this were all over."

"I know, Wendy. It must be hard for you. Let me ask one more question. Have you ever seen Sandy and Jonathan together? I thought they might have gone to the saloon together. We don't know for sure if they were dating."

"Yes, I have. Sandy dated a lot of men. Oh, not a lot. I shouldn't say that. She dated more than one man. I guess she wasn't the type to settle down. Scott wanted her to get married and start a family. He'd have loved to have had a great niece or nephew. They would have been almost like grandchildren. Anyway, to get back to your question, I saw Sandy with Jonathan a couple of times at the saloon. They came to listen to the bands Seth books on Saturday nights. Does that answer your question?"

"Yes, it does. Now we know he was her boyfriend."

"I'm not sure I'd call him her boyfriend. They were there together, but I don't know if they were serious about each other or not."

Jimmy's next call was to Betty at the trading post in Chinle, Arizona. She recognized his voice and laughed when he asked her what time it was there.

"That depends on whether you're on the reservation or not, Bird Man. You know how that works."

"Yes, I do, Betty. How've you been? Is it hot out there?"

"It's the middle of the summer. What do you think? Is it raining where you live there in the mountains, in your bird's nest?" She was laughing when she said it, obviously enjoying the banter.

"I have a question for you. Do you remember our conversation about Sandy Lynch? She's the young woman you said made a nuisance of herself at your ceremonials."

"How could I forget? But, I don't remember saying she was a nuisance. What about her?"

"Did you ever see her with a young man?" He described Jonathan.

"Yes. He wasn't bad looking for a *bilagaana*," she said, teasing. "But, I think it was just once. He was only with her on one trip. They came in the trading post together. Are you still looking for that murderer?"

"Yes. The man with Sandy might have been the killer."

"Oh," she said, "I shouldn't have asked. Just thinking about a killing might be bad luck."

"You've been a big help, Betty. Thank you."

"Bird Man?" she said. "When are you coming back out here to see us?"

"I don't know, Betty. Maybe one day."

"Rosa has been asking about you. She liked you. She's weaving a rug for you."

Jimmy was surprised. "I see. I'm honored. Why do you think she'd do that? She hardly knows me. We only met one time."

Betty giggled and said, "I think she wants you to meet her daughter."

Chapter 28

Jimmy awoke to the sound of rain on his tin roof. He had only a few days left before fall classes began and still had a lot of preparation to do. He was anxious to get started and into the routine of teaching and meeting with students. Jimmy sat up and stretched.

Yellow Dog did his stretches, too, extending his front legs in front of him. He yawned and stuck his rear in the air, curling his tail over his back. He went to the door, wanting out. Jimmy opened it and the dog hesitated before going out in the rain. He was back in less than two minutes. He shook the water from his coat in a sparkling arc.

Jimmy took a quick shower and got dressed. He made a light breakfast and ate at the table by the window. He considered lighting a fire in the woodstove, but worried that if the sun came out later, it'd be too hot in the cabin. He decided since he'd be gone most of the morning, he'd skip it.

Jane Smith had called him the day before saying Sandy wanted him to visit her in jail. She wanted to talk to him. Jimmy called the sheriff asking if he should go through with the visit. He'd said, sure, why not. Maybe Jimmy would learn something that would help with the case. Jimmy had agreed to visit her. He was to be there at ten o'clock.

He met with Jane in the jail's outer office. Her briefcase sat on the floor beside her.

"I don't mind telling you I don't like this. Everything I know about lawyering tells me it's a mistake for her to talk to you. You're not wearing a wire, are you?"

Jimmy laughed. "No, I'm not. A deputy searched me before they let me in here. They even took my belt. I don't even know what she wants to talk to me about. Do you?"

"Not for sure. She seems to think you'll help her. I don't know what you can do that I can't"

"I don't either. I guess I'll find out."

"Dr. Houston?" Smith said in a quiet voice. "Go easy on her. She's fragile right now. She's scared."

Jimmy nodded. He asked the deputy to take him to see Sandy. She was already in the small interview room when he entered. Her chains were secured to a ring in the floor. Someone had given her makeup, probably Jane, and she looked much better than when he'd seen her last. She was still a nice-looking woman. She smiled as he sat down.

"This is a terrible way to receive guests," she said. She made her chains rattle in their ring. "I asked them to take them off, but they wouldn't. I guess they were afraid I'd attack you or something."

"How are you doing, Sandy?" he asked. Not for the first time, he felt sorry for her.

"As well as can be expected, I guess. I'll never get used to being in jail, but I suppose it does get easier after a while."

"I'm not sure why I'm here. What do you want from me?"

"Oh, nothing really. I just wanted to see a friendly face. When you talked to me before, you seemed so...oh, I don't know, sincere. I need someone I trust to talk to. I just wanted you to know I'm innocent. I didn't kill Uncle Scott. It happened just like I said. It was Jonathan who did it. I don't know why I reacted like I did. I was scared. I should have called the police immediately, but I panicked."

"Yes, you should have. You wouldn't be here if you had. Were you afraid of Jonathan? Did he threaten you?"

"Yes, I was afraid of what he might do to me. He didn't directly say he'd harm me, but I could see it in his eyes. He was terrified. I guess he was full of adrenaline or something. He was in a panic. I thought if he killed Uncle Scott in a fit of rage, he'd do the same thing to me."

"Do you know if Jonathan had a gun?"

Sandy's eyes grew big. "Do you think he shot Sam?"

"I don't know. Do you think he'd be capable of that? It was a vicious attack. Whoever did it, wanted him dead. We think the shooter was trying to stop the investigation."

"Maybe. I think he had a gun. A rifle. He talked about it once. He was a Second Amendment guy. He talked about that once or twice. He was angry about all that stuff on TV about taking away our guns."

"The sheriff didn't find a gun in his house. Do you have any idea what he might have done with it?"

"No. I think he kept it in his house. Jane said the sheriff told her he'd run away. Maybe he took it with him. I think he kept it in his car sometimes." She dropped her eyes to the tabletop and said, "Do you think the prosecuting attorney will accept my plea deal? Jane thinks he will, but I'm not sure. I don't want to be blamed for Uncle Scott's death. I didn't kill him. You believe me, don't you?" She looked at him with pleading eyes. "Maybe you could talk to the sheriff and prosecuting attorney. They'd listen to you."

"I'm not a lawyer, but I think you have a good chance of having your deal accepted. It will help if the sheriff catches Jonathan, and he confesses to the killing. But, there will be some serious charges brought against you."

"Oh, I hope they catch him. I want him punished for killing Uncle Scott."

* * *

After leaving the jail, Jimmy returned to his cabin. He opened his laptop and began putting finishing touches on his class syllabus. He was looking forward to teaching the new course. He had not taught a course in plant morphology before and had done extensive research in preparation. He reviewed the required reading list he planned to hand out to his students and added one last reference. They'd groan when they saw it but would trudge through it as required. It would be a good course with lots of lab work. He hoped his students would like it.

Yellow Dog perked his ears and went to a window to look outside. Jimmy heard a car approaching his parking lot. He went to a window to look out, too. A nondescript sedan pulled to a stop beside his Cherokee. Jonathan Wright got out and opened the car's back door. He pulled out a military style rifle and worked the ejection lever. Jimmy sucked in a deep breath and backed away from the window. He looked frantically around the room for a weapon. His rifle was in a case in the back of the Cherokee. He ran into the kitchen and picked up his heavy cast-iron skillet. The dog began running around, too, excited by Jimmy's actions.

He stepped into his bedroom and looked for a place to hide. It was a very small room, and there was nothing that would provide concealment. He certainly wasn't going to get under the bed, and the closet would be a dead end. He pressed his back against the wall near the door and waited, the skillet raised. The dog sat down and looked at him, turning his head from side to side. Jimmy felt the vibrations of Jonathan's footsteps on the deck. He came closer and closer.

"Dr. Houston, are you in there? I want to talk to you. I won't hurt you, I promise."

Jimmy didn't answer. The cabin door opened, and Jimmy could hear him walk into the main room. "Come on, Doc. Why don't you come out and talk to me?"

The dog crawled under the bed. Jimmy held his breath. The skillet was getting heavy, but adrenaline gave him strength he didn't know he had. He heard Jonathan shuffling around in the room. His footsteps came closer. He was so close, now, Jimmy could hear him breathing. A floorboard creaked just outside the bedroom door.

"Are you in there, Doc? Do you have a gun?" Jonathan asked. His voice was high and tense. "I don't want to get shot."

Jimmy remained silent. He took in a small breath, hoping Jonathan wouldn't hear him. His hands shook with tension. Jonathan pushed the bedroom door open a crack and thrust the barrel of the gun through it. Jimmy waited, the skillet held high.

"Come on, Doc. I know you're in there. Come out and talk to me," Jonathan said.

The barrel extended even more into the room. Finally, Jimmy could see the hand that held the forearm of the gun. He brought the skillet down on it with all his might. Jonathan screamed and dropped the rifle.

Jimmy pushed through the door and shoved him to the floor ahead of him. He raised the skillet and was about to finish him off when Jonathan raised his hands and yelled, "I give up! I give up! Don't hit me with that thing."

"You were going to kill me. You have it coming."

"No, no! I wasn't going to kill you. I just wanted to talk. Geeze, I think you broke my wrist." He held his arm tenderly and worked his hand back and forth. "I think I can feel the bones grinding in there."

"You stay right there. Don't move." Jimmy said. He ran into the bedroom and returned with the rifle. He pointed it at Jonathan's head. "Just stay where you are." Jonathan lay back on the floor groaning with pain. Jimmy found the dog's leash and bound his hands behind his back. He moaned and rolled onto his side, a sheen of sweat appearing on his face.

"My hand hurts like hell, Doc. Why don't you untie me? I'm not going to hurt you."

Jimmy found a roll of duct tape and taped Jonathan's ankles together. When he had him bound up like a suckling pig, he relaxed and put the rifle on the table. He pulled out his phone and called Sam. He told him quickly what had happened. Sam said he'd be right there. Jimmy slumped onto a chair and stared at Jonathan. The dog crawled out from under the bed and approached Jonathan cautiously. He smelled his shoes then went to sit with Jimmy.

Jonathan wanted to talk, but Jimmy told him to shut up until Sam got there. Jimmy went to the kitchen sink and scooped up some water. He splashed it on his face and then dried it with a towel. His hands were still shaking, and he leaned on the counter to catch his breath. He had thought he was going to die. Jonathan shifted around on the floor and moaned. Jimmy didn't feel sorry for him.

A few minutes later, Sam arrived. He limped into the room and looked in amazement at Jonathan. They sat him upright on a chair, and Sam replaced the dog leash with handcuffs. He looked at the AR-15 laying on the table then back at Jimmy and asked, "Where's your gun, Jimmy?"

Jimmy mumbled something Sam didn't catch. Sam said, "What's that? Speak up. Where's your gun?"

Finally, Jimmy said, "It's out in the Jeep."

Sam shook his head then he said. "First, we need to call the sheriff. Then I want you to tell me everything that happened."

"I called him. He'll be here soon." Jimmy told him what Jonathan had done.

"So, let me get this straight. You took on a man with an AR-15 with a skillet?"

"Well, yes. I didn't have a choice."

Jonathan said, "I wasn't going to hurt him, Mr. Miller. I just wanted to talk to him." Both men looked at him as if he were a bug. "The gun wasn't even loaded."

Sam picked up the rifle and worked the ejection lever. It was empty. "What the hell? Why'd you threaten him with an empty gun? Are you nuts?"

"Like I said, I just wanted to talk. I know the sheriff's department is looking for me. I wanted Dr. Houston to help me. I want to turn myself in. I was going to give him the gun to take to the sheriff."

"Turn yourself in?" Sam asked incredulously. "Why didn't you just go to the sheriff's office and surrender?"

"I don't know. I guess I was afraid they'd shoot me. You hear about so many police shootings. They might have killed me before I could give up. That's why I wanted the Doc's help. He seems like a reasonable person, and he has a connection with the sheriff."

Sam said, "The sheriff is on the way. I suggest you just keep your mouth shut until he gets here. We'll let him sort this out."

When the sheriff arrived with a deputy, they unwrapped Jonathan's ankles and put him in the back of their cruiser. Jonathan complained about the injuries to his wrist and hand. The sheriff said they'd take him by the hospital on the way to jail. He waited sullenly in the car while the sheriff talked to Jimmy. After Jimmy had told him the details of his encounter with Jonathan, he picked up the gun, working the ejection lever. Sam told him the gun had been empty when he'd checked it.

Jimmy said, "I saw him take the gun out of the car and work the ejection lever. I thought he'd jacked a cartridge into the chamber. Jonathan said he was just checking to be sure the gun was empty. I have to admit, it scared the crap out of me."

The sheriff asked, "Where's your gun, Professor?"

Sam said with disgust in his voice, "It was out in his car. A lot of good it did him there."

The sheriff shook his head but didn't say anything. He walked out on the deck and took in the view. "What is this, some kind of fire tower?" He was referring to the cabin. "So, this is where you live. I'll bet it gets exciting when a big lightning storm rolls in. I wouldn't want to be here when that happens." Jimmy explained that his father had built it years ago. They'd used it for a hunting cabin. "It's a neat place. You can see forever out there," he said, nodding toward the horizon.

Jimmy asked, "What happens to Jonathan now, sheriff? I suppose you'll put him in jail with Sandy. How are you going to figure out who killed Scott? They're going to blame the killing on each other. Jonathan told me he didn't kill him."

"Yeah, I figure they will. I'll let the prosecuting attorney handle that. But, can you imagine taking them to trial? They'll blame each other, and a jury won't be able to decide which one did it. What a mess. Anyway, I'm glad we got Jonathan off the street."

Sam asked, "Bill, did you find out if the blood in Jonathan's washing machine was Scott's?"

"Yes, it was. That complicates things even more. It looks like Jonathan was there when Scott was killed, or at least came in contact with him somehow. But, it doesn't prove he's the one who crushed Scott's skull with a war club."

*   *   *

A few days later, Jimmy and Sam watched through a one-way window as the sheriff and prosecuting attorney interviewed Jonathan. Jonathan's lawyer sat beside him. Jonathan was wearing an orange jumpsuit like the one Sandy had worn earlier. His wrist, the one Jimmy had hit with his skillet, was covered with a thick cast. It ran halfway up his forearm and covered most of his hand.

The sheriff asked him to tell them what happened at Sandy's house at Thanksgiving last fall. Jonathan took a big breath and began. They had gone out a few times and Sandy invited him for Thanksgiving dinner. Jonathan didn't have relatives living nearby, so he accepted. His story was identical to Sandy's up to the time the arguing began.

"Sandy and her uncle got in a big argument. He was angry because she'd been smoking pot. She had an Indian pipe, and she liked to fire it up sometimes. Mr. Mitchell smelled it as soon as he came in the house. I smelled it, too. The odor's hard to get rid of, you know? Anyway, they argued for a while, and I thought they'd settled down. Then Sandy started in on him again, complaining about him giving his land to the tree huggers. That's what she called them, tree huggers."

The sheriff asked, "What were you doing while they were arguing?"

"Well, nothing. I just sat there. I'm not family or anything, so it really wasn't my business. Anyway, things settled down some, and I went to the bathroom to wash my hands because we were about ready to eat. While I was in there, I could hear Sandy yelling at him again." Jonathan stopped speaking and swallowed. He looked at his lawyer who nodded at Jonathan and told him to go on. Everything would be okay. "Then I heard a sound I hope I never hear again. It sounded like someone had hit a watermelon with a club. Then, I heard his body hit the floor. The sound was so loud, it rattled the windows."

"What did you do then?" the sheriff asked.

"I ran into the dining room, and there was Mr. Richmond on the floor with blood coming out of his head, and Sandy was standing there looking at him. An Indian club was on the floor beside him. I just stood there for a while and stared at them. Her face was white, and she looked terrified."

"Did she say anything to you?"

"No, not just then. I felt his neck for a pulse, but I couldn't feel anything. He wasn't moving, and I couldn't see him breathe."

"Other than feeling his neck for a pulse, did you touch him anywhere else?"

"Yeah, I guess I did. There was blood everywhere. I got some of it on my hands, and I wiped it off on my pants." Jonathan took a couple of deep breaths.

"Go on," the sheriff said.

"I said we needed to call 911, and she started blubbering and crying. She was frantic She begged me not to call them. I could see he was dead, so an ambulance wouldn't have done him any good anyway. Then, she changed. She seemed to calm down and started saying that I was involved, and I had to help her get rid of the body. I told her, no way. She said if I didn't she'd say I killed him."

"What did you say to that?"

"I told her I wasn't going to help her. It wasn't any of my business. She started screaming at me, making threats. That's when I took off. I drove home and washed my clothes. I figured she'd eventually come to her senses and call the cops, but she didn't. I didn't hear anything more about it until they found his body. I was worried she'd come for me sometime, and after that policeman was shot, I was *really* worried. That's when I bought the gun to protect myself. I should have called you guys then, but I didn't. I was scared. I didn't know what to do. And, then after a while, I was afraid if I called, it would be too late. I'd be blamed, or maybe charged with something for not calling it in."

"Did you ever see a gun at Sandy's house?"

"No, but one time, she talked about going shooting. I think she said she went up on the mountain somewhere. She only talked about it that one time."

"Why did you run away, Jonathan? You hung around after Scott's body was discovered. I'd think you'd have left immediately after that."

"I should have left when she killed him. But, when she was arrested, I just panicked. I packed my stuff and took off. Then, I realized I would be on the run the rest of my life. I decided I'd better come back."

"Is that when you came back to talk to Dr. Houston?"

"Yeah, I knew she'd try to lay this all on me. I figured it was time to come back and defend myself. Besides, with her in jail, I wasn't afraid she'd shoot me in my sleep."

"Why did you choose Dr. Houston?"

"Everyone who knew him spoke highly of him, and I read those articles in the paper about him and Mr. Miller. I thought maybe he'd help me."

Sam turned to Jimmy and said sarcastically, "There you go, Professor. You've proven the old axiom; no good deed goes unpunished.

Chapter 29

Sam, Jimmy and the sheriff met at a restaurant. While they ate their lunch, the sheriff brought them up to date on the case. He told them the prosecutor was pulling his hair out trying to put together a case against Sandy. Both he and the sheriff believed she was the one who killed Scott. She had a motive, but as far as they could tell, Jonathan didn't. He'd just been at the wrong place at the wrong time. His crime was leaving the scene of the killing and not calling the authorities. That and not being too bright. Why was it that sometimes technical wizards were short on common sense? After debating the pros and cons of the case, the prosecutor decided to charge Sandy and put her fate in the hands of a jury. In the meanwhile, they were both in jail.

Sam asked, "She hasn't admitted shooting me, has she?"

"No, she hasn't," the sheriff said. "And, we're not making any progress proving she did it. We looked everywhere for her rifle. We believe she had one because a neighbor said she'd seen her unload it from the car in front of her house. Sandy says she didn't own a gun. We checked to see if there was a record of her purchasing one but drew a blank."

"Where did you look for it?" Jimmy asked.

"We searched her house, her shop and her car. We searched Scott's house and outbuildings. We used metal detectors around his house and even had a dog search out there. We didn't find a thing. We're at a loss. We don't know where else to look."

"What about up on Dolly Sods? Maybe she chucked it over the hill from an overlook or something," Jimmy said. "Or, sunk it down in the bog."

"No, we didn't search for it up there. That's an idea, but if she threw it over the hill somewhere, we'll never find it. I'll send a deputy up there with a metal detector and a dog and have him search the area where the body was found. Maybe we'll get lucky."

Sam said, "Jimmy, you have a scientific mind. Put yourself in her place. Where would you hide it"

"Sorry, Sam. I left my Ouija board at home. Maybe if I just close my eyes and…"

"Come on, Professor. I'm serious. I want the person who shot me put behind bars."

"Okay, Sam. Sorry. Let me think about it." The three men ate in silence for a few minutes. A waitress came by and refilled their drinks. Jimmy said, "Sandy lived in Davis. There are several places she could have disposed of it near her house. If it were me doing it, I'd go out in Blackwater Falls State Park and toss it over the cliff at the overlook. It's hundreds of feet down to the river, and it would be hard to search for it. You'd need to rappel down in there. She could have waited in the parking lot until no one was around and tossed it over."

The sheriff said, "I don't have the manpower to make a search like that. I think all my deputies are afraid of heights, and I'm not doing it."

Sam said, "Maybe you could get a rock climbing club to help you out, Bill. I bet they'd be happy to help."

Jimmy said, "There's some other places I'd look first. Route 32 crosses the Blackwater River in two places. She could have dropped it in the river from either of those bridges. The water's so dark, it would be hard to spot even if the water were low."

"I hadn't thought of that. I'll get some men out there first thing in the morning." he said.

"If that doesn't pan out, I'd look in the river along the gravel road near the site of the old lumber mill. I fish that section all the time, and it would be easy to toss it in the water along there somewhere."

"I hope she didn't do that. There's several miles of road along the Blackwater up there. It could be anywhere. I say we take the low hanging fruit first. We'll try the water under the bridges."

*   *   *

The next day, Sam and Jimmy watched as deputies in a boat searched under the first bridge. They used fish finders and metal detectors to scan the river bottom. The water was shallow, and it didn't take them long to conclude the rifle wasn't there. They loaded their boats onto trailers, climbed into their trucks and drove to the bridge in the valley.

After they had all parked along the road, they stood at the low concrete bridge and looked into the sluggish, black water that flowed slowly through the valley. Brush and small trees crowded the narrow stream. The slow-moving water leached tannin and other chemicals from the boggy soil staining it the color of strong coffee. They couldn't see more than a few feet down in the water. The muddy bank and river bottom made it hard to do a search—it proved to be difficult to launch their small boats.

The deputies swore and growled as they rowed the boats along the narrow, curving river. The brush that hung over the water clutched at their clothing as they passed and threatened to knock their hats from their heads. Jimmy thought if the rifle were thrown in the river, this would be the place. The road was straight and narrow with little traffic. At night, a car could be seen approaching for hundreds of yards. All she had to do was to wait until the road was clear and drop it into the river. If Sandy hauled Scott's body in the trunk of her car to Dolly Sods, this bridge was along the way. The mud on the river's bottom would make the rifle hard to find. Jimmy had fished here several times. He'd given it up because it was too difficult to push his way through the brush, and he'd spent more time untangling his flies from the shrubs along the river than fishing.

He heard the beep of the metal finder, and a deputy shouted that they'd found something. It turned out to be a golf club someone had thrown in the river at the golf course near the river's headwaters.

Someone quipped it must be a par five river. They continued their search. They didn't find the rifle near the bridge, so they expanded their search downstream. Maybe high water had washed it farther away.

The metal finder beeped repeatedly, but they only found beer cans and other metal debris thrown into the river. Finally, Jimmy heard a deputy whoop and shout, "I think we found it!" Everyone crowded around as a muddy bundle was handed up to the men on the bridge. The sheriff put it on a tarp in the bed of a pickup truck and donned rubber gloves. The object was almost four feet long and wrapped in several layers of black plastic, secured with wire. Two bricks had been used to weight it all down. The sheriff used cutters to carefully remove the wire. He pulled the plastic back to expose a military style rifle. "This has to be it," he said.

Sam smiled grimly. He looked at Jimmy and nodded. He said, "You're better than any Ouija board, Professor."

*   *   *

Jimmy asked the sheriff and Sam to come to the cabin to talk. Jimmy set out a selection of drinks and dumped a large bag of ice into his ice chest. It had taken him an hour to scrub the fish smell out of it, but when he was done, it was usable. He put several glasses on the table along with a roll of paper towels. He'd forgotten to buy napkins.

The two men arrived at about the same time. Sam carried two large pizzas that Jimmy had asked him to pick up on his way. They naturally gravitated to the deck with food and drinks in hand. Jimmy dragged an extra chair from the kitchen onto the deck. The sheriff looked at the mountains and said he could understand why Jimmy liked it here. Sam teased Jimmy about being a hermit. The dog was the recipient of several generous pieces of pizza. He watched them carefully, hoping for more.

Bill told them about the rifle they'd found in the river. Sam asked, "Did you get any prints from it?"

"Yeah, we did, Sam. It was Sandy's AR-15. She made a mistake when she wrapped it in plastic. It kept it clean, and we found some prints. The gun was still loaded. She'd wiped it down with something like Windex but missed one cartridge. We got a good finger and thumb print from it. There's no doubt it was her gun."

"What about the ballistics report? Is it in yet?" Sam asked.

"Yes. It's the same gun that was used to shoot you. It was Sandy who almost killed you, Sam."

He got up from his chair and walked to the end of the deck and looked out toward the horizon. He still limped a little when he walked. Maybe he always would. Jimmy and Bill were silent as Sam stood there. When he returned to his chair, his eyes were clear and bright. "Well now, I'm glad that's over. It's always better to know than to not know."

"Have you confronted Sandy with this new evidence?" Jimmy asked.

"Yes. We had a conference with Sandy and her lawyer, Ms. Smith. When we told her the evidence we had against her, she broke down. Against her lawyer's advice, Sandy started crying and told us everything. We got it all on tape. She admitted that she'd struck Scott with the war club in a fit of anger. She confirmed that Jonathan was out of the room when it happened. Her confession confirmed everything Jonathan told us."

"Did she say how she got Scott's body up in that tree?" Sam asked.

The sheriff laughed grimly. "It was just about like you two suspected. She put him on an old tarp and dragged him down the trail to the tree. She used a ladder and ropes and pullies. She's an amateur rock climber, so it wasn't a big problem for her to hoist him up there. She did it all by herself. She's stronger than she looks. She said she wanted Jonathan to help, but he refused."

Jimmy asked, "Did she confess to shooting Sam?"

"Yeah. She said she panicked when she read about you two in the paper. She was more afraid of Sam than you, Professor, so she tried to stop the investigation by shooting him. She said to tell you she's sorry, Sam." The sheriff watched him, judging his reaction.

"Sam snorted. "She'll try anything to get off. I don't think you can trust her as far as you can throw her."

"I agree." The sheriff turned and looked Jimmy squarely in the eye and said, "Jimmy, she said she'd like for you to come in and visit her."

Jimmy shook his head. "Not a chance in the world, Sheriff. I won't go near her."

"Smart man."

"What will be the charges against her, Bill?" Sam asked. It sounds like you'll have a lot of choices."

"The prosecutor says he'll charge her with voluntary manslaughter for killing Scott. It was done in a fit of passion, so a charge of murder's probably out. Anyway, the penalty for manslaughter is pretty stiff. She'll also be charged with attempted murder. He may throw in a few other charges like improper disposal of a body, and so on."

"How much prison time do you think she'll get" Jimmy asked.

"It's hard to tell, but I'd guess she'll do twenty years. Maybe more. It depends on what a jury has to say about it."

"What about Jonathan? What'll happen to him?" Sam asked.

"Oh, not much. The prosecutor says he'll probably let him off with a suspended sentence. He just panicked." The sheriff chuckled. "Talk about a date gone bad!"

When the drinks and pizza were gone, Sam and the sheriff left. Jimmy watched them walk to their cars, Sam limping a little. Jimmy was proud to know them and to consider them friends. It had been an arduous task, but together they'd finished it. But, at what cost?

He'd call Wendy in the morning and tell her how everything had turned out. He hoped it would bring her closure. There would be lengthy court hearings, and he prayed she'd stay home and let the lawyers handle it. Life was too short to spend in a courtroom.

Epilogue

The ERJ-170 commercial aircraft banked steeply and made an abrupt landing at Albuquerque International Sunport. Passengers immediately stood and began dragging their luggage from overhead bins. They walked in single file through a covered walkway to the gate and then rushed to the luggage carousels.

Thirty minutes later, Jimmy and Dana drove their rental car into the brilliant New Mexico sunlight. She hadn't been to this part of the U.S. before, and Jimmy delighted in giving her a guided tour. He pointed out interesting plants along the highway and called her attention to the Shiprock formation far to the north. Dana marveled at the brilliant colors of the desert, and they gazed with amazement at the towering mesas and buttes. They laughed and talked, enjoying the time they were spending together. They ate tacos at a roadside stand and stopped for gas at a rundown station along a lonely stretch of highway.

Early the next morning, they ate a leisurely breakfast at a restaurant in Chinle. They stopped at the trading post to say hello to Betty and made arrangements for a Navajo elder to guide them into Canyon De Chelly the next day. Betty frowned briefly when Jimmy introduced Dana but soon was as friendly as ever. Jimmy joked and bantered with her, and she threatened to tell Dana his secret name.

They drove along the south canyon rim, stopping frequently at overlooks to marvel at its depth and impressive stone formations. They drove down the long, rutted driveway to Rosa's house and stopped at a respectable distance. It hadn't changed since his visit before. Dust devils swirled across the vast desert behind the house, dissolving as fast as they formed. The morning sun beat down on them, promising a hot autumn day. A dove called briefly from the chaparral. They waited.

Dana whispered to him that maybe Rosa wasn't home. Jimmy shook his head and said to just wait and see. After a considerable passage of time, the front door opened, and Rosa stepped out onto the porch.

Jimmy took Dana's hand and approached the lovely old woman. He spoke the Navajo greeting, "*ya at eeh*" to Rosa. He saw only a trace of disappointment cross her face when he introduced Dana. Rosa nodded and motioned, inviting them to sit down. A younger version of Rosa stepped through the door and introduced herself as Rosa's daughter. She said she'd translate, if Jimmy wanted her to. He accepted gratefully.

Upon Jimmy's urging, Dana recited the names of her parents and grandparents. Rosa listened carefully and when Dana was finished, nodded her head. Through their translator, Jimmy and Rosa talked about the weather, their long plane ride, his work at the college and his plans to tour the canyon the next day. She told him about her family and about her health. She predicted a long, hard winter.

Finally, Rosa said she was pleased he'd come for the rug. She had just finished it. She spoke to her daughter who went into the house and, minutes later, returned with the rug. She draped it over the bannister of the porch for them to see.

Dana caught her breath. It was beautiful. She told Jimmy it would look good on the wall of the cabin. It was much too precious to be used as a floor rug. He agreed. He felt a corner of it, rubbing it between finger and thumb. The wool was thick, heavy and tightly woven. Its colors were brilliant, the pattern intricate. Rosa had an extraordinary talent.

Later, they said their goodbyes with Jimmy saying "*hagoone*" in parting. Rosa smiled and looked at Dana's brilliant hair, glowing in the sunlight. She spoke to her daughter who giggled. Jimmy knew Dana now had a secret name and it had to do with her hair. He wondered what the Navajo name was for woodpecker. It was good that he would never know.

*   *   *

Days later, Jimmy looked out his office window at the brilliant fall colors that dotted the mountains in the far distance. The leaves of the sweet gum trees nearby were a brilliant yellow, and red maples were ablaze with crimson. Fall was well underway. He returned to his desk and looked at the stack of papers he needed to read and score. He decided they could wait until the next day. His new course was well underway, and his students seemed to like it. He'd completed two papers about his research in the rain forest and had submitted them to a scientific journal to be juried by his peers. With luck they'd be published in the spring. The fall semester was going well.

On the way home, he stopped at his mailbox at the bottom of the mountain and picked up a neat bundle of mail held together with a rubber band. If nothing else, the mail carrier was meticulous when sorting letters. He suspected most of it would be advertising. When he pulled into his parking area, he could see the dog watching him through the chain-link fence that surrounded his kennel. His front paws were on the fence and he had an intent look on his face. He quivered with anticipation. They played fetch with his sock stuffed with rags for a half hour before they went into the cabin.

Jimmy went online and pulled up the latest edition of the *Kanawha Daily Bugle*. Ray Lambert's column outlined the latest news of Sandy's run-in with the law. She had plead guilty to manslaughter and attempted murder. All other charges had been dropped. There had been a series of hearings, and the result was a sentence of fifteen years in the state penitentiary—less with good behavior. Sam had been called to testify in the sentencing hearing and had asked for a harsher sentence but had failed. Sandy had appeared in court dressed like a runway model and charmed everyone involved, including the judge.

For his involvement in the crime, Jonathan Wright was sentenced to one year in the county jail but was released on probation. When Lambert ran him down for an interview, he was living in his cabin in the valley writing false news stories for blogs on the Internet. He said his latest story was about the president's son-in-law being abducted by space aliens. He was sure it would make him a lot of money.

Lambert devoted considerable column space to Sandy's motive for killing her uncle. He described the endangered fern and its protection by the Endangered Species Act. Sandy had believed the Act would be repealed by the new president, and she would make a fortune when she sold the land for development. Ironically, the president's attempt to repeal the Act failed. The bill easily passed in the House but stalled in the Senate. One stubborn senator cast the deciding vote, giving it a thumb down.

He closed his laptop and pushed it aside. He unrolled the plans for his new house and spent an hour pouring over them. He penciled in the changes Dana had suggested. He stood back, looking at the modifications, and realized she was right. They made a vast improvement. He decided he'd talk to her about the plans again. Maybe she'd have other suggestions. It was good to have a woman's perspective.

He called Sam to see how he was progressing. He'd almost recovered from his injuries, but his left arm still bothered him, and his nagging limp had not improved. His doctors said the muscles in his side and hip had been badly damaged, and he might always have it. He went to rehab religiously, and if anyone could recover from such wounds it would be Sam. He asked about Sylvia. She and Sam had gone out on a few dates, but Jimmy didn't ask about that. It wasn't his business. He'd heard talk about them going on a cruise together, but he didn't ask—that wasn't his business either. They talked for a few minutes, but Jimmy could hear voices in the background, so he said goodbye.

He sorted through his mail, tossing the junk in the wastebasket. A fat, official looking letter from the highways department caught his eye. He wondered what it could be about. He used his pocket knife to slit open the envelope. It was a notice of condemnation. They had seized his property along the river. It would be used for the completion of the Corridor H highway. The land where his great-great grandfather's farmhouse had once stood would soon be used for an approach-way to a bridge across the Cheat River.

He dropped the letter on his desk and walked out on the deck. The wind had picked up and a few colorful leaves swirled into the void before the cabin. The nippy air held the first promise of frost. Workers would arrive soon to install insulation and weatherproof the cabin. He'd decided to stay through the winter.

He returned to his desk and reread the letter. He could challenge the condemnation, but he knew he'd lose. The highways people would claim eminent domain, and the bridge construction would proceed unimpeded. He would receive fair market value for the property, but how do you put a price on a family's heritage? Five generations had lived and worked on that tract of land and now it would come to an end. He shook his head and tossed the letter back on his desk. Yellow Dog sensing his master's sadness, whined and leaned against his leg. Jimmy stroked his ears.

He made supper of leftover black beans and rice and a chunk of homemade bread Dana had given him. He sat on the deck and ate while the sun set, watching a purple blanket advance over the mountains as darkness approached. He washed the dishes and stacked them in the rack to dry. Yellow Dog turned around and around in his bed and was soon asleep. Jimmy set up the telescope and looked at the Big Dipper and all the other constellations whose names he didn't know. He focused on the farm on the mountainside far away and saw a flaming brush pile tended by a woman with auburn hair and a big black dog.

Author's Notes

In writing fiction, it is the author's responsibility to provide accuracy in describing real places and events. The reader expects and deserves no less. I have attempted to do so but have exercised the writer's prerogative in some cases. Here are some examples where fiction overrides fact:

The Canaan Valley wood fern is fictional. I have given it the imaginary name *Dryopteris canaanensis*. However, the genus *Dryopteris* is real and contains several interesting wood and shield ferns.

State College, as described in this story, is fictional. The college and its employees are products of my imagination.

Jimmy's cabin, the Eyrie (also spelled *aerie)*, is fictional. Oxford Dictionaries define it as "a large nest of an eagle or other bird of prey, built high in a tree or on a cliff."

Adams County, West Virginia is entirely fictional. The real places described in this book such as highways, towns, mountains and streams, are set in this fictional county. The county sheriff and police force described herein are wholly fictional. All characters, except national figures, are fictional.

Red Creek Saloon is an imaginary bar located on Red Creek, a tributary whose headwaters arise in or near Dolly Sods Wilderness. The bar is a figment of the author's imagination.

Other places, organizations and resources are real but used fictionally. Here are some examples:

The *Organization for Tropical Studies* conducts research in rain forests, primarily in Central America. The *La Selva* research station, located in eastern Costa Rica, hosts scientists and students from around the world.

Canyon De Chelly National Monument, located on Navajo tribal lands, is situated near the town of Chinle in north-eastern Arizona. Its prominent features include an 800-foot sandstone formation, sandstone cliffs, prehistoric rock art, and remnants of ancient Puebloan villages.

Blackwater River is a thirty-four-mile-long tributary of Black Fork River located in the Allegheny Mountains of West Virginia. Its upper reaches flow through extensive wetlands where tannins leach from rotting vegetation, producing acidic water the color of coffee. The lower portion of the river provides prime trout fishing habitat.

Black Fork River is formed by the confluence of the Blackwater River and Dry Fork. It is a very short river, flowing only about four miles before being joined by Shavers Fork to form Cheat River near the town of Parsons, WV.

The Northland Loop Nature Trail in Dolly Sods Wilderness provided the site for the "burial" of Scott Richmond's body. The curious reader can find the large red maple tree with a Y-shaped trunk on the last quarter of the trail. It provided inspiration for this story.

Dolly Sods Wilderness is a wilderness area in the Allegheny Mountains near Davis, WV. Originally, it was simply referred to as Dolly Sods. It encompasses 27 square miles and has a highest elevation of 4700 feet.

The Endangered Species Act was enacted in 1973. It "provides for the conservation of species that are endangered or threatened throughout all or a significant portion of their range." To date, it has not been repealed.

I have drawn from the following resources: The National Audubon Society *Field Guide to the Southwestern States*, 1999; *West Virginia Atlas & Gazetteer*, 1997; The Rand McNally *Road Atlas*, 2014; The National Audubon Society *Sibley Guide to Birds*, 2000; West Virginia University *Flora of West Virginia*, 1970; *Life of Belden, the White Chief*, 1871.

Printed and bound by PG in the USA

USA2019PGIL